A TAPESTRY
OF DREAMS

For more information about Jessica Blair visit
www.jessicablair.co.uk

A TAPESTRY
OF DREAMS

Jessica Blair

piatkus

PIATKUS

First published in Great Britain in 2014 by Piatkus

c

retri
the pri   ted
in ar   d

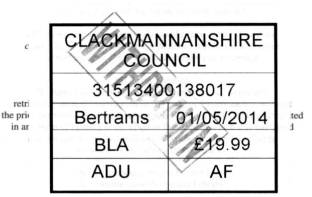

ISBN 978-0-7499-5911-1

Typeset in Times by M Rules
Printed and bound in Great Britain by
Clays Ltd, St Ives, plc

Papers used by Piatkus are from well-managed forests
and other responsible sources.

MIX
Paper from
responsible sources
FSC
www.fsc.org   FSC® C104740

Piatkus
An imprint of
Little, Brown Book Group
100 Victoria Embankment
London EC4Y 0DY

An Hachette UK Company
www.hachette.co.uk

www.piatkus.co.uk

JILL

Thank you for
happy memories

1

August 1850

The heavy oak doors opened smoothly, and light from several oil lamps in the hall of Griffin Manor streamed across the four stone steps and on to the wide gravelled drive. A group of high-spirited ladies and gentlemen poured on to the paved veranda at the front of the house. Laughter rang out on the balmy night air as one joke led to another. 'Goodnights' started to be exchanged. Mixed with arrangements to enjoy another night's gambling at the card and roulette tables soon were offers of other pleasures suggested by several elegant young women as they bestowed good-night kisses.

'Well, gentlemen, once more it has been a pleasure to have you here, and we look forward to seeing you all again soon.' These words were spoken by a very self-assured young lady and met with murmurs of agreement from all the dozen or so men who were leaving, but Daniel Bullen knew they were directed especially at him. All the young men had frequently taken their pleasures and entertainment at Griffin Manor after first visiting it six months ago, but Daniel was now a personal friend of one of the owners.

Situated in the rolling countryside of the Aire Valley,

pleasantly set away from the woollen mills of Keighley and the pollution rising from the woollen mills and workers' houses that crammed the conurbation of Leeds and Bradford, Griffin Manor had been bought by brother and sister Hugh and Penelope Huston early in 1849. They had seen the potential in developing the deserted and neglected manor house, situated near a stone bridge crossing the River Aire, as a place of entertainment for the young bucks of families riding high on the wealth generated by the West Riding's wool industry. They had tastefully renovated the old house and laid on unrestricted gaming amidst plenty of good food and the best wines, as well as certain other attractions.

Griffin Manor had turned into a moneyspinner for Hugh and Penelope, who were on their way to making a fortune. Its success was in no small measure due to Penelope's charm. Her striking looks and soft appealing voice made her difficult for any young man to overlook. That allure had enthralled Daniel Bullen from first seeing her, and Penelope, knowing what she might gain one way or another, was not slow to use her advantage. Now, as the young men milled outside the Manor, she made sure he saw the kiss she blew to him, knowing he would recall the other kisses, and more, they had shared in the privacy of her opulent turret room.

Heading for their traps and carriages, other gamblers, flush with winnings or regretting their losses, smiled as the group of young men burst into song. They straggled over to their horses, hitched to rails provided for this purpose on some grassland to the east of the house.

'Race you home,' someone shouted.

'Couldn't,' came the slurred answer. 'My head would drop off.'

'Let's see if it will,' someone else challenged.

2

'No, I couldn't manage without it and I must get home before midnight.'

'Like Cinderella?'

'Who's Cinderella?'

'Ignoramus!'

'Ignoramus! Ignoramus! Ignoramus!' the chant went up, to the embarrassment of the target, until they all reached their mounts.

Amid general struggling to get into their saddles, the young man who had just been taunted protested that he needed help.

'Better give him a hand, Jeremy,' said Daniel to the man beside him.

'Suppose so,' replied Jeremy, a trifle blearily.

They slid down and took hold of 'Ignoramus', with one heave lifting him on to his horse's back. With that Daniel slapped the animal's rump, sending it into a gallop, with the rider's startled cries soon fading into the distance.

Laughter broke out and the other men left the paddock and headed in various directions to their homes along the Aire Valley.

After a mile Jeremy bade Daniel goodnight and turned down a drive leading to a large house half concealed behind a stand of oaks.

Daniel, with a further mile to ride, was left to his own thoughts and in no hurry to have them interrupted by a barrage of questions when he arrived home at Ash Tree Villa.

No doubt his father would still be up, ostensibly dealing with business affairs though Daniel suspected it was really so as to remind his son what was expected of him – the mill should always be uppermost in his mind. Not that his father put any restrictions on Daniel's out-of-work pleasures, but always with the caveat that business came first. It rankled

3

with Daniel that he could not be more open with his father – speak to him man to man. After all, he knew from local rumours that Tristan Bullen had been no angel in his young days, and still at times discreetly sought his own diversions. But he also knew how much his father loved all his family. He had worked hard for them, seized opportunities, and now rode his luck to bring them a luxurious lifestyle.

Daniel slowed his horse to a leisurely walk, enjoying seeing the countryside tinged with an air of mystery by the white moonlight. Cloud shadows, driven by a freshening wind, chased each other along the slopes of the valley like riders in the night. He breathed deeply, drinking in air that still retained a trace of warmth on this late-August evening. He turned into the stableyard, slid from the saddle and quietly led his horse into its stall. He knew the grooms would all be asleep and did not mind settling his own mount for the night. Once that was done, he hurried to the back door and let himself into the house. He made his way quickly along the stone passage that led to the large stone-flagged hall, the focal point of Ash Tree Villa. He would have made straight for the stairs but, seeing a light under the door of his father's study, knew he was expected to glance in.

'Ah, you are back,' Tristan greeted him amiably, looking up from the sheaf of papers he was about to put into the top drawer of his grand mahogany desk. 'Sit down. Sit down,' he said, waving to a chair. 'But before you do, pour me another whisky. And get one for yourself.'

Pleased to find his father in a good mood, Daniel poured generous measures.

'Did you have a pleasant evening?' asked Tristan as they settled back in their chairs.

'Yes. I was at Roger's. Four of us are in the midst of a billiards contest,' Daniel lied.

'Did you win?' Tristan studied his son closely.

'Three of the matches. I lost the fourth, but that's not the end of it. When we decided on these meetings, we thought it best to play six contests so I can still come out on top.'

'See that you do.' There was almost a note of command in Tristan's voice, a warning that he would brook no failure. 'A Bullen must always win!'

About to counter that it was only a game between friends, Daniel decided not to; instead he asked, 'Have you been working all night, Father?'

'Yes.'

'You know you shouldn't . . . '

Tristan interrupted him with a dismissive wave of his hand. 'I like doing it. I get pleasure from the thought of all I will leave as your inheritance.'

'But you should think of your own health. You know Dr Withenhope advised you to cut back on work. Hand more over to me and to Thomas and Ralph. We can all help.'

Tristan looked at his son with an expression that Daniel knew spelled an end to the matter. 'My health is my own concern. And I'll be the judge of when all of you may take more responsibility and what direction that will take. Now, if you are thinking of preaching – don't!' He gave his son a meaningful look, drained his glass and replaced it on his desk. He stood up then and went to the door.

Daniel tightened his lips and shrugged his shoulders. He should have known better than to try and advise his father.

Tristan stood with his hand on the door knob and looked back at him. 'Those papers you saw me put in the drawer as you came in . . . I commissioned a report on wool supplies for the future. I want you to read it.' He did not wait for any response but left his son to it.

*

Daniel sat back in his chair, sipped his whisky, thought about the report and considered reading it, but then his mind slipped back to thoughts of Griffin Manor and Penelope Huston. The report was forgotten.

2

Tristan Bullen eased his large frame back in his chair at the head of the heavy oak table that stood in the elegant dining-room of Ash Tree Villa. The half-panelling of dark oak complemented the patterned wallpaper that his wife Ann had chosen. She had been careful that it did not draw attention from the oil paintings of Yorkshire scenes that she knew her husband treasured and which had influenced their son Thomas, who at the age of nineteen still enjoyed sketching. Ann noted Tristan's gaze flick over them as they always did at the end of the meal, before his final dismissal of them all.

He glanced back towards the table, noting the presence of each family member. Ann, of course, and the five children: Daniel, Jessie, Liza, Thomas and Ralph. Satisfied that they were paying attention, he let his gaze wander for a moment. They all waited, holding themselves in readiness with some trepidation. Whoever his eyes finally settled on must say the grace-after-meals, and woe betide them if they got a word of it wrong. Finally Tristan let his gaze rest on Ralph, the youngest child at sixteen.

Ralph felt his stomach churn. The last time he had got a word out of place he had suffered the lash of his father's tongue. He swallowed and began, 'We give you thanks, almighty God, for …' He paused. Twenty-one-year-old Jessie gripped her hands tightly together in her lap, the next word ready on her lips, willing her brother to say it. '…. these and all your benefits …' The rest of the grace tumbled out. Everyone's eyes turned to Tristan, who nodded and stood up. Everyone felt the tension drain away but no one else moved.

Tristan went to the far end of the table, holding out his right hand to his wife. She took it and stood up. Holding hands, they walked to the door. Their touch was special to each other; they both knew they had the love and respect of their partner.

Ann accepted that her husband was an enigma. He was master in their household and let no one question his authority. His rule was inflexible, his will iron-hard and the lash of his tongue as sharp as a leather thong; but she knew that his love for her and all their family was unbounded. He would show that when he thought it was merited, but he was not a man at ease with words of endearment. She also knew he never had, nor ever would, lay a hand in punishment on her or on their children, no matter how sorely provoked by disobedience. Punishment from Tristan came in other forms.

When he had started to court her at sixteen neither of them had any prospects except the drudgery of continued employment at a Keighley mill along with hundreds of their fellow workmates. Tristan's mother and father had succumbed to the harsh working conditions there when he was fourteen. He had escaped incarceration in the workhouse by hiding out in the woods until he'd ventured to join a queue seeking employment at Ellison's Mill. He was taken on, no questions asked. The wage was a pittance but it ensured he could feed himself legitimately, supplementing that which found its way into his pockets via his light fingers. But Tristan had a sharp mind and a determination to extricate himself from this harsh existence. He was determined to better his lot.

One day, walking hand in hand with Ann along the river-bank, he suddenly stopped and she noticed an expression in his eyes that she had never seen there before. She tried to penetrate that faraway air, but eventually asked, quietly as if she shouldn't, 'What is it, Tristan?'

He had hesitated at first, and then in a hushed tone told her, 'See those fine houses along the hillside, above the river's flood-line? One day we'll live in one like them.'

She had laughed, not with derision at his earnestness, but at the thought of herself, a factory girl, ever setting foot in such a place. But Tristan's promise had been kept. First he had persuaded Ann to leave the factory and go into service at one of the high-class houses. 'Learn how these people live so that, when we move in, their ways will not be strange to you. You will know how to be mistress and to handle your own domestic staff. Meanwhile I'll learn all there is to learn about the wool trade and running a big mill.'

He had done so, and had let his employer, Mr Ellison, see his ability and desire to achieve. These actions did not go unnoticed by the mill owner who quickly recognised that he had an asset in Tristan Bullen, a young man who was worth promoting. Tristan accepted those promotions and, in the knowledge that the mill owner had no son to take over from him, was ready to seize his chance when the owner fell indisposed due to a health problem.

Tristan made some far-reaching decisions which paid off, putting a substantial amount of money into Mr Ellison's bank account. A year later, recognising that his health was deteriorating again and wanting the business to continue to thrive and provide a good income for his wife and daughter,

Ellison put a proposal to Tristan: 'I need to recognise your loyalty and acumen. I will sign the mill over to you with the proviso that a quarter of the annual profits go to my wife and daughter, and that if ever the profits fall below ten per cent they will all go to my family.'

Tristan did not hesitate, except to add his own proviso that if ever the Ellisons wanted to sell their shares in the business, he had first refusal.

With this agreed Tristan was ready to take his place amongst the mill owners of the West Riding, but before that was made public knowledge he brought Ann out of her employment and enjoyed a moment of intense pride when he took her over the threshold of Millside House, close to the business he had taken over. In her turn Ann was proud of what he had achieved. Once he had built up the business and was able to buy out Mrs Ellison and her daughter they moved into Ash Tree Villa, placing Millside House in the hands of Tristan's trusted manager.

Now, glad to be to be holding her husband's hand as they walked together, Ann was pleased and relieved that Ralph had not jumbled his words. They were two steps from the door when Tristan stopped and turned back to view his children who were still sitting at the table, knowing they should not move until their parents had stepped into the hall.

'Well done, Ralph,' he said quietly.

Ann was pleased he had done so, and noticed her son swell with pride at his father's praise.

'Daniel, my study in ten minutes.' The sharp delivery of this sent a shiver through his eldest son, who, annoyed that he had reacted like a ten year old and not a man of twenty-two, tightened his lips in exasperation.

The door closed behind Ann and Tristan. Daniel's siblings

looked at him and, as they rose from their chairs, bombarded him with questions.

'What does Father want you for?'

'What have you been up to?'

When Daniel denied any wrongdoing, they poured scorn on him but he remained adamant. 'I'll know soon enough,' he added.

Ten minutes later, not a moment before or after, he knocked on the door of his father's study. He waited until he heard a gruff, 'Come in.'

Daniel stepped into the study to find his father seated behind the desk. He closed the door and, as he crossed the floor to the chair indicated by his father, tried to read his parent's expression, but it remained inscrutable. He sat down. Knowing his father's whims, he made sure that he sat with a straight back and determinedly held at bay any sign of nervousness.

'Do I need to remind you again of your responsibility to this family – to the business I have built up, enabling you to live in a style far beyond any I enjoyed at your age?' his father began. 'You have never known hardship, never known poverty, never known what it is to go hungry. Be thankful that you haven't! Don't let any behaviour of yours take you down that road – you wouldn't like it.' Tristan kept his eyes fixed firmly on his son as he spoke, allowing the warning to sink in.

Sensing the explosion that was about to follow, Daniel held his father's gaze, determined not to appear fearful.

His composure faltered when his father slammed both hands down hard on his desk, shattering the silence. Daniel was more than startled by it. He felt his defiance drain from him, but forced himself not to react. His father's tone of voice was harsh and remorseless as he began to speak again.

'As my eldest son you stand to inherit a mill which is not the biggest but decidedly the best in the area. It has taken me a lot of hard work, after seizing the opportunity that came my way, to bring it up to the standard I desired. The task required an understanding of people, and I couldn't have managed it without the faith and support of your mother. I will not see all that endeavour go to waste because of you! Heed this warning – you have two brothers, my will can easily be altered in their favour.'

Daniel spread his hands in a gesture of innocent supplication. 'What have I done, Father?'

'It's not just what you have done, but also what you haven't done. I think you know what I mean but I'll tell you, shall I?' His eyes remained fixed firmly on his son, who did not dare avert his gaze. 'You have a responsible position at the mill, but there are times when you absent yourself without any reason – setting the worst possible example to our employees. Orders that needed your approval for despatch have been held up, which does not please our customers; repairs to machinery that needed your sanction were delayed, with adverse consequences for production. The report that I put in that drawer has not been looked at; it remains exactly as I left it, and I have not received any indication that you pursued the new sources of supply I had identified.' He held up his hand to stem Daniel's protests. 'Stop! I don't want to hear any shoddy excuses; I don't want to be told what it is you get up to instead of devoting yourself to the business. Make no mistake, I know all about it.' His gaze became even more penetrating. 'Straighten your life out, Daniel, heed what I say. Continue on this path and you'll lose everything, finish up in the back streets. No decent girl will look at you then. Do you want to end up broken and penniless, without anyone to call on for help?

Those you call your friends now won't want to know you. Pull yourself together. It's your choice what you do with your life. Take the right road, Daniel.'

'But . . .'

'Wait a moment, let me finish. Maybe I should take some of the blame; perhaps I've spoiled you, been too easy-going . . . or maybe too severe at times. It's not easy to get the balance right, but I hope I've always been fair.' Tristan paused, waiting for Daniel to say something, but when nothing was forthcoming, added, 'All right, Daniel, I've had my say. Now all that remains is for you to choose which way you wish your life to go. It's up to you.' His tone softened a little. 'Don't disappoint your mother; don't break her heart.' He gave a nod of dismissal.

Knowing it would be useless to utter another word, Daniel stood up and walked briskly to the door. He was seething at the reprimand even while he realised it was justified. When he left the study, not wanting to be questioned by his siblings, he strode quickly to the stairs. Moments later he flung himself on to his bed and, with his father's words still echoing in his mind, stared blindly at the ceiling. There was only one thing for it – he must choose!

3

'Enjoy your ride, my dear.'

Eighteen-year-old Susannah Charlesworth smiled and blew a kiss to her father, who could not hide the love and pride he felt. She blew another to her uncle Gideon, standing beside Francis, his younger brother. The men watched her put her horse into a walk for about fifty yards before changing to a trot.

'She sits well,' commented Gideon.

'Her mother's teaching,' replied Francis, a little catch in his voice at the recollection of his wife, lost to him in death five years ago. 'They always rode together. Now our grooms are on the lookout for Susannah whenever she goes riding alone. She sometimes meets up with Rosalind Webster and her brother. As you know, they are about the same age and all get on well.'

They saw Susannah turn and wave then put her horse into a gallop. She was at one with the world she loved, here on the family estate on the northern edge of the Lincolnshire Wolds. She slowed her horse to ease the strain of the climb to the ridge from where there were panoramic views across the Humber and Yorkshire. Looking back, she silently thanked the sixteenth-century ancestors who had chosen to build Stockdale Manor below this ridge, taking advantage of the position to give the house a southerly aspect while protecting it from the winds that could bring icy blasts from as far away as the Arctic. Since that date the estate had been carefully developed and expanded by successive generations. At the same time the house had grown to its present size, two storeys and two substantial wings being added, giving it a solid, established look. As a little girl Susannah had loved to roam its many rooms and have adventures in her mind as she did so. She used to revel in the stories her father told her of how he and his elder brother had once done the same. Noticing her interest, her father had gently instilled in Susannah a love for this land.

He had not hesitated to take responsibility for the estate when Gideon had renounced all claim to it, in order to go into banking in Hull.

'I have no interest in the land as a living,' Gideon had told their father. 'You know I love it and that Stockdale will always be dear to my heart, but leave it to Francis; he'll care for it and make it his future, pass it on to a son when he marries.'

Their father, content in the knowledge that his younger son would cherish the estate, also recognised Gideon's capabilities and set him up as a banker in Hull, the thriving port on the banks of the Humber. The brothers supported each other after their parents were killed when their coach overturned while they were on the way to attend a civic reception in York. They had both settled to their independent lives, determined to be a credit to their parents,

Francis concentrated on improving his estate. Keeping his crop production at the same level and turning some wasteland into extra pasture, he was able to increase his flocks of wool-producing sheep, introducing the Lincolnshire

15

Longwool, which was noted for its prodigious quantity of coarse wool.

Gideon immersed himself in the banking world but, encouraged by his brother, often visited Stockdale. He had never married, having lost out in love to a rival. He nursed no jealousy, feeling only regret that he had been too slow to press his case. He held his lost love in his heart, and rejoiced on his brother's marriage to Rachel in 1830 and then again on the birth of their daughter two years later. After a number of miscarriages, tragedy struck when Rachel died in childbirth in 1845, the longed-for son with her.

Gideon became a more frequent visitor to Stockdale Manor then, which led Francis to confide in him later, 'If it hadn't been for you, I would have gone under. Thank you for making me see I still had a beautiful daughter, who deserved not just my love but the love that Rachel would have given her as well.' A strong family bond was strengthened even more and Susannah gained a special place in her uncle's heart.

'It's a lovely morning. Walk with me, Francis, I have some news for you.' Gideon cast a glance at his brother, and caught his momentary expression of mixed curiosity and surprise.

'Of course,' replied Francis. 'This sounds serious.'

Gideon gave a little laugh. 'Well, it is and it isn't. I'm opening an office in Bradford.'

At this unexpected announcement Francis stopped and stared unbelievingly at him. 'You are going to leave?'

'No! Let me explain before you jump to too many conclusions. But let us keep walking, there's no point in just standing here.' Gideon stepped out and Francis, all ears for the explanation, fell into step beside him. 'I have been thinking about other opportunities for a while. The business in Hull is running smoothly; I have a good staff who know my business operations and how I work. I pay them well so they would never betray my trust – they know it would only be their loss if they did. I have begun to feel I need a fresh challenge. I believe the West Riding textile trade offers that. It is an important industry that is showing signs of further expansion. I feel it presents a challenge I will find stimulating.'

'I can see that, and understand you don't wish to restrict your business to what you have already achieved. The textile trade in the West Riding could offer you what you need in the future, but have you thought it all through? Might you not find life over there alien? It will be very different from life in a Yorkshire port from which you have easy access to Stockdale, where you know you are always welcome. This is your second home. Won't you miss it if you move?'

'I will, but I'm not going to the end of the world. I'll still come back.'

'But you won't come as frequently, and both Susannah and I will miss you. I know she won't like the idea.'

Gideon tightened his lips for a moment then said, 'Francis, I have to tell you, I have been looking into the possibility of this expansion into the West Riding for some time.'

'You never said anything.' He made no attempt to disguise the hurt he felt at not being told before now.

'It was never meant as a snub to you, but I wanted to make a thorough investigation into the prospects there before I mentioned it to you. If I hadn't liked them, then no harm done. But I do like them, so I'm telling you now.'

'And how far have you got?'

'I can go into partnership in an established business. The owner, Mr Moorsom, is an ageing widower with no family;

17

he is looking for someone who would be interested in keeping the business going under his name; while he acts as sleeping partner. He operates from the Keighley side of Bradford so has as his clients mill owners from both places. This is an opportunity for me to buy into established connections while working towards an expanded business, to which Mr Moorsom has no objection.'

'Hmm. You seem to have gone into this thoroughly and your mind is already made up.'

Gideon nodded. 'I have.' He saw the disappointment in his brother's eyes. 'Don't look like that, Francis. I need a new challenge. After all, what else is there in life for me?'

'If only you hadn't lost that girl . . . how different things would be.'

'Let's not talk of it. Just a brief episode that's better overlooked,' said Gideon brusquely. He never referred to his disappointed hopes if it could be avoided, and his brother did not even know the identity of the lady in question.

Francis nodded. 'I'll say just one thing more: there are other ladies out there. It is never too late.'

Gideon gave a wan smile and shrugged his shoulders. Francis knew now was the moment to revert to the subject of his brother's move. 'So you have fixed up the new partnership. What about your living arrangements? I presume you'll move over there?'

'I'll buy a house close by, but I'll not give up my home in Hull. After all, I will be spending time in both places.'

'Have you looked at any properties?'

'Not really. There are several possibilities but I . . . '

'You don't know yet. So I suggest that you and I and Susannah take a look at them together. You'll need an opinion from a female, and I'm sure Susannah is more than capable.'

18

'That would be marvellous. We'll arrange it for when I have more details of the properties I fancy . . . that may take me a little while.' He left a moment's pause then added, 'Thank you, Francis. I had baulked a bit at telling you my plans.'

Francis looked him in the eye. 'Who am I to stand in my brother's way?'

Gideon smiled and gave him a friendly slap on the shoulder. 'Let's walk some more.' As they fell into step Gideon momentarily considered his brother's comment about finding love again, then dismissed the thought. Too late for that now, he told himself.

4

Daniel rolled out of bed. For the past four days that word 'choose' had haunted him. Two futures beckoned and he constantly wavered between them, weighing up their individual merits in his mind.

The mill offered him security, assuring him of a good life devoid of any of the hardship his father had experienced in his own younger days. Daniel knew the workings of the mill, understood what was needed to keep it profitable, and reckoned he was capable of taking it over when the time came, but he lacked the real drive and enthusiasm for it that consumed his father. After Tristan's criticism of him and threat to make his brothers heirs to the business instead Daniel knew he would have to tread carefully, show more enthusiasm for the wool trade, amend his slipshod approach to his role at the mill and ease up on the night life at Griffin Manor. But that did not mean he could put thoughts of Penelope from his mind. Maybe she was his future . . . but he was sure his father would not approve of that.

Penelope . . . while he dressed he considered a life with her instead of working for his father. Daniel felt sure he could exploit her love for him in order to gain a stake in Griffin Manor; *that* would be more to his liking than spending endless dreary days at the mill. He gave a little chuckle – what would his father say if he ever raised the possibility? But would Penelope condone a business partnership? And what would her brother Hugh think to that idea? Penelope was the stronger of the two, of course. If he could win her over it was as good as achieved. Daniel straightened his blue stock as he observed his reflection in the mirror. Yes, his new future could lie at Griffin Manor. He began to turn away but stopped and eyed himself again in the mirror.

'Fool!' he hissed to himself, his eyes narrowing. 'Fool! Why choose? Couldn't I have the mill and Griffin Manor as well? Couldn't I be richer even than my father?' With an expression of determination he strode across his bedroom and chose a royal blue brocade waistcoat from the wardrobe. He fastened it, turned and eyed himself anew in the cheval glass. As was his habit, he flicked the lapels of the waistcoat with his long fingers. Satisfied, he chose a single-breasted, knee-length coat of grey cloth and pulled on highly polished soft leather ankle-boots before hurrying from the room.

He took the curving staircase to the hall and made straight for the dining-room where his mother and brother Thomas were already enjoying their breakfast.

'Good morning, Mother,' he called brightly as he crossed the room to kiss her.

She smiled her thanks; the light in her eyes betrayed her love for Daniel, her eldest child.

'Father?' he queried.

'Already gone,' Thomas was quick to reply, implying by his tone that they had better not be too long before they followed him.

'Ralph?' asked Daniel as he ladled himself some porridge from the tureen on the sideboard.

As if on cue the door opened and Ralph, with his usual cheery smile, said, 'I'm here! My sisters are still primping themselves.'

'They have all day,' returned Thomas. 'If you are to ride with us, you'd better hurry.'

Fifteen minutes later the three of them were bidding their mother goodbye. As they crossed the hall they called to their sisters who were coming down the stairs deep in conversation.

'Didn't you get it all said last night?' queried Ralph, lightly.

'Will they ever?' said Thomas with a despairing look to the heavens. 'Do you think they will, Daniel?'

'Oh, who cares? Come on,' he snapped. 'We'd better not be late.'

'Oh, Father been at you again, has he?' asked Ralph, turning his light-hearted mockery on his brother.

Daniel made no reply but Ralph reckoned he knew the answer by the glare his brother gave him and the bad-tempered way he flung open the door.

Three horses, attended by a groom and a stable-boy, awaited them. Within a matter of minutes they were riding away from Ash Tree Villa heading for Keighley.

With Daniel in the lead, Thomas looked across at Ralph. He pointed ahead and made a face. Ralph grinned and nodded as he placed a finger to his lips. They were both curious about the state of things between their father and Daniel, but were wise enough not to question their brother in his present mood.

When the usual chatter from his brothers was missing, Daniel guessed what they were wondering. He was pleased that his moments of play-acting were having the desired effect and enabling him to concentrate on his thoughts, which were not as they surmised. He had made a decision, though he needed to think carefully about it. He did not want the inane chattering of his brothers distracting him right now.

They rode at a brisk pace, knowing their father would be standing at his office window, pocket watch in hand, to note the time of their arrival. He would have already confirmed the presence of his various managers, who in turn knew they were expected to check on the punctuality of the workers for whom they were responsible. Men, women and children streamed towards the wide archway that gave access to the large mill yard from where they would make their way to their various places of work. The road seemed to be packed with human bodies, jostling towards the arch where the tall wooden gates had been thrown wide. The clatter of clogs filled the air; another day at the mill was beginning.

Most of the workers were thankful to have a job that put brass in their purses or pockets – whether it provided food for a family or was swilled away in local public houses. Most accepted hard grind as their lot; envy of the three young men who rode towards the mill might enter their minds for a brief moment, only to be dismissed in the knowledge that none of them would have courage or insight to do what the youngsters' father, Tristan Bullen, had done. The workers were thankful that on becoming master of the mill he'd never lost sight of his humble beginnings, and appreciated what he owed his operatives by keeping their wages a coin or two higher than they could get at other mills. There were those among them who already wondered what would happen when the eldest son Daniel succeeded to the mill.

The riders slowed their horses to a walk when they neared the throng heading for the archway. Workers pushed each other aside to allow the master's sons access. Body jostled against body. Some men touched their flat caps in deference to authority. Young women eyed the riders with different eyes and speculative whispers.

'Fancy him, Liza?'

'Aye. Any time.'

'Which one?'

'Be nice to change about.'

'I could teach that young 'un a thing or two in bed.'

'What are you – a school-marm?'

Her friend laughed. 'It would be an education right enough!'

'What about Mr Daniel?'

Her companion shook her head. 'Take more than our charms to move him. I hear tell he's doing all right at Griffin Manor. There's class there, and we ain't got it.'

The horses were past.

'Better stop dreaming,' commented Liza wistfully. 'Let's get the looms turning and earn our crust.'

As soon as the three riders appeared in the yard stable-boys appeared. They briskly took charge of the horses and led them into the stables situated in one corner of the yard, which was bordered on three sides by tall brick buildings, looking solid enough to see out Mr Tristan and his descendants stretching far into the future. As he walked away from the stables Daniel glanced around – it was that air of solidity heralding a long future, and the thought of all these employees turning wool into money for him for many a long year, that satisfied him he had made the right decision about his future. There was an excellent basis for it here; anything he could add would be a further bonus and line his pockets even more – all he need do was manoeuvre Penelope into his way of thinking. He would have to play that carefully. Not rush things.

Daniel sat down behind his large desk, positioned so that he could see the comings and goings in the yard below. He knew Tristan had been right when he had warned him about neglecting (Daniel preferred the word postponing) some aspects of his work, but from now on things at the mill would change. Though he would find time for his pleasures, Daniel would be more careful about when he took them. There would be no more absenting himself from the business, even when his father was not around. He grimaced at the thought. Penelope would not be pleased. But he told himself he could charm her into accepting the new scheme of things.

On reaching Griffin Manor that evening Daniel immediately questioned the footman on duty in the hall. 'Miss Penelope?' he asked.

'In her room, sir,' replied the footman, resplendent in a livery especially designed for Griffin Manor. He nodded towards the heavy oak door inlaid with the gilded motif of a griffin. 'Shall I announce you, sir?' He put the question even though he knew what the answer would be because of the special privileges Miss Huston extended to Mr Daniel Bullen.

'Is she alone?' Daniel asked.

'Yes, sir.'

'Then it won't be necessary, thank you.'

'Very good, sir.'

Daniel turned away and the footman moved off to attend to two people who had just entered the building.

Daniel crossed the hall briskly and gave three sharp raps on the door the footman had indicated, paused then gave two more. He waited a moment, listening intently for a response. It came almost immediately. He opened the door and slipped inside, closing the door smoothly behind him. Penelope had already left her chair to greet him.

'Our signal worked again,' Daniel commented with a smile, and held out his arms to her.

'Always good to know when to expect you,' she replied, eyes twinkling in a way that sent shivers of pleasure coursing through him. She slid into his arms and kissed him, letting her lips linger, promising to fulfil any desire. Then she let the moment pass, leaned back against his arms and looked at him intently.

'Something is not right,' she said quietly.

'It's nothing,' he replied.

'Daniel!' She hardened her voice and, still holding him, let her direct look bore into him. 'I've known you less than a year but I think I know you very well. Daniel, something is wrong and I think it concerns me.'

He tightened his lips as he hesitated to answer.

'Come on, out with it,' she prompted, with a snap in her voice he could not ignore.

'I'm going to have to cut back on our daytime meetings ... probably cut them out altogether,' he replied with apprehension, not sure in his mind how she would take this.

'Oh, is that all?' said Penelope dismissively. In fact she felt relief, but was careful not to show it.

'You don't mind?' asked Daniel, surprised that a resounding objection had not been raised.

'You must have a perfectly good reason,' she replied casually.

'I have.'

'Then tell me.'

'Somewhere more comfortable where we won't be disturbed?' he suggested.

She gave a smile, took his hand and led him to a door in

the wall behind her desk. It led to a private room above so that she had no need to use the staircase from the hall if she did not want to. 'I think we had better not be disturbed while you tell me.' She unlocked the door and stood aside to let him pass, saying as he did so, 'You know the way.'

She locked the door behind her and followed him up the stairs, which led into a large tastefully furnished room with a bay widow that gave panoramic views along the Aire Valley that could be enjoyed from a settee positioned in the bay. A mahogany table with two chairs stood against one wall, and a matching secretaire and chair were positioned on another so that windowlight fell across the desk top from the left. Daniel knew that the door beyond, slightly ajar, gave access to a bedroom with a large four-poster.

'Make yourself comfortable,' Penelope invited, indicating the chairs to either side of the fireplace. She crossed to a table on which stood two decanters and some glasses. 'The usual, no doubt?' she queried, but was already pouring a glass of whisky for him.

Daniel raised it to her. 'To us,' he said.

She acknowledged his toast and sat down. 'Well, why no more daylight meetings?' she enquired, as he made himself comfortable. 'I have so enjoyed escaping into the country-side with you or to Bradford or Leeds. Is it your father?'

'Yes. He's laying down the law about work. I let some jobs slip and he's found out.'

'That was a bit foolish of you.'

'I know,' Daniel replied. 'I've got to be careful it doesn't happen again; he's threatened to cut me off.'

Penelope hid the alarm which surged through her. That must not happen. She had too much to lose. Riches beck-oned. She wanted a secure future and saw that with Daniel Bullen she could have it, so have it she would. Love? Oh

27

yes, if pressed she would admit that at their first meeting she had fallen in love with this handsome young man whom she knew many other women coveted. She recalled her grandmother's words: 'Penelope, when you fall in love, be sure to love where there is money.' She had done just that and felt sure Daniel loved her in return. She would do anything to keep him.

He went on to tell her of the interview with his father, saying that he was determined not to lose out on the mill.

'Does he know about me?' she asked.

'No, not yet.'

'Let's keep it that way, for the time being. I think he may not approve of Griffin Manor. The right moment will come for us. In the meantime, I think it would be wisest for us not to meet for three months.' She kissed Daniel, arousing waves of desire in him. Then she took his hand and led him towards the bedroom door. 'Let's make our last daylight encounter memorable, shall we?'

5

'Are you going riding today, my dear?' Francis asked his daughter over breakfast.

'Yes,' Susannah replied. 'I arranged to meet Rosalind and Roland at ten o'clock if the weather was fine.'

'And it is,' her father said. 'I took my usual look outside as I came down. It's a nice brisk morning for the first of September and it appears settled for the day.'

'Does that mean harvesting starts soon?'

'Within the next week, if the weather holds good.'

Susannah went to the sideboard to help herself from the tempting breakfast dishes, which one of the maids had laid out a few minutes previously.

Coming to the table she asked, 'Will we be joining the Websters for the Mell Supper?'

'Yes, Mrs Webster did mention it to me a couple of weeks ago. She's planning on both sets of employees celebrating together as usual, in their large barn.'

'It's good of her to keep doing it.'

Francis gave a knowing little smile. 'Marjorie likes organising, and is keen to keep up some of the traditions she and your mother instituted for the two estates. I must ask her if there is anything she wishes me to see to.'

'I can ask her,' offered Susannah. 'I was invited to take lunch there today after our ride.'

'Splendid. Then I'll leave it to you. I presume you'll be crossing Last Brook?'

'Yes, using the bridge rather than the ford downstream.'

'So you'll be going via Penny Acre Field?'

'Yes.'

'Just cast your eyes over the flock in that field, will you? As a precaution. They should be all right. I was going to go myself but there is a job at the opposite side of the estate that I need to check on; it will save me time if you have a look at the Longwools.'

'I can easily do that. I'm meeting Rosalind and Roland at the bridge.'

Susannah was pleased that her father had involved her. From an early age she had been interested in the estate, especially the sheep which had become the mainstay of its income. Her father had continued to follow the policy of his own in concentrating on sheep carrying a good yield of wool, having seen the potential of supplying the expanding mill businesses in the West Riding of Yorkshire. The fleeces were transported there by the convenient river, canal and road systems. In the past two years he had introduced the ancient breed of Lincoln Longwool sheep alongside the large flocks of Leicesters which formed the bulk of his stock. He hoped the mill owners would be attracted not only by the exceptional yield of the strain but also by the lustre of the strong dense wool.

'Are you pleased with the new flock?' Susannah asked him.

'So far, yes. They have done well since we introduced them and I'm thinking of increasing their number and doing some cross-breeding with the Leicesters, for a firmer wool.'

'I'll give them a good look over.'

'I know you will.'

Francis was relieved that Susannah showed such a deep interest in the estate and all that went with it; after all, as his only child, she would inherit it one day. He hoped her interest would never wane and that she would marry someone who would be as committed to the estate as she was.

'I'll get off a bit earlier so I can do that for you before Rosalind and Roland arrive.'

'Have a good time,' Francis said as they parted at the foot of the stairs. 'Enjoy your ride and lunch. I'll be away most of the day, so I will see you this evening.'

'You have a good day too, Father.' She kissed him on the cheek and hurried up the stairs to change.

Twenty minutes later Susannah was riding away from Stockdale Manor. She studied the sky. Her father was right; this was one of those days when the weather looked settled. The slight breeze could hardly be bothered to ripple the leaves on the trees. Everything seemed to be at rest. Unwilling to disturb the tranquillity, she kept her horse to a walking pace. The sheep, lazing in the grass, ignored her.

Reaching the stone bridge over Last Brook she slid from the saddle, led the horse over the bridge and let it have freedom to champ on the grass. She strolled back on to the bridge, leaned on the parapet and looked down into the gently flowing brook which chattered to her as it swirled around the stones and across the muddy bed, reminding her of the times when, as a little girl, she had stood here with her mother. She could still hear Mama saying, 'Listen, Susannah, it's telling you of your dreams.' Even now, after all these years, she could hear her mother's gentle voice, flowing like the brook, slipping effortlessly into a story.

How she wished she had her mother now; someone to talk

to and ask the sort of questions she could not ask her father. Rosalind was a confidante up to a point; Rosalind's mother had been helpful too, but held back from going too far for fear of upsetting Susannah's father. She missed her mother so much. Her throat tightened. She bit her lip but could not prevent a single tear from sliding down her cheek and dropping into the water beneath.

The sound of horses' hoofs startled her. The sun had warmed the air a little more. 'How long have ... ?' She banished her dreams. 'Oh, my goodness – the Longwools!' She turned away from the parapet. Rosalind and Roland were galloping towards her. Her horse jittered away from the sound but calmed on hearing her voice call out reassuringly.

'Beat you!' Rosalind told her brother as she hauled her horse to a halt where the track rose to the bridge.

Roland ignored her; instead he turned his attention on their friend. 'Good morning, Susannah.' His broad smile held warmth and pleasure.

'Good morning to both of you,' she replied.

'Sorry if we're late,' said Roland. 'Blame her,' he added with a teasing note, inclining his head towards his sister. 'Primping, as usual.'

'Making excuses for delaying me,' said Rosalind, returning his banter as she steadied her horse. 'Take no notice of him.'

'As if I would,' returned Susannah.

'Oh, that breaks my heart,' replied Roland, placing his hand on his breast and mimicking collapse.

'Oh, sit up, Roland,' scolded Rosalind.

'I can't. Only Susannah knows how that can be achieved.'

She laughed and blew him a kiss. 'There, that will have to do.'

Roland put on a glum face. 'I suppose it will. It's better than nothing.'

'Good,' said Susannah. 'Now both of you can help me. My father asked me to inspect the Longwools. I meant to have it done before you arrived.'

'We're at your command,' replied Roland. 'You want your horse?'

'Please.'

As he turned his mount away from the bridge, Rosalind queried quietly, 'Dreaming?'

Susannah gave a wan smile and nodded. She knew her friend realised what this place meant to her.

'Will you be all right?'

Susannah brightened. 'Of course. We are going to have a good day. A nice ride, the three of us together, and then what I know will be a very enjoyable luncheon with your mother.'

'We certainly will,' replied Rosalind.

'There you are,' said Roland, handing the reins of her horse to Susannah. He straightened in his saddle. Susannah had always admired the way he sat a horse, with such assurance and control, even from when he was ten years old and she a novice rider of eight. 'Right, where are the sheep?'

'Penny Acre Field. You know, the big one adjoining your estate.'

Roland knew it. As he grew up he had become interested in the history of his home and surrounding land. He had learned that the estate had originally belonged to Harthill Priory, which had been established by a small group of Augustinian monks who had lived a peaceful life there, following their religious beliefs and doing good works, beneficial to the district in which they lived. That peaceful life had been shattered when they had been driven out by Henry VIII's Commissioners and their land sold off. Roland had discovered that in the early-seventeenth century the land and the priory, which by then had been turned into a substantial country house, had been sold to one of his ancestors, Wulfstan Webster. He had also learned that at about the same time some of the land had been bought by Dudley Charlesworth who had built Stockdale Manor. From ancient letters and documents he realised the two families were friends then, leaving a legacy that persisted to the present day.

'Penny Acre Field it is,' called Roland.

'Sorry about this,' Susannah apologised again as they set their horses to a walking pace. 'I should have got it done before you arrived.'

'We are all entitled to day-dream,' returned Rosalind.

'Are we looking for anything in particular?' Roland asked.

'No. Just checking that everything is all right with the flock. You know how particular Father is about the Longwools, especially after taking that advice from your father.'

'I'm sure everything will be in order,' Roland reassured her.

So it proved. They could see nothing untoward with the flock, and once they had left Penny Acre Field they settled down to enjoy their planned ride.

Their chatter was light and free; they all enjoyed their close friendship and wanted nothing to spoil it. They were open with each other but knew when not to pry; if they suspected there was something afoot they would wait to be informed without asking questions. Susannah envied Rosalind's totally relaxed attitude with young men of her own age; it was easier for her – she had a brother. Even when riding with the hunt, attending balls or parties, Susannah was not totally relaxed in masculine company.

Roland was different. They had known each other since childhood and in her opinion their relationship was that of siblings.

As she snuggled into her feather-bed that night she thought how fortunate she was to have two such loyal friends as Rosalind and Roland, and hoped their friendship would last a lifetime. But at that moment a meeting was taking place that would test their closeness.

6

When the study door opened in Ash Tree Villa the three young men immediately curtailed their jocular exchanges, but Thomas managed a wink at Ralph who had to force his expression to remain serious. It was always the same when they gathered for the monthly meeting with their father to discuss progress at the mill; Thomas would try to provoke his younger brother into making a gaffe when their father appeared, but Ralph was adamant that he would never do so.

Tristan closed the door and made for his seat behind the desk, saying, 'Charge them, Daniel.'

'Yes, sir.' Daniel sprang to his feet and went to the sideboard where, as usual, a bottle of whisky had been set alongside four glasses in readiness for this meeting.

'Your mother and sisters are with their books, embroidery and piano,' Tristan announced. Daniel placed a glass of whisky to one side of the papers that his father had set in front of him.

Daniel brought a glass to Thomas and one to Ralph, knowing that his father and mother believed it better to allow them to have a drink, provided they never overindulged, than to try and enforce a ban and drive the desire underground.

As Daniel sat down his father raised his glass. 'To Bullen and Sons, may it continue to prosper.'

They all repeated the toast and drank.

'Reports,' he said.

'Two looms broke down today. Nothing serious,' said Thomas. 'I arranged to have them repaired this evening, to be ready by the time the workers start tomorrow morning.'

Tristan nodded. 'Good. Are breakdowns becoming more frequent?'

'No, sir. These two looms are old and the recent extra production has taken its toll, but after Sinclair Brothers have repaired them they'll give us a lot more service.'

'You know this firm?' asked Tristan, surprised that a new firm of repairers had been consulted.

'Yes, sir. I made it in my way to look them over just after our last monthly meeting. I took Ralph with me. He can comment on their excellent workmanship.'

'I can, sir,' put in Ralph quickly. 'That engineering apprenticeship you let me do paid off. I knew what I was looking for and can vouch for Sinclair Brothers' work. It won't be bettered round here.'

'Good, good,' muttered Tristan, not wanting to appear over-enthusiastic. He had been against Ralph's doing that apprenticeship and never liked being proved wrong; it had been Ann's persuasive powers that had won the day. 'Let the boy do it. It will do him good to get out and mix with the likes of such people. Don't you ever forget your roots and where you came from, Tristan Bullen,' she had added. 'It's something the boy wants to do. Mark my words, he'll make a success of it.'

Tristan had reluctantly given way, trying to conceal the fact that his wife could twist him round her finger, something he counterbalanced by being less receptive to other people's ideas.

'I hope you are right about their competence,' Tristan said. He looked back at Thomas. 'Are the rest of the looms working well?'

'Yes, sir.'

'And the workers still happy on them?'

'Yes. The extra pennies on their wages you surprised them with a couple of weeks ago have settled any rumblings of discontent, as I hear is happening at some of the mills in Bradford.'

Tristan gave a sharp nod of satisfaction. 'Keeping them happy keeps trouble from our door. Remember that, all of you. Have you anything else to add, Thomas?'

'Production is keeping up with orders. In fact, we are a little ahead so won't miss the two looms being out of action, providing they are soon back in operation.'

'They will be,' put in Ralph.

Tristan made no comment but he liked his youngest son's positive approach to his work, and reckoned Ralph would always have the mill as his priority. He turned to Daniel then. 'I'm pleased with your changed attitude since we spoke a few weeks ago,' he told his eldest son.

'Thank you, sir.'

'Keep it that way.' Though he surmised that Daniel still visited Griffin Manor, Tristan knew the visits were less frequent and were not interfering with his work at the mill. Nevertheless he suspected that there was some attraction at Griffin Manor other than gambling, drinking and good food, a girl maybe, but at this juncture he would not pry.

'I will, sir.' With this firm assurance Daniel brought his father's thoughts back to the present.

'Good. Have you anything to report?'

'No, supplies are good, but I do have a suggestion to make.' He paused, waiting for a reaction.

'Very well, let us hear it.'

'You know we buy Lincoln Longwool fleece, because of its quality, from the Stockdale estate in the North Lincolnshire Wolds? At present we mix it with wool from other flocks.'

'Yes.'

'I think we should use more of the pure unadulterated Lincoln Longwool. We should make sure of a greater supply. The Lincoln's worth has already been proved on the looms of Norfolk. I believe we are in a position to take on more of that trade, by expanding our use of the finer wool by the sheep bred on the Wolds ... in other words, expanding our worsted trade.'

Tristan was a little taken aback by the enthusiasm in Daniel's voice. He was pleased his son seemed to have taken heed of his warning and had been making himself better informed as to of the prospects for future trading. A shrewd judge of people's expressions, he had been observing the facial reactions of his other sons while the eldest had been speaking. He had seen interest dawning brightly in their faces. It would be easy to curb their enthusiasm but Tristan judged it would be better to encourage it by looking further into Daniel's suggestion.

'You have put forward an idea I believe is worthy of consideration. You have put some thought into this, Daniel, and I can see interest is being shown by your brothers.' He looked thoughtful for a moment, and then said with enthusiasm, 'Here is what we will do. Thomas, you can look into what new equipment we will need to expand our worsted trade; Ralph, you can report on the space and workforce needed. Daniel, you decide on the manufacturing capacity we can reach, and the potential widening of sales outlets. I do like the idea but its execution will depend on securing an increased supply of wool. When we know more, I will write to Mr Charlesworth and enquire about that.'

'When do you want the information from us, sir?' asked Daniel.

'I detect from your voice that you are keen to explore this avenue as soon as possible,' said Tristan, eyeing his son closely.

'I think if the idea is plausible we should not hold back on taking these first steps and should keep an eye to the future. If possible I'd like everything in place by next shearing time.'

Tristan raised an eyebrow. 'So, before next June?'

'Yes, sir.'

He looked searchingly at his other two sons. 'Can you manage it?'

They were both surprised, as was Daniel, that their father was consulting them when in the past he would simply have made the decision and that would have been the end of the matter as far as they were concerned. Now he was giving each of them more responsibility.

'Yes, sir,' Thomas and Ralph said together. They liked being consulted and did not want to mar it. Thomas added, 'We can be ready by June but the immediate time limit needed is for the preliminary reports. We should set a date for those to be ready.'

'Quite right, Thomas,' agreed Tristan. 'What about meeting a week today to discuss this idea only? Can each of you have a report ready by then?'

There was a positive response from all of them.

'Good, then a week today it is.' Tristan raised his glass again. 'To the success of our expansion.'

*

The next day, knowing his father and mother had gone to Leeds, Daniel called his brothers to his office.

'What do you make of yesterday's meeting?' he asked.

'To put it mildly, I was surprised,' said Thomas. 'We were being consulted, asked for our opinion, not being ordered to carry out a specific task.'

'Exactly,' agreed Daniel.

'I like being given responsibility,' said Ralph. 'It's the first time Father has put trust in me . . . I mean, proper trust.'

Daniel nodded. 'What's behind it?' he mused. 'Has this visit to Leeds today something to do with it?

'Does it matter?' said Thomas. 'Whatever is in his mind, we seem to be part of it.'

'Then we should make sure that the reports he wants from us are complete and convincing. It seems that he wants to see the firm sound and secure in our hands.'

'Maybe he's thinking of retiring?' gasped Ralph.

'Retiring?' chorused Daniel and Thomas.

'Not Father,' added Daniel. 'He'll never retire. He's put too much of himself into this firm to give it up by retiring. Besides he was keen on expansion, which I think we want to make sure happens. It will be to our benefit when he does finally have to give up.'

'We could speculate all day and never find an answer,' said Ralph.

'So why not give up and concentrate on those reports?' said Thomas.

Six days later, after the evening meal at Ash Tree Villa, they awaited their father's arrival in his study. They had spent part of the previous day at the mill comparing their findings and suggestions. Although they all thought their reports were good they felt apprehensive when awaiting their father's arrival. No one wanted a flaw in a report to mar the possibility of expanding the business.

'Sit down, sit down,' Tristan said with an irritable shake of his hand in the direction of three chairs once he arrived. He took his own seat behind the desk.

'Have you all got your reports for me?'

'Yes, sir,' they chorused.

'Good – let me hear Thomas's first. Equipment required for expansion?'

He pulled out a sheaf of six pages from a folder. 'To make this expansion worthwhile, I recommend we buy three new looms with an option on two more.' Thomas's heart sank a little when he saw his father grimace at the proposal. 'We could manage with two, but if we are thinking seriously of expanding, particularly if it is to be in the worsted trade, then we should think big. That has traditionally been in the hands of the Norfolk weavers but, being in flat land, they don't have the water power we have in our hill country. That is hindering their expansion; we don't suffer in the same way and can expand in the knowledge that we will always have a plentiful supply. Convince the suppliers and buyers of this and we should not fail.'

'Sounds very plausible,' said Tristan, but Thomas thought he detected a doubtful note in the statement, and was wondering how to counteract it when Ralph stepped in.

'When Thomas suggested three new looms with the possibility of others, I knew it would mean finding space for them all. We could accommodate one more in the present weaving shed but any more than that will mean looking at acquiring more space so I made enquiries about the vacant building adjoining the mill.'

Tristan shook his head. 'No chance of that! When I took over I tried to buy it. It was in the hands of a firm of lawyers who said they would contact the owner. They did, but there was an immediate refusal together with an order for them never to broach the subject again. I asked the lawyers for a personal introduction to the owner, but met with refusal; they said they had strict orders from the owner never to reveal his identity.'

'So we have encountered a blank wall,' muttered Daniel.

'No, we haven't,' put in Ralph.

All eyes turned to him with surprise.

'I only found out yesterday, only verified it today, only made contact this afternoon and hadn't time to tell anyone before our evening meal . . . you know the strict instruction, no business talk at the table? I thought this would be the time to tell you all.' He paused; everyone looked at him, eager for him to continue.

He took a deep breath. 'First I went to see Sinclair Brothers. They will make us three new looms and have them ready by the stipulated time.'

'So they know of our plans to expand?' Tristan frowned.

Ralph went on quickly, 'Only partially, and I've sworn them to secrecy at this stage, threatening them with losing the order if word gets out through them.'

'Do you trust them?' asked Tristan.

'Yes, sir. I would have done so even if I hadn't threatened them, but thought it best to lay all my cards on the table. I told them there might be more orders if we were able to expand further and that I was trying to find out who owns the property next to ours. I was flabbergasted when they told me they knew.'

'What?'

'Were they willing to tell you?' demanded Daniel, feeling he had been outplayed by his young brother.

'Yes. They saw no reason not to.'

'Go on,' urged Tristan, beginning to see great possibilities for his firm.

'The owner died three months ago. They never knew him but they know the young lady to whom the estate has been left, a Miss Helen Forbes. She is twenty-two and a close descendant.'

'So why wasn't this generally known?' asked Thomas.

'Apparently she is descended from an illegitimate child of the former owner. He wanted to leave her his fortune, but it was not to be known until after his death; apparently in life he did not wish to be associated with his misdemeanour.'

'So we will have to find Miss Helen Forbes?' said Daniel.

Ralph caused general surprise again. 'I have done so this afternoon. She lives not far away. She sees no reason not to sell the property and seemed amenable to our having it, since our proposed expansion will be providing local people with work.'

'Something of a philanthropist then?' commented Thomas.

'I don't know if I would go that far,' replied Ralph.

'So now there is every possibility of getting our idea off the ground,' commented Daniel.

'Everything is coming together at the same time. This must be meant to be,' said Tristan. 'But first we must close the deal to buy the property from Miss Forbes. You and I will start on that tomorrow. Once it is agreed we'll look over the property and get any necessary alterations underway. When we have done so we can bring in Sinclair Brothers and order the new looms right away so they can engage more staff if necessary. Then, with all that in place, we must look into means of transporting the new wool from North Lincolnshire.'

'We must be sure we have secured the fleeces first,'

pointed out Daniel. 'We don't want Mr Charlesworth selling elsewhere.'

'I said I would write to him. I'll offer to buy all he can produce, provided they are of the same standard we have come to expect from him. I'll suggest a penny more a pound than he would get elsewhere,' Tristan said.

He leaned back in his chair with a grunt of satisfaction. 'You have all done well. You must like the idea. Now let's make it a reality.'

7

Marjorie Webster swept into the stable-yard of Stockdale Manor. As she pulled her trap to a halt, a groomsman and a stable-boy hurried out to take charge. The boy took the reins from her and soothed the horse while the groomsman held out a steadying hand to the visitor as she stepped to the ground.

'Thank you, Gerard,' she said with a pleasant smile.

'Good morning, Ma'am,' he returned. He liked Mrs Webster. She was a vivacious lady who always seemed to be enjoying life, greeting everything she was doing with enthusiasm. She was also a dark-haired beauty, who knew how to use both looks and charm to twist others round her finger. No one could refuse to be part of any scheme in which she was involved.

'Is Mr Charlesworth at home?' she asked.

'No, Ma'am. He was away early. He wanted to make good while this spell of wonderful weather lasts.'

'I thought he might be. How is the harvest?'

'A good one, Ma'am. The last cutting should be in Penny Farthing Field in three days, by all accounts.'

'Splendid. We are at the same stage at Harthill. That should work well for the Mell Supper. I'll go and see Miss Susannah about the arrangements. She is at home?'

'Yes, Ma'am. She'll be riding out to the field this afternoon. I'll get one of the maids to escort you.'

She gave a little smile. 'No need to stand on ceremony, Gerard. I know my way. I'm almost one of the family.'

He touched his forehead respectfully as she made for the house.

Marjorie used the nearest entrance and rang the bell. A maid welcomed her and escorted her to the hall from which there were magnificent views across fields where the stubble of harvested wheat glowed in the sunshine, their acreage only outdone by the grassland supporting large flocks of sheep.

The maid knocked on the drawing-room door. Almost immediately they heard Susannah's, 'Come in.'

As the maid opened the door Mrs Webster saw Susannah sitting on the window seat of the large bow window. When she saw her visitor she dropped her book. 'Mrs Webster! How nice.' She rose to her feet eagerly and they embraced in a way that expressed their close friendship.

Susannah appreciated the way Marjorie Webster had taken the place of a mother to her. She had done so without being overpowering, and without any thought of usurping Rachel Charlesworth's place in her daughter's thoughts. Their closeness was based on a solid understanding, and a special kind of love that had brought the two families close.

Arm in arm, they went to the window seat and sat down together.

'We're close to finishing harvest,' commented Marjorie.

'And you've come about the Mell Supper?'

'Yes. I propose we do the same as before. Our large barn is the best place to accommodate all the farmworkers. Your Mrs Goodson can do the savoury pies and meats, Mrs Jordan will look after the fruit pies, puddings and cakes, and the menfolk will look after the drinks.'

'That is agreeable to me,' said Susannah, 'if it is with you?'

'It is,' replied Marjorie. 'And I'm sure neither Mrs Jordan nor Mrs Goodson would want their jobs altering. We'd have a riot on our hands if we tried that.'

'Anything to keep the peace,' said Susannah, smiling.

Early the following afternoon Susannah was about to leave the house to go to Penny Farthing Field when she was approached by one of the maids to tell her she had a visitor who was waiting in the drawing room.

'Who is it?' asked Susannah.

'He told me I was not to say,' the maid replied.

Surprised to hear it, Susannah nodded and the maid left her. This sort of situation annoyed her, but thankfully it very rarely happened; generally a visitor was polite enough to present a card or give a name. Feeling irritated, she hurried down the stairs; she wanted no delay in getting to the harvest celebrations. She walked quickly across the hall and swept the drawing-room door open. As soon as she stepped inside, all exasperation left her. 'Uncle Gideon!' Her face was lit by joy and laughter. 'You've come! We hadn't heard from you for so long.'

He eased her from his embrace but held her hands at arm's length. 'You're as lovely as ever. Of course I've come! I wouldn't miss the end of harvest and Mell Supper at Harthill Priory, because that involves Stockdale Manor too and we always give the best Mell Suppers.'

'Ah, so that is why you've come, not to see me or Father?' she scolded him. 'Where have you been? What has kept you away from us?'

'I've been very busy, but I'll tell you more after I've seen your father.'

'I can't wait that long.' she protested.

Gideon laughed, 'You'll have to, young lady.'

'Very well, I'll take you to see Father now. He's at Penny Farthing Field.' She grasped her uncle by the arm and started for the door.

'Hold on, my dear. I've only just arrived ... I need to restore myself. The groom's taken my horse and trap.'

'You are staying? You can't mean you are going on to Hull?'

Gideon laughed at her concern. 'Of course I'm staying. That is, if you'll have me?'

'Have you?' Susannah looked shocked that such a question should be asked, but then she turned her expression to one of doubt. 'Well, I don't know. You haven't kept in touch as often as you should have done.'

'Oh dear, then maybe I should retrieve my trap and leave where I'm not wanted?' The teasing light in Gideon's eyes betrayed his real feelings.

'Well,' she said, 'I think I can forgive you. I'll tell Mrs Ainsworth you are here and will be staying.' She started for a door in a corner of the hall, but it opened before she reached it. 'Ah, Mrs Ainsworth, I was just coming to find you. We have a visitor.'

'Mr Gideon! Welcome,' said the housekeeper. 'I'm pleased to see you. I hope you are in good health?'

'I am indeed, Mrs Ainsworth.'

'Uncle Gideon will be staying, Mrs Ainsworth.'

'Couldn't miss the Mell Supper, I expect.'

'Of course not.' Susannah smiled. 'Your room is always kept ready for you, Uncle. I'll have the maid light a fire and put a warming pan in your bed.'

'Thank you,' he replied.

'You take your time, Uncle, I'll organise a horse for you.' Susannah hurried from the house.

He admired her as he watched her go; she seemed to brim with happiness. It had always been the same whenever he came to Stockdale Manor. Now his visits would not be as frequent. He would still spend time here; family ties were too strong for him not to. But what of this visit? He must have a word with his brother about the moment he would break the important news to his niece . . .

When Gideon came downstairs again he found Susannah sitting in the hall, patiently awaiting him.

'I'm sorry if I have kept you waiting,' he apologised.

'Not at all, Uncle. I was pondering on how nice it is to have you with us again,' she said as she rose from her chair. 'I hope you found everything you required?'

'As always.' He smiled. 'Now let's go and find my brother. That's a new riding habit, I believe?' he added as they made for the door.

'It is,' she replied, pleased that he had noticed. 'Do you like it?' She made a little twirl, showing off her long navy blue skirt, dropping in folds from a tight-fitting waist. Her matching figure-hugging jacket with light blue lapels was buttoned at the front. A length of delicate white lace, tied around her black top hat, was allowed to tumble down her back to waist-level.

'Very becoming,' he approved.

'Thank you. I see you came prepared to ride,' she said, noting his attire.

'Of course. No point in coming to Stockdale Manor without.'

'Does that mean you are going to be with us for some time?'

50

'It depends how long you and my brother will have me.'

They had reached the door and as he opened it for her she gave him a little smile. 'And that depends on how you behave yourself.'

He returned a gesture of surrender. 'Then I will be a paragon of virtue.'

He bowed and she stepped past him. They found Gerard waiting outside with two horses ready for them.

'Your favourite, sir,' he said, touching his forehead.

'Thank you,' replied Gideon. 'You have kept her in good shape.'

'She has had regular exercise and good grooming by young Garth Sigsworth here,' he said, nodding towards the boy holding the horse intended for Susannah's uncle.

'A new recruit?' Gideon asked the boy.

'Yes, sir.'

'He came to us shortly after your last visit,' explained Gerard. 'He's mad about horses.'

Gideon nodded at Garth. 'You'll like it here then.'

'I do, sir, I do,' he replied enthusiastically, his chubby face breaking into a broad smile, the apprehension he had felt at the thought of meeting Mr Gideon Charlesworth for the first time vanishing as he spoke.

'Work well, and I know you'll be happy here,' said Gideon in a friendly tone.

'I will, sir. Thank you, sir.' The boy soothed the horse with a quiet lilt in his voice as he held it while Gideon helped his niece into the saddle.

Once on his horse Gideon checked that Susannah was ready. They raised their hands in thanks to Gerard and Garth then put their mounts into a walking pace away from the house. Once clear they moved them into a steady trot.

'It's good to be back at Stockdale,' Gideon said as he drew a deep breath.

'You shouldn't have stayed away so long.'

'Business called,' he replied.

'It must have been important.'

'It was.'

She waited for further explanation but it was not forth-coming.

He sensed her expectations and after a few moments said, 'All will be revealed after I have talked with your father.'

'This all sounds very mysterious.'

He laughed. 'It's not really, so don't let your expectations run away with you.'

'To stop that you had better tell me now.'

He shook his head. 'No, young lady, you will have to wait. The present time is not appropriate.'

She gave a mock pout of annoyance, but he just laughed and set his horse at a quicker pace.

Francis, chatting to his manager who was supervising the progress of the harvest, stopped in mid-sentence when he recognised two riders top a rise some distance away. Susannah and . . . 'Gideon!' he exclaimed, and turned to his manager. 'You have everything in hand. I'll let Mr Webster know we'll be ready tomorrow.'

'We'll be done by then, sir.'

'Good. I'll be out here early.' Francis hurried to his horse and was soon answering a wave from Susannah. Within a few moments he had reached the new arrivals.

'Gideon, it's good to see you!'

The two men leaned across from their saddles to shake hands.

'I couldn't miss the joy of the harvest and the Mell Supper.'

'I told him that's what he's come for, not to see us,' said Susannah.

'Maybe you are right,' quipped her father.

'Don't you side with her,' Gideon objected with a grin. 'You know I've had a lot to see to.'

Susannah picked up on the implication quickly. 'Do you know something, Father?'

He shook his head. 'No, but whatever it is must be serious if Gideon's had much to see to.'

'He told me he had to see you first,' said Susannah. She turned to her uncle. 'Well, here he is. Now you've seen him, you can tell me what has kept you away.'

'No,' replied Gideon. 'As I said on the way here, this is not the appropriate time.'

'There's your answer, Susannah. It seems we'll both have to go on waiting.'

It was only when she had gone to her room to change that the two men were able to be alone together.

'I take it you are near to making your final plans and are thinking about breaking the news to Susannah?' commented Francis.

'I believe this might be a good time. I am near to completing a firm agreement about the business, and I have several houses in mind from which to make my choice. I think Susannah should be told before she hears any rumours. I wouldn't like her to think that I had deliberately kept this from her.'

8

'That was a delicious meal,' said Gideon appreciatively. 'Let us make ourselves comfortable in the drawing-room: I think this is the time to tell you my news.'

Susannah nearly missed the almost imperceptible nod her father directed at his brother. She felt a little surge of annoyance; so her father already knew whatever her uncle was to reveal. She said nothing, but led the way into the drawing-room where Francis poured them each a glass of Marsala before settling down in one of the chairs that Gideon had drawn close together. When Susannah saw this she thought, This must be something serious. She waited for her uncle to start, not knowing whether she should feel apprehensive or excited.

Gideon settled himself, cleared his throat, took a sip of his wine and placed his glass on the small table beside his chair.

'As you both know, my banking business in Hull is doing well. I have a reliable staff of five, under the supervision of Mr Peterswill. However, I have felt for some time the need for a further challenge and looked for fresh opportunities in banking. I have found something in the West Riding of Yorkshire.'

Susannah felt cold with surprise. 'But . . . you can't leave.' Tears brimmed in her eyes.

'Susannah, hear Uncle Gideon out,' said her father gently.

'I know this has been a shock for you,' Gideon put in sympathetically. 'Let me explain. I am not deserting you. I will still be a regular visitor. Let me assure you it has taken me a lot of serious thought before I finally reached a decision about this.'

'But you are going to a different place,' protested Susannah. 'It may take you away from us. You may find other friends who will come to mean more than us.'

'Never!' he said emphatically. 'There are bound to be new people to meet but they will never take your places in my affections.'

'Susannah, be happy for your uncle, he is doing something he wants to do. It is good for a man to try to achieve an objective on which he has set his heart. And he is not going far; it is not as if he is going to leave England.'

'I am keeping the business in Hull, so if things do not work out for me over in the West Riding I will always have something to return to.'

It was on the tip of Susannah's tongue to say, 'I hope they don't,' but she fought with her feelings and held the words back; they would be unkind. She thought too much of her uncle to hurt him. As betrayed as she felt, she got out of her chair and went to kiss him. 'I hope your plan works out.'

Gideon took her hand with relief. 'Thank you,'

Still holding his hand, Susannah slid to the floor at the foot of his chair. 'Tell me more about it, please.'

'It's another banking venture, an established firm where the original owner will act as sleeping partner, and occasionally step in whenever I am away.'

'So you will be able to come and see us?'

'That's right. And you will be able to visit.'

'But I've heard it's all dirty towns and mills there.' Susannah grimaced.

Gideon chuckled. 'Not all. There's a lot of fine country-side nearby. As a matter of fact, the houses I have been looking at are in open countryside. You and your father must come and help me choose which one I should have, and then you, Susannah, must advise me on decorations and furniture. I will not be removing anything from my house in Hull. I'll be keeping my housekeeper there, too, so you and your father can still have use of it whenever you are visiting the town.'

'So things are not as black as you first imagined,' her father pointed out.

But that observation was no consolation in the darkness of the night when, unusually, she woke several times, disturbed by this new upheaval that was coming in to her life. Ever since her mother had died Susannah had taken comfort from having her father and uncle close at hand; now that was at an end. She had not closed the curtains. The moon's pale light, fitfully obscured by passing clouds, did little to ease her troubled thoughts.

She awoke to bright sunshine, stretched to drive away sleep and allowed the new day to take over. She swung out of bed, slid her feet into her slippers and drew her silk robe around her. She went to the window and saw the Lincolnshire countryside bathed in the morning light that seemed to be telling her she had much to be thankful for. Today would be full of activity. The harvest would be completed as quickly as possible so that the celebrations could begin and be enjoyed by all. Happiness would be spilling over; she must not spoil the mood. She shouldn't dwell on her disappointment. Her uncle's move to the West Riding

56

should be viewed as a new step in her life too. She should not feel this as a loss; her uncle would still visit; she had her father; the Stockdale employees were loyal and there were friends here, especially the Webster family, in particular Roland and Rosalind.

She rang for her maid who helped her carry out her toilette and dress for the morning. Being young and aware that fashions were changing for the better, Susannah had been quick to seize the chance to move away from the previous restrictions of feminine attire, especially in her choice of everyday clothing. Today, knowing she would be using a trap, she chose a loose-fitting, ankle-length fustian skirt, its grey colour brightened by a green jacket buttoned loosely at the front over a white blouse.

Reaching the dining-room, she learned that her father and uncle had already left the house. She took a quick breakfast and then collected a small bonnet of the same shade of green as her jacket, which she held in place with a ribbon tied beneath her chin.

Leaving the house by the front door she found the stableboy arriving with her horse and trap.

'Good morning, Garth,' she said with a smile.

He touched his forehead as he said, 'Good morning, Miss.' He held the horse steady while she climbed on to her seat and then handed her the reins. As he did so he said, 'Your father said to tell you he was going back to Penny Farthing Field, Miss.'

'Thank you, Garth.' Susannah flicked the reins and in a few moments was leaving Stockdale Manor behind.

She let her gaze wander across the rolling countryside which sparkled in the sunshine under the immensity of the wide sky. She sighed to herself. Why had she been so upset last night? Why had she let Uncle Gideon's news upset her and allowed it to disturb her sleep? Wasn't she acting self-ishly in expecting things to remain the same? Her uncle was doing what he wanted, shouldn't she be glad for him? She shook herself back to the present and, when she reached Penny Farthing Field, found the line of men swinging their scythes rhythmically, determined that all would be finished soon. As the corn was cut, workers stepped forward and nimbly tied it into sheaves. Banter was prevalent and only interrupted when orders were shouted and work redirected.

'Here's Susannah,' said Francis, seeing her turning the trap into the field.

'Now it's time to start enjoying today,' put in Francis 'What do you think to the wagon, my dear?' he asked, indicating the vehicle which would form the centrepiece of the parade.

Multi-coloured ribbons were tied around the wheels and twisted along the shafts. Bright cloths hung from the sides of the wagon; a special stand had been erected in the centre, and because sheep were the main produce of both estates, a replica of one had been shaped from corn-stalks and was awaiting the final cutting from which some final straws would be woven into the replica.

'It's beautiful, even better than last year's,' replied Susannah. 'Who was responsible for the sheep? It's a novel idea.'

'Two of Webster's men made it but I think it was Roland's idea,' said her father. 'You can ask him, here he comes.'

Roland pulled his horse to a halt alongside the wagon. 'Hello, Susannah,' he said brightly. He turned to Gideon. 'Hello, sir. It is good to see you here.'

Susannah, surprised not to see Roland's sister with him, asked, 'Where is Rosalind?'

'Mother insisted she should come in the trap driven by

Edgerton, who wasn't too pleased. He thought as head groom he should be supervising the final decorations of the Shire horses.'

'Now you'll have to accompany me, Roland. I'm off to gather the provisions from Stockdale to take to your barn. I only came here to see how things were progressing, but I think all will be finished by mid-afternoon. So I'd better get our supplies to your mother.'

'It will be my pleasure to ride with you,' said Roland with a warm smile which was not lost on Gideon and made him wonder if there was more behind it. Roland slid from his saddle, fastened his horse by its reins to the back of the trap and climbed on to the seat beside Susannah to take the reins.

'When will you all be moving off for Harthill? We must be back for the procession,' Susannah asked her father.

'Let's say three o'clock.'

'Until then.' Roland sent the trap in motion.

As it rumbled away, Gideon said, 'I believe that young man thinks more than a little of Susannah.'

Francis was surprised by this remark coming from someone he regarded as a confirmed bachelor. 'They're just good friends.'

'You don't see more to it?'

'No. They've been friends all their lives, and friends they will remain.'

9

'I'm pleased your uncle was able to be here,' said Roland as the trap rumbled out of the gateway. 'I don't remember him ever missing the Mell Supper.'

'He hasn't as far as I know,' replied Susannah. 'It wouldn't be the same without him, but I was beginning to wonder if he would make it this year.'

'He's left it very late. However, better late than never,' observed Roland. 'What kept him until now? It must have been something very important.'

'He has told us he is widening his business to the West Riding of Yorkshire and had some details to settle there before he could return.'

Roland raised his eyebrows. 'That does surprise me. I've always thought this was his home.'

'Uncle Gideon is not giving up the Hull office, or his house there, but he is looking for a second house in the West Riding.' She went on to explain about her uncle's pending move and concluded, 'He wants Father and me to look over some houses he has his eye on. And then, when he finally chooses one, he wants my opinions and suggestions about furnishings and decorations.'

Roland gave a little nod of approval as he said, 'That will

be interesting for you. No doubt he has in mind how delighted your father was with the way your suggestions for altering the large drawing room at Stockdale turned out. I recall my mother commenting on them and remarking that she thought you had a hidden talent.'

Susannah blushed at the praise. 'They were only a few ideas for how the room could be made more comfortable and enjoyable.'

'I think they turned out extremely well.' Roland left a little pause and then asked, 'Do you ever see yourself leaving Stockdale Manor and the Wolds?'

'Not if I can help it.' She shot him a quick glance. 'Whatever made you ask that?'

He shrugged his shoulders. 'I don't know. Maybe because you had been telling me about your uncle leaving.'

'He's not leaving, he's just finding another business interest.'

'I suppose so.'

She glanced at him. 'What about you?'

'My life will be bound by the Harthill Estate. Besides I like the open spaces here, Lincolnshire's big sky and the rolling Wolds. Nothing could tear me away. But. . . ' He hesitated as he turned the trap through the gates of Stockdale Manor and directed the horse to the secondary drive that led to the back of the house, giving direct access to the large kitchen.

Sensing from his hesitation that there was more to come, Susannah prompted, 'But what?'

'I'll have to tell you later,' he replied, with a glance at the five traps lined up in the back courtyard. Servants were hurrying back and forth, loading them with prepared food from the kitchen.

'Mother has certainly got things organised and running smoothly by the look of it.'

61

'And no doubt it will be the same at Harthill,' said Susannah with respect for Mrs Webster showing in her tone.

'I'll leave my horse tethered to the trap. When we've taken the first lot of provisions to Harthill, I'll leave it there and help you with the rest of the food.'

'Thank you.' She smiled her appreciation of his offer.

A stable-boy ran to steady the horse while Roland jumped from the trap and came to help Susannah to the ground. They were about to go in when another trap, driven by Edgerton, rattled over the cobbles.

'Rosalind's here,' said Roland. He crossed the yard to help his sister to the ground while a stable-boy steadied the horse.

'Hello, you two,' said Rosalind brightly. She glanced around. 'It's all bustle here,' she commented as she noted two under-grooms from Stockdale emerge from the house with baskets of food and put them into the two traps nearest the back door.

'I like your dress,' said Susannah admiringly.

'Thank you,' replied Rosalind. 'It's all right for now, but you can't really look your best when there's work to be done.'

'You look right at any time,' commented Susannah, a little enviously.

Rosalind had a way of looking good in whatever she wore, having a slim waist that seemed automatically to allow a dress to fall into its most attractive lines.

'I don't know about that,' she replied with a laugh, though she was pleased she had aroused her friend's admiration. 'Now let's see what there is to take.' She headed for the door, followed by Susannah and Roland.

'Good morning, Mrs Goodson,' Roland said breezily as they entered the bustling world of Stockdale Manor's kitchen, 'and to all your staff.' His smile swept across them all.

'Good morning, sir,' they all choroused, the younger ones bashfully appraising this handsome young man.

'I see you have recruited two more to help you in the kitchen today, Mrs Goodson,' said Rosalind.

'Aye, Miss. We need the extra hands.'

'How much food has already gone?' asked Susannah.

'Two traps have left; two more in the yard are about to leave. These helpers,' Mrs Goodson indicated four people packing some boxes alongside the kitchen staff, 'will be taking two more traps in a few minutes, and then it will be your turn. You'll all need to make several trips. There are a lot of hungry mouths to feed.'

'We'll start packing,' said Susannah. 'Mr Roland is here to help.'

'Good,' Cook approved, and then called to one of the kitchen maids. 'Sally, run and tell Mr Gerard that he can send young Garth to help now.'

'Yes, Mrs Goodson.' The girl left the box she was packing with meat pies and hurried from the kitchen.

'I'll take the boxes, you take the baskets,' said Roland.

Susannah appreciated his desire to relieve her of the heavier containers.

When Sally returned with the stable-boy, now free from his grooming duties, Cook ordered, 'Garth, help Miss Susannah.'

'Yes, Mrs Goodson,' he replied, a keen edge to his voice. This was the first year he had been actively involved with the preparations for the Mell Supper. Previous years he had merely attended as a member of his family, his father being employed on the Stockdale Estate. Now he was enjoying the feeling of being a proper participant.

Two more traps left and then it was the turn of Susannah and Rosalind. With their traps loaded, they left for Harthill Priory.

'What should I do now, Mrs Goodson?' Garth asked.

'You'll be needed here to continue helping with the packing and loading so you can start off by helping Sally.'

He went to the table where she was working. He was pleased; he liked Sally who was only a year older than he. She gave him a warm smile when he joined her. 'We've these pies to pack in these baskets. Be careful not to break the pastry and keep each pie level. I did it last year. Watch me pack this basket and then you have a go.'

'Yes, Sal,' he said lightly, and gave her a wink.

'Hey, don't you be so cheeky,' she said, putting on a serious face to match her critical tone. She saw disappointment banish his smile. She waited a moment then leaned towards him and whispered, 'But I like it.'

Garth's face broke into a grin and his eyes sparkled. 'See you at the Supper. You can sit with us, Ma won't mind.' He knew Sally had worked at Stockdale just over a year and that she had come from Boston in the south of the county so had no one close enough to join her at the celebrations.

'I'd like that, Garth,' she said appreciatively. 'Better get on, Mrs Goodson's eyeing us.'

On reaching Harthill Priory, Roland directed the horse to the open doors of the large barn which was a scene of high activity.

'I suppose things are getting done even though everyone appears to be rushing around aimlessly,' he commented with a grin.

'Your mother's organisation is second to none. Everything will be in place by the precise time,' Susannah reassured him.

'How right you are. I've never known a slip-up and I don't suppose there will be one this year. Tradition must prevail.'

'And rightly so,' said Susannah. 'Harthill Priory wouldn't be the same without its Mell Supper. It's even enticed Uncle Gideon to visit us again.'

'And I hope it always will,' said Roland sincerely. 'Here's Mother,' he added as he drew the trap to a halt outside the doors.

Mrs Webster was attired sensibly in an ankle-length dress of printed cotton with a fitted bodice buttoned from the neck to the waist. Three-quarter-length sleeves left her wrists and hands free from any hindrance to activity on this busy day. Her dark copper-tinted hair was tied up and held in place by a practical yet colourful lawn cap, with a frilled edge and a crown higher in the front than the back.

'Your mother looks very elegant,' commented Susannah, noting the practicality of Mrs Webster's choice of attire. 'Rosalind must take after her. Good morning, Mrs Webster,' she called out as Roland's mother hurried over to them.

'Good morning, my dear,' Marjorie called back. Then, with the organisation of the day in mind, added, 'You may as well take the food straight to the tables at the far end of the barn. You too, Rosalind. The ladies there will arrange it as I have instructed.' She turned to two men who had just put some bales of hay in position to form tiered seating beside one wall overlooking the space left in the centre of the barn. 'Harry, Gus, help unload these two traps and then back to the good work you are doing.'

'Yes, Ma'am.' They readily set about their new task; a welcome change from humping bales.

The traps were soon empty, the baskets and boxes taken over by the ladies who transferred the mouth-watering contents on to trays and plates, setting them out on rows of trestle tables that had been arranged down the full length of the barn.

'I need you here, Rosalind, to check that plates are available and set correctly,' said her mother. 'Edgerton, you can resume your other duties.'

'Yes, Ma'am,' the groom acknowledged.

'Mama, I'll just let Susannah know I am staying.'

'Very well, but don't stand chatting.'

'I won't,' replied Rosalind, and hurried over to her friend, 'Mama wants me here. I'll see you at the Supper.'

'I look forward to it,' said Susannah, noticing Roland waving from the trap.

They headed back to Stockdale Manor. Each time they made the trip from there to Harthill they found further progress had been made.

'Mother's enjoying this,' remarked Roland when they brought the penultimate load of food from Stockdale Manor.

'I'm sure she is, and she does it with great efficiency and without needless fuss,' observed Susannah. 'And you and I play our part with magnificent teamwork,' she said with a flourish.

'Of course we do,' agreed Roland with smile. 'And now I'm going to claim the first dance from you, before anyone else can beat me to it.'

'It's yours.'

'Thank you.' He bowed his head. 'When we have made our last delivery, I'll drive you home for a rest and to change. We'll all meet up in Penny Farthing Field at three o' clock to join the harvest procession.'

When Susannah reached Stockdale she enquired from Mrs Ainsworth where her father was.

'He and Mr Gideon are in the study, Miss.'

Susannah peeped round the door and said, 'I'm home, Papa. I am going to change. Roland has suggested that we all meet up in Penny Farthing Field at three. Is that all right, Papa?'

'Yes, my dear, that suits us very well.' He glanced at his brother who gave a nod of agreement. 'Be here in the study in an hour.'

When she rejoined the two men, Francis rang the bell that would summon the housekeeper.

'Are the staff ready?' he enquired.

'Yes, sir.'

'Good. Let them all go as soon as you are satisfied.'

'I will, sir. Have a splendid time.'

Once they were in the trap they lost no time in heading for Penny Farthing Field. Before they even reached it they could hear the accumulation of joyful sounds rising on the air.

"We couldn't have picked a better day,' observed Gideon, his eyes sweeping the sky's light blue canopy.

'The early mist was a good herald of what was to come,' said Susannah. 'It sounds as if there are a lot of people at the field already.'

'They'll waste no time when there's feasting ahead.'

They turned into the field and positioned the trap to leave the gateway clear. They had hardly stopped when Garth came dashing over to them, leaving the wagon he had been helping to decorate.

'Been looking out for you, sir,' he called, grasping hold of the horse's bridle. 'I'll tether her to yon stake.'

'Thank you, Garth,' Francis replied.

They were swept into the jovial atmosphere of the gathering crowd. Even though Stockdale Manor and Harthill Priory did not grow an abundance of corn, concentrating more on the wealth that came from their flocks of sheep, their harvest celebrations had to follow tradition.

'There are the Websters,' said Susannah, waving enthusiastically, and broke into a run to meet her friends.

'I wish she would show more decorum,' said Francis with a sigh.

'Oh, let her be, Francis, she should enjoy her young life.'

With Gideon's words in mind Francis watched the three young people greet each other and wondered what the future held for them all.

'Most of our employees and their families must already be here,' said Roland as they set off for the wagon with the straw sheep securely mounted for all to see.

For many years the two estates had shared this celebration, with the result that employees knew each other well and seemed delighted to be meeting in a large gathering again. People mingled easily but Roland noticed a family looking on from the sidelines.

'There's the Dobson family looking rather forlorn. He's one of our new employees,' he explained to Susannah. 'I'll go and make sure they join in. We don't want them to forget their first Mell Supper at Harthill.'

Rosalind and Susannah were swept into the excitement and laughter resounding across the field. Young children chased around the cart; others a little older kept aloof from games they had left behind. Boys and girls were still gathered in their own groups, eyeing each other from a distance, passing opinions about which boy or girl they fancied but at this juncture of the day were too embarrassed to approach. The parade would ease the barriers of their own making. Later in the day these would be demolished entirely as a relaxed atmosphere prevailed, helped by the tasty food and drink.

'Come and have a word with Papa,' said Rosalind. 'He's over there with your father and uncle.'

'I am pleased to see you here, sir,' said Susannah. 'Are you fully recovered?'

'Oh, yes, yes.' He dismissed what lay behind the enquiry with a wave of his hand. 'It was nothing, just a lot of fuss.'

Roland, who had rejoined his family, was about to enlighten the others but caught a sharp look from his father and remained quiet.

'This is a splendid day and everyone is in high good humour,' commented Mr Webster, diverting attention from himself.

'Do you like it?' asked Gideon, indicating the wagon where two men were putting the last touches to the straw-sheep.

'We think it's grand,' replied Roland, his enthusiasm unmistakable.

'We do,' agreed Susannah. 'It's a marvellous idea to bring sheep into the festivities.'

'I'm glad you do,' said Mr Webster. 'They may not have anything to do with harvest time, but they are the mainstay of our two estates and should be celebrated. So there stands the sheep.'

One of the men on the wagon straightened up and called out, 'Mr Webster, sir, the wagon is all ready.'

'Thank you, Mason. The horses should be here soon.'

His words acted like a signal; a few moments later two magnificent Shire horses were led into the field by Edgerton and another groom from the Webster stables. The horses, decked out with ribbons and flowers, their great manes and fetlocks groomed to perfection, stepped out proudly as if aware that they were the centre of atten-tion. As they were being hitched to the wagon, people gathered round to watch and admire. Three more wagons, drawn by equally attractive horses, appeared in the field, ready to transport passengers to the great barn at Harthill Priory.

Ten minutes later, Mr Webster checked that everyone was ready for the parade to begin. Finding they were, he moved a little distance away, raised his rifle to his shoulder and fired a shot into the air: the signal to anyone not in the field that the procession was about to leave. As the sound died away everyone cheered and the wagons started to roll, with those who had chosen to walk streaming alongside. In a matter of moments, amidst the cheering and banter, someone started to sing. Soon the air was filled with happy voices to match the colourful parade.

Garth looked for Sally and, seeing her caught up in the throng, pushed his way towards her until he was able to take her arm. 'Sally, do you want to come with me?' he asked as the wagons started to move.

Looking relieved, she said, 'Yes, we'll stay together, if you don't mind. Some of the other girls are not particularly friendly, they're a bit older than me.'

'Of course I don't mind,' Garth said brightly, pleased that Sally was seeing him as her friend. Chatting and laughing, they marched with the parade. As it neared Harthill, those who had not been able to get to Penny Farthing Field began to stream up to meet it at various points and add to the laughter and singing until it was in full flow when it reached Harthill. The wagon was placed in a prominent position near the barn. Once the other wagons were empty they were taken to a convenient place where the horses could be made comfortable until the end of the celebrations, when they would return the farmworkers to their homes or quarters.

Mr Webster and Mr Charlesworth were standing at the entrance to the barn. Word flowed quickly through the gathering and an expectant silence fell across the crowd. Mr

Webster took a step forward and raised his hands, a gesture which stilled any final exchanges.

'On behalf of myself and my family, I welcome you all to Harthill Priory for another Mell Supper. It has been a good harvest and our sheep are in good health too so it is right we should celebrate in our usual way. I welcome all the regular workers and their families from both this estate and Stockdale Manor. We like to see familiar faces, but we also like to see new people joining us; to those we say welcome, and we hope you enjoy your first Mell Supper with us and will partake in many more. So, with no more ado, let us celebrate.'

Cheers rang out and applause filled the air until Mr Webster and Mr Charlesworth, smiling in acknowledgement, moved away. The gathering broke up to pursue their own celebrations as a fiddle and a concertina began a lively jig to which few could resist dancing. It set a joyous tone for the rest of the day and into the night. There was food a-plenty; pies, home-made bread, big pats of butter stamped with a sheep or sheaf of corn, cheese, home-made pickles of every kind, succulent hams and sides of beef were there for the carving, all to be followed by cakes, scones, honeycombs, a variety of home-made jams and the special gingerbread from Harthill. Beer flowed from the barrels conveniently positioned on trestle-tables.

With several fiddle and concertina players present, the music and dancing were almost continuous, through jigs, reels, quadrilles, the waltz, and the more recent innovation to reach the Lincolnshire Wolds, the polka. It took little time for those who had already mastered it to find willing pupils, who caused much laughter with their attempts. The musicians were given respite when a merry sing-song of popular songs was organised by the leaders of the local church choir.

Susanna and Rosalind loved dancing and did not hold back whenever they were asked by Roland, Mr Webster and Susannah's father and uncle. Nor did they do so when shyly approached by the head butlers and grooms from both estates, believing it right to accept on this occasion.

Susannah smiled at the sight of Sally trying to teach Garth some elementary dance steps and avoid his clumsy feet. She was pleased to see that his ineptitude was not marring their relationship, which she noticed had blossomed today; it was a friendship which had won the approval of Garth's family, leaving Sally blessing the moment he had been sent to help her in the kitchen at Stockdale.

Shortly before midnight Roland drew Susannah aside. 'Our families will soon be going home. I have something I want to tell you first.' He took her hand and led her to a seat in a corner of the barn.

'I hadn't forgotten but I thought the frivolities had driven it from your mind,' said Susannah as she sat down.

'No. I was trying to find courage to speak after spending such a pleasant evening.'

'This sounds serious,' she said, casting him a questioning look.

Roland gave a weak smile. 'Well, it is something I wish I didn't have to say.'

'This sounds even more serious.'

'I am going away. I won't be home for Christmas.'

'Oh, Roland.' A note of disappointment rose in her voice. 'But you've always been with us at Christmas.'

'I know. And want to be here. This will be the first Christmas all of us have not been together.'

'It won't be the same.'

'Nor for me.'

'Where are you going?'

'Father wants me to travel; he believes I should have my outlook broadened even though he knows I want nothing more than to devote my life to Harthill. I think he believes that by making this journey I will either forget that or else feel it even more strongly. In other words he believes that seeing other worlds will test my devotion to Harthill. I have tried to convince him that there is no need for this sort of test, my heart is here and always will be, but he is adamant about it and so I must go.'

'How long will you be gone?'

He gave a little grimace. 'A year. I insisted I should be back for next year's Mell Supper. Father agreed. A year will certainly be too long for me.'

Susannah laid a sympathetic hand on his arm. She met the confusion in his eyes. 'It will be an experience . . . make the most of it. Time will pass quickly. I'll miss you, Roland.'

Thinking that the future would take care of itself, he said no more.

They walked in silence to join their families.

It wasn't until dawn's light was beginning to pale the sky in the east that the field finally emptied and the celebrations were over.

10

Daniel Bullen glanced over his shoulder at the dark threatening clouds behind him, and urged his horse on to try to beat the coming rain.

The mill, the mill, the mill ... work, work, work, thrummed in his mind to the beat of the hoofs.

The first drops stung his face. He looked heavenwards and cursed his father. Even this evening, after a long day's work, Tristan had left him to peruse some orders, saying, 'They *must* be dealt with now, so the orders can be dispatched first thing tomorrow.'

As he pressed the horse for more speed, Daniel tightened his lips. Couldn't his father afford to relax a little? Work was ever his master, and he expected his three sons to eye the mill with the same devotion. They must never be allowed to forget that it provided them with a life of opulence, wrested from the looming spectre of poverty. Couldn't he see that his attitude to the business was different from theirs?

Daniel had not visited Griffin Manor for three months, nor had he seen Penelope in that time. He was glad he had arranged this separation with her after his father had issued his ultimatum. Once he had demonstrated more interest in the mill, the atmosphere had swung in his favour and his relations with his father grew markedly more amiable. Now the three months' separation was up and he had decided this evening to rekindle his relationship with Penelope.

The rain became more persistent, the storm broke. The sky darkened and wind lashed at man and horse. The delay caused by his father meant a soaking for Daniel. His cursing was lost in a crash of thunder, but uttering his rage did nothing to alleviate his temper. He urged his mount on, faster and faster, hoofs pounding the turf.

Griffin Manor was lost in the darkness that had dropped from the heavens. Daniel almost missed the gateway, so thick was the rain. He hauled at the animal to change course and turned it through the open double doors into the large stable where other horses were tethered in stalls, and coaches and traps awaited their owners.

Two stablemen hurried to him, one taking charge of the animal, the other helping Daniel out of his water-proofed cape, leaving him unencumbered to hurry along the stone passage to the house. He rang the bell and the door swung open almost immediately.

'Good evening, Mr Bullen,' greeted a footman.

'Not bloody good at all, Bates,' rapped Daniel.

'It will improve now you are inside, sir,' the man said as he stepped behind Daniel to take his dripping cloak and cap.

'I hope so, Bates, I hope so. My day needs improving.'

'Start the evening off with a Roman Punch, sir. Miss Huston ordered one to be ready for new arrivals, to counteract the damp.'

'Very thoughtful, Bates, very thoughtful.'

'In the small drawing-room, sir.'

'Thank you. Let Miss Huston know I am here.'

'I will, sir.'

Daniel crossed the half-panelled hall to the small drawing-room where he found a punch-bowl, ladle and glasses arranged on a table beside the fire, the sight of which immediately set the new arrival on the way to forgetting his unpleasant ride. The punch, well laced with rum, helped to mitigate the memory of the driving rain, and Daniel's ill humour was completely dismissed when the door opened and Penelope walked in.

'Hello, Daniel. I am pleased to see you here again,' she said, her seductive voice ensnaring him once more.

'And I am more than pleased to be here,' he replied, his enquiring gaze trying to interpret the warmth of her welcome.

She stepped towards him. 'I have missed you,' she said quietly, allowing the huskiness in her tone to tease and promise at the same time.

'No more than I missed you,' he returned. He reached out, spanned her waist with his hands, pulled her to him and kissed her.

Her arms came around his neck and she held his kiss with mounting passion, only breaking it for a moment to murmur huskily, 'It's been too long. We have time to make up.'

They ignored his unfinished drink and left the room.

With passion gratified they lay side by side, basking in the sensation of being together. Time stretched unendingly ahead now that they were reunited.

'Daniel, when will I see you again?' Penelope asked, wary of the answer she might receive.

'Soon,' he promised.

'But how soon?'

'As soon as possible.'

'Possible? What does that mean?'

He twisted round so he could meet her eyes with his. 'You know the situation. You know I dare not risk daytime meetings. There is too much at stake. But I'll do my best to come as often as I can at other times.'

'You'll do your very best?'

'Of course. After . . . ' He left the inference unspoken but said, 'How could I keep away?'

She slid her arms round his neck. 'I love you, Daniel.' She pulled his head down to her and kissed him with a hunger that more than emphasised what lay behind those words.

'And I you,' he said quietly. Then added, 'Don't you think we should make an appearance at the gaming tables?'

'I suppose so,' she said reluctantly.

'And I am ready for any sustenance you care to provide.'

Penelope gave a little sigh. 'Trust you to think of your stomach.' She pushed him away and swung out of the bed.

They walked slowly down the curving staircase, each aware of the attraction that sparked between them.

Reaching the bottom of the stairs, Penelope paused. 'I'm going to check the dining-room. Will you play the tables?'

'Yes,' he replied, and then added, with a teasing twinkle in his eyes, 'I've got to make my visit worthwhile!'

'Oh, so you think I haven't done that already?'

He watched the sensuous sway of her body as she walked away, aware that she knew his eyes were on her. When the dining-room door had closed without Penelope looking back at him, he went to the gaming room. Once inside, he stood still and looked about him in surprise at the alterations; the room was larger and the tasteful decorations added a sumptuous feeling to the atmosphere. The silence of concentration on cards, dice and roulette enveloped him. He stood and watched the scene, taking in who else had been tempted to Griffin Manor this evening.

Someone spotted him. 'Daniel!'

The cry alerted the other gamblers, who looked up from their games.

'Welcome back!' 'The Prodigal Son returns!' 'Where have you been? Found someone else to amuse you?' 'Father let you off the leash this evening?' The questions and comments flowed, with no malice in them, and Daniel took them all in good part. He realised how much he had missed the Manor. Eventually his friends settled down to continue their gaming.

He strolled among the tables, pausing to watch a game of whist, the turn of the cards in faro, poker and vingt-et-un, the toss of the dice in hazard and the roll of the ball and the spin of the wheel at the roulette tables. He quipped with friends and acquaintances and gave a pleasant word to strangers, who wondered who this handsome and popular young man was.

He began to realise just how hungry he was. He left the room and went in search of food. Judging from the noise there were as many in the dining-room as there were gambling.

Two long tables arranged against one wall were set with a wide variety of tempting cold meats, savoury pies, pickles, salads and piquant sauces; a separate table was filled with mouth-watering desserts, and another with a variety of wines. People helped themselves, stood and talked while they ate or found one of the small tables arranged in an adjacent room whose double-doors were open wide in welcome. There were only a few seats vacant. Conversation flowed, adding to the hubbub in the two rooms.

Daniel weaved his way to the savouries table. He was about to pick up an empty plate when a voice said, 'I thought you were never coming.'

He turned and smiled. 'My dear Penelope, I'm overwhelmed. I had heard that you had started on the plans you once told me about, but I doubted you would make the changes all at once. Certainly your alterations and decorations have made the place even more attractive. How have you managed to attract so many new people?'

'I decided, that apart from making the actual building more inviting, I would introduce more gambling tables, thereby giving visitors further opportunity to lose their money and enhance my bank balance. But most importantly we upgraded our offerings in the dining-room. Hugh did exceptionally well at spreading word of what we had done. Our usual clientele liked it, and newcomers came out of curiosity and were tempted to try the gaming rooms. You've seen the result tonight.'

'Excellent, but the true results will be seen in the profits you make,' he said, with no particular emphasis on his desire to be told all about these.

'Very true,' Penelope agreed. In her euphoria she added, 'The results are better than either I or Hugh ever imagined. We are determined to keep our standards high.'

He raised an eyebrow. 'What about the girls?'

'Very, very discreet now. They no longer live on the premises. I call them in only if a gentleman makes a special request. So that side of the business is kept to word of mouth and all requests are strictly vetted by me.'

'You are aiming the whole enterprise towards a more exclusive and wealthy market. That's a good idea.'

'I'm glad you approve. Where the money is, that's where I want Griffin Manor to be.'

'From the number and type of customers you have this evening, I'm sure you are on the way to achieving your desire,' commented Daniel with unmistakable enthusiasm.

'Now let us have something to eat. While you were in the gaming room I arranged a table for us.'

When they were seated, Daniel raised his glass. 'To you, my patient Penelope.'

She acknowledged this with a gesture in return. 'It is good to have you back.'

He savoured the wine. 'Heavenly,' he said, and leaning forward, added, 'Almost as heavenly as you.'

Penelope smiled. 'I aim to please.'

They sat for a few minutes chatting in general about how Penelope had transformed Griffin Manor until she suggested, 'I think you should try the offerings on that table.' She rose from her chair and he followed to make his choice.

Five minutes after they had returned to their table, Daniel dabbed his lips with his white napkin and said, 'If the rest of the food I have chosen is as delicious as those first mouthfuls, I will be sampling everything on that table.'

Penelope laughed. 'You'd never manage that. But I take it as a compliment and will tell the cooks.'

'Cooks? More than one?' he said, emphasising his surprise by the raising of an eyebrow.

'You don't think only one person made all of this, do you?'

'I suppose not.'

'I have three main cooks, each capable of producing any of the dishes you see on that table but each expert in one particular culinary field. That way I get the best from them and all our customers' tastes are satisfied.'

'Marvellous, my dear,' said Daniel. 'And no doubt all your efforts will soon be giving you an excellent return.'

Though it was a statement, Penelope sensed the question behind it. In the excitement of her achievement she was about to reveal more, but something told her not to and she held back from disclosing the specific fruits of their endeavours, contenting herself with a demure smile.

As he rode home in the dark of the late-October night Daniel thought of all Penelope had achieved and foresaw what the future might bring if Griffin Manor continued to be handled right. 'A valuable addition to the business,' he muttered to himself. 'If eggs spill from one basket, the other could catch them.' But he knew his father would not approve of involving his beloved mill in an enterprise so different from the woollen industry.

Penelope snuggled down in the comfort of her featherbed, her mind dwelling on the hours with Daniel. He was back in her arms and they had made up for lost time! Apart from that, she could tell his surprise at the transformation of Griffin Manor contained not only shock but approval. She was sure the financial potential of the enterprise had attracted him, and that he would like to get his hands on it. She smiled. For her that could prove to be a stepping stone to the wealth generated by the mill, and with two different enterprises there would be no chance of ever being penniless again should one of the ventures fail which, at this juncture, seemed very unlikely. The future for the cloth industry looked secure; people would always want it, there was nothing to threaten that, and there were people who would always be gamblers, lovers of good food or wealthy gentlemen who sought out pleasure with attractive and available girls.

She let her thoughts drift, confident that the future ahead of her was bright. Her immediate attention should be given to Christmas and the opportunity it presented to make the delights of Griffin Manor even more widely known.

11

'This November meeting will be our last before Christmas,' announced Tristan as his sons settled down in his study. 'I am pleased to say that the purchase of Miss Forbes's property was completed amicably, with both parties satisfied with the price negotiated. As you know, Ralph played a big part in discovering the identity of the owner. I involved him closely in the subsequent negotiations and I think he learned a lot, which will stand him in good stead if we see opportunities to expand further in the future. On the occasions that we brought you into those discussions, Daniel, you did well with the points you raised; there were two or three that I certainly would have missed.' He left a slight pause and then, with a little smile, added, 'I suppose an older mind is not so alert as a young one. I was pleased with the way everything was signed and sealed so quickly, enabling us to start work on the buildings.' He glanced at Daniel, inviting his report.

'You've all seen the progress we have already made with the new buildings and I believe you will be pleased with the end result. How are the looms coming along, Ralph?'

'They are just ahead of schedule,' his brother reported.

'Good, but make sure there's no falling behind. It's essential that everything is in place to start as soon as the extra fleeces are delivered,' warned Daniel. He turned to his father. 'Have you heard from Mr Charlesworth? Are we sure we will get the full amount we need?'

'I have, Daniel. I have his letter here.' Tristan held it up for them to see. 'I'll read it to you:

'Dear Mr Bullen,

I was delighted to receive your letter and to learn that you would like to take all Stockdale's fleeces at the next shearing, and at a penny more per pound depending on the quality of the wool. I thank you for that offer but I will have to inform my other customers of the changes. When that is cleared I will accept your offer under the conditions you mention. I have no doubt that the quality of the wool will be as good as, if not better than, previous years. I was pleased that your offer was for all the wool we produce. It comes at a time when the additions to our flocks of Longwools are making good progress and will add considerably to our output.

'I quite understand that you would like your son to be here at shearing time to check the yield and quality of the wool and make a final assessment of the transaction. I understand he will have your full authority to close the deal. May I add that as your representative, your son will be a welcome guest in my home, as you have been in the past. I look forward to meeting him and hope it leads to a continuation of the good-will you and I have built up. As before, your foreman will be welcome and have a room above the stables.

'I expect shearing to be in late-April or early-May. I will give you a more precise date nearer the time.

'I remain yours faithfully,

Francis Charlesworth.'

Tristan looked up from the letter. 'I think that is satisfactory. It would appear the Stockdale Estate is now supporting more sheep. Maybe we won't have to look any further to obtain all the wool we need for the new venture. Daniel, it is up to you to judge that, and the quality of the wool, when you are there. This is your first visit to Stockdale Manor. It is now your responsibility to see that negotiations go through amicably and to the satisfaction of both parties. We want a good outcome for our business, but not one that leaves a bitter taste at Stockdale. Remember, there is a future for both Mr Charlesworth and for us.'

'I will not forget that, Father, and I am sure that in the years ahead we will all benefit from our association.'

'I am pleased to hear that. Now I think we should be giving thought to the transporting of the wool from North Lincolnshire to the West Riding. Can we find a more efficient way than the one we are using?'

'Father, Ralph and I have already been thinking about that,' said Thomas. 'We have studied a possible route, bearing in mind our need for greater loads. We have come to the conclusion that we might have to use a combination of road, river and canal. We have a rough idea of a route and are presently engaged in making a costing. It would be better for us to finish that before disclosing our ideas to you.'

Tristan nodded thoughtfully. 'Will you have it ready for our first meeting in February?'

Thomas glanced at Ralph, who spoke up. 'We should

have, provided the weather isn't too severe to stop us travelling. We need to assess the route ourselves, get some more information and permissions to use the waterways we have in mind.'

'Very well, do your best. You have all done well. I have put Steve Craston in charge of hiring more workers; he has good judgement. He tells me he anticipates no problems in recruiting the number of new workers we require. There are workers clamouring for jobs, it is simply a matter of picking the best. I have implicit faith in his judgement. I hope you all agree?' There were murmurs of approval. 'Good,' Tristan continued. 'Keep things moving, but enjoy Christmas when it arrives. Then it's back to producing more cloth and putting more money in the bank.'

'Papa, have you heard if Uncle Gideon is coming for Christmas?' Susannah asked when she came into the dining-room one lunchtime in November.

'No,' he replied. 'The letter I had from him a month ago implied that he hoped to have everything in the West Riding completed so that in spring we will be able to take a look at some houses for him.'

There was knock on the door. It opened and a maid came in holding a round silver tray on which lay two envelopes. She walked briskly over to the table and held it out to Francis.

'These have just arrived, sir. '

'Is someone waiting for an answer?'

'No, sir. The boy who brought them said he was not to wait.'

'Thank you, Rose.'

Francis took the envelopes and letter opener from the tray, nodded, and the maid left the room. He glanced at the neatly executed copperplate writing, but did not recognise the originator's hand.

'Good heavens, one is for your uncle.'

'Why has it come here?'

'Curious,' he muttered.

'Maybe there's an explanation in yours. Who are they from, Papa?' Susannah asked.

'I don't know the writing.'

'Well, you'll have to open your envelope and find out. You'll never know if you just stare at it,' Susannah said with a chuckle.

'I suppose not.' He slit the sealed flap, took out a card and a sheet of paper that had fitted neatly into the envelope.

'Well?' prompted Susannah when her father seemed to be taking time to digest what he was reading.

His eyes had widened with surprise and curiosity. He read the printed card on which certain gaps had been filled in by the same immaculate copperplate writing used on the envelope:

The Honourable Geoffrey Smallwood-Brown and Mrs Elisia Smallwood-Brown have the pleasure of inviting. Mr Francis Charlesworth, and Miss Susannah Charlesworth to a New Year's Eve Ball to be held at Ashworth Towers on 31st December at 8 p.m. until 9 a.m. January 1st.

'Oh, my goodness,' he gasped.

'Ashworth Towers!' All Susannah's excitement was expressed in those two words. 'I've always wondered what that big house was like inside. Now I'll know!'

'Hold on, young lady. I haven't accepted yet,' cautioned her father.

'Oh, but you can't refuse, Father, you just can't. Now

there's a chance to see inside Ashworth Towers and meet the Smallwood-Browns!

'Maybe there's some explanation on that sheet of paper you have in front of you,' she prompted.

'Oh, yes, maybe . . . I was forgetting it,' Francis spluttered, still trying to make sense of this unexpected invitation. He unfolded the sheet of paper.

Dear Mr Charlesworth,

I enclose an invitation which I hope you and your daughter will be able to accept. I have been informed that Mr Gideon Charlesworth will be staying with you at this time; therefore I am taking the liberty of also sending an invitation for him. I would be grateful if you could reply on his behalf.

Yours in gratitude,

Elisia Smallwood-Brown

'That is kind of them,' said Susannah. 'Uncle Gideon *will* get a surprise. Oh, I do hope he will accept. If he's coming for Christmas he can stay on for this party.'

Francis shook his head. 'I'm still puzzled by it.'

Susannah made no immediate reply.

'Aren't you?' he asked, eyeing her with a questioning look. 'You don't seem as baffled as I am.'

'Well, I do know a little,' she replied hesitantly.

Her father's lips tightened. He fixed his eyes fixed firmly on her, awaiting an explanation.

'We don't know the Smallwood-Browns but Rosalind does,' said Susannah.

'How? I never knew.'

'Nor did I until very recently. She asked me not say anything until this invitation came.'

88

'You knew about this?'

'I knew it was a possibility.'

'Go on, tell me more.'

'The Smallwood-Browns have a son called Henry and a daughter called Felicity. She met Rosalind at a tennis match and they enjoyed each other's company so much that Rosalind was invited to tea at Ashworth Towers. Henry was there and a month later was making a request to Mr Webster for Rosalind to accompany him to an event in Lincoln. And I believe it went very well.'

'But why have we received an invitation?'

'I don't really know but maybe it was through Rosalind. I'm going over there tomorrow. I'll find out then.'

Francis nodded thoughtfully. 'I'll wait until you return before I answer this.'

'Oh, Papa, you've got to say yes! You must.' There was pleading in her voice. 'It would be bad manners not to accept.'

'We'll see.' He laid the invitation down. Susannah knew it was no use trying any further to persuade him.

The following afternoon, the clock above the front door of Harthill Priory showed two o'clock when Gerard drew the trap to a halt. He sprang from his seat and was helping Susannah to the ground when the front door burst open and Rosalind came running out.

'Susannah! Welcome!' Exuberance filled the air as Rosalind flung her arms round her friend and hugged her tight.

'It's good to see you, Rosalind.'

'Good day, Gerard,' Rosalind said, looking over Susannah's shoulder.

'Good day, Miss,' he replied

'Collect me at six, Gerard,' said Susannah.

'Very well, Miss.' He climbed into the trap and sent the horse on its way.

'Come and say hello to Mama, then we can take a stroll in the garden.'

Rosalind couldn't hold back any longer. She gripped her friend's arm and turned to face her. 'Did you get it?' she asked eagerly.

'Yes,' replied Susannah, her eyes bright with excitement. 'It came as a complete surprise to Father.'

'You hadn't told him it was coming?'

'No. I'm pleased you told me about it last week but I thought it best for him to know nothing about it until it arrived,' she said as they entered the house.

'Henry told me when his mother was going to send out the invitations. I knew your father would receive his yesterday; that's why I invited you over today. How did he react? Oh, I'm dying to know, but it will have to wait! Mother will wonder where we are. She's in the small reading room writing some letters.' Rosalind led the way briskly and, on opening the door with a flourish, announced, 'Here's Susannah, Mama.'

Marjorie turned and held out her hand to Susannah. 'Hello, my dear.'

'Hello, Mrs Webster.' Susannah took her hand and kissed her on the cheek. 'I hope you are well?'

'Blooming,' she replied with a broad smile.

'And Mr Webster?'

'Much better than he was when you saw him at the Mell Supper,' Marjorie replied brightly. 'Thank you for asking. And what are you two going to do until afternoon tea at four?'

'We'll walk in the gardens.'

Marjorie nodded 'Very pleasant. It's a nice day for the season and still has some warmth in it.'

'We'll leave you in peace, Mama,' laughed Rosalind. 'Come on, Susannah.' She started for the door.

'I'll see you shortly, Mrs Webster.' Susannah smiled at her hostess and followed her friend from the room.

'Come quickly, I need to know,' Rosalind urged as they crossed the hall, pausing only for her to grab a cloak, a warm bonnet and an ermine muff.

Once outside they fell into an easy stroll as Susannah told of her father's reaction to the invitation. 'He was astounded. I told him about you and Henry and suggested it was because we are friends.'

'So you'll be coming?'

'He didn't say yes and he didn't say no. He said he would wait until I had visited you today.'

'You will love Ashworth Towers. Henry's mother and father are so kind. I'm sure your papa and uncle will like them, and Felicity too.'

'It will do Father good,' said Susannah. 'He doesn't get out and about much. I know he still misses Mama, even after all this time, and that is understandable, but I would like him to mix with more people.'

'And it would do you good if he did. You would have more freedom to enjoy yourself.'

'Oh, I'm all right, Rosalind.'

'Susannah, you should be finding yourself a young man. Time ticks away too fast. Even from our young days it was my dream that you and Roland would marry and we would become sisters. But ... ' Rosalind gave shrug of her shoulders.

'Have you heard from him since he left?

'Yes. When he last wrote he was in Belgium. He seems to

91

be having a wonderful time, but we don't know where he is likely to be at Christmas.'

'Oh, I will so miss him at the ball,' sighed Susannah, 'he is such a good dancer.'

'Well, perhaps you'll find a very special partner for New Year!' said Rosalind with a mischievous twinkle in her eye.

12

Thomas Bullen stood with his back to the fire that was blazing in the large grate in the study of Ash Tree Villa, parodying his father's gestures to the amusement of his brothers. He coughed, put on a stern face. 'Now see here, you three, I will not have you slacking at the mill. You must set . . . ' His perfect impersonation was stopped when they heard footsteps in the hall nearing the study door. Thomas scuttled to a vacant chair and they all assumed relaxed positions. When their father walked in, they jumped to their feet. He gestured them to sit down. Ralph winked at Thomas, almost causing him to laugh.

'Reports!' snapped Tristan as he sat down.

Each of his sons delivered up-to date information about the work in the mill and an update on their part in the new undertaking.

Tristan listened intently, nodding whenever something pleased him. When they had finished he waited a few moments as if weighing up all he had heard. 'Good, good, very satisfactory. Everything appears to be going well and on schedule. You are all doing well, and that pleases me. We will not close the mill over Christmas but I have issued orders to the managers of each department to work out rosters so that each man gets a full day off to be with their family or whatever, and no pay will be deducted for that day.'

'That will please the workers,' commented Daniel.

'Have you any objection?' asked his father, challenging his son with a frown.

'No, sir. I was merely making an observation.'

His father nodded. 'Always remember, all of you, the workers are the people who keep you in wealth and comfort. I'm not like some other mill owners who do not care about the conditions of their force; I believe that rewarding them now and again keeps them happy in their own sphere, makes sure there's no trouble at the mill.' His eyes swept over the three of them and they all chorused, 'Yes, sir.'

'Good. I am placing no restrictions on you over Christmas and New Year. You may come and go as you please, you are old enough to be responsible for your own lives, but I will say: do not besmirch the name of Bullen. If I hear one word that there has been trouble caused by any of you, I will deal with the culprit in my own way. I'll remind you that I worked hard to bring my family from near poverty to where we are today. Don't sully our reputation. Enjoy yourselves over this period but there are one or two things I must insist on: I expect you to attend Christmas Day morning service and we will dine as a family on that day. If you are to be absent for any other meal, let your mother know. No sense in preparing more food than is necessary. Oh, and I think your mother is planning a couple of parties, She will expect you to attend and be sociable – if there are any of your friends you would like to invite, let her know.' He glanced round at them. 'Any questions?'

'Are we to continue these meetings in the New Year?' Daniel asked.

'Of course, but we will make the next one on the first Thursday in February, here in the evening, after we have dined.'

The early snow had cleared from the Lincolnshire Wolds but they were now coated with a hoar frost, its sharpness clouding Rosalind's breath as she rode to Stockdale Manor.

Hearing the sound of hoofs Garth came from the stable, where he was mucking out the stalls, to see if the approaching rider needed his attention. His face lit up with a smile on seeing Rosalind. He came to steady the horse while she dismounted.

'Good morning, Miss.' He touched the peak of his cap before taking hold of the reins.

'Good morning, Garth,' Rosalind replied brightly. She patted the horse's neck. 'Keep her warm, I'll probably be here an hour.'

'Yes, Miss.'

Rosalind hurried to the house and within a few minutes Sally was opening the front door and telling her that Susannah was in the reading room. Taking her cloak and hat, the maid led the way and announced her.

Rosalind's appearance brought a smile to Susannah's face. She rose quickly from the settee, leaving behind the book she had been reading. She hugged her friend and kissed her lightly on her cheek.

'It's good to see you, Rosalind. It must have been a cold ride. Come, make yourself warm.' She indicated the settee drawn up to the bright fire.

'Yes, it was, but so exhilarating.'

'I'll ring for a warming drink,' offered Susannah as her friend sat down and held her hands out to the fire.

'That would be welcome,' replied Rosalind.

They settled to exchanging niceties until the hot chocolate and biscuits had been brought. Rosalind watched her friend pour. She accepted the cup and took a sip.

'I've had another letter from Roland,' she said.

'He's become a good correspondent,' Susannah remarked.

'He has. He didn't want to go in the first place, but now that he has got settled I think he feels obliged to make up for his objections.'

'Is he well?' enquired Susannah.

'Yes. At present he is still in Bruges. He has made some good friends there who are visiting relations in The Hague at Christmas and have invited him to accompany them. He hints at the possibilities of extending his tour if Father agrees. Papa is pleased, believing it will do him good to broaden his outlook even further and may stimulate ideas that will benefit the Harthill Estate.'

'I hope your father is right and it doesn't deflect Roland from a future at Harthill.'

'I think its lure will be strong enough to bring him back when he is ready,' said Rosalind, emphasising her words as she glanced at her friend.

Wanting to change the subject, Susannah asked, 'Are your preparations ready for Christmas?'

'I think so.' Rosalind gave a little smile. 'You know Mother, nothing must be left to chance, and she has a great ally in our housekeeper. What about you?'

'Papa told me yesterday that Uncle Gideon will be coming as usual, and that pleases me. No doubt your family will be visiting us on Christmas Eve?'

'Nothing is more certain, and the ritual will continue with your visit to us on Boxing Day,' said Rosalind. 'You know, I think Roland will miss that.'

'Oh, I'm not so sure. He'll have new and different customs to attract him,' commented Susannah wryly.

'And so shall we, with the New Year's Eve Ball at Ashworth Towers,' reminded Rosalind brightly.

'Papa is under the illusion that I have plenty of dresses to choose from without getting a new one.' Susannah pulled a face as she informed her friend of this.

'What? Just like a man.' Rosalind threw up her arms in disgust. 'Well, I must see that he changes his mind,' she added firmly.

Susannah knew her friend to be a hatcher of plots; even now she could be turning over something in her mind, but Susannah did not ask. If Rosalind was, it would soon manifest itself.

But it came sooner than expected.

An hour later the visitor said, 'I really must be going.' And, standing up, she added, 'I don't want to outstay my welcome.'

'You know you never could do that,' Susannah assured her.

Outside the house, Rosalind quickened her step towards the stables. Susannah was a little surprised but in a moment realised why she'd chosen this moment to depart.

'I purposely sat in the window to look out for your papa returning,' Rosalind explained. 'Come on, I want a word with him before he goes to get changed.'

They reached the stable-yard just as Francis appeared heading for the house.

'Hello, Mr Charlesworth,' Rosalind called brightly.

'Hello, Rosalind,' he returned. 'No doubt you two have been having a good chat.'

'We certainly have,' replied Rosalind. 'I was hoping I might see you, to ask if Susannah could come to stay at

Harthill for two or three days when Mother arranges for Miss Bosworth to come about our dresses for the ball at Ashworth Towers. It would be convenient for her to measure Susannah at the same time.' Francis gave a little grimace of disapproval. Rosalind noted it and added quickly, 'Oh, Mr Charlesworth you can't say no. You simply mustn't. Mama and I are having new dresses; you must let Susannah look as pretty as us.'

Francis tightened his lips and gave a slow shake of his head. 'Well, young lady, I can tell you are plotting again,' he said sternly.

'But, Mr Charlesworth, don't you want your daughter to be . . . ' He had raised a finger and Rosalind let her words fade away.

'I believe, that to some extent you were instrumental in our receiving invitations.' A faint smile touched his lips. 'Now you are backing me into a corner where I can't say no to a new gown for Susannah.'

'You are a very perceptive gentleman, Mr Charlesworth,' she said with a beguiling smile.

He gave a shrug of his shoulders. 'Ah, well, who could resist the wiles of a charming young lady? And how can I refuse my own lovely daughter?'

Broad smiles crossed the faces of both girls and, with a shout of joy, they embraced each other as they thanked Francis.

He laughed at their exuberance. 'I'd better inform my brother we'll be going, and formally accept the invitation from the Smallwood-Browns. And you two had better organise the dressmaker's visit with your mother, Rosalind.'

Four days later Susannah said goodbye to her father and climbed into the trap held steady for her by Garth. After making sure his passenger was comfortable and protected from the sharp air by a thick rug across her knees, Gerard took the reins beside her and set the horse in motion. Susannah blew her father a kiss which he returned with a cry of, 'Enjoy yourself.'

Susannah breathed deep of the chilly air and settled herself to enjoy the ride. The sun was weak and there was no wind, allowing the hoar frost to retain its pallid grip. She knew Gerard was respectfully waiting for her to open a conversation if she wished to do so. For a little while she just allowed her thoughts to dwell with some enthusiasm on what material she might choose for her dress, but she let that consideration die away, knowing Rosalind would direct the choosing, based on Miss Bosworth's suggestions, with enthusiasm.

'I see our shepherds have been preparing the barns and open shelters for the sheep,' she commented.

'Yes, Miss. The head shepherd tells me he is delighted with the new flocks of Longwools and wants to make sure they have adequate cover if we get snow. He's a man who always likes to be prepared, as you know.'

'I do like the breed. They look so attractive when their fleeces are long.'

'Yes. I think they are going to yield well come shearing time.'

'That's good news. The horses look in fine fettle too.'

'They are, Miss,' replied Gerard, a touch of pride in his voice. 'Young Garth is working out well too. I thought his initial enthusiasm might just be for show but, once he got settled, I could see it was based on a real desire to work with horses. He has a natural gift with them and is quick and ready to learn.'

'I am pleased to hear that and to know you think he will be an asset to the stable.'

'He will be. He has the makings of a fine young man.'

Susannah fell silent then, her thoughts conjuring up an image of Sally and Garth together and with it impressions of what she and Roland had been like at their age. She wondered if he would regret not being at home for Christmas, but that was no concern of hers – he had made his choice.

As Gerard drew the trap to a halt outside the front door of Stockdale Manor and jumped down to help Susannah to the ground, Rosalind hurried out, followed by one of the manservants and a maid.

'Welcome,' she called, and embraced her friend with evident delight.

The manservant took Susannah's dressing-case from Gerard; the maid stood by to take her spare cape and hatbox.

'Goodbye, Miss,' said Gerard, and climbed back on to the trap.

The two young ladies linked arms and walked up the steps to the front door. In the hall they followed the maid and manservant, who were already halfway up the stairs.

'We've put you in a room next to mine at the front of the house,' explained Rosalind.

They entered the room, in which a fire burned brightly. The manservant left but the maid remained.

'This is Agnes,' said Rosalind, 'she'll look after you while you are here.'

'Thank you,' said Susannah, and then turned to the maid, smiled and said, 'I'm sure we'll get on very well, Agnes.'

The girl bobbed a curtsey. 'Yes, Miss,' she said shyly.

'Susannah, get yourself settled and then come down to the drawing-room when you are ready,' Rosalind suggested.

'Thank you, I won't be too long.'

After she had gone, Agnes said, 'I understand, Miss, that you have stayed here before, so you'll know where everything is?'

'Yes,' replied Susannah. 'You weren't here then.'

'I'm new,' replied Agnes. 'I've been here two months.'

'Do you like it?'

'Oh, yes, Miss. If there is anything you need, just let me know.'

'Thank you. You can start on my dressing-case while I wash up after the journey.'

'Yes, Miss.' Agnes opened a door. 'Towels and soap are laid out for you in here and I brought hot water for you. It should be cool enough now.'

'Thank you, Agnes.'

Half an hour later, Susannah was entering the drawing-room where she found Mrs Webster and Rosalind waiting for her.

'Hello, Mrs Webster,' she said and crossed the room to kiss her on both cheeks. 'It is so kind of you to have me and arrange for Miss Bosworth to come.'

'It is good to see you, Susannah, and far better this way than Miss Bosworth having to make two separate journeys.'

As they had been speaking Rosalind had rung the bell and within a few minutes two maids came in with the tea trays. They set them down and poured the first cups, then left the room.

Susannah settled comfortably, relaxing in what she had always regarded as her second home.

'Ah, I see you have remembered my favourite,' she commented with pleasure at the sight of the jam sponge.

'But first you must have one of the scones,' said Mrs Webster. 'Cook has experimented with a new flavour.'

'Then I won't disappoint her,' said Susannah, selecting one from the plate.

'We've had another letter today from Roland. You'll be interested in what he says.'

'And you'll get a surprise,' put in Rosalind, then paused to take a sip of tea.

'Has he changed his mind about spending Christmas in Holland?' Susannah asked.

'Oh, no, that's not it,' continued Rosalind. 'His Christmas is going to be rather different and I sensed in his letter that he will miss our traditions. I'll read it to you. She put down her tea-cup and picked up an envelope from the table beside her. She cleared her throat and read:

'Dear Mother, Father and Rosalind,

'Firstly, I must assure you that I am well and that I am enjoying being in Holland. The friends I have made here are very welcoming. Two families who are especially kind to me are developing a flower and bulb trade. It is doing very well and is most interesting.

'One of these families, by the name of Gersen, has invited me to spend Christmas with them and extend it to the New Year. The Dutch have their main festivities on December 6th, St Nicholas's Day, instead of the 25th. I have been informed that they give small, neatly wrapped gifts, which are accompanied by a short poem that relates to the gift and recipient. I don't particularly care for that idea – I was never any good at rhyming! These small gifts are anonymous and contain a note about where the recipient's main gifts can be found.

'I'm told the Christmas fare is similar to ours, but again they have it on St Nicholas's Eve. There is

102

always a letter-cake each, which is a small confection made in the shape of the first letter of the person's Christian name.

'It will be strange celebrating so early, but it will be a new experience for me. I will think of you all and remember our festivities at Stockdale and Harthill.

'I hope you are all in good health.

'Have a wonderful Christmas and give my regards to the Charlesworths. I'm sorry not to be with you for the holiday.

'Your loving son,

'Roland.

'There you are, Susannah, now we know where my brother is going to be.'

'Thank you for reading me the letter. It is good to know he has settled in to his travels, though it does sound as though he misses some aspects of life at home.'

'Ah, well, he could have returned but chose to stay on the Continent,' said Rosalind, with a note of regret in her voice.

'A pity,' put in Marjorie. 'We'll all miss him but we won't let that spoil our Christmas – and we have the New Year's Ball at Ashworth Towers to look forward to this year. Miss Bosworth will be here tomorrow with her assistant, fabrics and patterns. I have set aside three rooms in the guest house for her use. She thinks a two-night stay will be sufficient. I've informed her about the occasion we will be attending so she will offer advice with patterns and material, if you want it. She will do the measuring and if things work out may get a preliminary cutting done, certainly of one dress, so we get some idea of what her timing will be. She will return to her premises in Hull to do the work and be back a week later for a fitting, and four days after that with the completed garments.'

'This is so exciting!' said Susannah. 'I'm looking forward to all of it. It's making Christmas last right into New Year.'

13

Marjorie Webster sat in a chair she had positioned to face the double-doors leading into the hall. As composed as she appeared, she couldn't have denied the flutter of excited anticipation she was experiencing. Miss Bosworth stood beside but slightly behind her, back straight, hands clasped below her ample bosom, confident that her work would win approval.

The moments passed, only the steady, soothing 'tick-tock' of the long-case clock breaking the silence.

Then the double-doors opened and two smiling young ladies stood there side by side. Mrs Webster gave a little gasp but quickly controlled her reaction, except for her expression of obvious approval. Though Miss Bosworth could not see Mrs Webster's reaction, she sensed it and was filled with pride.

Rosalind and Susannah exchanged a quick glance, a little nod, and then walked elegantly forward, to pause in front of the two spectators.

'Miss Bosworth, you have done a wonderful job,' said Marjorie, looking with admiration at the two girls. 'Your advice on pattern and colour has been perfect.' She made a little gesture with her hand saying, 'Promenade.'

The girls paraded elegantly around the room. The floral pattern and white broche silk of her ball dress complemented Rosalind's complexion to perfection. Her shoulder-length copper-tinted hair was held in place by a band of colours that matched those of the waist-band. The neckline dipped from the shoulders and the bodice came in tight at the waist, allowing the skirt to flare attractively.

'I could not have wished for anything better for my daughter, Miss Bosworth,' sighed Mrs Webster.

'Thank you, Ma'am.'

'And I can say the same about Miss Charlesworth's dress. It is perfection. The extra two pleats in the skirt and the higher neckline suit her admirably. Your choice of pale blue silk with a pattern of tiny pink roses does so much for her delicate skin. Delightful, Mrs Bosworth, truly delightful. I'm sure Mr Charlesworth will be enchanted too. Don't you think so, Susannah?'

'Oh, I'm certain he will,' she replied enthusiastically. 'It's wonderful, Miss Bosworth.'

'Thank you, Miss.' The dressmaker turned to Mrs Webster. 'I don't think the dresses will need any more attention, but if you think they do, between now and the ball, then let me know.'

'Thank you.' Marjorie rose from her chair and accompanied her to the hall where Miss Bosworth quickly made ready for her departure.

When Marjorie returned to the room she found the girls pirouetting across the floor. 'The practising must stop.' She smiled. 'Off you go, out of those dresses! Next time you don them will be for the ball.'

'Oh, but . . . '

Marjorie cut short Rosalind's protest. 'I think you should keep them as a surprise for the men. Leave your dress here,

Susannah. Agnes will look after it for you. Use the room you had when you stayed with us. I will suggest to your father that you, he and your uncle come here to dress and we all travel together in our carriage.'

'That will be lovely,' replied Susannah. 'It's going to be a splendid occasion.'

'Roland doesn't know what he is missing,' said Rosalind.

Her observation brought no visible reaction from Susannah, and both girls hurried away to change and leave their dresses in the hands of the maids.

As arranged, Francis, Gideon and Susannah left Stockdale Manor for Harthill Priory at two o'clock on New Year's Eve and were warmly welcomed by Peter, Marjorie and Rosalind. They were settled in and were relaxing in pleasant conversation when tea was served at three o'clock. Anticipating the splendid continuous buffet that would be served at Ashworth Towers, Marjorie had instructed Cook to arrange only a very light meal later for anyone who wanted it.

Looking forward to showing off their ball dresses and surprising the men, Susannah and Rosalind were too excited to eat. After a brief visit to the dining-room they went off to prepare for the Ball.

Agnes, who had already seen Susannah's dress, was still in awe of it, fearing she might mark or even carelessly tear it. Her expression of relief when it was safely on brought a merry smile from Susannah.

'That wasn't so bad, was it?' she asked.

Agnes gulped, content that her worst fears had not been realised. 'No, Miss.'

'I must make sure I don't spill anything on it.'

No more could be said as at that moment there was a

knock on the door. Agnes went to it but only opened it when Susannah was out of sight in the adjacent bedroom.

'Miss Rosalind,' she said, loud enough for Susannah to hear.

Susannah stepped into the dressing room to greet her friend. 'Was there anyone in the hall as you came along the landing?'

'I couldn't see; I could only hear voices. Two, I would say, your father and mine.' Rosalind glanced at the maid. 'Agnes, you'd better do as we planned now,' she said.

'Yes, Miss.' The maid went to the door and opened it slightly so she could see the top of the stairs without being observed.

The two girls were on tenterhooks, watching her.

'What a good idea of your mother's, to serve drinks in the hall so that you and I could make our grand entrance,' whispered Susannah.

Rosalind nodded. They saw Agnes raise her hand. A few moments later she turned and mouthed, 'Mr Gideon.' The girls nodded their understanding. It seemed an eternity before Agnes's next signal came and they knew Rosalind's mother was on her way downstairs. They waited a little longer. Agnes pushed the door gently open. Voices grew clearer, a little louder, then settled as the men finished greeting Marjorie.

'Now?' asked Rosalind,

Susannah nodded. They stepped out and moved quietly to the top of the stairs. They paused there, knowing they could not be seen by the people in the hall until they had reached the landing at the top of the wide flight that gave final access to the hall. Arriving on that landing they paused, then with matching steps started down the ultimate flight. The buzz of conversation rising from the small group below stopped. The atmosphere changed, charged with admiration. Their relations watched, hardly daring to breathe, lest they destroy the magic of the occasion.

With the girls five steps from the bottom, Gideon started to clap. Immediately everyone followed suit and let the applause rise to a crescendo until they reached the hall and stopped. A few moments later Marjorie rushed forward and managed to whisper to them before the men arrived, 'It worked perfectly, my dears!'

Francis, ignoring his daughter's precious dress, hugged her tight. 'Beautiful,' he whispered. His voice grew ragged as he added, 'I've lost my little girl but gained a grown-up daughter. You are so like your mother.' Tears filled his eyes but he stemmed the flow. He must not mar Susannah's day.

Peter Webster held his daughter at arm's length and said in all sincerity, 'The duckling has gone, leaving the swan to fly.' Delight was brimming in Rosalind's eyes as she stepped forward and embraced him. 'I'll always treasure those words, Father.'

'A dream come true,' said Gideon as he bent to kiss his niece. He turned to Rosalind. 'And you match her. What a wonderful way to start this New Year's Ball. My wish is for everyone here to have a brilliant year, and to start it right by dancing it in with joy in your hearts.' He raised his glass and the others followed suit.

When they were all gathering in the hall to leave for Ashworth Towers, Susannah, standing thoughtfully on her own, recalled her father's words: 'I've lost my little girl but I've gained a grown-up daughter.' They had made her feel different somehow and now she was stepping out into a whole new experience. What would Ashworth Towers offer her?

*

Knowing his parents were alone in the drawing-room, Thomas Bullen took the opportunity to make a request. 'Mother, Father, we've had a very enjoyable Christmas and I appreciate the freedom we have enjoyed. I want you to know that on Boxing Day I happened to meet with a young lady and subsequently dined with her at the Astoria in Keighley. I was wondering if you would allow me to bring her here on New Year's Eve?'

'Do we know her?' asked his father, laying down the newspaper he had been reading.

'Mama doesn't but you, Father, have met her.'

Tristan was curious. 'Where?'

'It's Miss Helen Forbes.'

'Oh.' Tristan did not hide his surprise. He glanced at his wife and gave her an explanation. 'She's the young lady from whom we bought that derelict building close to the mill.'

'Is she an agreeable person?' Ann asked her husband.

'I have only met her in a business way,' he replied.

'She's very pleasant,' put in Thomas, 'you'll like her, Mama.'

'We'll see.' She glanced at her husband. 'I think we should say yes to Thomas.'

'Very well,' he agreed, bowing to her wisdom.

'Thank you,' said Thomas, beaming with delight. 'Will seven o'clock be all right?'

'I think you ought to make it before. That is, if it will suit the young lady. Why not half-past five? It will give us a chance to talk to her before we dine and see the New Year in. Does she live far away?'

'No, Mama. In a large house this side of Keighley. There are a line of them, but standing in their own grounds.'

'Ah, yes, I know where you mean, fine houses.' Ann gave a nod of approval.

'The young lady was left well provided for, and our buying the old property she inherited will have made her quite independent,' put in Tristan to reassure his wife.

Ann looked at her son. 'You will collect her, Thomas, and see her safely home.'

'Yes, Mama.'

'Who else will be with us for New Year's Eve?' Tristan asked.

'Ralph and Liza,' replied his wife. 'Jessie has been invited to see the New Year in with her old schoolfriend's family in Sutton-in-Craven, and Daniel asked to be excused as he would like to celebrate with some of his friends. I gave both of them permission.'

Tristan nodded. He liked Ann to take charge of such family matters, knowing she would consult him if there was ever a problem; it left him more time for his beloved mill.

The snow flurries on New Year's Eve were few and far between but the weather remained cold. Thomas was reminded of that when he poked his head round the drawing-room door and said, 'Mama, I'm off now to collect Miss Forbes.'

'Very well,' replied his mother. 'Make sure she is comfortable for the ride. You have a rug for her?'

The question was never answered; Thomas was already on his way. Ann smiled to herself. Her son was in love. She hoped his dreams would never be crushed.

Jessie had been collected by her friend and the friend's brother half an hour ago. Ann was pleased to see them so easy together and knew it would be good for Jessie to be away from the family for an evening. She sighed, thoughts drifting back to the time when she was their age and Tristan

111

was telling her of his dreams, stirring similar ones in her as she realised how serious he was about achieving them. If anyone had made his dreams come true it was her husband, and she thanked God for him.

Daniel lay in bed in Griffin Manor with Penelope in his arms, running his fingers slowly and seductively down her back. He knew they should go downstairs to socialise with the customers, gamblers and diners, and welcome in the New Year, but that could wait. He lay picturing the day when Griffin Manor and all its profits would be his.

Penelope dreamed of how she could twist the man who lay beside her around her little finger and never want for anything again; the Bullen Mill and Griffin Manor would be united one day.

Ralph and Liza came out of their rooms at almost the same time and walked to the top of the stairs together.

'That's a pretty dress,' Ralph commented.

Liza felt surprised. Her brother had never made such an observation before. He must be growing up and she had not noticed. Then she recalled that Miss Forbes was coming to dine. Ralph had met her, but Thomas was bringing her here. There couldn't be jealousy stirring, could there? No, Thomas and Ralph were too close for that. She dismissed the idea and replaced it with thoughts of a beau of her own coming to whisk her away. One day it might even come true!

So the evening moved on. Lives had come together and drifted apart. Dreams had been dreamed, some lingering hopefully while others lay shattered. But everyone reflected on the future.

14

The chatter, which had been lively since leaving Harthill Priory, subsided as the coach turned through imposing iron gates marking the drive up to Ashworth Towers. Susannah was eagerly anticipating her first proper sight of the house, which so far she had only seen from a distance. Now it was completely hidden from view by the night.

The coach creaked, leather against metal. Hoofs clattered on the stony core of the drive; horses panted from the effort and the coachmen called encouragingly to them. Breath clouded on the frosty air. The coach swung with the curving drive. The moon, escaping a passing veil of cloud, revealed the fine building at the bottom of a slight but sheltering incline in the rounded landscape.

Susannah suppressed the gasp that came to her lips; it would not be lady-like to show wonderment at the sight of the great house. The central façade was two storeys high and surmounted by a stone balustrade. At each end was a wing of the same height stretching at right angles from the main front and so forming a sheltered oblong courtyard through which the drive ended in front of a flight of steps. At the corner of each wing, rising from the second storey, was a round tower with a steeply pitched conical roof. 'My fairytale castle,' Susannah whispered to herself, recalling a picture from one of her childhood books that had conjured up all sorts of romantic dreams in her young mind. Tonight looked set to live up to them.

The coach rattled to a halt. The main door to the house opened and three footmen, attired in what Susannah thought would be their dress uniforms for special occasions, hurried down the stairs to assist the new arrivals. Stable-boys had appeared and a groomsman was speaking to the newly arrived coachmen, directing them where to take their vehicles and then avail themselves of the rooms set aside for their stay.

Entering the building, they were met by the head butler and three maids. The footmen who had met them at the coach took outdoor clothes from the men and the maids attended to the ladies. The butler asked their names and escorted them to an ante-room to the left. He opened the door and stood there while he checked the situation with a glance. Then, seeing that the previous arrivals were moving on, he announced: 'Mr and Mrs Peter Webster, Mr Francis Charlesworth, Mr Gideon Charlesworth, Miss Rosalind Webster and Miss Susannah Charlesworth.'

He stepped to one side and with an inclination of his head indicated that the guests should move towards their hosts, who were waiting to welcome them. By the time Susannah's turn came to be greeted, she could sense the gentle warmth and acceptance emanating from the Honourable Geoffrey Smallwood-Brown and his wife. She had feared a different sort of greeting even though Rosalind had reassured her that the family were not the type to harbour snobbish feelings. When she felt the touch of his hand, saw the bright friendly eyes, she knew she liked their host. Moving on to be greeted by his wife, she had the same feeling. All speculation about what the people who lived in Ashworth Towers were like was banished.

'So you are Miss Charlesworth, Rosalind's friend.' The young man who greeted her next bowed graciously as he took her hand. 'I'm Henry. I have already heard a lot about you from Rosalind, I am so pleased to meet you.'

'Thank you,' replied Susannah quietly. 'It is my pleasure.'

'I trust you will enjoy your evening, and you must reserve some dances for me on your card.'

'I will be delighted to do so.'

He half-turned to the young lady next to him. 'This is my sister Felicity.' The two young ladies exchanged greetings. Susannah found the same warmth and friendliness coming from this young woman, and knew already from Rosalind that they shared the same year of birth.

'If you would like to go through that door,' said Felicity, 'the footman will direct you.'

A servant stepped forward and escorted them to open double-doors where they were greeted by a wave of sound. Other guests were busy meeting friends, renewing acquaintanceships or joining in conversation with people they had never met before, but nothing detracted from the convivial atmosphere.

Following the Websters, Susannah cast a quick glance around the room. 'About a hundred guests?' she queried in a whisper.

Rosalind nodded. 'Henry said around that number had been invited.'

'This is a fine room,' commented Susannah, eyeing the half-panelling above which white-painted walls ran up to the ceiling from which hung stucco stalactite decorations. Several oil paintings of classical subjects adorned the walls.

'This is the main drawing-room,' Rosalind explained.

They accepted a glass of Madeira from the silver tray offered by a liveried manservant.

The buzz of conversation and laughter mounted. The majority of the older guests were welcoming in their approaches to Susannah, and many commented on the style of her dress. She soon found herself receiving the attention of younger guests, too, especially men of her own age who were eager to put their names on her dance-card.

'Miss Charlesworth, I would be honoured if you would add my name to your dance-card.'

Susannah turned to the young man who had made the request. 'Mr Bradley, it is so nice to see you again; it seems a long time since our childhood parties. I will put you down for the first waltz after the interval.' She wrote Ian Bradley on her card.

'Thank you, Miss Charlesworth, I look forward to that and I hope I will be able to tell you about my travels at some time.'

'Is your father here this evening?' she asked.

'Sadly, no,' he replied, regret coming to his lively eyes. 'He has a business meeting which was planned a considerable time ago and he couldn't alter it. I know he would have enjoyed meeting with your father again. They don't meet often enough with Father having to spend time in Grimsby and Hull on business. He has fingers in so many enterprises that take up much of his time.'

With the booming of a gong, struck by one of the servants at a signal from Mrs Smallwood-Brown, the head butler announced, 'Please take your seats at the table. Your choice of refreshments will be served.'

People began to drift towards the dining-room.

'May I escort you?' Ian crooked his arm.

'Thank you. If you would be kind enough to take me to my father, I'd be grateful. Perhaps you would care to join us?'

'I'm sorry, Miss Charlesworth, I have already agreed to dine with Henry Smallwood-Brown, but I look forward to our dance.'

After a brief word with her father, Ian departed and Susannah sat down.

'A most attentive young man,' Francis commented.

'Yes, Father, he is on my dance-card for the waltz. Are you enjoying the evening?' she asked.

'Better than I thought I would,' he whispered.

'Then I'm pleased. It is good to see you socialising more.'

'Oh, I'm quite content,' he replied.

'Yes, but look at Uncle Gideon. He's the centre of a whole group of men.'

'I know, but he's a banker and you'll always get those with financial interests wanting to talk business, even at events like this.'

'Ah, but look at him now,' Susannah pointed out, seeing her uncle move away from the men and sit down between two young ladies.

Francis gave a little smile, 'Oh, that's your uncle – always was a man for the ladies.'

'Then it's a wonder he never married.'

'There was someone once, but your mother and I never knew who. It came to nothing, apparently, though we never found out why. And are you enjoying the evening, my dear?'

'Very much so, Father. This food is splendid and I am looking forward to the dancing.' This was turning out to be a memorable evening for Susannah and she recognised, once again, that she was advancing deeper into the adult world, with all the changes and new expectations that entailed. There was a wider world ahead of her than the one she knew, wider even than her beloved Lincolnshire Wolds, though they would always be dear to her heart, the centre of her life.

Pleasant music drifted through the house, and when the first dance was called the ballroom was turned into a whirl of colours. The opening quadrille was followed by minuets, gavottes, polkas, the Lancers (newly arrived from Paris), and the ever-popular swirling waltz. Susannah was so thankful that her father had permitted their housekeeper, Mrs Ainsworth, to teach her some of these dances, knowing that it was what his wife would have done. He swelled with pride as he watched her and her partner waltz past. Francis was started out of his reverie by a tap on the shoulder and a voice saying, 'She's wonderful, and enjoying every moment.'

Francis turned to his brother. 'She is, isn't she?'

'Then let us charge a glass and drink a toast to her.'

So the evening progressed towards midnight. Everyone gathered in the ballroom and the musicians changed tempo until for a few minutes they fell silent. From the hall the loud tolling of a grandfather clock marked the first stroke of midnight. Silence fell on the room and then, as the seconds were counted down, the musicians quietly started to play 'Auld Lang Syne' letting the strains rise loudly to the twelfth stroke. Cheering rang out. Cries of 'Happy New Year' were exchanged. Laughter abounded. Finally the musicians picked up their playing again and the dancing continued.

The New Year moved on. Finally it was announced that breakfast was being served to anyone who gave an order to one of the servants. There were a few takers, who wanted to prolong their visit, but after consultation the Websters and Charlesworths, still happy after their earlier foray to the dining-room, decided they should leave. Rosalind managed to secure a parting kiss from Henry and a promise that they would meet again soon. Thanks, laced with praise for a wonderful time, were offered to their host and hostess, who insisted they should keep in touch and visit again. The Smallwood-Browns privately expressed their delight and approval of their son's interest in Rosalind to Mr and Mrs Webster.

In a joyous mood, the Websters and Charlesworths climbed into their coach which had been brought to the front of the house. Once the coachman saw they were settled he sent the carriage on its way, leaving the crisp morning air filled with shouts of thanks as the guests waved goodbye.

The Charlesworths changed into their own coach at Harthill Priory, and once again thanks and parting exchanges were made. As they got underway, the three occupants sank back in the seats with sighs of pleasure.

'That was a lovely night,' commented Susannah, with some regret that it was all over.

'It was,' agreed Francis and Gideon together.

'I suppose we all have a lot to say about it, but I think it would be better left until tomorrow,' Francis suggested.

'Don't you mean today, Papa?' corrected Susannah.

The rest of the journey passed in sleepy silence. At Stockdale Manor they climbed wearily from the coach, and, with only a mumbled goodnight to each other, went to their rooms and were soon in bed, letting thoughts of their evening at Ashworth Towers lull them to sleep.

*

The clock had boomed the twelve strokes of midnight through Ash Tree Villa, bringing Tristan, Anne, Liza, Ralph, Thomas and Helen Forbes to their feet to exchange good wishes for the New Year. They had enjoyed dining together; the Bullens using it as a chance to get to know the charming young woman who had entered their lives. Having had to fend for herself and combat adversity during the last three years, Helen was independent-minded but adaptable, a good conversationalist and a lively character.

Laughter had rung through out the house during a session of parlour games before Helen declared that she should leave. With goodnights made, Thomas escorted her home. He jumped from the trap in front of her house and helped her to the ground. He took her arm as they walked to the front door and stood by while she sought the key in her reticule, having released the maid from her duties earlier in the evening.

Helen inserted the key in the lock and, turning to Thomas, said, 'Thank you so much for a most pleasant evening. I enjoyed meeting your mother and some of your family – and, of course, conversing with your father again without its being on a business footing. Thank you.' She held out her hand to him. He took it and, when he held it a little longer than decorum demanded, she added with a teasing twinkle in her eyes, 'Ah, Thomas, before I make the invitation you might have in mind, you have to earn it.' Before he could comment, she added, 'Let's say goodbye. For now at least.'

He smiled. 'So that, when we meet again, you can have a better opinion of me?'

'If the weather is fine, you can take me to Skipton on Saturday morning.'

'Very well, I will do that. I am at your command.' He

made a little inclination of his head and walked down the path whistling 'Choose Me Your Valentine'.

She smiled and went into the house and locked the door.

'I liked Helen,' commented Ann to her husband as they prepared for bed.

'So did I,' agreed Tristan. 'A capable young woman as I already knew, but tonight I encountered a warm personality. Thomas could not do better.'

Ann nodded. 'I can see him happily settled with her. I hope Daniel will soon meet a suitable young lady.'

'He will,' replied Tristan. 'He's of a different nature to Thomas; needs to find his own way. But he will do, and discover someone worthy of him.'

'I hope so. We never get as close to him as we do to Thomas and Ralph. It's as if there are sides to him he doesn't want us to see.'

'I'm sure you are exaggerating, my dear. He has knuckled down to work much more readily than he used to. I've not had to discipline him at all recently. His capabilities are finally showing themselves. I can see he will be a credit to us one day.'

'I hope you are right, Tristan,' said Ann, before climbing into bed and seeking reassurance in his arms.

15

'Oh, I'm so pleased this weather didn't come before the ball,' said Susannah, looking out of the drawing-room window.

There had been heavy frosts for two days and now snow was falling steadily as if it was determined to be around for some time.

Gideon came up beside her and surveyed the sky. 'It looks as if you will have to put up with me for a little while longer.'

'That will be a bonus for Father and me,' said Susannah. 'But what about your business?'

'My staff are competent enough to get on without me breathing down their necks, so I've no worries about not being there. Besides they'll be longer without me when I move, though then we will be in regular correspondence. There'll come a time, though, when I need to be back in Hull or things there will pile up and make my move to the West Riding more awkward.'

'Have you a date fixed for us to help you choose your house?'

'As soon as this snow clears and I've visited Hull, I'll return here for the three of us to go to Keighley together.'

'I'm looking forward to helping you. It will be an adventure.'

The door opened and Francis walked in. He was still in the clothes in which he had left the house earlier in the day, with the exception of his outdoor coat, hat, gloves and boots. Expelling a deep breath, he flopped into a chair.

'Has it been difficult, Papa?' asked Susannah.

He gave a brief nod. 'It has today. Two sheep were missing. We searched hard until we found them in a drift. Numb-headed things had strayed out of their shelter.'

'Were they all right?' asked Susannah with concern.

'They were, thank goodness,' he replied. 'Needed prolonged attention from three of the men, but they brought them through all right.'

'Here. Drink this.' Gideon thrust a glass of whisky at his brother.

'Thanks,' said Francis, raising the glass. He took a drink and smacked his lips. 'Just the reviver I needed.'

'You shouldn't have been out there,' said Gideon.

'The men appreciate me being with them at times like this.'

'I know, but be careful you don't overdo it.'

'I'll double my watch over him,' said Susannah.

'Don't you start, young lady,' chided Francis.

She came to him, kneeled down and hugged him. 'I will if necessary,' she replied, and kissed him on the cheek, but she knew that where the sheep were concerned she would lose the battle. He would rally the estate workers and work alongside them to fight the adverse weather and see that his flocks were safe and able to use the shelters that had been prepared for them. Any animal that showed signs of distress was brought into the protection and warmth of a large barn kept free throughout the winter for this purpose.

'And what have you been doing with yourself all day?' he asked.

'I've played four games of draughts with Uncle Gideon.

I beat him every time, so then he got the sulks and wouldn't play again.' Susannah grinned at the face her uncle pulled at her and went on, 'He said he had some figures he must study but I think it was an excuse to avoid another beating. So I went back to the usual, reading sewing and writing letters, ready for Sally to collect and Gerard to see on to the mail coach.'

'And no doubt dreaming of the ball?' Francis had seen his chance to learn a little more about her deeper reaction to that night, which had eluded him until now.

'It was a wonderful event. I so enjoyed it. I loved it all, but the dancing the most.'

'Mrs Ainsworth had taught you well.'

'Oh, Papa, I'm so glad you allowed her to do that. Rosalind told me before we left that several of the young men commented to her on my dancing. She was sure I would receive other invitations.'

Francis took a sip of his whisky that allowed him a pause to think about his reply, but he never made it because Susannah, feeling in her reticule, jumped to her feet, saying, 'I need a handkerchief,' and hurried from the room, thankful that her father had not been able to reply.

When the door closed behind her, Gideon looked at his brother. 'You were starting to fish,' he said.

'Isn't it a father's right to know what his daughter thinks about such things?'

'Of course it is, but you have to be careful how you do it, and choose the right time to go about it.' He looked sharply at his brother. 'Let me remind you, Susannah is growing into a beautiful young lady. I believe she left much of her girlhood behind at that ball. This is a delicate time for her. Be careful how you handle it.'

Francis took another sip and looked hard at his brother but

held back from making any argument. Francis knew that whatever his brother said about family matters was always uttered in good faith.

Susannah, who preferred to do the morning combing of her hair herself, laid the brush down, looked critically in the mirror of her dressing table, made another assessment, patted a wayward curl into place and picked up her dance card from the ball. It took her mind back three weeks to that evening and to all the people who had signed it.

She smiled in recollection. Here was her father's rounded hand, here Uncle Gideon's flourish. Henry Smallwood-Brown's careful letters recalled his lightness of foot. She peered closely at a name, barely able to make out the handwriting – Monty Weir. Oh, dear, his feet had been as uncontrollable as his scrawl; Cary Pearson whose deep blue eyes sparkled with interest; Gordon Chambers who thought a lot about himself and tried to impress her by telling her what he would do when he joined the Army as a commissioned officer – the only bore of the night. Good-looking Ian Bradley had danced so divinely she did not know her feet were touching the floor. He had flattered her by claiming two more dances, which Susannah had granted readily. Recalling this she laid her card down, wondering if she would hear from him again in accordance with the promise he had made.

She rose from her chair and walked into the neighbouring dressing-room, where her maid was waiting. Susannah selected a morning dress which she put on with the maid's help and then went down to the dining-room to join her father and uncle for breakfast.

'Good morning, my dear,' said Gideon. 'I was just saying to your father, after three weeks of poor weather some signs of it relenting at last these last couple of days have made me decide I must make an effort to return to Hull.'

'You are sure it will be safe to do so?' she asked with some concern as she sat down at the table.

'It has been quite a rapid thaw, a little unusual but I think the journey will be possible. I'll see what it is like in an hour's time.'

An hour later the sun was out, the sky was blue and the weather promised to hold fair.

'I'll travel light on horseback and leave my trap here, if that is all right, Francis?' said Gideon when they had gathered in the drawing room to make the decision.

'You know it is, without asking.'

'I've already told Gerard to have my horse ready. He should have it brought round any time now. I'll get my things. I won't be long.' Gideon stepped quickly to the door. When it had closed, Francis smiled at his daughter. 'That's your Uncle Gideon. Takes time to make up his mind but when he does it's all go.'

'I'll get Cook to put some food together,' said Susannah, starting for the door.

'I've already done that,' said her father. 'I could tell he had made up his mind to go, so I instructed her.'

A few minutes later Gideon hurried in. The usually calm, steady attitude had been overtaken by a bustling, mind-made-up figure. 'Right, I'm off.' He took Francis's hand and wrung it warmly, then turned to Susannah, gave her a hug and a quick kiss on the cheek. He stepped into the hall, shrugged on his warm redingote, crammed his hat on his head, pulled on his gloves and headed for the door. Francis and Susannah followed. He stopped and turned to face them.

'Don't come out, it's cold even though it's bright. I'm dressed for it, you are not.' He glanced out of the glass doors.

'Your man has taken my saddle-bags and Cook's contribution, Garth has my horse, so I'm ready. I'll let you know when I need you to view the houses. Goodbye.' And with that he was gone.

As father and daughter watched him go, Susannah said, 'Well, I've seen something of the anxious side of him before, but never as marked as today.'

'I suppose the weather has something to do with it. He doesn't want to be isolated any longer, he's been away from his business too long.'

Susannah gave a little laugh. 'He's been dragging his heels about choosing a house, so if today's mood returns and he gives us a date we'd better be ready for the journey.'

Francis grunted. 'We certainly had, but don't let this side of him fool you. He'll have thought about those houses very carefully and will have in mind just the right time for us to look them over. We'll have a whirlwind visit when he lets us know. Oh, he's off.'

Gideon was in the saddle. He waved, and without further ado, sent his horse away from Stockdale Manor.

About the same time Daniel Bullen pushed himself from his chair and went to the window in his office. He was glad the weather had taken a turn for the better and hoped it would stay so; it would make a lot of difference. There would be fewer absentees from the mill. His father was more sympathetic to the workers in the poor conditions that had prevailed recently.

Men and women had slithered through snow turned to slush by hundreds of feet marching their way daily along uneven streets, to earn just enough to keep them alive. Those at the Bullen Mill counted themselves lucky to be working for a thoughtful owner who had once been one of them. Daniel knew that was why his father was sympathetic to his

127

workers in the bad weather – he himself had tramped through snow and afterwards stood at the loom with wet feet. But Daniel knew there were also those among the workers who played on his father's sympathetic nature at times like these. As he watched some of them trudging across the yard, which still had some thawing snow visible that had not been cleared, he swore when he took over there would be no one seeking to prey on his sympathies.

He turned back to his desk, sat down, picked up a pencil to get some production figures ready for his father ... but paused before making a mark on the paper and let his mind drift to Griffin Manor. Soon he would be lying naked with Penelope again – he cursed the weather for missed opportunities, but now, with the changing skies, there would be no obstacle in his way.

Thomas had left the mill early, thankful that the improving weather was holding good. The snow that had hit the West Riding had prevented him from seeing Helen again. He had been on tenterhooks, hoping it had not affected his chance of furthering their relationship, so once the weather had started to improve he sent her a note.

Dear Miss Forbes,
    Now that it is easier to move more freely, I ask you to do me the honour of accompanying me to Sunday lunch at the Worthy Arms in Silsden. If your answer is yes I will call for you at noon.
    Yours in admiration,
    Thomas

He had awaited the answer in some uneasiness but that was banished when it came with a grateful acceptance of his suggestion.

At noon on Sunday he jumped down from his trap in front of Helen's house, secured his horse and straightened his redingote. Whistling once more 'Choose Me Your Valentine', he stepped jauntily along the path.

He pulled the doorbell and a few minutes later the maid opened the door. Recognising the visitor and knowing he was expected, she said brightly, 'Good afternoon, Mr Bullen, Miss Forbes is expecting you.' She stepped to one side, allowing him to enter the hall. 'Please follow me.' She led the way to the drawing-room. 'Mr Bullen, Miss.' She stepped to one side to allow him to enter, and closed the door.

Helen rose from her chair with a welcoming smile. She held out her hands to him and Thomas put one to his lips.

'It is good to see you again, Helen, looking so well and pretty in that outfit.'

She inclined her head, accepting his compliment with a gracious smile. 'It is kind of you to say so.'

Thomas took her pale blue cape, which the maid had left ready, and held it for her. She slipped her arms through the open sleeves and picked up the grey muff that matched her plain full skirt.

'Do you know the Worthy Arms?' she asked, as she tucked her hair in neatly at the sides of the bonnet.

'Yes. I have been there before, and have got to know the landlord. He runs a good dining-room.'

'Good, then I look forward to trying it.'

They left the house in good humour, both determined to enjoy their day.

'You handle the horse very gently,' observed Helen when it had got into its stride.

'Thank you,' replied Thomas. His lips tightened. 'Daniel

can be a little rough with them at times. It annoys me, but as you know a younger brother has to be careful with the criticism he makes.'

'He takes umbrage if you object?' asked Helen with a modicum of surprise.

'He certainly does, and more so if it concerns work.'

'And being the eldest, he's in charge after your father?'

'Yes, he'll take over the mill one day.'

Helen detected a hint of concern in Thomas's remark but made no comment, deeming it no concern of hers. 'I only met him when we negotiated the sale of my property. He wasn't with us on New Year's Eve.'

'He was away with friends,' replied Thomas dismissively.

'One day I hope I'll meet him on social terms.'

At that remark Thomas felt a warm glow. It hinted that Helen wanted to continue her friendship with him.

'I must paint that village church ... it is so nicely situated,' he mused.

'Do you paint?' she asked.

'Yes, I've always been interested. It is only a pastime. I don't have as much time for it as I would like.'

'You must show me.'

'You wouldn't be interested.'

She smiled. 'That is where you are wrong. I do know a little about art, I had good teachers.'

Their conversation continued pleasantly as they discussed each other's interests during the rest of the drive and throughout their meal, when they received every attention from the landlord and his staff.

'That was a most pleasant meal. Thank you,' said Helen as they drove away from the Worthy Arms.

'It was my pleasure,' replied Thomas, turning the horse in the direction of Keighley.

Helen sensed something was troubling him when his usual ebullient flow of conversation began to dry up.

'Thomas, I never beat about the bush ... what is the matter? We've had a lovely day. I hope I haven't done anything to spoil it?' she asked.

'No, you haven't,' he replied quickly.

'So what is it?'

'I'm not going to be able to see you for a while,' he replied glumly.

'Oh! Why not?'

'Work,' he replied. 'Since we have put extra looms in the building we bought from you, we will be buying more wool. Father has negotiated extra supplies of fleeces and Ralph and I have to check the route for transporting it from North Lincolnshire to our mill. We have done some preliminary work and think we have a feasible plan but we still have to negotiate means of transport, rights of waterways, carriers and so on. It will take me away – I don't know for how long – just as I'm getting to know you.'

'I'll still be here when you return.'

'I wish Father had given the job to Daniel. That would ... ' he continued as if she had not spoken, then realising what she had just said, he stopped, drew the trap to a halt, turned to her and said, wide-eyed, 'You mean that?'

'I don't say things I don't mean, Thomas. Of course I'll be here.'

'Waiting for me?'

'Yes.'

'And I was dreading telling you.'

'It's work, Thomas. I understand if it sometimes takes you away. I understand a little about the wool trade, and knowing the role your father has designated for the building I sold him, I realise everything has to be made ready by shearing time, especially the transporting of the fleeces. You've work to do, Thomas, work I know you will do successfully, to ensure the future of the mill. Think of me when you are in Lincolnshire or wherever, and recall the happy time we have had together today.'

'I will, Helen, I will,' he answered fervently. 'It will keep me going until I'm back again.'

'Thomas.' She looked deep into his eyes. 'You may kiss me now and have something else to remember me by.'

16

'This spring weather is holding splendidly,' commented Francis as he and Susannah leaned on a fence and admired the healthy lambs. 'Lambing is nearly over. I hope we don't hear from Uncle Gideon about Keighley until the last one is born.'

'I wonder what is holding him back,' said Susannah. 'Maybe there'll be word when we go in to lunch.'

'I hope so. I thought early-spring might be the time he would choose to visit the West Riding but it is drawing on. He knows full well I get busier later on.'

They hung their outdoor clothing in the small cloakroom off the entrance and changed their boots for indoor shoes before going into the hall.

'How long have we?' said Susannah, glancing at the grandfather clock standing like a sentry near the bottom of the stairs, its steady tick marking the passing seconds.

'Ten minutes,' said her father. 'Time to wash our hands. He headed for the cloakroom while his daughter took the stairs.

The clock was chiming the hour when they entered the dining-room together.

'There are letters,' said Susannah, having noted that a

silver salver on which two envelopes were neatly laid had been set near her father's place.

'One from my brother, I hope,' Francis said as he sat down. He picked up the two envelopes and glanced at the writing. 'Yes, one from Gideon,' he exclaimed thankfully. 'Oh, this one's addressed to you,' he added with a note of curiosity coming into his voice.

Susannah came to collect her letter. Who could be writing to her? She sat down in her place again, puzzled by the writing she did not recognise.

Even though he felt a need to know who was communicating with his daughter, Francis curbed his interest and waited to open his letter until the soup had been served. He scanned it quickly and said, 'Your Uncle Gideon is planning to be here in four days' time and suggests we leave for Keighley the following day. He takes it that it will be convenient for us to fall in with his plans.'

'Is it agreeable to you, Papa?' asked Susannah, selecting a piece of bread.

'I'll make it so. I really do think your uncle is dragging out this house-move too long.'

'I hope one of the properties he has in mind will be suitable and that he settles there quickly,' commented Susannah, leaving her bread on her side plate and eagerly picking up her own letter. She slit the envelope carefully and extracted a card. 'Oh, my goodness,' she gasped. Looking up at her father, her face drained of colour, she said, 'It's an invitation.'

Gideon's advice returned to Francis's mind. He knew he must be careful how he handled this situation – the first personal invitation his daughter had received.

'Who is it from?' he asked gently.

'Ian Bradley,' she said with a slight tremor in her voice.

'He was at the Smallwood-Browns' New Year's Eve Ball. I danced with him several times.'

'A very good-looking young fellow, I recall.'

'Yes.'

'I noticed you had several conversations with him too and he was most attentive at the buffet,' commented Francis. 'So what is the occasion for this invitation?'

She read out, '"*Mr Ian Bradley requests the company of Miss Susannah Charlesworth at an informal party for thirty friends to be held at Woodhouse Grange on 6th April 1851, 6 p.m. until 10 p.m.*"'

Francis knew his daughter was in a state of nervous tension, wondering what his reply would be. He hesitated a few moments, took a spoonful of soup and then looked at her and said, 'You must answer quickly and politely to accept. After all, they are our neighbours, even though five miles separate our two properties on the south bank of the Humber.'

Susannah was hardly able to believe what she had just heard. Her father had always been so protective and an invitation like this, a first for her, would once have needed endless scrutiny. Perhaps it was different now she was older. Maybe in these last few months he had come to realise she was a young lady and, having seen her in Mr Bradley's company at the ball, had not only formed an opinion of him but maybe even made enquiries about the man. But no matter if he had and no matter what had gone through his mind . . . her father had said yes!

She jumped from her chair, rounded the table and flung her arms round his neck. 'Oh, thank you, Papa, thank you.'

Francis smiled and patted her hand. 'Now, let us get on with our lunch. We'll talk about this afterwards.'

Susannah was in a happy frame of mind as she walked into the drawing-room with her father. She felt she had moved another step away from the boundaries that had restricted her younger life; in fact, they were gone for ever.

She poured the coffee that been placed ready in the drawing-room a few moments before their arrival. She put one cup on the small table set beside her father's chair to the left of the fireplace. She brought her own to another table, close to a chair set to the other side of the fireplace in which flames burned brightly.

Francis took some sugar and stirred his coffee thoughtfully. 'Susannah, your mother would have been proud of you. You owe much to her, you know. Though she died when you were young, she made sure that Mrs Ainsworth knew the ideals she wished to impart to you. Mrs Ainsworth has been a gem in seeing you were brought up just as your mother wanted.'

'No doubt you played your part too, Papa.'

He gave a wan smile. 'I hope so. What I am clumsily hinting at is this. Be a credit to your mother. Don't do anything she would not want you to do. Always do what is right. Always be strong and be your own person. You are old enough to understand what I am saying. Always love where it is returned and you will have a happy life. Now enough of this. Let us deal with that invitation. Had you an idea that it was coming?'

'No, Papa. Mr Bradley did say he hoped we could meet again, but that was all.'

'You don't know anyone else who will be going?'

'Not definitely but I would expect Rosalind to be there. Henry Smallwood-Brown and Mr Bradley are close friends.'

'We'll check that. It would be nice for you to have her there and as a companion to accompany you. We could ride over to Harthill Priory tomorrow, and if she has been invited

I will suggest that, when the time comes, Gerard drives you there and collects Rosalind on the way.'

'That would be splendid, Papa.'

'That's settled. The comfortable satisfaction in his voice pleased Susannah. She was even more contented when he went on, 'As you know, I've met Mr Bradley, Ian's father, on a few occasions, and I must say he struck me as a pleasant friendly person. He has shipping interests in Grimsby. At one time he was considering developing suitable sites along the south bank of the Humber to try to stimulate trade with Hull but more particularly to open up connections with suitable inland points. That possibility seems to have waned a little but with a man like him it could be resurrected any time, especially with his wealth.'

'Rosalind told me that Ian Bradley's mother has wealth in her own right which is tied up so only she can handle it. But she does back her husband's enterprises and, unusually for a lady in her circumstances, takes an interest in them and does not hold back any advice if she believes it will help him.'

'A lady before her time,' commented Francis, showing by his tone that he admired this trait.

The following morning was sunny and showing the first signs of the year warming up. With her father taking the reins, Susannah made herself comfortable to enjoy the ride which would take them through the rolling terrain of the Wolds. The fields had shed winter's harshness and were teeming with new life. The grass was showing goodness and sheep were revelling in the freedom of being outside

'Our flocks are looking well,' Susannah observed.

'Yes, I'm pleased that they took no harm in those trying conditions, though as you know it was touch and go for some of them. But they survived and all is well.'

They were greeted with pleasure by Marjorie Webster, who insisted that they stay for lunch.

After a morning drink, she knew she would be alone until the meal was served; Rosalind and Susannah were already engrossed in conversation and would be walking in the garden; Francis and Peter would talk sheep and farming, but Marjorie didn't mind. She liked having visitors, didn't stand on ceremony, and if there was the opportunity to do whatever took her fancy, she would do it. As she watched them walk away she gave a little sigh of regret; she still missed Susannah's mother even after all this time.

She was sitting on the veranda at the front of the house when Peter and Francis returned to join her and await lunch. Ten minutes later Rosalind and Susannah returned and flopped into the two vacant chairs,

'Mama, Papa, I've said yes. You're always saying I can't make up my mind ... well, I have, I've said yes,' announced Rosalind, wide-eyed with excitement.

Marjorie and Peter looked surprised, and then exchanged a glance of bewilderment.

Rosalind, taken aback by their expressions, stared at them and then started laughing. She could hardly get her words out in her merriment. 'Oh, dear, you thought I was telling you I'd agreed to Henry coming to ask you for my hand in marriage? No, no, it's not that. Well, not yet, and then only if he asks me. Maybe he won't, but I think he will – sometime.'

'Rosalind, slow down, slow down,' said her father, gesticulating with his hands. 'Who have you said yes to?'

'And about what?' put in her mother.

'Susannah. She's been invited by Ian Bradley too. She is accepting. Gerard will be driving her so she has suggested that they come this way for me. That is what I've said yes to.'

Francis, smiling quietly at Rosalind's exuberance, said, 'Marjorie, Peter, I'm sorry if I have caused all this. The purpose of our visit was to tell you about Susannah's invitation and volunteer to take Rosalind as well, but when you invited us to stay I thought I would mention it at lunch once we were all settled together.'

'Oh, dear,' said Susannah. 'I'm sorry I mentioned it to Rosalind.'

'It doesn't matter,' said Peter with a dismissive wave of his hand. 'No harm done.'

The lunch gong sounded.

'I have received a letter from Mr Charlesworth,' said Tristan, walking into Daniel's office.

He laid down his pen and, with an enquiring look, waited for his father to go on.

Tristan sat down opposite him and glanced at the piece of paper in his hand to verify he had its contents right. 'He says the sheep are in good fettle and the quality of the fleeces is among of the best he has seen. Increasing the size of his flock has naturally led to a bigger yield. It seems we made a good investment in buying the old building from Miss Forbes.'

'Good,' said Daniel. 'The looms are waiting. Does Mr Charlesworth say when he would like to see me?'

'He says he expects shearing to start in three weeks' time.'

Daniel glanced at the calendar, prominently placed on the wall and easily visible from his chair. 'The twenty-fifth.'

'We must check the route with Thomas and Ralph. Fetch them. Everything had better be in place or I'll want to know why.'

Blanching at the implication that lay behind those words, Daniel headed for the door. He knew what the cutting edge of his father's tongue could be like. Halfway there he stopped. 'Sir, if you don't mind the suggestion, it would be easier if we went to their office. I know they have the relevant maps there.'

Tristan grunted, 'Very well.' He pushed himself from his chair and by the time he reached the door Daniel had it open for him. He walked down the corridor with an extra-brisk step. Daniel raised his eyebrows as he tried to catch up. That briskness did not augur well for Thomas and Ralph if the route was causing problems.

Tristan threw open the door and the bang it made caused the two young men to jump away from the map they had been poring over. 'I've had no report about the route for a while. You were having problems with one section, I believe. I expected you to have it settled by now.' He glared at them. 'Well?'

'We were away two days last week, sir,' replied Thomas, a little warily.

'And?'

'We were unable to find an answer,' he confessed. 'It isn't always easy to discover who owns rights of way, and has access to waterways.'

'We do have something else to look into,' put in Ralph timidly.

'Get it done!' thundered Tristan. 'This whole enterprise could be scuppered by your incompetence.'

'Sir, it has been difficult ... '

'I want no excuses. You've been spending too much time with your sketchbook. I will not have that hobby threatening the mill. Shearing will be starting in three weeks' time.' He waved the letter at them. 'Mr Charlesworth will be expecting those fleeces to be moving then.' His eyes narrowed. 'You'd better see that they are.'

Tristan stormed out of the room.

Daniel gave a little shrug as if to say, I can't do anything about it. With a faint twitch of his lips he said, 'You'd better get on with it, brothers. Throw that damned sketchbook away, Thomas, and all your paintings. As Father says, the only important thing in this family is the mill.' He followed Tristan from the room.

Ralph looked askance at his brother, 'What are we going to do, Thomas? The increase in the number of fleeces means more wagons. The stretch of the old route that we need to complete our new idea is not fit for wagons after the severe winter has left it in a terrible condition; far worse than I had imagined. The wagons could be in danger of breaking in the ruts. The new route we devised using more waterways to make the transporting of the fleeces more efficient was looking good. This last stretch is all we need to complete the route as we visualise it.'

Thomas had been looking at the map spread out on the wide oak table. He smoothed it with the flat of his hands, a habit he had developed since first becoming engaged in this task.

'Trying to conjure up a solution with your magic fingers?' said Ralph, coming to stand beside him.

Thomas made no comment but instinctively performed the action again. Ralph's eyes automatically followed the movement of his fingers.

'Thomas, maybe we've been looking in the wrong place for this last stage,' he said, his voice rising with excitement.

'What do you mean?' asked his brother, straightening.

'Look,' said Ralph, directing his attention back to the map. 'We've got a connection to the River Don from where we were aiming to use a canal to the River Aire, bringing us into the West Riding near Keighley.'

141

'Right,' agreed Thomas, watching Ralph's finger trace that route on the map.

'Naturally we have always looked west from Stockdale Manor, here.' He tapped the map. 'It's that area that is causing the problems. But maybe we should have been looking north from Stockdale.'

'North? But that's ... '

Ralph let him go no further. 'If the land north of Stockdale has not suffered in the same way as that to the west, then there might well be a suitable way to the Humber, and that would lead us to the canals and the Aire which we have already included in our route.' Excitement was rising in Ralph's voice, and it forced Thomas to reconsider their plans.

It only took him a moment to see what his brother was driving at. 'You've solved it!' he cried, slapping him appreciatively on the back.

'Hold on, we've got to see if it's possible first,' cautioned Ralph.

'Then let's get on with it. We can be on our way in an hour. Say nothing to Father or Daniel, but we'll have to call in at home to mention it to Mother and she can tell Father we've gone to solve the problem. If we tell him and Daniel, they will only hold us up wanting to hear more about it. Come on, let's get home and make ready.'

17

The inn Thomas and Ralph found for the night was in a pleasant situation overlooking a village pond occupied by ten white ducks. Opposite the inn was a row of ten well-cared-for cottages. Similar cottages stood in a line to either side of the inn, and beyond the row on the right was a fine stand of oaks. The landlord, a well-built man with a friendly face and smile, gave them a warm welcome. In answer to their enquiry about rooms for the night, he called out, 'Sara!' A well-proportioned lady came from the back room, wiping her hands on a piece of cloth hanging from the belt round her waist. Her rounded face and rosy cheeks, coupled with bright eyes and a welcoming smile, spoke of contentment. Ralph thought they had picked a good place to stay.

'My good wife Sara,' said the landlord by way of introduction, 'and I'm Roger.' He held out a big hand to the brothers whom he judged had money behind them.

'Thomas, and this is my brother Ralph.'

'Pleased to meet you, gentlemen. Sara, two rooms for tonight.' He glanced at Thomas. 'Would you like food this evening?'

'Please, if that is possible?'

'Always possible, sir,' Sara replied. 'Rabbit pie, meat pie or one of my special stews?'

'I'll have a special, please,' said Ralph.

'And I'll have the rabbit,' said Thomas.

'Very good,' Sara said. 'If you follow me, I'll show you to your rooms.'

They picked up their saddlebags and followed her.

'When you are ready, come down for a jar of ale on the house,' called Roger as they followed his wife.

'Very civil of you, landlord,' called Thomas.

They had a quick wash from the filled ewers in their rooms and came downstairs to claim their ale. They exchanged greetings with four customers in the bar and found a corner table. By the time they had finished their meal, for which they had nothing but praise, they had formulated their plan for the next day.

They were in their saddles soon after an early breakfast, and thankful that the weather looked set fair.

'Are you sure this is the right way to go about this?' queried a cautious Ralph. 'Just turning up and seeking help from Mr Charlesworth might be frowned upon.'

'I don't think he'll protest. They're his fleeces we are seeking to transport, and we are only asking for advice based on his local knowledge.'

But they met with deep disappointment when they reached Stockdale Manor and asked for Mr Charlesworth.

'I'm sorry, sir, he's not at home,' said the maid who had answered the door to them.'

'It is a business matter. Do you know when he will be back?'

'I'll find out, sir, if you care to wait?'

'Thank you,' said Thomas.

The maid closed the door.

A few minutes later the door opened again.

'I'm Mrs Ainsworth, Mr Charlesworth's housekeeper,' said a prim, neatly dressed lady with an air of authority. 'I'm afraid the master is away and I am uncertain when he will be back.' She had quickly summed up the two strangers and had made a favourable assessment of them, otherwise she would have been careful in what she told them. 'If it is a business call you should see his manager, Jack Weldon. I have just seen him go into his office. You will find that at the back of the house in a building that stands alone on the west side of the courtyard.'

'Thank you, Ma'am. We are sorry we won't see Mr Charlesworth but I'm sure his manager will be of help.' They doffed their caps and left the house.

Reaching the building to which they had been directed, Ralph used the doorknocker then opened the door on the call of, 'Come in!'

A middle-aged man, with skin roughened by wind and sun, looked up to see the two young men coming in. His quick assessment of their clothing and bearing told him they were not looking for employment.

'Good day, gentlemen,' he said.

'Good day,' they replied brightly. Thomas carried on, 'The housekeeper directed us to you. I'm Thomas Bullen and this is my brother Ralph.'

The manager rose from his chair and extended his hand to them. 'Jack Weldon. Have you come about the sheep? I thought it was arranged for Mr Daniel Bullen to be here at shearing time?'

'He will be here then. This is something else. Neither he nor our father knows we are here.' Thomas noted a quick flash of curiosity and doubt cross the manager's face then.

145

'This visit is all above board,' Thomas said quickly. 'Let me explain.' He paused and the manager chose that moment to gesture for them to be seated.

Once they were comfortably settled Thomas explained how he and Ralph had come up against an obstacle in the usual route to the mill, and how they needed to investigate a solution. 'We'd like to go across country from here to the Humber, using that to reach the canals on which we have already arranged transport,' he explained.

Jack Weldon listened carefully; after all, it was in Stockdale's interest to help move the fleeces. Thomas had seen interest in the manager's expression when he had finished his explanation and hope soared when Jack said, 'There would be no problem crossing Stockdale land, that section of the estate is better draining land and we have a private track across it.'

'Does it go as far as the Humber?' asked Ralph, hope in his voice.

Weldon gave a wry smile. 'Alas, no. The land between ours and the Humber is owned by a man by the name of Jules Bradley.'

'Where can we find him?' asked Thomas.

'Woodhouse Grange,' said Jack and, seeing the Bullens look mystified, added, 'Leave that for the moment. We have always found Mr Bradley a considerate and helpful neighbour, though as far as our adjacent holdings are concerned little of note has arisen. Should he need to use our track, for personal reasons, he is at liberty to do so. In turn he has extended the track across his land to the Humber, again for personal use only. Now, whether he would consider allowing it to be used for commercial purposes, I do not know. I must point out that he is a very rich man with shipping interests in Grimsby and would appear to have no need to

146

use the land to add to his fortune. Although I should add rumours circulated about a year ago that he was thinking of developing a harbour or two, to try to facilitate more trade across the Humber and inland. I do know some preliminary work was done on one site, though to what extent I do not know.'

'This sounds very interesting and might offer a possibility,' said Thomas. 'How do we get to Woodhouse Grange?'

'I'd better take you, it's a lonely place. I wouldn't live there, but the Bradleys like it. Mind you, they have a big house on the Wolds beyond Grimsby and a town house in London too.'

Ralph raised an eyebrow. 'Not short of a bob or two.'

Weldon laughed. 'Not them.'

'Will they be at Woodhouse Grange now?'

'Oh, yes. They always come at this time of year. I know they are here now, I've seen them in the distance out riding.' Jack pushed himself to his feet, saying, 'Let's go then.'

Within ten minutes they were riding north, and two hours later they were sitting down with Jules Bradley.

He listened carefully to the Bullens' story, but said nothing until it was finished. He then rubbed his chin thoughtfully as he considered the facts presented to him. Finally he looked up and eyed the three men watching him hopefully.

'I have no objection to your crossing my land to the Humber,' he said in a quiet deliberate manner, 'provided you stick to the extension of the Stockdale track. It may need some repairs in places, but I will see to that.'

'Thank you, Mr Bradley, that's part of our problem solved,' said Ralph with relief.

Jules Bradley gave a little smile. 'Ah, but that's the easy part of your problem. Now, what about the remainder?'

The three man, hanging on his words, realised this was not the moment to pass an opinion. They waited.

Bradley leaned forward over his desk. 'Mr Weldon, you would be aware that I have done some preliminary work on a section of land along the Humber?'

'Yes, sir. Rumour had it that you were seeking to develop a small harbour there.'

'That was the idea. Then I held the project in abeyance while I conducted more research on its possible uses on this side of the Humber. I got one or two interested parties, but nothing that spurred me on to sink more money into the venture. Shipping fleeces from Stockdale now ... once other farmers and agricultural dealers hereabouts see this enterprise taking off they'll want to use the facilities themselves.' He paused, then, with a determined slap of his hands, said, 'We start right away. I will have a labour gang taking up the harbour work tomorrow. We have a deadline to meet – the first shipment of fleeces. Not long, but if we concentrate on getting the harbour deep enough to use, all the rest can be put in place afterwards. How does that sound?'

'Excellent, sir. This solves our problem.'

'Then I'll have documents drawn up and have everything between us put on a legal basis. It's best for both sides as you will realise, but in the meantime a handshake will do.' He stood up and Thomas and Ralph were on their feet to shake hands on a deal that they hoped would have far-reaching consequences for the future.

18

'From what we have seen these last three days,' said Francis, after looking at the houses Gideon had chosen for his brother and niece to view, 'I think you would be wise to choose one of the two properties you have picked on the outskirts of Skipton within easy access of Keighley. There is a good road, but even more tempting is the fact that there is now a rail connection between the towns.'

'So that comes down to a choice of two. Which do you like, Susannah?'

'There is little to choose between them in terms of accommodation, Uncle, but I think you'd be happier in the second one we looked at, Barden House. It gives you some fine hill views, an extra-large garden which has been well cared for, and the big fields on all sides are included, which should suit someone who likes his privacy.'

Gideon smiled. 'You make it sound as if I want to cut myself off.'

'No, I don't mean that, Uncle Gideon,' she protested. 'But I know that there are times when you like to escape, and Barden House would help you to do that. Don't you agree, Papa?'

'I do. I can see your uncle living there.'

'Right, then Barden House it is,' said Gideon decisively.

The owners were pleased to get the sale settled because the date of their move to the southern counties was approaching. The problem of staff was also solved for Gideon when the owners announced that they would not be taking any of their employees with them. Seizing on this information and the owner's recommendation, Gideon counted himself lucky and re-engaged the staff.

Susannah eased his mind on a further point about the decorations. 'I think they are quite adequate; for now. Best if you live in the house for a while, and decide gradually how you would like to use it and which parts will need work.'

'Splendid! I wouldn't have thought of that myself but you have made me see the sense of it. When I have decided, I'll bring in decorators to get the house exactly to my liking.'

The next day, Gideon quickly dealt with any documents that needed his signature and left the rest of the work in the hands of the solicitors he had employed to oversee the purchase of the banking business. That evening the three of them enjoyed a celebratory dinner and made an early start the following day for Lincolnshire.

Learning of their arrival at Stockdale Manor, the farm manager sent a message to Francis, asking him for a meeting as soon as possible as he wished to inform him of some important developments.

'Now, Jack, what had you to tell me?' Francis asked on entering the manager's office.

Jack Weldon quickly enlightened him about Thomas and Ralph's visit and the outcome of the interview with Jules Bradley.

'This is very good news, Jack. You have handled things well and I approve of your actions. I will contact Mr Bradley myself and assure him all is well. Will he definitely have the

150

dock ready to handle the fleeces? It is getting near to shearing time.'

'He assured me that all would be ready. It won't be the finished harbour, but he has drafted in a big workforce and will keep them at it right up to the first shipment. With that out of the way, he proposes to improve the port and hopefully attract more customers. He sees this as the chance to fulfil a dream that he has for this side of the Humber. He hopes that you will be pleased with what he has to offer now and will continue your interest.'

'Will he be at the site tomorrow?' Francis asked.

'He's never away. Said he wouldn't be until the shipment of your fleeces had been dealt with.'

'Good. Then I'll see him in the morning.' Francis turned to go then asked, 'The two young men ... '

'Thomas and Ralph Bullen.'

'Yes. They knew what they were about?'

'They certainly were aware what was needed to get the fleeces back to the West Riding. They had everything in place except how to circumvent a track that had become unusable, and they didn't lose a moment once I mentioned that Mr Bradley might offer a solution.'

'Good. It must be their brother who is coming to check the wool at shearing time.'

Once Thomas and Ralph had reached an agreement with Mr Bradley they made haste to return to Keighley. They went straight to the mill to find their father and brother anxiously awaiting their return, hoping they would be bringing good news. It was joy all round when the explanation was made.

'You have done well,' praised their father. 'At one time I thought we wouldn't find a solution, so you are to be highly commended for what you've achieved. This will ensure the smooth running of future shipments, and, if the quality of our wool becomes known abroad, the contact you have made with Mr Bradley could mean we have access to the necessary shipping facilities.' There was excitement in his voice, betraying the vision he had in mind. He turned to Daniel. 'You be ready to leave for Stockdale soon. Warn Reuben Yates, who will be going with you. Keep Mr Bradley's ideas for expansion along the Humber in mind when you go to Stockdale; they might even encourage Mr Charlesworth to enlarge his flocks even more. We could be on the verge of great things.'

Rosalind eagerly accepted Susannah's invitation to tea one May afternoon, the first time they had met since Ian Bradley's party.

'Are we on our own?' she enquired as they settled down together in the drawing-room.

'Yes, Father is busy with something or other so I thought it a good time for us to talk in private.'

'Very sensible,' Rosalind agreed.

Susannah poured the tea, and they settled down. Their conversation soon turned to the party.

'It was most enjoyable,' Rosalind sighed, remembering.

'With a small number of guests, you certainly get to know people better.'

'And it leaves more space for anyone wanting to dance,' said Rosalind with a little shake of her shoulders.

'Oh, I did enjoy that! Ian Bradley danced so well, I felt as though I were walking on air with him.'

'Oh, dear, you sound as if you ... '

'And he's so handsome,' cut in Susannah. 'And he said he hoped we would meet again soon.'

'Careful, Susannah, that was only a general comment.'

'I think it was more than that.'

'No, it's you wanting it to be more than that.'

'But you didn't see the look in his eyes.'

'You saw what you wanted to see, Susannah. You aren't the first one to fall under his spell. He doesn't do it intentionally, he has no ulterior motive; it's just his natural charm. But I must tell you that he is expected to marry Lavinia Cherwell, and no doubt will. You would understand if you saw them together; they are right for each other. It's a pity she wasn't there for the party, she's studying in France.'

'Oh!' There was no mistaking the disappointment in Susannah's voice and her face turned pale. 'Just when . . . '

'Don't take it to heart, my dear. There are plenty of other young . . . '

'Who cares?' said Susannah bitterly. 'It seems I am doomed.'

'Don't be sad. You have your whole life before you.'

'To be spent as a spinster!'

Rosalind laughed. 'I can just see you, sitting there all alone with your knitting.'

'Don't make fun of me,' grumbled Susannah. 'I start taking an interest in men and am immediately faced with life on the shelf!'

'Boo-hoo,' mocked her friend. 'No doubt you will find someone else. You're young and pretty. Stop feeling sorry for yourself.'

Two weeks later Daniel rode in the gathering darkness along the Aire Valley, following the meandering river until he left the track to turn through the gateway to Griffin Manor. A lackey took his green wool coat, silk top hat and leather gloves, and, knowing Mr Bullen to be a regular visitor, left him to make his own way to whatever pleasurable pastimes he sought. After a quick glance in the gaming rooms and dining-room, his search for Penelope was only interrupted by brief acknowledgements to friends. Unable to find her downstairs, he went to her office on the first floor. He knocked on the door and, hearing her call, went in.

On seeing him Penelope rose quickly from her seat and, smiling with pleasure, came round her desk to greet him. Her brother Hugh was with her and he and Daniel exchanged polite greetings.

Penelope slipped her arm under Daniel's and said, 'It is good to see you.'

'You too,' he replied, with a smile and a sidelong glance at Hugh.

She read his meaning and frowned at her brother.

Hugh rose from his chair. 'I must see how our new dealer is coming on. I will see you shortly, Daniel.'

'I'll be down soon to try my luck,' he replied.

When the door closed behind Hugh Penelope pressed herself into Daniel's arms and their lips met, promising much more to come.

'I have something to tell you,' he said as they reluctantly separated. She went to pour them each a whisky. He settled on a sofa and she sat down beside him. They raised their glasses to each other.

'What is it?' she asked.

'At the end of next week I will be going away for a while,' he said quietly.

She pouted.

'What for this time?'

'Work. I have to go to Lincolnshire to look over the quality of the fleeces we are buying.'

'You've never had to do that before,' she said with a frown of disappointment.

'No, Father has always done it previously. I believe he wants me to broaden my knowledge and experience.'

'But why you? Couldn't Thomas or Ralph have gone?'

He reached out and took Penelope's hand. 'You forget, I'll be owner of the mill one day. Cross Father in any way now and he would change that with the scratch of a pen. And neither you nor I would want that, would we?'

'I know, I'm sorry if I seem to be protesting, but I miss you when you go away.'

'I hope so.'

'I do, Daniel, I do. You know that. Is it the same for you?'

He did not answer but stood up and went to the door to turn the key. Penelope began to discard her clothes. The desire in her eyes implored him to do the same. He needed no bidding.

'Thank goodness the drizzle of yesterday has been blown away,' Daniel remarked as he and Reuben Yates rode away from the inn in which they had stayed the night. He was glad he had decided they would take two days for the journey. The overnight stay was refreshing and put him in a better state to concentrate on the purpose of his visit.

'Fine country,' he commented.

'It is that, sir. Gentler than our Pennines.'

'You've been to Stockdale many times, Reuben, what's it like?'

'It's a fine estate, sir. What acreage I do not know. I suspect Mr Charlesworth keeps buying and selling land in order to expand and find better grassland for sheep rearing. I believe it has been in his family for centuries.'

'A well-established line then, and no doubt wealthy?'

'Who can tell, sir? It would seem so, but it could all disappear.'

155

'Disappear? How do you mean?'

'I'm not up in these things, but as I understand it the estate should pass to the eldest son but there is none.'

'No heir to the estate?' Daniel showed surprise.

'No, sir. Mr Charlesworth only has the one daughter.'

Daniel raised no further questions about the family. He had some intriguing information already. He would make sure he learned more in due course.

'A fine-looking house,' he commented as they approached Stockdale Manor. He had had distant sightings of it from afar but this one, viewed from a turning in the long drive, made him halt his horse and stare in admiration.

'It is indeed, sir,' agreed Reuben as he pulled his own mount to a halt beside Daniel's. 'Your father always stopped here to admire the view and I was always glad when he did so.'

'Whoever chose this site knew what they were about. On a nice rise, looking south, but positioned below the summit so that there is shelter from the north winds. A wise man,' commented Daniel. He tapped his horse forward but remained silent for the rest of the ride, drinking in the fine proportions of the ancient building.

They dismounted in front of the house. Reuben remained with the horses while Daniel went to the front door. A few moments later it was opened by a manservant.

'Mr Daniel Bullen to see Mr Charlesworth.'

'Yes, sir. You are expected. Please step inside.' As Daniel did so he saw the man look beyond him. 'I see you have your usual foreman with you. I will send word to the head groom. He will look after him and see that your horses are cared for.'

'Thank you,' said Daniel cordially. He followed the servant into a small reception room off the hall. 'If you will wait here, sir, I'll inform Mr Charlesworth you have arrived.'

A few minutes later Francis came hurrying in. His smile was warm. 'Welcome to Stockdale Manor, Mr Bullen.'

'Thank you, sir. My father sends greetings and apologises that he isn't with you this year.'

'I'm sorry too. I trust his health is not the reason for his absence?' Francis enquired.

'No, sir, it isn't, though he gets a little tired at times. I try to ease the burden of the mill for him, but as you probably know his heart and soul is in it. I think he wanted me to come here for experience and to meet the people with whom we deal.'

Francis nodded. 'Now, let us get you settled.'

As he had spoken Francis had gone to the bell-pull and a few moments later a valet appeared. 'This is Calvert,' said Francis. 'He has only been with us two months but he is very efficient and quickly fell into our ways. The head butler has assigned him to you for the duration of your stay.'

'Thank you,' said Daniel. 'I'm sure we'll get on very well.'

'Show Mr Bullen to his room, Calvert.'

'Yes, sir.'

As they crossed the hall, Calvert picked up the saddlebags that had been brought into the house.

'You have been assigned a south-facing room,' said the man as he opened a door.

Daniel stifled a gasp at the sight of the sumptuous room. He crossed it to look out of the window. He had admired the view from ground level, but with the extra height of the first floor it was even more impressive.

*

When Daniel walked into the drawing-room Francis rose from his chair, saying, 'Is everything to your liking, Mr Bullen?'

'Indeed, sir, it is.'

'Come and meet my daughter Susannah.'

There was a movement from the wing-chair placed so that its back was to the door. Daniel had not seen its occupant when he entered the room.

He hoped he managed to hide his surprise when the person who had been sitting there rose gracefully and turned to greet him. He had been expecting a schoolgirl, not the beauty who faced him now.

'Good day, Mr Bullen. Welcome to Stockdale Manor. I hope your visit will be a pleasant and profitable one.'

'Thank you, Miss Charlesworth. I'm sure it will be.' He took her proffered hand, bowed and carried it towards his lips.

'Please, do sit down. We will take tea.' As she sat down again Susannah said, 'We take dinner at six-thirty, informal dress unless it is a very special occasion. Father and I don't stand on ceremony.'

The tea arrived and Daniel was soon singing the praises of the baked goods that accompanied it, but his eyes dwelt on the beauty of his young hostess whom he judged would be only a little younger than himself.

Their conversation drifted into generalities, with Daniel respecting Mr Charlesworth's desire to leave talk of business until the morrow, the day before shearing would begin. Susannah eventually excused herself, saying, 'I have some things to discuss with our housekeeper,' and her father told Daniel that he needed to verify that all the shearers had arrived. 'Please make yourself at home,' he said.

'Thank you, sir. It is a pleasant afternoon, I'll take a turn in the garden, if you don't mind?'

'Do. I hope you find it interesting.'

As he strolled through the garden Daniel remained unaware of his surroundings, too intent on the loveliness of Miss Charlesworth and in musing on the possible consequences of his visit to Stockdale.

19

Having completed the domestic tasks that needed her attention, Susannah went to her room. Time enough to be sociable. Besides her father would quickly make himself free to do that. Idly she wandered across the room and looked down into the garden. Mr Bullen was sitting on a seat, his back to the house, his eyes fixed on something in front of him. Anxious that she should not be seen, she stepped back from the window but found her curiosity about their visitor had been aroused. She edged back towards it, positioning herself so that she could see without being seen.

He had laid his hat beside him on the seat, thus affording her a three-quarters view of his face over his left shoulder from above. The angle brought out his rugged handsome features clearly and the pose he had adopted accentuated the determined set of his jaw. She could not see his eyes but recalled that they were a startling light blue. She surprised herself – she had been unaware previously that she had even noticed their colour and shade. Irritated with herself for being caught out, she turned away from the window and sat down in an armchair close by. What had caused her to notice such things about him? And why? This made her think about her reactions to the two invitations she had recently received, and how her interest had been stirred in the young men she had met on those occasions. She even found herself wondering about Roland. Why had she never had these feelings for him when he was around? Familiarity precluding any closer interest? Would she feel differently towards him after his long absence? She gave a little shake of her head. No, to her he would always be just Roland, Rosalind's brother.

When she stood up and looked out of the window again, Daniel Bullen was nowhere to be seen.

Her father and Daniel were already in the drawing room when Susannah came down half an hour before the evening meal would be served.

'Ah, my dear, here you are,' said Francis, rising to his feet.

'Good evening, Miss Charlesworth,' said Daniel, standing up. She inclined her head in acknowledgement and added, 'Mr Bullen, you are to be our guest for a few days so I think the use of Christian names is permitted. Don't you agree, Father?'

'Indeed,' he said quickly.

'Then it is Susannah, Mr Bullen,' she said, pleased that they would be less formal with each other.

'It is my privilege to use such a pretty and fitting name, Susannah. You have the beating of me – Daniel is hardly a match for it.'

'Ah, but he survived the lion's den. With such a strong name you will surely survive Stockdale Manor.'

'I have already fallen under its spell,' he replied gallantly.

'Is this your first visit to Lincolnshire, Daniel?' she asked.

'It is.'

'Your two brothers beat you to it. I was sorry we were away when they were here.'

'I've told Daniel, tomorrow I'll take him to see what they

achieved,' said her father. 'Do you want to come along? You've never seen what Mr Bradley has been busy with, have you?' He glanced at Daniel. 'Susannah has always shown an interest in the estate so it is as well she knows what is going on nearby.'

'I'd love that, Father,' she replied.

'Good. Daniel's foreman and Jack Weldon will accompany us.' He looked at Daniel. 'Then it's Sunday so the sheep shearing will have to wait. It will begin in earnest on Monday.'

'Where do you go for the Sunday service, sir?' Daniel asked.

'The local village church in Thornton Curtis; it is a nice church with a good vicar. I hope we don't lose him. He knows when to end his sermon – always the sign of a good cleric.' Francis gave a little chuckle. 'If I rub my chin during his sermon, he knows I think he's said enough and ends with a few brief words.'

'Well, sir, I must say that sounds like a very good partnership,' said Daniel. 'Would you allow me to accompany you and Miss Charlesworth on Sunday?'

'By all means, young man.'

By the note in Mr Charlesworth's voice Daniel knew he had done the right thing. He was pleased to see it verified by the flash of approval he glimpsed on Susannah's face.

'You'll be able to meet our neighbours and dearest friends from Harthill Priory, Mr and Mrs Webster and their daughter Rosalind, who is the same age as I am. You won't meet Roland, who is a year older. His father wanted him to broaden his experience so sent him to tour the Continent.'

'I'll look forward to meeting your neighbours.' Daniel left a little pause then queried, 'Harthill Priory?' emphasising the word 'Priory'.

'No longer a religious house,' said Susannah, 'Henry the Eighth saw to that. It passed through many different hands over the years until eventually the ancestors of the present Webster family bought it. They have done some wonderful restoration work and turned it into a beautiful country home. You'll be able to judge for yourself – they are sure to ask us over. You'll like them.'

Daniel thought to himself, I'll make sure I do. They could be useful allies if ever the idea, now forming in his mind, needed some approval and support.

'Father, have you told Daniel about Uncle Gideon and how we came to be in Keighley recently?'

'No. We've had so much else to talk about.' Francis glanced at the clock. 'We'll tell him over dinner.'

But Daniel had picked up on Susannah's reference to the West Riding and he was wondering what it might mean for the future.

He had to curb his impatience until dessert was served, taking in all the information he could about their visit to the West Riding and about Gideon Charlesworth's banking enterprise.

'That is most interesting. My father will be sorry he did not know you were in Keighley. He would have been glad to have entertained you, but no doubt that can all be put right when you next visit your brother, Mr Charlesworth. Both of you would be welcome at any time.'

'Thank you, we will bear it in mind.'

Daniel looked thoughtful when he said, 'Why don't I have a word with Father about moving our banking business to your uncle's house? Although we don't currently do business with Mr Moorsom's bank, we know the firm is sound and profitable.'

'Oh, no, Daniel, please don't do that. I have nothing to do with Gideon's work and would not wish to appear to interfere in it. I know what his answer would be even if you approached him directly. He would instantly refuse and would never budge from that decision. He has always encouraged cordial relationships with other banks. No doubt he will continue that policy in Yorkshire. He wouldn't want any bad blood with your present bankers. So please leave things as they are.'

'Very well, sir, I understand.'

'Thank you.'

The remainder of the meal passed off cordially, with Daniel asking for his compliments to be passed to the cook on the delicious menu she had provided. On moving to the drawing-room, they spent a pleasant evening talking; Daniel and Susannah learning more about each other and their families and friends without making it obvious that their true interest was personal.

As he lay in bed, Daniel sifted the information he had gained and filed it away in his mind, hoping to use it one day to bring to fruition the ambitions already forming there.

Susannah thought about the young man who was presently under their roof, feeling pleased that she had this chance to get to know him. She knew she must not seem forward or show any partiality towards him. Any interest must come from the young man, but she was beginning to hope that it would.

After a leisurely breakfast they left Stockdale Manor for the Bradley workings on the Humber.

Susannah was pleased that it was a bright morning. They kept to a leisurely pace, and with everyone in good humour it made for a pleasant expedition. Daniel silently admired the way Susannah sat side-saddle and handled her horse with easy skill that spoke of its being a partnership, whereas he regarded his own mount merely as a means of getting from one place to another. In fact, he felt better off the animal than he did seated on it. With a little smile he thought, but I could learn to ride with greater skill and finesse, especially if my tutor were as charming as Miss Charlesworth.

Susannah hung back when her father was talking to Daniel and was startled to find herself observing his seat and the way he handled his horse. Both were clumsy and rough without any thought for the animal's welfare. But, she thought, I've been brought up with horses, he probably hasn't. He really should have some instruction.

On reaching the workings on the Humber they were amazed by the transformation that was taking place there and delighted when Jules Bradley told them that the harbour, though still under construction, would be usable for the first shipment of fleeces.

That news set the atmosphere for the rest of Daniel's visit. The following day Mr Charlesworth drove the trap to the church in Thornton Curtis. The vicar was pleased to meet Daniel, and he in turn complimented the clergyman on his sermon, and in particular its length. 'Just right, sir. Any longer and your meaning would have been clouded.'

'Thank you, young man. How perspicacious of you. I hope you will join my congregation at another service.' He turned away to speak to another parishioner.

Daniel caught the amused twitch of Susannah's lips and gave her a sly wink.

This was noted by Rosalind, who had been curious about the young man accompanying the Charlesworths at church.

'Rosalind, please meet Mr Daniel Bullen. He is here to

look at the quality and quantity of this year's wool,' Susannah introduced them.

'I am pleased to meet you, Mr Bullen,' said Rosalind.

'And I you, Miss Webster,' he said, with a smile as he bowed to her. Straightening up, he said quietly, just loud enough for them both to hear, 'Are all the young ladies in North Lincolnshire as beautiful as the two who assail my eyes now?'

Susannah blushed, but Rosalind rose to the compliment. 'I don't think we should allow you to find out! We must keep you fully occupied at teatime this afternoon. Three o'clock at Harthill Priory. Susannah knows the way.' Mrs Webster was approaching them. 'Mama, this is Mr Daniel Bullen ... you know, Susannah's father told us he would be coming. I've asked him to join us for tea this afternoon.'

'Very well, my dear.' Marjorie turned to Daniel. 'I'm pleased to meet you, Mr Bullen. Don't mind my daughter.' She glanced in the direction of Rosalind who had slipped her hand into Susannah's and was whisking her off to meet one of the parishioners. 'She's always a whirlwind, but who would have her any other way? That is Rosalind.'

'And she is a delight,' said Daniel. 'No doubt they have been close friends from an early age?'

'Indeed you are right, Mr Bullen. There is a special friendship between our two girls, something for which I am truly grateful. Now you must excuse me. I need to have a word with that lady nearing her trap before she gets away.' Marjorie started off at a brisk pace but made sure she called back, 'I will see you at tea, Mr Bullen.'

He watched her go and thought, You would have been just like your daughter when you were young. Wondering where Susannah and Rosalind were, he saw them detach themselves from a group of young people and start in his

166

direction. They were obviously in good humour and his immediate thought was, Love me, love my friend. Words he stored away to help him further a scheme he'd had no thought of until he came to Stockdale Manor.

Daniel had seen sheep sheared before, but the speed and dexterity of the team that had come in to deal with the Stockdale flock amazed him. When he remarked on this to Susannah later on Monday, she replied, 'Yes, I've been watching it done since I was a little girl. It is such a special skill. I understand the fleeces are of excellent quality this year?'

'Yes, they are,' he replied. 'We'll be producing an exceptional quality of cloth. I hope it continues in the future.'

'There is no reason why it shouldn't, Daniel.'

He liked the way his name sounded from her lips. With her father in earshot he lowered his voice when he replied, 'And I will have the added bonus of seeing you whenever I come to examine the fleeces.' He noted the answering blush that rose to Susannah's cheeks.

Two weeks later they had seen the final consignment shipped out of Bradley's Harbour, as the new construction had been christened. Hopes were high for this development when traders in other goods saw the advantages of using the new harbour.

As Daniel and Susannah watched the barge move off into midstream he said, somewhat regretfully, 'There it goes, and that means I will be leaving tomorrow. You have been a wonderful hostess and your father a most considerate and friendly host.'

'It has been our pleasure. I am pleased that you haven't been pining for town. Our way of life must be so different.'

He gave a wry smile. 'It is. I must say I wondered what I would be coming to, but it has been a delightful visit amongst the work. Whenever you come to visit your uncle, you must let me know.'

They turned to their horses. Seeing Susannah's father approaching, Daniel stopped and said quickly, 'Miss Charlesworth, would you allow me the honour of writing to you occasionally?'

Susannah's hesitation was only momentary. Her father approached them. 'Yes, Daniel, I would like that, but you had better ask Father's permission too.'

'Well, Daniel, are you pleased with the arrangements here for transporting the fleeces?' asked Francis as he brought his horse alongside.

'I am, sir. My brothers explained how this section of the route would work, but it is even better than I had anticipated. I must congratulate them both on their vision.'

'Do that from all of us,' said Francis.

As the two men had been exchanging comments, Susannah, sensing what might be coming next, had let her horse walk on. Daniel was not slow to notice her move away from them and saw it as a sign of encouragement for him to make his request now.

'I will, sir. Father will be eager to hear your views, you may depend on it. I have much to tell him myself, but there is one more thing I must ask of you.' He hesitated slightly.

Curious, Francis pressed him, 'What is that?'

'Sir, may I have permission to write to your daughter?'

Francis reined in his horse. His little girl . . . and the beautiful young woman she had become. His wife came to mind then, together with the silent question, What do I say, Rachel? How he wished she was with him now.

Daniel had stopped beside him and was watching him

anxiously, wondering if he should say more, but deciding that at this moment silence was his ally.

'This is a surprise, Daniel, utterly and completely. I had no idea that you had any leanings toward my daughter.'

'Sir, I have been delighted to meet Susannah and have come to admire her greatly even after this short time. It would give me such pleasure if you would allow me to write to her.'

Francis looked thoughtful for a moment then he called, 'Susannah!'

She turned her horse and rode back to them. 'Yes, Father?'

'I rather think you might know why I have called you back?'

'Yes, Father, I think I do.'

Susannah could not hide the smile of delighted anticipation that broke out at her father's question.

'Very well, you may write to each other,' Francis said.

'Thank you, Father.'

'Thank you, sir,' added Daniel humbly.

The young people smiled at each other, and Francis saw the warmth in those smiles, How quickly his world could change. How different it would become if . . . He shut off the thought. It might never happen.

20

Susannah came in after her ride glowing from the warm morning air. As she crossed the hall to the stairs she caught sight of five envelopes laid out on the console table. She went over to it more in hope than expectation, for she had begun to think Daniel had not been sincere in saying he wanted to write to her. Then she saw her name, written in flowing script, on one of the envelopes. Her heart missed a beat; she seized the envelope and hurried up the stairs. She sent the door to her room swinging shut behind her as she crossed to the chair set in front of the dressing table. With clumsy fingers she slit the envelope open and withdrew a sheet of paper.

10th July 1851

Dear Miss Charlesworth,

It is with great respect that I write this first letter to you. I have the most pleasant memories of the days I was privileged to spend with you at Stockdale Manor.

Having spent all my life until then in Keighley and its vicinity, I had no idea what I was coming to. As I rode further into Lincolnshire I was charmed by the beauty of the countryside, and then I found myself in what I can only describe as the most friendly, welcoming house.

But a house alone cannot extend a welcome – it is people who do that. Who better to do so than you, your father and the staff you have gathered around you? I am truly grateful that you were there and that I was able to spend time in your company. I hope I might have that privilege again. In the meantime, I am thankful that we can correspond.

I remain, yours in friendship,
Daniel Bullen

Susannah gave a contented sigh; she had heard from him! Her thoughts sped in confusion from one thing to another until she mustered them to her will and chided herself for being scatterbrained. She read the letter again. There was no hint of any affection, but what had she expected at this early stage? There was a recognised timescale in the ritual of courtship, and it was slow and protracted. She looked at the letter again then rose from her chair and headed for the small mahogany-veneer bureau. She must acknowledge Daniel's letter at once. Then she stopped herself.

'Susannah,' she said aloud. 'Stop. You must not appear so eager. You must not act like a lovesick schoolgirl: be your age, don't reply for a few days. Employ decorum. There is nothing in this but friendship, at least for the time being. Anything at all might happen in the future. Have no expect-ations and then you cannot get hurt.'

Having calmed herself, she went back to her dressing table and placed the letter in a drawer. Then she proceeded to discard her riding habit and change for luncheon.

*

When her father came in she told him she had received a letter from Daniel. 'He was very polite. Says he enjoyed his time here and thanks us for our hospitality.'

Francis smiled to himself when nothing else was forthcoming.

'Come on, Susannah, what does he say?' pressed Rosalind eagerly as soon as she arrived that afternoon.

'Who?' said Susannah, feigning ignorance.

'You know who,' came Rosalind's retort. 'I can read you like a book. Your demeanour tells me something has happened. You are trying to hide it, but you can't. Well certainly not from me. I've known you too long.'

'Let's walk in the garden,' said Susannah.

'All right, but don't try use it as an excuse not to tell me.'

Susannah laughed. 'I won't! But we'll be out of earshot outside.'

'That sounds as though there's something to hide?' Rosalind suggested.

'No, it doesn't. It's only your interpretation that views it that way,' Susannah corrected,

Rosalind gave a little shrug. 'Well, perhaps. But come on, do tell!'

They strolled out into the rose garden, where the healthy-looking bushes were promising a fine display before too long.

Susannah was enjoying keeping her friend on tenter-hooks; it had so far been very much the other way as Rosalind had flirted with more boys at parties than Susannah cared to remember.

'You were right, I did receive a letter from Daniel today . . . '

'There, I knew it!' chimed Rosalind triumphantly.

172

'It's nothing to get excited about,' warned Susannah.

'Don't tell me that. The fact that he has written is exciting enough. First letters will always be expressed cautiously. It's what comes later that causes the real excitement, but there's always a hint in the first one if you look for it. So what did he hint?'

'Nothing,' came Susannah's quick retort, 'and it is no good your trying to read something into that.'

'Very well, but mark my words: there will be more to come. You forget, I saw the way he looked at you when he was here.'

'You have a vivid imagination, Rosalind.' Wanting to move away from this topic, she added quickly, 'What about you and Henry?'

'Coldish at the moment. He's away in London.'

'Poor you.'

Rosalind shrugged her shoulders. 'It can't be helped. But I have had a letter from him and he will be home soon. Oh, by the way, we heard from Roland again.'

'How is he?'

'He says he is in good health and still enjoying his stay. He has been befriended now by a family with six daughters.'

'Six? Good gracious!'

'Plenty for him to pick from,' laughed Rosalind.

'Do you ever think he may not wish to return?'

'I have sometimes wondered if Father made a mistake in sending him abroad, but then I think the pull of Harthill will always be strong, and he has said in this recent letter that he misses Lincolnshire.'

'But the temptations a young lady can offer might be stronger even than that?'

'And could the life offered by a young man from Keighley be just as tempting to a young lady not far from me at the

173

moment?' Rosalind's eyes twinkled with mischief but Susannah ignored the question.

Four weeks later a letter arrived for Francis. Seeing that it was from his brother, he quickly scanned the letter.

'Your uncle Gideon writes from Hull to tell us that he has had some decorating done at the house in Skipton and has also acquired new furniture. He would like us to visit him there and be his first guests. He suggests we go a week on Monday, if that is convenient for us. He suggests he comes here the day before and we travel to Skipton together.'

'It is up to you, Father.'

'I think we should go. It would be unkind not to.'

'Very well, Father.' Susannah hesitated for a moment and then added, 'We could make it an opportunity for you to see Mr Bullen.'

He smiled. 'Ah, but which Mr Bullen?'

'Daniel's father,' she replied, blushing at the inference she knew lay behind her father's words.

'I suppose it is more than likely we may bump into Daniel too?' he added. 'I think it would only be polite to inform him that we are coming to Skipton and Keighley, and that you hope there might be a convenient time for us to meet.

'Will you write to him today, my dear? I will write to Gideon to agree with his plans.'

Letters were swiftly exchanged, and when Francis, Gideon and Susannah left Stockdale Manor they knew that they would be staying for five nights with Gideon, and on the evening of their second day in Skipton they would be dining at the Bullen residence in the Aire Valley.

21

As the carriage rolled to a stop in front of Barden House, the front door opened and a tall thin lady, her black dress drawn in to emphasise her slim waist, stepped out and came down the steps to greet the new arrivals. She was followed by the head butler, middle-aged with an imposing bearing and an open face in which darted eyes bent on missing nothing.

'Good day, Mr Charlesworth, welcome to Barden House,' said the woman.

'May I add similar greetings also?' the man said.

Gideon smiled, thanked them, turned to Francis and Susannah and introduced the housekeeper, Mrs Studley, and his head butler, Mr Gorton.

Susannah did not see the signal but knew one must have been made when the two menservants, who had been waiting near the front door, hurried forward to take charge of the luggage. Two maids stood by ready to be of service if required.

'I hope you are going to enjoy your uncle's new home,' said the housekeeper to Susannah as they walked to the front door together.

'I'm sure I shall,' she replied, and added with a touch of excitement in her voice, 'I'm looking forward to seeing what decisions Uncle Gideon finally made about the decorations and furnishings. Father and I gave him some preliminary advice and thought he might want to consult us again, but he went ahead without further ado. I am rather interested to see what he decided.'

'I really think you will like it, Miss.'

So it proved. Susannah, eager to see what her uncle had done, hustled him quickly through the house to show her.

'But you can't be seeing it properly,' he protested as she sped from one room to another.

'The first impression counts for a great deal,' she told him. 'And it is most favourable.'

At the end of this whirlwind tour they found Mrs Studley had arranged tea for them in the dining-room. When they were seated at the table, Mrs Studley brought in the cook and introduced her as Mrs Carbery. Susannah took an instant liking to her, a homely woman with an air of calm. Her smile embraced everyone and her voice was gentle. She made quite a contrast to the gaunt housekeeper who adopted a serious expression, though Susannah could tell that these two women got on extremely well; her uncle had been fortunate in 'inheriting' them.

When finally Susannah and her father had settled in, she took the opportunity before the evening meal to make a more leisurely appraisal of the house.

'Uncle Gideon, I love it,' she finally declared. 'I'm sorry I didn't get to help you make your decisions but I approve of what you have done. Don't you think he has done well, Father?'

'I do. Far better than I would have done on my own,' replied Francis.

'I have to confess, I was not entirely on my own. Mrs Studley knows the house well so she helped, but took into account my tastes.'

'I can tell already that you will be happy here, but I hope it will not lead you to desert us?' said Francis.

'Of course it won't,' replied Gideon. 'Stockdale and Hull are my real homes.'

Susannah settled comfortably in her bed but was kept awake by thoughts of their visit to Ash Tree Villa and the prospect of meeting Daniel again. She had had two more letters from him in which she had sensed caution, as if he feared appearing too forward in his approach. She respected him for that but was nervous of her own feelings for him. The days they had spent together, even though they had always been in company, had left such pleasant memories ... She fell asleep, hoping the stay here in the West Riding would be as memorable.

The following day was spent relaxing around the house and the adjacent land owned by Gideon. At six in the evening they all took the carriage which Daniel had sent from Ash Tree Villa.

On entering the house they were greeted warmly by Tristan, who introduced his wife Ann and the rest of the family.

As they mingled Daniel drew Susannah into conversation with his brothers and sisters. She found them all friendly, and with Thomas and Ralph found common ground in their visit to the Stockdale estate while she was away. Thomas she found naturally jovial and friendly; she soon realised he thought a good deal of Helen Forbes, who at his request had also been invited this evening. Susannah liked Helen and felt she was a person with whom she would like to become better acquainted. Ralph was quietly attentive, someone she sensed would be ever willing to help if needed. The sisters Jessie and Liza were very close, but she sensed that they would accept her as one of them if her relationship with Daniel blossomed. Her conversations with him throughout the evening were guarded, but she sensed he wished they could have more time together. She realised he was making an attempt at this when his father made the offer, 'I'll show you over the mill tomorrow afternoon, if you would care to see what happens to the fleeces we buy from you?'

'That would be most interesting,' said Francis. 'I would like that. What about you, Gideon?'

'I'll look forward to it,' his brother replied. 'It will be a new experience for me and could be useful if ever I am approached about investing in some aspect of the woollen trade.'

Seeing Susannah was about to reply, Daniel put in quickly, 'I don't think it is a good idea for the ladies. After all, there's dirt and dust involved, and some of our employees are rather rough and crude in their speech. I believe Liza and Jessie are going to Helen's where we are all going to meet for afternoon tea, so I suggest I take Miss Charlesworth and Mother for a walk by the river first.'

Tristan glanced at his wife who answered the query in his eyes by saying, 'I think that's a splendid idea. I'm sure Miss Charlesworth will enjoy that more than touring a dirty old mill. I most certainly will.'

Tristan gave a little laugh. 'Very well, but don't forget . . . where there's dirt there's money.'

'Quite right,' chuckled Gideon, who had taken to Tristan, quietly admiring a man who had pulled himself up from poverty to riches and who made no bones about using his native West Riding accent. He also liked the devotion Tristan showed to his wife, whom he also admired for being able to live on equal terms with other mill owners' wives while still giving down-to-earth solid support to her husband and raising a large and likeable family.

Gideon was pleased that his impressions were favourable because he had seen this evening that Daniel was attracted to Susannah, and that the attraction was reciprocated. He must have a word with Francis.

Daniel took his mother and Susannah along a path that ran by the riverbank. It was much used by people on Sundays, but mid-week was almost deserted. They had been walking for half an hour when Ann, indicating a wooden seat, said, 'I could do with a rest, but don't let me hold you two back. It's a long straight stretch here, I'll be in sight.'

Whether his mother was genuinely in need of a rest or not, Daniel was never sure but he was not going to miss the opportunity she was presenting.

'Will you be all right here?' he asked as she sat down.

'Would you like us to sit with you?' queried Susannah solicitously.

'No, no.' Ann waved away their concerns. 'Enjoy your stroll.'

'If you are sure you'll be all right, Mrs Bullen?'

'Of course I will.'

The two young people set off at an easy pace.

'Your mother is very thoughtful,' said Susannah.

'I hoped you would get on well with her.'

'I like your whole family,' she added, 'and Helen fits in well. Thomas has made a good choice.'

'As good a choice as I have made,' he said.

Susannah was startled. She hadn't realised that Daniel had someone in mind. 'Why isn't she with us today then?' she asked, rather tartly.

'But she is ... standing in front of me now,' he said quietly, but with a note of firm resolve in his tone.

'Me?'

'Who else is standing here?'

'Are you proposing, Daniel?'

'If you want to interpret my words that way, then the answer is yes.'

'Oh, Daniel, it's too soon! We don't really know each other.'

'I know all I want to know. I hope you feel the same?'

Susannah tightened her lips. 'It's a big step for me, bigger than for you. I am an only child ... I have my father to consider,' She saw objections to this reasoning rising on his lips, so added quickly, 'I'm not saying no, but I'm not saying yes. Please let us carry on with our letter writing for the moment, but rest assured – I do treasure your proposal. I promise to think seriously about it and reach a decision as soon as possible. Please bear with me until then.' She laid a hand on his forearm, pleading for understanding.

He nodded. 'Very well, Susannah, if that is the way you want it. I will respect your wishes and tell my heart to content itself with the love it feels for you.'

'Thank you, Daniel.'

As they walked on Susannah stole a glance at the lone figure sitting behind them on the bench and wondered once again if Daniel's mother had contrived for them to be alone together? If she had, was this contrivance a sign of her approval?

Gideon, Francis and Susannah stayed another three days at Barden House, during which time Tristan arranged for Gideon to meet some of the business community in Keighley and Gideon entertained the Bullen family in his new home.

Susannah used the time to get to know the family better and to work out whose loyalties lay where. With no siblings of her own, she realised she would have to find allies in the Bullen family to help her through what would be a dramatic change in her life if she took the step desired by Daniel.

She left without making any hint to him as to what her decision might be.

As they neared Stockdale Manor, Gideon said, 'Do you mind if I stay for a couple of days?'

'Gideon, you know you don't have to ask,' replied his brother. 'It's always a pleasure to have you.'

'There is nothing demanding my immediate return to Hull; I know everything there is in safe hands. But our visit to Keighley had brought some financial prospects to the fore and I'd like to spend some time here thinking about them.'

'I wondered if anything had arisen from your meeting with those businessmen. You have been more thoughtful than usual since then.'

Gideon shrugged his shoulders and gave a little nod. 'Queries have arisen in my mind which could pose a problem. That is why I would appreciate some time here in the tranquillity of our beloved Stockdale. The peace here is a balm to the mind.'

'Then stay as long as you like. I know our home will help you solve your problem.'

'Thank you. It is good to know you believe that. When the right time comes I will share my thinking with you. I believe you can help me solve it, but now is not the right time.'

The next morning, feeling a strong desire to tell Rosalind about her visit to Yorkshire, Susannah made her way to

Harthill Priory. She was greeted by an effervescent Rosalind who, as soon as her friend was out of the trap, whisked her away to the privacy of part of the gardens.

'I know you'll have lots to tell me, Susannah,' she enthused, 'but you just have to let me tell you my news first, you just have to!'

Susannah laughed at her excitement. 'Go on then.'

'Roland's getting married!'

Susannah's laughter disappeared. 'What?'

'Roland's getting mar—' Rosalind's words faded away. She had seen a shadow cross Susanna's face, and with it traces of sorrow and regret. Rosalind laid a hand on her arm. 'Oh, I'm sorry. I didn't realise that you ...'

'No, no,' cut in Susannah. 'It's all right. It just came as a surprise.'

Rosalind nodded and said weakly, 'It did to us too.'

Susannah shifted into a more comfortable position. 'You must let me have Roland's address so I can send him our congratulations. Now tell me all.'

Rosalind related all she knew, and as her story unfolded Susannah wondered if this was an omen. Maybe she could test that by telling Rosalind her own news, but she hesitated.

'You hinted that you had something to tell me?' prompted Rosalind.

'Daniel has said he wants to marry me.'

'Oh, how wonderful!' Rosalind embraced her friend with renewed excitement. 'You must have said yes?'

'I don't know what to do.'

'But surely,' cried Rosalind, 'you ...'

'There's a lot for me to consider first – my father, Uncle Gideon, Stockdale. Could I leave Lincolnshire and live ...'

'There's only one consideration: do you love him?'

My Dear Susannah,

I know I have cast the usual formalities aside by not addressing you as 'Dear Miss Charlesworth' but I hope that, since I have made known my feelings for you, you will allow me to continue to address you in this manner.

I trust you enjoyed your visit to the West Riding and went home thinking of your time spent here, and that you will continue to do so. It was a joy for me to be with you. It made me feel I have known you for ever. I hope I will always have that feeling, and that you will think the same way about me.

Dear Susannah, please ease my aching heart with the answer I long for.

Yours for ever,

Daniel

Susannah took the letter into a quiet corner and reread it. The time spent with Daniel and his family came back to her vividly; the clarity of her recall shocked her. Was that a sign that they, especially Daniel, had stolen a place in her heart? But what of her own family, her father and Uncle Gideon? What would it mean to them if she accepted Daniel? She knew she must carefully balance every aspect of the course her future life would take. She needed time, but sensed that Daniel would want an answer soon.

22

The Bullen men were feeling well content as they walked into Tristan's study after a very enjoyable meal. They took their places facing the chair set handy for their father to reach the glass of whisky placed near the corner of his desk. The three younger men were expressing satisfaction with the progress of production at the mill as they awaited his arrival for their October meeting. They had left him, as was usual on these evenings, making sure that their mother and their sisters were comfortable in the drawing-room until their business was concluded.

'That new order will boost our sales for this quarter,' commented Thomas as they made themselves comfortable. 'Is it likely to be ongoing?'

'Father will probably answer that,' said Daniel, looking round from the decanter he was pouring. 'He hasn't said anything to me but was probably saving the announcement for this meeting.'

Ralph gave a little shiver.

'Cold?' asked Thomas.

'No.'

'Someone must have walked over your grave,' added Thomas.

'Not mine, I hope,' he countered with a frown.

A scream, penetrating the room from the direction of the hall, startled them.

'Liza!' gasped Ralph, who sprang to his feet and ran towards the drawing-room. The others were only a stride behind him but the door burst open before they reached it. Liza flew out, her face contorted with fear.

'Quick! Quick!' she screamed at them. 'It's Father!'

The brothers found Tristan sprawled on the settee with their mother and Jessie kneeling beside him.

'What happened?' Daniel stepped quickly to his mother's side and dropped on one knee beside her.

'He was getting up to come to you,' explained Jessie, 'when he keeled over on to the settee.' Realising her mother was in shock and that someone must take charge of the situation, she took it on herself to do so. 'Ralph . . . ' She glanced back at her brother, and saw his face drained of colour. 'Ralph!' This time she put a snap in her voice to jerk him out of his stupor. 'Send for the doctor! Quick!' She shot a glance at her sister. 'Liza, stop that crying! Get Mrs White! Now!'

Startled by the sharpness of her sister's voice, Liza pulled herself together and ran from the room.

Thomas strode quickly to the sideboard and poured a good measure of whisky into a glass. He fell to his knees beside Daniel who was loosening the cravat around his father's neck and unfastening his collar.

'Mother, drink some of this,' said Thomas, pressing the glass to his mother's lips.

Confused and numbed by what was happening, Ann automatically did as her son told her. The liquid hit her throat. Its sharpness caused her to cough and gasp for air, but it brought back some measure of awareness to her mind.

185

She saw her husband's eyes flicker. 'Make him more comfortable, Daniel.'

The housekeeper and Liza, who was wiping tears from her eyes, hurried into the room.

'Oh, ma'am,' gasped the housekeeper, face full of concern, anxious for her employer and wanting to do all she could to help. She was shocked by Mr Bullen's colour. She had seen that before when her husband had died in similar circumstances while only thirty. Before she could offer help or advice, Tristan reached out and took hold of his wife's hand.

With eyes full of devotion, he gave a weak smile. 'Thank you, my dear,' he croaked. 'Than ... k ... you for ... all you h ... ave done for me.' He jerked with a spasm of pain, fell back and was gone.

'No! No!' Ann wailed, then hugged him with tears streaming down her cheeks.

Daniel felt his stomach churn as an awareness of the heavy responsibility that had been thrust upon him dawned.

Thomas was numb. He stared in disbelief at his father, unable to grasp that he would never issue an order again.

Ralph couldn't comprehend what was happening. His father should be getting up to attend the usual meeting with them, but he seemed to be making no effort to do so.

Liza was sobbing again.

Jessie appeared to be completely in charge of herself but kept hidden from the others how she truly felt. Even now, she found herself trying to visualise the changes this tragedy would bring about for them all.

The doctor came, certified that Tristan Bullen was dead, gave Ann some laudanum and left to answer another urgent call

The silence that settled over the house weighed heavily on every mind, but more so on Daniel's when he realised that now he would be in charge of the mill and the owner of this house and the land on which it stood – he would henceforth be regarded as head of the family, and even in these tragic moments he felt a sense of satisfaction at the power that had come to him. He was finally in a position to act as he pleased. He felt the urge to share this with someone, and who better than Penelope? He hurried quickly to the stables, where, after a moment's commiseration with the man who was now their employer, the groomsman and stable-boy soon had his horse ready.

Even in these few minutes they were aware of a change in Daniel Bullen. His sharp tongue carried an air of impatient authority that could not be put down simply to the loss of his father. They felt life here would never be the same; they would be given less consideration than they had been by Mr Tristan. The reins on Daniel had been cast aside; now his newfound authority and unbending belief that he was right would prevail.

As they watched him ride away into the gathering darkness the groom shook his head dolefully. 'Jimmy, my boy, times won't ever be the same.'

Once clear of Keighley's houses, Daniel put his horse to a gallop and urged it faster and faster. The beast responded as if it knew its master wanted to live a new life as soon as possible. The thrum of the hoofs drove his plans relentlessly into his mind, obliterating the recent tragedy with the lure of a beckoning future. Daniel had plans to fulfil.

Reaching Griffin Manor, he was quickly out of the saddle and throwing the reins to a lackey. Daniel hurried into the house.

'Good evening, sir, it is good to see you back.' The friendliness of the greeting from the two menservants made him feel that nothing had interrupted his regular visits, but it had and there was time to be made up. While one of the men took his outdoor garments, he glanced at the other and made a little gesture towards the stairs. The man interpreted his silent question and gave a small nod. Daniel went up them without undue haste, but once on the landing and out of sight he strode quickly to Penelope's door.

'Good evening, Mr Bullen,' said the maid, loud enough for her mistress to hear, and immediately stepped on to the landing to take up duties downstairs.

The door had only just closed when a rustle of silk heralded Penelope's appearance. Her eyes dazzled and danced with joy as she rushed to the arms held open for her. 'Daniel!' As his embrace closed around her she said, 'Oh, how I've missed you. Never, ever leave me so long again.' Her lips sought his and he met them hungrily.

When he stepped back she sensed something was wrong. 'What is it, Daniel?'

'Father died a short while ago.'

'Oh, no,' she gasped. 'Sit down.' She took him to the sofa. 'You need a drink.' He drained the whisky glass but waved aside the offer of a refill. 'Do you want to talk about it?' Penelope asked tentatively.

'We were about to have a meeting at home. Thomas, Ralph and I were waiting in his study when we heard the women scream. We reached him but in a matter of moments he was gone.'

She laid a sympathetic hand on his arm. 'You know, if there is anything I can do ... '

'I know. Thank you, Penelope. Naturally we have made no plans yet. I came here because I wanted you to hear this from me.'

'I thank you for that, Daniel.'

'I don't know when the funeral will be, but whenever it is I would rather you did not come.'

'Are you ashamed of me?' she asked with a tremor in her voice.

'No, my love. I just wanted to spare you. I would not get any time with you, and I may not over the coming weeks. There'll be a lot to see to and I'll have a lot more responsibility.'

'I hope that is not going to get in the way of what we mean to each other?'

'It won't. Remember that. And also remember that everything I do is for us both.'

'That sounds as if you have made plans?'

'I have, but now is not the time to tell you what they are except that riches await us. The mill is mine. Griffin Manor is yours. But if my plans work out . . . ' He paused then said, 'No, not if. That should be when . . . when my plans work out, we will be rich beyond anything you dream of.'

'Tell me!' she pressed.

He shook his head. 'No. You'll have to wait.' He stood up before he could succumb to her wiles. 'I must get back.'

She took him in her arms. 'Don't stay away too long.'

'I won't.' He kissed her again and hurried from the room.

Penelope stood looking at the closed door, wondering what Daniel's schemes were and what part she would play in them.

Daniel and Jessie endeavoured to bring some order and stability to the household over the next few days by concentrating on all the things that needed to be done leading up to the funeral.

Two days after the tragedy Daniel found a few moments to pen a letter he wished he didn't need to write.

My dear Susannah,

It pains me to tell you that two days ago my father suffered a severe heart attack from which he died almost instantly. We have at least the small comfort that all the family were with him at the time. We are trying to come to terms with our loss but at the moment are finding it hard.

Please forgive me if I write no more now. I will do so when things are quieter after the funeral, which is set for a week today.

Ever yours,
Daniel

Under normal circumstances Susannah would have experienced a racing heart on recognising the handwriting on the envelope, but the black edges around it sent a chill through her. She had just managed to read Daniel's message when her father, anticipating a pleasant lunch with his daughter, walked in.

He pulled up short on seeing her ashen face. Concerned, he asked, 'What is it, Susannah?' She lifted the envelope. He saw the black edges. 'Oh, my goodness . . . who?'

'Mr Bullen, Daniel's father,' she said hoarsely, holding the letter out to him.

He took it and read then pulled out a chair to sit beside her and take her hand. 'I'm sorry to hear this.' He scanned the letter and said, 'The funeral must be today. We should write at once. I'll write to Mr Bullen; you write to Daniel. If we do it now I'll send one of the men to despatch the letters and hopefully they will soon reach the Bullens.'

The news of Tristan Bullen's death had spread like wildfire through the mills of the West Riding and beyond, with the result that, on the dreary autumn day of the funeral, the route from Ash Tree Villa along the Aire Valley and into Keighley was lined with people. The church was full to overflowing so that many mourners, muffled against the damp air, stood outside to pay their last respects. The service was short and dignified, and when people filed away they knew they had seen laid to rest a man who had showed what someone of lowly origins could achieve; for that, even his enemies respected him. They all wondered if Daniel Bullen could take his place.

23

Dear Susannah,

It is with regret that I cannot write in more affectionate terms to you at the moment, the appropriate words do not flow from my pen, but please rest assured that they are there in my mind and hopefully winging their way to you. Thanks to what you have expressed in your kind letters, you are the pillar on which I lean.

This time has been trying. A death does not stop the work of a mill. Responsibility for its continued success has been thrust upon me. I am determined to succeed but am finding there is much to deal with that my father had kept from us. It will take some time to sort out his affairs, but we are working hard to do so. The sooner things settle down – within my mourning period, I hope – then you and I can think seriously about our future and put this setback behind us.

Ever yours,
Daniel

Susannah read the letter again, wishing she was able to give him more support. She had toyed with the idea of visiting her uncle but knew that was impractical. Gideon was constantly on the move while in the West Riding, consolidating his business; besides, she knew her father would not countenance any action that he would deem as being too forward. She would have to be patient and live on the letters that passed between her and Daniel until his mourning period was over. She sensed from the tone of them that he would openly profess his love for her then and seek her hand in marriage. Such conclusions set Susannah wondering how she really felt about him.

Christmas was subdued for the Bullen family. Daniel knew that Susannah's thoughts would be with him at this time, and hoped his gift to her of a porcelain brooch would bring happy recollections of their time together.

The day their six months' mourning period was over, Daniel, Thomas and Ralph threw off their dark suits and discarded their black gloves, hatbands and cravats. Jessie and Liza bemoaned the fact they were expected to wear mourning for another six months.

'That is what you will do,' said Daniel firmly. 'I'll remind you that I am head of this household now. We will follow all due conventions. We have appearances to keep up. I won't have fingers pointed at us. You know very well Mama would want you to follow the full mourning period, so see to it that you do.

'Just because she can no longer express an opinion does not mean we should do as we choose. I'm afraid I don't think she will ever fully recover, and the doctor thinks the same. We will wait a little longer, but if there is no improvement, alternative arrangements will need to be made.'

'An asylum?' gasped a shocked Liza.

'It might come to that, unless you wish to take sole responsibility for her?'

Liza blanched at the thought. There was no support to be had from Jessie.

'Hmm, you've both made it perfectly clear where you stand. I'm not surprised. So as head of this house, I will put a suggestion to you.' Daniel paused and smirked as he continued, 'You each have a small legacy left to you by Father. Use it wisely because at the end of your mourning period I will expect you to move out of what is now my property. In other words, find yourselves rich husbands.'

The two young women were abashed, not only by the suddenness of this confrontation but particularly by the callousness of the ultimatum. They only now realised the extent of their father's influence over Daniel.

As the door closed behind him Jessie looked at Liza. 'So he wants us out,' she hissed with unmistakable disgust.

'Let's see if Thomas can help,' Liza suggested.

'Would you really want to stay after Daniel has ordered us out?'

'No,' replied Liza, 'but let us tell Thomas.'

'All right, he'll have to know sometime. It may as well be now.'

Liza was already halfway to the door and soon returned with their brother.

'What's this about?' he asked on seeing Jessie with a serious expression to match Liza's. He listened carefully as they related their interview with Daniel.

'In a way, I'm not surprised. I've seen his high-and-mighty attitude creeping in at work, and he constantly reminds Ralph and me who's boss. Ralph is young and placid enough to take it at the present time, but who knows about the future? I tell you, things are changing at the mill. I thought this might happen when Father died, and must admit I am finding it more and more difficult to work with Daniel.'

'So what are you planning to do?' asked a surprised Jessie.

'At the moment I don't know, but now you've told me about his attitude to you, I'm going to make a decision soon. Most probably I will leave. If you want my advice, you should do so too. But please let us keep all this to ourselves for now.'

Liza looked at Jessie. 'So all we have to do is find ourselves nice rich men to marry.' At first she chuckled at the thought. By the time Thomas was leaving the room, both his sisters were laughing aloud rather than give way to the tears that threatened.

That evening two Bullen men left Ash Tree Villa within half an hour of each other.

Thomas made his way to a house in Keighley. His knock was answered quickly but he just managed to catch a brief exchange at the other side of the front door.

'I'll get it, Alice.'

'Yes, Miss.'

There was a moment of silence and then the door opened.

'I thought you might come. I hoped you would.'

He stepped inside. The door closed behind him as he was welcomed into the arms of Helen Forbes.

'It's been too long,' she whispered close to his ear. 'But the neighbours would have talked if we hadn't observed etiquette.'

'We've time to make up,' he said, leaning close so he could look her in the eyes with all the love he could muster. 'Will you marry me, Helen Forbes?'

'With all my heart,' she whispered, and their kiss sealed a lifetime commitment.

Once the euphoria of committing themselves to each other had lessened and they were seated to enjoy the simple meal the cook had quickly prepared for them, Thomas told her about Daniel's ultimatum to his sisters and his own unease about developments at the mill.

'I would leave tomorrow if I knew what to do,' he concluded.

Helen looked thoughtful. He knew the expression and awaited her conclusion. 'If you are not happy at the mill then you should leave.'

'It isn't as easy as that. I'd be losing good money. I'd need to find another job first and where would I find an opening? Besides, who would want me?'

'Stop that, Thomas Bullen.' She raised a finger. 'Think positive. My brain has been working overtime in these last few moments. You've asked me to marry you and I've said yes, so let us do so as soon as possible.'

'But ... '

She stopped him immediately and looked sternly at him as she said, 'There you go again. There is nothing to stop us. I don't want a grand wedding. I've no relations. Do you want a big wedding?'

'No, my darling, I just want you.'

'There you are then. Let's get it organised right away. We don't even have to find a house ... we have this one. Once we are married it will be yours. You can still keep working at the mill until you find something more to your liking. How does that sound?'

Thomas stood up. Taking her hands in his, he helped her to her feet. All the time his eyes were fixed adoringly on her. 'It sounds as if I have found a gem. Thank you, my love.'

3rd May 1852

My Dear Susannah,

I am happy to say that work at the mill is settling down, enabling me now to consider the direction in which I wish my life to go. I think my correspondence with you has given you a glimpse of my feelings. I propose therefore to write to your father very soon and ask his permission for your hand in marriage. If this does not accord with your wishes then please let me know before I contact him.

I sincerely hope you will not feel you have to write such a letter. I will await your reply within the next three weeks and live in hope that it will not rend my heart asunder. A future with you is one of my most cherished dreams. It now rests in your hands.

Yours with deep affection,
Daniel

P.S. Ours won't be the first marriage in the family. Thomas has just told me that he and Helen are to marry and will arrange it to take place immediately we are all out of mourning. It will be a small wedding, immediate family only, as Helen has no one.

These words sent Susannah's heart racing even faster. She devoured them a second time and, not wanting to be disturbed by anyone, hurried upstairs to her room. She sank on to her bed and read the letter for a third time. A proposal of marriage! She would not be left on the shelf! Father must agree – he really must. She would write to Daniel immediately and give him permission to write to Francis. She sat down at her table with pen and paper, stared at the blank page for a few minutes, deciding the best way to reply, then she picked up the pen and started to write.

Dear Daniel,
You brought joy to . . .

Abruptly she stopped. The enormity of her decision weighed on her for a moment.

Leave Lincolnshire for the West Riding. Leave the estate where she had roamed since childhood. Move into a different world with Daniel. She fought against such thoughts with the determination that marriage to him would make no difference to her love of the life she knew here; she would merge both worlds successfully. Her husband would help her to do that.

Susannah picked up the pen and gave him permission to write to her father, and then followed this up with a letter of congratulations to Thomas and Helen.

Ten days later when she came into lunch her father was sitting at the table with a letter. His lips were tight; countenance serious – Susannah guessed what he was reading. She did not make her usual greeting but went to her place and sat down.

Francis looked across the table at his daughter, holding up the letter. 'I suppose you know what this is?'

'Yes, Father, I think I do.' Her voice shook a little.

'Daniel Bullen asks me for your hand in marriage,' he said quietly.

Susannah met his gaze but said nothing.

'If I agree it will mean a big change in your life. That is something you should give careful consideration to.' Seeing her about to speak, he held up his hand to stop her.

'I consider myself here to give advice, not to say yes or no, though one of those words will have to be said after your final consideration. I don't want to lose you; you have been, and still are, so much a part of my life here at Stockdale. Losing you will leave a big hole, but I cannot refuse and thereby possibly condemn you to a spinster's life. Your happiness is the most important thing to me; therefore I am hoping it will be a long engagement so that you can weigh things up carefully before you make your final declaration. After all, you have not been meeting Daniel regularly.'

Susannah rose from her chair, came to her father and kissed him on the cheek.

Her intention of making a quick reply to Daniel had been put in perspective, making her realise her father's last remark was sound.

It was a quiet meal, each of them occupied with their thoughts. When Susannah left the dining room she went straight to her room and penned a letter.

My dear Daniel,

I am honoured that you have asked my father for my hand in marriage. I would now ask that you give me a little more time before I make a final commitment to you. It is a big decision for me to make, to move away from the estate in which I have spent all my life to date. Please grant me this extra time so that our life together can be made more perfect. You will have my final answer in four weeks.

Yours affectionately,
Susannah

She sealed the envelope and went to tell her father of the

decision she had made. 'I did not give the real reason for my decision,' she explained to him, 'I thought it might seem strange to Daniel, but I want Uncle Gideon to know before I commit myself.' She saw relief flash momentarily across her father's face. 'And as you told me he would be visiting us this weekend, I thought it presented an ideal opportunity to tell him.'

'I am glad you have acted as you have, and I know that your uncle will be pleased that you considered him. After all, he has been very much a part of your life, especially since your mother died. Almost a second father to you. He will be arriving on Friday afternoon. You can tell him after dinner that evening. This is a big step you are thinking of taking, so between now and then please consider all the implications.'

Susannah made no comment; her mind felt clouded and uncertain. She had received an offer of marriage. There were no other young men in her life. Dare she ignore this opportunity in the knowledge that she might never receive another?

24

Gideon received his usual enthusiastic welcome on arriving at Stockdale Manor but sensed more vivacity than usual in Susannah's attitude. He knew better than to question his niece; he would be told in good time what had prompted this emotion in her.

Once he had rid himself of his travel stains, Gideon strolled on to the veranda to join his brother and niece for a drink before dinner. Comfortable in the balmy air, the men enjoyed their whisky and Susannah her Madeira.

Gideon cast his eyes across the green landscape and took a deep breath. 'Ah, that's a wonderful sight. It's good to breathe in pure air and see so much greenery.'

'Do you miss it?' asked Francis, seeing an opportunity to draw his daughter's attention to Gideon's observations.

He pursed his lips thoughtfully. 'At times I do, but there are compensations wherever you are, if you look for them. Most West Riding people are friendly and down-to-earth; they call a spade a spade but generally know their station. There's money to be made in the mills. Men have risen above their background there. They have worked hard, used their brains, and are thankful for that bit of luck that let them get where they are today. In most cases they have never lost sight of their roots. It will be interesting to see how their sons make out without having to struggle as their fathers did.'

Though she read something of Daniel's situation in her uncle's observation, Susannah made no comment but asked, 'Have you made any more changes to Barden House?'

'No, I am happy with it as it is.'

The flow of conversation was halted momentarily when the butler announced that dinner was served, but it was soon taken up again once they were seated at the dining table. Francis made sure it did not flag; he wanted to keep Susannah from thinking about breaking the news to her uncle while the servants were in and out, busy with the meal. He knew it would happen once they were seated again in the drawing-room, so it came as no surprise when his daughter cast a querying glance in his direction. He gave a slight nod.

'Uncle Gideon, I have something to tell you,' Susannah began nervously.

His attention was drawn by the tremor in her voice. He looked at her and waited for her to continue.

'I have had a proposal of marriage.'

'May I ask from whom and if you have accepted?'

'Mr Daniel Bullen, and I have not yet accepted. Father advised me to give it some more thought.'

'Very wise,' agreed Gideon.

'I have informed Daniel that I need time to consider his proposal and said that I will give him an answer in four weeks.'

'Do you know now what your answer will be?' her uncle asked.

'I am not absolutely sure yet, but I think it will be yes.'

Questions and advice poured into his mind but Gideon never uttered them; it was not his place to do that, and he was sure his brother would already have spoken.

'Four weeks,' he mused. 'Then use them to think carefully about the big step you will be taking if you accept.'

Susannah jumped up from her chair and hugged her uncle, saying, 'I will, Uncle, I will.'

Gideon held her a moment longer while he whispered, through a catch in his throat, 'Be happy, whatever you decide.'

By unspoken consensus the matter was allowed to drop. It was only raised again after Susannah had bidden the two men goodnight and Gideon suggested a nightcap. Once the whisky was poured and the first sip taken, he asked, 'Francis, are you happy about this marriage?'

'No, but only in the sense that I will be losing my daughter who will no longer be at Stockdale. Who am I to stand in the way of Susannah's happiness if this is where she seeks to find it?'

Gideon nodded. 'Do you think she will settle in the West Riding and into a life so different from that she is used to here?'

Francis gave a little shrug of his shoulders. 'How can I know? Life isn't plain sailing. We make decisions, and then we have to make them work. If Susannah accepts then I hope she can do that.'

Gideon took a thoughtful sip of his whisky. 'Do you remember when we returned here after you had visited Skipton?'

'Yes. You stayed for a few days, believing it would help you sort out something you had on your mind.'

'That's right. You asked me what it was and I said I would tell you if ever the time was right. It wasn't then.'

Francis nodded.

'Well,' went on Gideon, 'the time is right now.'

The announcement left a charged silence in its wake. Francis waited for his brother to elaborate.

'I had an idea after that visit that something deeper than friendship was developing between Susannah and Daniel Bullen. I felt uneasy about it but had no grounds for saying so. As you know, I let the matter go unspoken but now, with what I have been told this evening, I think I should speak to you about it.' He took a sip of his whisky.

Sensing he was a little embarrassed, Francis reached for the decanter and topped up his brother's glass. 'There, that might help.'

Gideon nodded his thanks and after another sip continued, 'I would not normally interfere between father and daughter, but you know how dear Susannah is to me.'

'I have always known that, Gideon, and have been thankful for it, especially after Rachel's untimely death. I know you have always had Susannah's interests at heart. So what is it that is bothering you about this possible marriage?'

'It isn't the marriage that bothers me. I know nothing of the feelings between Susannah and Daniel, and can only hope for their mutual happiness. No, it is the financial aspects of that match that worry me.'

'I don't think you need have worries on that score. After all, there is a thriving mill as well as this estate. Susannah should want for nothing.'

'Very true, but you know as well as I that once the marriage takes place, whatever the wife owns becomes the husband's. Susannah has a lot to lose.'

Francis looked thoughtful. 'Is there anything we can do about that?'

25

At the end of their evening meal, Thomas announced to his family that the date of his marriage to Helen was fixed for two weeks' time.

Ralph was the only one who looked shocked. It was something he hadn't contemplated happening so soon, but he quietly offered his congratulations and his feelings were somewhat alleviated when Thomas asked him to be his best man.

Daniel showed no reaction except to ask, 'Where will you live? Don't expect to move Helen in here.'

'I wouldn't dream of it,' replied Thomas coolly. 'Besides, Helen already has a house.'

'How convenient,' sneered his brother.

Thomas held back his retort; instead he turned to his two sisters. 'You know Helen has no one, so she is going to ask you both to be bridesmaids. Don't let on I've told you.'

A sparkle of excitement gleamed in their eyes. 'She won't even guess we know,' said Jessie.

'No, she won't,' agreed Liza, equally as excited as her sister.

The following afternoon Helen called at Ash Tree Villa, and from that moment on the days were hectic, with only

Daniel standing aloof from it all. He was already visualising his own wedding as a grand affair, though Susannah had yet to say yes.

Helen Forbes married Thomas Bullen in a quiet dignified ceremony in their local church. Daniel made his congratulations brief and, after toasting the bride and groom, absented himself from the rest of the quiet celebrations which were held in a local hostelry.

Helen had planned it that they would delay their honeymoon for a week so that they could move Thomas's belongings into the house and make it feel as if it was truly his home. She did this very skilfully, and when the last item came through the door and was in place she took him in her arms

'Welcome home, Thomas. May we have many years of happiness here,' she told him, with love overflowing from her eyes.

His answering smile told her how much he appreciated those first two words, and his kiss assured her that the rest of his life would be spent loving her.

'Come,' she said, 'I want us to walk into every room together, hand in hand, to make every room *ours*.'

'Oh, we haven't dealt with these,' Helen said as they entered the back room. She indicated two large folders propped against a wall. 'I don't remember bringing them in.'

'I brought them when you were doing something upstairs. I meant to move them into the shed outside. I'll do it now.'

'What are they?' she asked.

Thomas did not answer but started to pick one folder up, spreading his arms wide to do so.

'Show me,' Helen said quietly. 'We have decided together where everything else should go. I think we should do the same with these, rather than just condemn them to the shed.'

A little reluctantly he lowered the folder. 'They aren't important.'

'Let me see and be a judge of that.' Helen stepped forward and opened a folder. A gasp escaped her lips. 'What ...?' She was staring wide-eyed at a painting of a river scene. Thomas made no comment or explanation. She carefully lifted the painting to reveal another one, a portrait that she knew instantly was of Thomas's mother. One by one she studied six more paintings without speaking then she indicated the second folder. 'More?' she asked.

His nod revealed embarrassment.

She looked at the contents without comment, and then said, 'And you painted them all?'

He nodded.

'Why haven't you told me about them, and that you like to paint? You mention sketching, but that is all.'

'I just did them for my own pleasure. I haven't painted for a couple of years.'

'Why not?'

'I was too busy at the mill.'

'Does anyone in your family know about these?'

'Yes, but they showed little interest in my work, even though Father did collect paintings.'

Helen straightened up. With arms akimbo she fixed her husband with a solemn gaze. 'Thomas Bullen, you are a talented artist. And don't look so surprised. That is a fact, not just a prejudiced opinion because you are the man I love. I do know, up to a point, what I am talking about. Oh, here I am criticising you for not telling me about your painting when I have never told you about my own interest in art and how it came about. Suffice it to say that after my time at the orphanage, I came into the care of an art dealer. Nathan Hopkins and his wife Olivia taught me to love paintings and how to view them. I've never used the knowledge I gained from them except for my own enjoyment. Now, seeing your work, I know God has finally seen a way to let me use my expertise.'

'Helen, what are you talking about?'

'Your work is of professional standard. It will sell, if displayed in the right places.'

'Who would want any painting of mine?'

'Frankly, nobody at the moment, because you have kept your talent hidden so well. I suspect that is because you thought of it as an embarrassment when you were living in a different world. But you have admitted to me you would leave the mill tomorrow. These paintings are your passport to do that.'

'But . . . '

Helen sensed the objections that were coming, and stopped him. 'We won't go into your position at the mill at the moment. You must carry on there as if it is your chosen path in life. But let me take you to visit this very knowledgeable couple who taught me what I know, let them judge your talent, and from their opinion we will map out our new life together.' Still he hesitated. She begged, 'Please, Thomas, let me do this, let it be your wedding present to me?'

And he could not refuse to grant such a request.

The meeting between Thomas and the Hopkinses took place on cordial grounds, with Nathan and Olivia admiring Thomas's work and talent to such an extent that they took some work away with them.

'It might be a while before we can get some opinions but please be patient. You certainly have a future in the art world.'

Daniel had decided to retain the monthly meetings that his father had instigated. He saw them not only as a means of keeping his brothers' interest in the mill at the forefront of their minds but also as a way of imposing his own authority at the mill and on his employees – among whom he now regarded his brothers.

They were puzzled when he called an extra meeting, two weeks after the last one. They were even more puzzled when they walked into the study at Ash Tree Villa and found their sisters sitting there as well.

'What's going on?' asked Thomas. 'Daniel called this a business meeting.'

'I don't know,' said Jessie. 'He told us he was having a meeting with you and that he wanted us to attend.'

'No doubt we'll know in a few minutes,' said Ralph. 'There were several letters on the table in the hall earlier in the day, all addressed to him.'

'I hope calling this extra meeting hasn't upset anyone's plans,' said Ralph sympathetically. 'Daniel's far from considerate.'

'Too fond of holding the reins too much,' commented Thomas, with a touch of bitterness in his voice.

Before anyone could say more, Daniel walked in. Liza shot her sister a look which said, He's in a jaunty mood, what's happened?

Daniel sat down, placed his hands on the desk and said solemnly, 'I have called this extra meeting because some serious matters have arisen which I must bring to your notice.' He paused, gave a little laugh and then allowed amusement to flicker in his eyes. 'You look as though you all expect to hear something very serious. Maybe it is ... depending how you look at it.' He left a little pause then announced loud and clear, 'Ralph, charge the glasses. Thomas, give him a hand.'

His brothers got to their feet and quickly obeyed in case

Daniel's light mood altered. A few minutes more and they were waiting expectantly to hear what Daniel had to say.

He raised his glass. 'Here's to us all.'

Still puzzled, they drank to that.

'And may life continue to shine on us.'

They drank again.

Daniel settled back more comfortably in his chair. 'I received two letters today from the brothers Mr Lawrence Gaskell and Mr Defoe Gaskell. Mr Lawrence asked if he may correspond with you, Jessie, and Mr Defoe with you, Liza.'

The sisters looked at each other in astonishment. This was something so unexpected that they waited in silence for their brother to go on.

'Though I have heard their names mentioned in the company I keep, I knew little of them so I did some detective work today. Suffice it to say that my enquiries revealed they have been kept so wrapped up in work under their father's eye they have had little time until now to consider marriage. Now it seems, with business booming based on six haberdashery shops and two more in preparation, their minds are turning to thoughts of matrimony. It seems to me they would both be good catches. They provide chances of a well-established and well-off future for you both. I think you would be well advised to consider their requests carefully.'

'But we know nothing about them. We have never even met them,' protested Liza.

'I've told you the most important things. I can also tell you that Mr Lawrence is thirty and Mr Defoe a year younger. I suggest you allow me to give them permission to write to you. You may correspond with them, and at a suitable juncture, we'll invite them both to dine here.'

The quick glance the sisters exchanged indicated that they

were minded to accept Daniel's suggestion. This could mark their escape from under his thumb, and married to brothers they would, no doubt, be able to remain closely in touch with each other.

'Very well,' said Jessie for them both.

'Good,' said Daniel with satisfaction. Then, with deeper satisfaction still, he announced without any preamble, 'And I am to be married!'

A hush settled over the room.

'I had a letter this morning from Miss Susannah Charlesworth, accepting my proposal.'

'Of Stockdale Manor?' gasped Thomas.

'Yes. You all looked surprised,' he queried.

'Well, this is quite unexpected,' said Jessie. 'We never knew ...'

'We thought ...' said Liza. She left the sentence incomplete. 'Did this start when Miss Charlesworth was here with her father and uncle?

Daniel shook his head. 'No, when I went to Stockdale Manor for the sheep shearing. Before I left, I asked permission of her father to write to Susannah. We have been corresponding ever since. And of course there was the visit here that you mentioned, Liza.'

'So when will you marry and where will the wedding be?' asked Jessie.

'Nothing has been settled yet. We are hoping to meet in the near future.' He glanced at his youngest brother. 'You are looking despondent, Ralph. Aren't you happy for me?'

Ralph started. His thoughts had been dwelling on the outcome for him of all this unexpected news. 'Yes, I'm happy for you. And I liked Miss Charlesworth when she was here.'

'Good, then why so glum?'

'What is going to happen to me if you all get married?'

211

'You'll have nothing to worry about,' Daniel hastened to reassure him. 'Since these possibilities came to mind I have been thinking how to arrange things. Thomas is settled. If Jessie and Liza work things to their advantage both the girls will be well provided for and comfortably settled in fine houses on the outskirts of Bradford. I will be here in this house with my bride. Which leaves you and Mother, Ralph. The west wing can easily be converted so that Mother may be looked after there by a nurse and maid, and the remainder of it can be yours, Ralph, until you too find a bride.'

'You have it all planned out,' said Jessie, a little suspiciously.

'It is no good hanging back,' said Daniel. 'You've got to plan ahead as best you can.'

'And it seems that things have worked out well for you,' Liza commented.

'Only if you and Jessie marry the Gaskell brothers, which I think you will. The offers are too good to turn down.'

'And the mill? Or are you likely to be persuaded to live in Lincolnshire?' asked Thomas.

Daniel gave a little laugh. 'What makes you think I'd move there?' He didn't give his brother time to answer. 'You know very well the mill has been my life ... still is and always will be. However, as Susannah is an only child, and I know she and her father are devoted to each other, I will probably have to spend some time at Stockdale Manor. After all, it would be a big wrench for her to move away completely. However, that is still some way off. There is my wedding to plan and two others in the offing. Whatever happens, Thomas, it looks as though you will have to accept more responsibility for running the mill.'

26

As Thomas walked home he considered the news he would take to Helen and, knowing her, realised it would be best to come straight to the point. His intention was thwarted the moment he walked in.

Hearing the front door open, she rushed into the hall to meet him. 'Thomas! Come quickly, I've some good news. Take your coat off and come and sit down.'

As much as he had been dwelling on his own thoughts, he could not help but laugh at her excitement. It pleased him to see her this way for whatever she had to tell him might ease the impact of what he had to reveal.

He shrugged himself out of his overcoat and allowed her to bustle him into the drawing-room and sit him down on the sofa.

'Don't move,' Helen ordered. She stepped quickly back into the hall and reappeared moments later. She came to stand in front of him, and as she did so she turned a painting round so he could see it. 'I have arranged for Mr Hopkins to come and give his opinion of this,' she announced.

'You've what?' Surprise filled Thomas's voice as he looked at her in disbelief. 'When?'

'He's a very busy man, but as a favour to me he can manage a week today. It can't come quickly enough for me.'

Thomas held his hands up to try and stem her enthusiasm. 'Steady on, Helen. This is wonderful news but we must not get carried away. This is only one painting. Mr Hopkins may conclude from it that I have no talent.'

'He won't, I'm certain of it! This opportunity will help you fulfil your desire to leave the mill. You will still have an income from the shares your father left you.'

'But that will be small and I won't have anything else.'

'I set aside some of the money from the sale of the old property. That will ... '

'Helen, stop! I can't live off you.'

She sat down beside him and took his hands in hers. 'Thomas, by law what I have is yours so ... '

'No, Helen. That may be the law, but I won't take advantage of it. I will stay on at the mill until we see how things turn out.'

'Very well then, we will say no more on that point. But don't refuse to see Mr Hopkins; don't throw this opportunity away. I believe you have talent, but if at any time the people who see your work don't have equal faith in you, I will submit to their assessment.'

'Very well,' he agreed.

With her eyes shining brightly and a tremor of excitement running through her, she leaned closer to him, kissed him and whispered a heartfelt, 'Thank you. I know you will never regret it.' After a little pause she added, 'Now what have you to tell me?'

'You and I are going to a wedding.'

'Whose?'

'Daniel and Miss Charlesworth's.'

'Ah.' Helen raised a finger and ran it gently down his cheek. 'But I got the best of the Bullen brothers.'

He gave a little smile which disappeared as he said, 'Daniel announced it at a family gathering this evening. That was why I told you I would be late home.'

'I sincerely hope they will be happy. I think Daniel might be hard to live with, so if Miss Charlesworth needs a friend I hope she can find one in me. I liked her. It will be a wrench for her to leave her country home and move here. I hope she will settle.'

'I hope so too,' said Thomas.

'You are looking anxious.'

'Not about that.'

'What then?'

Thomas tightened his lips and said, 'Daniel has said he expects me to work more hours as he may be spending more time in Lincolnshire.'

'Can't you tell him that will not be possible?' she protested.

'Hardly. I do have responsibilities.'

'Just consider your own future, Thomas. You might like to take it in a different direction. Whatever you decide, I will support you.'

27

Daniel paced his office, his mind not on his work. How could he tell Penelope of his coming wedding? Still unsure how he would manage it, he was soon in the saddle and riding along the Aire Valley.

'You are early today,' Penelope remarked with curiosity when he walked into her room unannounced. 'I'm pleased we'll have longer together.' She kissed him but was taken aback when she received no sign of a response from him. 'What's wrong with you?' she snapped. She stood back and eyed him, trying to fathom the answer to her question. When there was no immediate reply she sensed trouble. 'Tell me!' Her brittle tone was heightened by her defiant stance and the penetrating expression in her eyes.

'I'm getting married!' he blurted out.

The words dazed her. Surely he didn't mean it . . . Then every possible interpretation but one was driven from her mind.

'Daniel!' she screamed with excitement. 'A blunter proposal than I expected, but the answer is still the same. Yes! Yes!' She flung her arms round him and hugged him tight. 'When, Daniel, when?'

'I don't know.'

She leaned back and stared at him. 'Then we'd better decide now!'

'We can't.'

'Why not?'

'Because it's not you I'm going to marry.'

Aghast, she stared at him, her face draining of all colour. 'I don't understand.'

'I have plans . . .'

'Plans? What do you mean?' she screamed venomously. 'You bastard . . . you want rid of me! After all I've done for you!' In a fury she flung herself on him, pummelling at his chest with clenched fists as she screamed obscenities. 'Why? Aren't I good enough for you now you're a mill owner? You damned bastard!' Her fingers became claws, reaching out to tear at his face, but he managed to ward off her flailing arms and grab her wrists. He was determined to hold on tight, just as she was determined to wrest herself free from his grip and scratch his eyes out.

'Stop! Stop!' he ordered. 'Calm down.' He met her wild eyes without flinching, full of determination to make her listen. 'Hear me out, damn you.' She fell against him, sobbing. Gingerly he loosened his hold on her wrist and with his free hand smoothed back her hair.

'Calm down,' he ordered firmly. 'You need to hear what I have to say.'

He pulled her closer. Penelope turned her head to look up into his eyes, seeking the answer she wanted.

'Do you want to be rich beyond anything you can make at Griffin Manor?'

'Yes, but only if it is with you.'

'I have the mill.'

'I know.'

'Would you like to be Lady of the Manor?'

She stared at him enquiringly. 'You talk in riddles.'

'I do not. Eventually that is what you will be, after I marry Susannah Charlesworth of Stockdale Manor.'

'And who is *she*? And how long have ... ?' Penelope's eyes flared.

'Listen carefully,' he interrupted in a tone that told her he was deadly serious in what he was about to say. 'Susannah Charlesworth is an only child. Her father's brother is his only surviving male relative. She stands to inherit a fortune in land as well as money. All told her father and uncle are very, very rich, and one day it will all come to her. And, as I will be her husband, it will all then be mine.' He paused a moment to let his words sink in, then added, 'And when it is mine, you will share it with me.'

Penelope's nimble mind was assessing this scheme. 'You will be extremely rich, won't you?'

He gave her a knowing smile and nodded. 'So rich it will enable us to spend much more time together.'

She pondered. He did not interrupt her thoughts.

'You want me to be your mistress while you are married to this rich innocent?'

'If you put it that way, yes.'

She pursed her lips then started to unbutton her dress. 'Then let's you and I seal the bargain in the best way we know.'

He stepped towards her. 'That will be my pleasure.'

28

'Susannah, I would ask you to consider carefully all the implications of this engagement,' her father pleaded. 'It has been six months since you accepted Daniel's proposal and he has visited us here only once since he asked you to marry him. I think he should have come more often.'

'He has been extremely busy at the mill,' she said in his defence.

Francis wondered just how busy Daniel had been, but said nothing more on the subject. Instead he made a suggestion. 'Invite him to stay for three days before winter really sets in. You will have an opportunity to discuss dates and arrangements for the wedding.'

Susannah brightened. 'That would be wonderful! I will write to him as soon as we get back.'

'You can also make a preliminary suggestion to him: that you get married here at the beginning of July next year, with your guests attending; then we'll have a service of blessing in his parish. For most people that would solve the problem of travelling a long distance. If anyone wants to attend both, it is up to them.'

'That's a sensible idea, Papa. I'm sure he will agree. It will be a most suitable thing for his mother who is housebound.

Apparently she has never got over the shock of Mr Bullen's death and has deteriorated rather quickly.'

Autumn 1852

Dear Susannah,

I thank you for your most encouraging letter. Now the day that I long for seems so much nearer. I respect your father's wish to fix the date for July next year. The suggestion at least enables us to plan the day I am sure we are both longing to share.

His consideration towards our guests is most commendable and I am sure two separate celebrations will answer everyone's needs.

I am most grateful for your father's letter and kind invitation to me to visit. I am writing to him to accept and look forward to seeing him again. Though of course the most important aspect of the visit will be to see you once more.

Yours in admiration,
Daniel

Susannah looked up from the letter and saw a small smile twitch on her father's lips as he laid his own down on the table beside him.

'Has Daniel amused you?' she asked.

'He is doing all he can to impress me and assure me that your happiness is the most important thing to him. I appreciate that. It is the flowery language he is using to do so that makes me smile.'

'And may I hear it?' she asked.

'Not for you to know,' replied her father, still showing signs of amusement at what he had read. 'He will be visiting on the days we suggested. Will you inform Mrs Ainsworth?'

'I will, Father,' Susannah replied. And may I arrange for Rosalind to visit and reacquaint herself with Daniel as she will be our chief bridesmaid?'

'Of course. Maybe we should extend the invitation to her mother and father too, by way of a small celebration of your engagement.'

'Father, you are so kind and thoughtful,' Susannah enthused, and kissed him on the cheek.

'Whatever I do is all for you, my dear.'

On the day of Daniel's arrival Susannah could hardly contain her excitement. She and her father both came to the front door to greet their guest.

'Good day, sir,' said Daniel with a joyous smile as he took Francis's proffered hand in a warm grip.

'Welcome to Stockdale Manor once more.'

'Thank you, sir. It is most kind of you. I am pleased to see you looking so well. Of course, it is a delight to see your lovely daughter again.' As he was speaking Daniel turned to her, his pale eyes alight with warmth. He held out his hands to Susannah and kissed her. She knew he could read the depth of her feeling in her eyes.

'Are all your family well?' she enquired, leading him straight into the drawing-room, reluctant to miss a minute of his company by standing on ceremony and showing him to his room.

'Mother is not well but she is cared for. Ralph is having to take on much more responsibility at the mill. He is finding it strange to be in a position of authority, but he is managing.'

'And Thomas and Helen? Are they thriving?' queried Susannah.

'Yes. He is very efficient as my right-hand man and they

are happily settled. Oh, and I must tell you that Jessie and Liza are being courted by two brothers.'

'Does that please you?' Susannah asked.

'Yes. The gentlemen have an extensive haberdashery business, with several shops throughout the West Riding, and are very attentive to my sisters. The girls were wary of my choices of suitor for a time, but they have come to appreciate the brothers' good qualities.' Changing the subject, he informed Francis, 'I've heard your brother is finding Skipton to his liking. It's a lovely area.'

'You've seen him?' Francis asked.

'No, I haven't. I should make it in my way to do so but I have been extremely busy. I'm sure he'll find Skipton convenient for Keighley and yet far enough to feel his work is not on top of him all the time.'

'Gideon has always been capable of keeping his private and business lives apart – he can leave one behind when he enters the other.'

'A gift indeed, sir,' approved Daniel. 'I wish I could do that easily but it still takes an effort for me to do so. Maybe Susannah will be able to help me emulate her uncle in that respect.'

'I'll do my best,' she replied.

'Now,' said Francis. 'I know you have just arrived, but time will pass quickly and there are things we must discuss and put in place for this wedding. Firstly . . . Susannah, you tell him.'

'I want you to meet up with Rosalind again, especially as she is to be chief bridesmaid. While we're on that point, I expect you would like your two sisters to be bridesmaids also?'

'Naturally they would love to attend you, along with Rosalind.'

'And of course the young men paying them attention will be invited guests.'

'That will please them.' Daniel gave a little smile. 'And who knows? It may result in their all making up their minds sooner than we expect.'

'Will one of your brothers be best man?' asked Francis.

'I think it must be Thomas.'

Susannah was pleased with this choice.

'We'll visit the church in Thornton Curtis tomorrow; the vicar is expecting us,' said Francis. 'Have you made any enquiries about having a blessing at your home church, Daniel?'

'Yes, sir. The vicar is perfectly willing to perform a small ceremony. It can only be blessing as the marriage will already have taken place.'

'Good,' said Francis, with a measure of relief. 'I thought he might object to not performing the full ceremony.'

'He's a very understanding man, sir, and in cases like this takes the view that it should be the bride's prerogative where the actual marriage ceremony takes place.'

The following day the vicar of Thornton Curtis was delighted to see them again, and his attention to all the details of what he thought would be best for 'the great day' left them in no doubt that the ceremony would go smoothly.

Mr and Mrs Webster and Rosalind enjoyed meeting Daniel again; the men escaping when Susannah sought her chance to discuss bridesmaids' dresses with Mrs Webster and Rosalind.

'As Miss Bosworth is ill, will Mrs O'Leary be making all the dresses?' said Mrs Webster.

'Yes. I have heard no complaints about her work,' replied Susannah. 'I intend to write to Daniel's sisters to say that I will ask Mrs O' Leary if she or her assistant can go to Keighley to take their measurements and then return for the fittings.'

'Splendid,' agreed Mrs Webster. 'They must stay at Harthill for the wedding, then all the bridesmaids will be together to travel to the church.'

'That is most kind of you,' said Susannah with a smile of thanks.

'You've got everything settled then?' queried Francis when the men rejoined the ladies.

'We have,' said Susannah. 'Daniel will have to inform his sisters of our ideas. I will write to them also.'

'We shouldn't impose on him,' said Francis. 'I think you and I should visit Gideon, at a time Daniel believes will be convenient for you to talk about dresses with his sisters.'

'A splendid idea, sir,' agreed Daniel. 'Where dresses are concerned, I'm sure I would have got it wrong. Should we say two weeks from today? I could contact your brother when I return the day after tomorrow. Do you know if he will be in Skipton then?'

'Yes. He is there now and has informed me that he intends to stay for the next three weeks. I will write him a letter, and if you would take it, it would make for a speedier delivery.'

On the morning of his departure, knowing that Susannah's father had been called by his farm manager to deal with a sudden crisis, Daniel seized some moments alone with Susannah. 'I'm sorry we haven't managed more time in private together,' he said regretfully.

'So am I,' she replied, laying her hand on his arm. 'It was understandable, with so much to be arranged. But bear in mind, we will have a lifetime together.'

He smiled. 'So we shall.' He drew her into his arms then and his kiss held a promise for the future.

A week after Daniel's departure Francis received a letter from his brother welcoming him and Susannah to stay with him in Skipton. It turned out to be a busy but valuable visit. Jessie and Liza were delighted with the choice of material that Susannah had made for their dresses, and were also pleased to confirm that the invitations to their suitors to accompany them to both wedding and blessing had been accepted. Susannah was pleased that the courtships were turning out so well, and also to meet up with Thomas and Helen again.

As the days progressed through winter and spring the arrangements continued to be made, so that everything flowed smoothly towards the wedding day.

Susannah lay in her bed watching the rising sun gradually flood her room with the soft light of the July morning. She stretched and luxuriated in the softness of her feather bed. Before noon she would be Mrs Bullen. 'Bullen' – she let the word come to her lips, but suddenly it did nothing for her. 'Charlesworth.' Ah, now that had a better ring to it. It meant something, whereas Bullen now seemed to have no merit to it at all. She frowned. But that was who she would become – Mrs Bullen. Unless ... o, my goodness, suppose Daniel hadn't arrived? Intimations of disaster gripped her mind, even though it would mean she would never have to use the name Bullen if he hadn't. She ignored the chill in the room, panicking as she flung on her robe. Daniel had planned to arrive yesterday. Now she was wishing they hadn't agreed to stay apart until she walked down the aisle to join him.

She rushed towards the door but never reached it. A knock

on the other side stopped her. She stood still and called out, 'Come in.'

The door opened and her lady's maid stepped in.

'Oh, you are up, Miss.'

'Yes, Lillian, I'm up,' said Susannah, trying to calm herself.

'Are you all right, Miss? You look a little flushed.'

Susannah smiled to herself. You couldn't keep anything from Lillian. 'Yes, I'm perfectly all right. I've just been wondering what I would do if Mr Daniel hadn't arrived. I'm afraid I panicked.'

Lillian smiled. 'You need have no fear of that, Miss. Mr Daniel is here. Young Garth saw him in the village yesterday evening. So you can concentrate on looking your best when you walk down that aisle. You nip back into bed, Miss, you've plenty of time. I'll bring your breakfast and then I'll help you get ready.'

'Thank you, Lillian.'

When the door closed behind the maid, a feeling of loneliness settled on Susannah. 'Oh, Mama, how I wish you were here!' Her eyes dampened and her mind drifted to the far-off days of her childhood. 'Mama . . . '

I am here. Take heart, I'll be with you.

Susannah started. She glanced all around the room. Even though she was certain no one would be there, she would always swear that her mother had spoken to her. She would tell no one of this but she would heed her mother's message.

When Lillian came in with the breakfast tray, Susannah realised that her appetite had returned. Though she did not comment, Lillian was pleased to note her young mistress's eyes were bright again and her smile was warm once more.

So began a hectic morning in Stockdale Manor. It was no less so at Harthill Priory where Rosalind, Jessie and Liza were slipping into their dresses amidst much delight at the dressmaker's skill in completing the three matching pale blue full-skirted gowns with their tight waists and boned bodices.

With the minimum of fuss, Mrs Ainsworth and Lillian helped Susannah dress. When Mrs Ainsworth was finally satisfied, they stepped back and could do nothing more than express their admiration for the bride.

'You look beautiful, Miss,' said Lillian with a catch in her throat, 'Doesn't she, Mrs Ainsworth?'

The housekeeper, hands clasped in front of her, nodded. 'You certainly do. No one will match you today.'

Susannah stepped in front of the cheval glass to admire the dressmaker's handiwork again. The white sheer plain-weave linen bodice and three-tiered skirt fitted her to perfection and were matched by triple-flounced pagoda sleeves. The calf-length train fell from the back of a small tight-fitting bonnet trimmed around the front edge with a row of pearls.

She told them, 'Thank you both so much for all your help.'

'Your father will be very proud of you,' said the house-keeper.

As if on cue there was a tap on the door. Lillian opened it quickly.

'Is my daughter ready?'

'Yes, sir.'

'Come in, Father.'

Francis stepped into the room and stopped short. He stared at Susannah for a moment. 'You look so beautiful.' He held out his hands and stepped over to her, careful that he did not brush against the dress. As she took them he said quietly, 'And so like your mother.'

She smiled without saying a word but the eyes of both father and daughter were damp.

He crooked his arm. She linked hers inside it. They moved out on to the landing and took the first step into her new life.

29

Susannah felt as if she was in a dream world. She was sitting in an open carriage beside her father who looked very elegant in his morning suit. Two white horses were guided by liveried coachmen, there to see that the beautiful young bride reached her destination without mishap.

There had been no send off. The Stockdale Manor employees would all be at the church, and as soon as Mr Charlesworth had taken Susannah on his arm, Mrs Ainsworth and Lillian had left by trap.

Francis leaned towards his daughter and took her hand. Susannah smiled reassurance at him, then waved at the people who had come out on to their doorsteps to express their good wishes.

'I did not expect all this,' she remarked when they received the same reception from many other cottages along the route.

'Folk always like a wedding,' her father commented.

'Oh, my goodness,' she gasped when they reached the village and she saw the street to the church lined with people ready to express their joy for the bride-to-be.

'Enjoy it, my dear. It will happen only once.'

There was a crowd at the lych-gate and other spectators

lined the path to the church. She only had a moment to have a word with the bridesmaids excitedly awaiting her arrival.

They paused at the church door where the vicar expressed his welcome then left them to take up position at the altar. In those few moments Rosalind cast her eyes over the bride's dress and made a few minor adjustments to the fall of the train. The organist, who had been playing gently, let the music fade and almost immediately struck up with the appropriate fanfare.

Francis glanced at Susannah. She nodded. Seeing the signal, the bridesmaids led the bridal procession into the church, which was so packed that Susannah was almost overwhelmed. She had expected the invited guests to occupy half the church, but had never anticipated that people from the surrounding area would fill the rest of it to capacity.

She was halfway down the aisle when she saw that Daniel could no longer resist the temptation; he turned and seemed dazzled by the sight of the beautiful young lady walking towards him, her wonderful smile blazing out to greet him.

His mind twisted and tumbled, besieging him with warring thoughts. Here were innocence and riches; back in Keighley there was Penelope, neither innocent nor as rich as she would like to be, but his always and for ever.

The service started. Vows were exchanged; a blessing bestowed. The organ rang out.

When Susannah and Daniel stepped outside the cheers and cries resounded from every side. The couple stopped to acknowledge the crowd whose good wishes filled the air. Daniel smiled and said, 'Hello, Mrs Bullen.' Then added with a twinkle in his eyes, 'Want a kiss?'

She blushed. 'Not here, Daniel.'

He laughed. 'What's the harm in a man kissing his wife?

230

They'll all approve.' He gestured to the cheering crowd then took her arm. 'Come on, we'll find a quieter place.' He grasped her hand, helped her on to the carriage and, with cheers ringing after them, they headed for Stockdale Manor.

When the guests arrived the house was filled with joyous laughter which continued throughout the rest of the day and into the early evening. Accompanied by her bridesmaids Susannah went to her room, where they helped her into her white muslin leaving-dress with its deep flounces patterned in black, orange and green. The bell-shaped, three-quarter length sleeves were similarly flounced. Her short brimmed bonnet, set back from her face, allowed everyone in the hall to see the happiness radiating from her smile as she came slowly down the stairs amid clapping and renewed good wishes.

Daniel met her at the bottom and escorted her to the trap held steady by Garth.

Her father and uncle, standing beside it, made their farewells and then stood shoulder to shoulder, watching her husband drive Susannah away. It was only when the rousing send-off from the guests began to fade behind them that Daniel took his wife's hand. 'Happy?' he asked.

She nodded. 'Oh, yes! We'll have such a wonderful life together. Thank you for marrying me.'

He smiled. 'And thank you.' He did not add his next thought – for this land and all the riches that one day will come to me. Instead he asked, 'The lodge that your father had renovated, where is it?'

'Wait and see,' she teased, and then deliberately kept the conversation on themselves while directing him through the lanes towards their destination. A little wood blocked the view from the final turn but when Daniel had negotiated it he pulled the horse to a stop.

He sat for a moment transfixed by the view. The track they were on dropped steadily to a narrow valley surrounded by low rounded hills. A little below them and a hundred yards to their right stood a stone, two-storey building. It looked solid and secure. Daniel realised whoever had built it had chosen this site not only for the wonderful view but also for its seclusion, for the tracks along which Susannah had directed him would not be easy to find.

'This is wonderful,' he said.

'My great-grandfather built it as a hideaway. Grandfather had little use for it. When our feelings for each other became obvious, Father immediately set to work having it completely renovated. He told me what he was doing, but would not let me come to see it and said I should say nothing to you. Daniel, it is my father's wedding gift to us.'

'That is more than generous,' he gasped.

'I think he hopes we will spend some time here – I know he will miss having me around.'

'Of course we will, and if business prevents me from coming there is no reason why you can't avail yourself of this wonderful place. I know what this part of the world means to you.'

'But my place is beside my husband,' Susannah said sincerely.

Daniel made no reply, merely squeezed her hand and then sent the horse forward at a walking pace, imagining what it would be like to own all this as well as the mill and its assets.

Seven days later they returned to Stockdale Manor to an effusive welcome from Susannah's father and uncle, who had stayed on to keep Francis company.

Both Daniel and Susannah expressed their thanks to her father for his wedding present. Once they had settled,

Francis drew Susannah's attention to a letter that had arrived for her. She recognised the writing and said to Daniel, 'Do you mind if I read this now?'

He was curious but felt trapped because with her father and uncle there he could not refuse. 'Of course I don't,' he said pleasantly.

She thanked him. Turning to her father and uncle, she said, 'Please excuse me?'

They both nodded.

Susannah went to the small drawing-room, sat down at the satinwood secretaire, drew a letter-opener from the left-hand drawer and slit the envelope open. She drew out a sheet of paper and another sealed envelope. She unfolded the sheet of paper and read.

Dear Susannah,

You will have wondered why I have not answered your kind invitation before now. The truth of the matter is that I received it too late. I regret that, because I should have been there to see my dear friend, from what seems long ago, married. However it was not to be, so all I can do now is to wish you both every happiness.

As Rosalind may have told you I, too, am going to be married. Saskia is the sweetest girl in the world; I am sure you will adore her when you meet.

I have been asked by her parents to enclose a formal invitation to our wedding for you and your husband. I hope you will come.

Always your friend,
Roland

Susannah speedily slit the enclosed envelope and withdrew the invitation. She stared at the words without seeing them, adrift on a wave of nostalgia. Childhood days were gone; time was so fleeting. Now Roland and Rosalind too were on the verge of getting married.

She would love to attend the wedding . . . but it was probably the wrong time to go travelling. She stood up and hurried to rejoin the men.

'A letter from Roland,' she announced, and then added by way of explanation to Daniel, 'Rosalind's brother.'

'Ah, yes, I remember. The Websters were sorry he was not at our wedding.'

'And now he is getting married himself. Mr and Mrs Gersen have sent us an invitation, Daniel.'

Her father held up an envelope. 'I have one too.'

'Would you like to go?' Daniel asked.

She made no immediate reply.

'I see you would, my darling,' he said gracefully. 'I'm afraid I cannot spare the time away from the mill. Thomas and I have a very important meeting with some valuable customers from the south of England . . . they have insisted that I attend . . . but I don't see why you should not take the opportunity to go with your father.'

'No, I should be with you.'

'This opportunity won't arise again. You and I have a lifetime ahead of us. Don't you think she should take advantage of this chance, Mr Charlesworth?'

'That is up to Susannah. It would be very agreeable for me to have her as a travelling companion.'

'There you are, my love,' said Daniel. 'Don't disappoint your father. The Websters will be going, why not travel with them? We'll stay here another day, if your father is agreeable, then tomorrow you could call on them.' So it was arranged that Susannah would return to Stockdale Manor in a month's time; then she and her father would leave with the Websters who would organise their passage to Holland.

Two days after Susannah and Daniel had returned to Ash Tree Villa, he informed her, 'While we have been away, matters relating to the mill that only I can deal with have piled up. I will be working late this evening, don't wait up for me.'

When he left the mill, earlier than he had implied, he turned his horse in the direction of Griffin Manor. Into more open country by the river, he put the horse into a gallop that stirred his desires for what lay ahead.

When the liveried doorman had made his usual polite greeting, he added, 'The gaming room, sir.'

Daniel nodded his thanks and strolled into the first room. A quick glance told him that Penelope must be in the second gaming room. He made a quiet entry and saw a small crowd watching the play of eight men around an oval table in the centre of the room. The atmosphere was charged and he noted Penelope standing by in a supervisory capacity, as she did whenever word was brought to her that large sums of money were involved.

Even in her concentration she was aware of the door opening and closing. She glanced up and her eyes met his. He noticed a flush of pleasure tinge her face, and her forefinger brushed across her right cheek, a signal that he knew meant 'five minutes'. He watched the game until the minutes had passed then strolled casually from the room. A few moments later he felt an arm steal round him from behind, and Penelope whispered, 'Welcome back. I have something to see to in the kitchen ... I'll only be a few minutes. Here's the key.'

Later she lay in his arms and asked about the wedding. He skipped over it quickly, and when he had finished, said, 'It may interest you to know that my new bride is soon leaving me.'

She twisted over to look at him. 'Don't talk in riddles, I don't like them.'

'You will this one,' he chuckled.

'Go on then, see if I do.'

'My dearly beloved wife is going to a wedding in Holland!'

Penelope's eyes widened. 'When?'

'She'll be leaving a month today and I'm not going!' replied Daniel gleefully.

'Oh, how lovely!' Penelope laughed, and fell on him with further kisses.

Susannah found it difficult to settle to her new life in strange surroundings. Ash Tree Villa, as big as it was, was not Stockdale Manor. The atmosphere of the building itself was more sombre, something that Susannah could only put down to the materials of which it was built. The stone of the mill-stone grit country was dark, in marked contrast to the lighter stone from the quarries of the Lincolnshire Wolds. There were times when Susannah sensed a menacing feeling about the house, but she was always quick to overcome it; to encourage it could be fatal. Knowing that Daniel would mock her, she kept these thoughts to herself, dismissing them with memories of Stockdale and the wide Lincolnshire skies. She tried to overcome her feelings of homesickness by visiting Jessie and Liza regularly in the cottage that Daniel had provided for them two miles along the Aire Valley.

One fine day, three weeks into her homecoming, Susannah had Garth saddle her horse, glad she had brought both him and Sally with her from Stockdale. Garth escorted her to the Bullen sisters' cottage.

Jessie and Liza were more than delighted to see her. News was exchanged and, when tea and cakes were produced, Susannah felt confident enough to say, 'I was surprised when Daniel and I came ho— to Ash Tree Villa . . . '

Jessie interrupted her. 'It's all right, Susannah, we don't mind you calling it home. That is what it is to you now.'

'But I expected you still to be there. I hope you didn't leave on my account? After all, you were brought up there. It must have been a wrench for you to leave.'

'Daniel wanted us out,' Liza exclaimed.

Susannah frowned.

'You were not to blame,' soothed Jessie.

'He really wants us married so he's rid of all responsibility. He gave us to understand the sooner the better,' added Liza, bitterness coming into her tone. 'He has virtually isolated Mother and Ralph, though our brother at least has his work and can escape into the outside world more easily.'

'So, do I understand you rightly . . . my husband forced you into your present positions?' asked Susannah, disturbed by what she was learning from what had been a simple enquiry.

'Well,' Jessie hesitated a moment, 'forced might be too strong, but I suppose in a way we had no alternative but to go. He provided this cottage, and we cannot fault his choice of would-be husbands for us, but it did hurt that we had to leave Ash Tree Villa.'

Liza nodded her agreement.

'I'm so sorry about this. I will . . . '

Jessie interrupted Susannah quickly. 'I know what you are going to say, but please don't. If you do, you might upset Daniel and that in turn would elicit retaliation against us for talking out of turn.'

Susannah paused thoughtfully before answering. 'Very

well,' she said, surreptitiously crossing her fingers behind her back to make the promise unbinding.

She was troubled as she rode home. Being an only child, doted on and protected from life's harshness by her father's love, yet schooled to be strong in her outlook, trouble in a family was something unknown and alien to her. She felt she could not let the matter rest. She waited until she was sitting with her husband at their evening meal.'

'Daniel, I visited Jessie and Liza today.'

He looked up, eyes sharpening with a hint of disapproval. 'And were they well?' he asked with no real interest in his voice.

'They were, but I was troubled to hear that you had told them to leave this house. I took them to mean that you had made it clear you wanted it for us alone, bar the arrangements you made for your mother and Ralph.'

Daniel laid down his knife and fork, touched his lips with his lily-white napkin and glared down the table at his wife. She felt a little shiver run through her in response. He spoke to her very precisely and clearly after dismissing the maid.

'Firstly, Susannah, you do not bring up family matters when we are at meals. There are too many servants about and they are notorious gossips. Secondly, please don't believe everything my sisters might have told you. They were upset when I asked them to live in the cottage I had provided for them, but I know they are comfortable there and can now lead their own lives as they wish. I think you know as well as I do that they are satisfied with the choice of husbands I have made for them. You saw them all comfortable enough together at our wedding.' She was about to speak but he halted her with a raised hand. 'As regards my mother, she has rooms of her own in a private suite in what was an unused wing of the house. I have also provided her with constant care. Ralph, I believe, is more content in an apartment of his own, part of the wing where Mother is. There he has much more freedom than he would have had living with us.' Daniel rested one hand on the table with a deliberate gesture. 'That, my dear, is the truth of things. In future it would be better if you did not interfere ... '

She was annoyed by his attitude. What he had said might have had a grain of truth in it, just as what she had heard from Jessie and Liza might have, but she remembered her father telling her, 'Wherever you are, one side will say they are in the right, the other side will say the same, but the truth lies in the middle.' She knew she had to subdue these doubts, though, and said, 'I'm sorry, Daniel, I did not intend to interfere.'

He leaned forward, arms resting on the table, and stared at her until her gaze gave way. 'You have been meddling in things that don't concern you. I will overlook it this once, but don't *ever* meddle in my business again.' Each word was deliberately and precisely delivered. 'Now, get on with your meal.'

As much as her stomach churned inside her, she picked up her knife and fork and cut at a slice of lamb.

Daniel eyed Susannah a moment as she concentrated on her plate. He had seen her independent streak occasionally at Stockdale. He cautioned himself now to beware, watch out for it and stifle it. Nothing must get in the way of his own ambitions and dreams.

He lightened the atmosphere over the following days, wanting her departure with her father for Roland Webster's wedding in Holland to be pleasant and the visit to be memorable.

Three days before the wedding Susannah and her father

joined the Websters who were travelling on one of Mr Bradley's ships trading from Hull to Amsterdam. They were met at the port by Roland, who was delighted to see them and to introduce them to Saskia.

They were transported in two vehicles to Harlem where accommodation had been booked for them close to the church.

Susannah enjoyed the week. The Gersen family were kindness itself, and she was pleased to see the choice of bride Roland had made for himself. In a quiet moment that they managed to seize together, Susannah told him she liked Saskia and followed that with the query, 'Will this marriage preclude your return to Harthill?'

'Oh, no, after all it is my inheritance, but my father is still young enough to continue running the estate. I would not want to supersede him until he finds he can cope no longer. It is only then that I will return permanently.' Roland gave a little laugh. 'I might even be an old man myself by then – my father looks fit enough to make that so. I am happy enough in Holland at the moment. Obviously we will divide our time between the countries.' He smiled then added, 'That's as far as we've planned. We'll focus on whatever comes along in the meantime and make the best of it.'

'That's something I will always remember,' she said, taking in the wisdom of his simple philosophy. 'Be happy, Roland.'

'You too,' he replied.

Susannah had treasured memories in her mind as the Dutch coast fell out of sight. The voyage back was pleasant, and after a night at Stockdale Manor she left for Ash Tree Villa. It was mid-afternoon when she reached her destination to feel disappointed when Daniel wasn't there to greet her.

He rushed in an hour later, flinging his overcoat off in the hall and hurrying into the drawing-room. 'Susannah, my love, I'm sorry I wasn't here but there was something at the mill that held my attention.' He took her into his arms and kissed her. 'Have you had a wonderful time?'

'Marvellous.'

'Good, good. You must tell me all about it. But first, a drink. He went to the decanter on the sideboard. 'What will you have, my dear?' he asked over his shoulder as he poured himself a large whisky,

'Nothing, thank you,' she said.

He swung round, 'Oh, we must celebrate your return.'

She gave a little smile. 'I have another cause for celebration,' she said. 'I'm expecting a child.'

30

'A son . . . the baby must be a boy! Someone to see that the name of Bullen remains above the door of the mill! I'll expand the business for him – a cloth empire second to none in the West Riding. No, second to none in the world.'

Susannah laughed at the excitement Daniel displayed. 'What if the baby is a girl?'

'It can't be! It's got to be a boy. You must see to that.'

'I can't do that, Daniel, but I'll hope it is so and then you can fulfil those dreams.'

'Make them a reality, my love,' he said, swinging her into his arms.

When they announced the news around their family, congratulations poured in. Francis expressed his delight but added a word of caution. 'Take care of yourself, my dear. Remaining in good health is important for you and the baby.' Gideon made his joy known by saying, 'I'm looking forward to being a great-uncle.' Thomas and Helen were overjoyed, with Helen expressing the hope that one day soon she would emulate Susannah. Ralph wondered what all the fuss was about but enjoyed the celebrations. Jessie and Liza hoped that the news would prompt a reaction from the Gaskell brothers and save the sisters from becoming maiden aunts.

Daniel broke the news to his mother and for a few moments thought it had sunk in, but then she slipped away from him again.

Early November 1853

My Dear Rosalind,

I have such news for you. I am going to have a baby! Daniel is delighted and is being the most caring of husbands. Married life is so wonderful. I did not think I could be this happy. You must tell Henry.

I will keep you informed of my progress, and in the meantime, dear friend, write soon.

With affection,
Susannah

A week later she received a reply.

Dear Susannah,

I was doubly delighted to have your news, firstly for you and Daniel and secondly for myself. Why for me? When I told Henry, he proposed immediately. Your letter must have given him the impetus to say what I believe he has wanted to say for a long time, but heretofore fought shy of. When I read your letter to him his shyness fell away, and he became very romantic and then excited when I said yes.

He wants lots of children. Natural, I suppose; in the past the Smallwood-Browns have always had big families, though Henry only has one sister. To everyone's regret his mother never conceived again. So one of my babies *has* to be a boy, the family name of Smallwood-Brown can't be left to perish. Wish me luck!

The date for the wedding is still to be set. There are a lot of things to be taken into consideration but the signs are that it will be next June, so you should be back to full strength before then.

Keep well, dear friend,

Love,

Rosalind

During Susannah's confinement Daniel was the most concerned husband possible. He saw that her every need was provided for, and with the coming of what was expected to be the last week of the pregnancy, insisted that the doctor visited every day and that a nurse was in the house at all times. He put Thomas in charge of the mill so that he could be at home. Thomas made sure he received news of Susannah whenever he could so that he could report the latest developments to Helen. Though Ralph knew little about the procedure once a woman was pregnant, he still wondered why there was all this fuss about what appeared to him to be a natural progression. Not wanting to become closely involved, he spent more time with friends in Keighley and kept to his own rooms when he was at home.

Uncomfortable with her expanding body and its unfamiliarity, Susannah longed for the birth to take place. The people around her gave her all the support and encouragement that they could, but she was at the centre of the situation, the one who physically had to see it through.

'Ma'am, you should have your feet up,' Sally scolded mildly as she crossed to the bay window in the drawing room where Susannah was sitting looking pensively at the garden.

'Oh, Sally, I am so weary I wish it was all over but it is so nice for me to have a familiar face from Stockdale.'

As the estimated day for the baby's arrival dawned, Susannah became more anxious which only heightened the painful spasms which had begun in the night.

'Doctor, can't you do something about them? Can't you ease the pain?' Daniel pressed him early in the morning. 'My wife has had a terrible night.'

'Was the nurse with her all the time?'

'Yes.'

'I'll have a word with her.' The doctor immediately started for the stairs. Daniel was only one step behind when they reached the landing. 'Wait here, Mr Bullen,' the doctor ordered in a tone that would brook no protest. He opened the bedroom door and stepped inside, leaving Daniel to pace the carpet while wondering what was happening. They were a long five minutes for him.

'Well?' he asked when the doctor reappeared.

'There is no need for alarm. Everything appears to be taking its natural course but very slowly. I think it might be another forty-eight hours.'

Daniel's lips tightened with renewed anxiety as he said, 'In the meantime my wife has to suffer.'

'I can ease the pain with chloroform but I will need your permission to administer it. Chloroform has been successfully used for a number of medical conditions and, more recently, in some cases of childbirth. Doctors have been wary of using it in such cases in the past but I am sure it will become more widespread, especially when it becomes generally known that the Queen approved its use when she was having her seventh child.'

'Then use it! Use it!' said Daniel without hesitation.

'Very well, sir. I will make all the arrangements, but first there is just one thing.' The doctor opened the bedroom door and called quietly, 'Nurse.'

The middle-aged woman stepped out on to the landing.

'Mr Bullen, please will you inform the nurse what you have just ordered me to do?' Daniel looked askance at the doctor. 'I just need a witness to your authorisation.'

Daniel nodded and turned to the nurse. 'I have just told the doctor that he can give my wife chloroform to ease the pains of childbirth.'

A baby boy of six and a half pounds was delivered safely at eight in the evening of 20th July 1854.

Once the baby had been born and everything had been cleaned and tidied up, Daniel was allowed in to see mother and child.

He took Susannah's hand. 'You look radiant,' he said, eyes sparkling with admiration. He had not expected his wife to look this way after what she must have been through.

'I had a lovely sleep and when I woke up ... there he was,' said Susannah.

'A boy!' he said, looking at the bundle his wife held in her arms.

She smiled. 'I managed to do as you asked.'

Daniel bent over her and kissed her. 'Thank you.'

'We never talked about a name,' she said. 'Perhaps we both fought shy of discussing it in case it was a girl. You wanted a boy, so you choose. If the next one is a girl, I'll decide!'

'Very well. We'll call him William.'

Susannah looked at her son and said quietly, 'I wonder what the future has in store for you?'

Life at Ash Tree Villa reassumed its routine. A nurse was engaged to look after William whose wonderful smile captivated everybody. It even brought a response from his Granny Bullen whenever he was taken in for her to see.

Once the news was received by Francis he informed Gideon, who was in Hull at that time. He hastened to Stockdale and the brothers left together for Gideon's house near Skipton.

They both experienced a sense of deep relief when they saw Susannah looking so radiant, and were charmed by William's happy demeanour.

Their visits were interspersed with calls from Thomas and Helen, Liza and Jessie, until their lives settled down once more. Susannah longed to take on more of the role of mother, but apart from feeding the newborn she was relieved of daily tasks by the nurse and the maid allocated from the staff to help her.

July 1854

Dear Susannah,

Thank you for letting me know of William's birth. I am so happy for you and Daniel. Children are such a blessing. I know you always indicated you wanted to be a full-time mother but don't undermine your health; let others do the hard work, you enjoy the sewing – I know you have the skill to make pretty things. Try to establish a routine and follow your previous interests again.

Enough of my sermon.

I will keep you in my thoughts and prayers.

Your loving friend,

Rosalind

Susannah tried to follow this advice and organise things in which she was interested. She found it a little hard because before this her passions had been bounded by the country life she had known in Lincolnshire; her life here was very different and the atmosphere was one of industry and hard labour by a mass of people. Even though Ash Tree Villa was, like other homes belonging to mill owners, situated in the countryside, it was near enough the mill towns to sense the harshness of existence there.

Helen was the only one who truly sympathised with Susannah, for she had been free from all ties long enough to realise when someone felt themselves to be restricted by their life. Thomas understood too; seeing his wife was good company for his sister-in-law he quietly encouraged Helen's visits to Susannah, who was thankful for them. Their friendship deepened as they recognised the good qualities in each other.

After the euphoria of becoming a father wearing thin, tedium took over for Daniel. With Susannah taking every care to return herself to full health, he found himself occupying a bed in his dressing room more frequently, after finding solace in Penelope's arms.

He also absorbed himself in the running of the mill. Because he knew that he had the sole authority to make the final decision on future developments, he was always on the lookout to expand. He was driven by the memory of what his father had achieved by buying all the Longwool fleeces from Mr Charlesworth, and expanding their worsted trade. As he became more and more steeped in the business of the mill, Daniel became driven by a desire to emulate him, but always held in the back of his mind thoughts of what he would gain one day through his wife.

Rosalind kept Susannah informed of her own wedding arrangements, which unfortunately had had to be postponed two months due to the ill-health of Henry's favourite grandmother. The wedding would now take place in September, in Lincoln Cathedral as planned.

Daniel was not slow to express his unease at having to attend what would be a very formal occasion considering the standing of the Smallwood-Browns in the Lincolnshire landed community, and the fact that the ceremony's venue would be the great Gothic cathedral.

As the day of Rosalind's wedding neared he was still trying to talk his way out of attending but Susannah insisted. When she reached the point of countering his protests by threatening, 'Very well, Daniel, I shall travel alone,' he could do nothing but give way, but he insisted that they should return home the day after the ceremony. Susannah was disappointed that he was not living up to his promise to return frequently to visit her old home.

Susannah and Rosalind managed only a short while together at the reception held at Harthill Priory. Everything had gone exactly as planned and all the relations and guests had reached Harthill without mishap.

'I'm so pleased you came,' said Rosalind with great joy. 'I'm sorry I'm not going to get a lot of time with you. There are so many Smallwood-Browns – aunts and uncles and that sort of thing – who want to meet Henry's bride. Forgive me. We are going to live at Kelskey Grange, near Market Rasen. You must come and visit Lincolnshire again soon. Ah, here's Roland and Saskia! I will have to go, but I'm sure you will all have a great deal to catch up on.' She kissed Susannah on the cheek. 'Take care, my dear friend. Do keep up our correspondence.' And she hurried away to chat with two distinguished-looking middle-aged men and their wives.

Knowing his sister's effervescence, Roland raised his eyebrows and said in explanation of the guests she had joined, 'Sir James Furze and Lady Furze with the Honourable Gascoigne Jensen and his wife. Henry expects Rosalind to keep up with all these people; she rather enjoys it. Now, Susannah, it is good to see you again. You will remember my dear wife Saskia?'

Susannah smiled and took his wife's hand in hers, saying 'Of course I do. I hope you are looking after him?' Saskia smiled and nodded.

Susannah remarked, 'Rosalind has married well. I hope she never forgets us.'

Roland pursed his lips. 'Rosalind would never do that. She loves Lincolnshire and everyone connected with it, and has found a man who does too. Because he's heir to his family's estates here she'll never be far from her roots.'

Saskia caught a wistful expression cross Susannah's face then and changed the subject.

The conversation was cut short when Daniel strode up to them. 'Susannah, we are leaving. You should have a rest. We travel tomorrow and I want to be away early,' he said brusquely. 'I've told your father who has said I must take the trap. He'll get one of the Websters' grooms to drive him over.'

'Oh.' He had taken hold of her arm and given it a firm squeeze that conveyed to her he would not condone any objection. 'I am sorry about this,' she said to Roland and Saskia, with a downcast expression.

The reassuring smiles they gave her conveyed their understanding of her dilemma.

'Goodbye,' she said. 'I hope to meet you again soon.'

Daniel hurried her away, muttering, 'We'll see about that.'

In spite of his hustling she caught his words and pulled up sharp, causing him to stop. She glared at him. 'Those are my friends,' she said defiantly.

'I'll not have you mixing with those snobs!'

'You can't say that, you don't know them.'

He sneered, 'From what I've seen and heard today most

of them, with their posh accents, look down on a Yorkshireman who runs a woollen mill.'

She laughed. 'It is you who are being objectionable, Daniel, but unfortunately you don't realise it.'

He jerked her arm and snapped, 'Come on.'

She could not resist and once he was beside her in the trap he drove away.

Susannah was mortified. Their disagreement and the manner of their departure must have been seen by some of the guests. 'Please, Daniel, don't humiliate me in front of my friends.' As soon as she had spoken she wished the words unsaid.

'I've told you before: don't ever tell me what to do! I'll do what I like and you'll do as I say,' snapped Daniel. 'That is the role of a wife – to obey and to follow her husband in all things. Or have you forgotten your wedding vows?'

The trap rocked dangerously; Susannah gripped the seat. 'Slow down! Slow down!'

'What have I just told you?' he yelled.

Susannah, judging the best course was to say no more, remained silent until Daniel pulled the sweating horse to a halt at Stockdale Manor. He jumped down from the trap and started for the house.

'Aren't you going to help me down?'

He turned back without a word and helped her to the ground, letting her follow him into the house.

He poured himself a whisky and swallowed it in one go. It seemed to drive the fury from him. As he put the glass down he said quietly, 'I'm sorry, my love, but a tiresome couple I had just been talking to got on my nerves. I shouldn't have reacted as I did, especially with you. And I shouldn't have driven as I did.' He reached out, took her into his arms and kissed her. 'Forgiven?'

She softened, feeling the charm in him she had always admired wipe away the memories of her reaction at Harthill. 'I'm sorry too. Say no more about it. Let it all be washed away by the news that I am expecting again! I did not tell you before because you would have used it as an excuse for us not to attend the wedding.'

For a moment he looked surprised, but that was immediately forgotten in her pleasure at the kiss that erased any trace of the disagreement between them.

As their lips parted she reminded him, 'Don't forget, if it's a girl I choose her name. It will be Estelle.'

'You can forget that. I have a boy's name ready,' he teased.

Seven months later Estelle was born.

It had been an extremely difficult birth and the use of chloroform had done little to ease Susannah's pain.

A routine visit by the doctor two days later raised concerns in him. After a thorough examination at which the nurse who always worked with him at births was present, he sought out Daniel before he left.

'I am still concerned about your wife, Mr Bullen. She must have complete rest until I say otherwise.'

'I'll make sure she complies with your order, Doctor,' replied Daniel resolutely. 'She will have every care.'

'Good. I will call each day until I am satisfied that Mrs Bullen can leave her bed. I am pleased you have engaged the same nurse you had for Mrs Bullen's first confinement. The familiarity will give your wife confidence, which is important now. There is one other thing, Mr Bullen.' Daniel was struck by the sombre tone that had come into the doctor's voice. 'From the nature of the birth and what Mrs Bullen has had to endure, she has been left in a distressed state. That, together with what I have learned from my examinations, leads me to believe it would be unwise for her to become a mother again.' Daniel was taken aback and it showed on his face. 'I'm sorry Mr Bullen. I know you were set on a big family, but my advice is, forget that.'

Daniel nodded. After a moment, he said, 'I understand. It is a blow but I understand.' He paused then added, 'May I ask one thing? Please will you say nothing of this to anyone? I will break the news to my wife.'

'If that is what you wish then I agree. I will, of course, have to make a note of my findings in my records, but they are strictly confidential.'

'Thank you, Doctor.'

Daniel walked with him to his trap where the doctor gave him a final word of advice. 'Mrs Bullen's health is the most important thing. See that she is well looked after.'

Daniel watched him drive away then walked slowly back into the house. He went to his study, poured himself a large whisky, and sat down heavily on his chair. He stared into the glass. The vision he had always nurtured of a Bullen textile empire, linked to vast landholdings in Lincolnshire, all its many aspects run by his numerous sons, was submerged under the strong spirit.

'Damn!'

Or maybe the doctor was being over-cautious. Daniel poured himself a second large measure of whisky and pushed the warning from his mind.

31

At the same time as Daniel was stiffening his mind with whisky, Thomas, at the mill, was receiving a message that, if acted on, would change the course of a number of lives. The note had been delivered by an untidy urchin who had been sharp enough to outwit the two guards on the Bullen Mill gates and reach the office. There he had made such loud protests when two clerks tried forcefully to eject him that Thomas came from his office to see what all the noise was about.

'What is it, lad?' he asked in a kindly voice that brought a curious look from the boy.

'You Mr Thomas?' the urchin asked, still with a note of hostility in his voice.

'Aye, none other,' he returned, imitating the boy's broad West Riding accent.

'Prove it,' countered the urchin.

Thomas laughed. He turned to the door of his office which was left open. 'Can you read?' he asked, looking at the lad.

'Aye, a bit.'

'Read that,' ordered Thomas as he pulled his office door shut and pointed at the letters on the glass panel.

'T . . . th . . . om . . . as. Same as on this paper.' He held up the note he had been clutching.

'Any other word?' asked Thomas.

The boy looked at the paper and read in a stuttering voice as he grappled with the letters, 'Bu . . . ll . . . en . . . Bullen.'

'That's right,' said Thomas, 'and it's there on the glass.'

The boy looked at the letters. 'Aye.'

'That's me,' said Thomas.

'Y' better 'ave this.' He thrust the piece of paper at Thomas who took it and scanned the words quickly. He delved into his pocket, took out a coin and flipped it into the air, saying, 'Catch.'

The boy deftly took the coin as it dropped, grinned and said, 'Thank y', sir.' He scooted out of the room pulling a face at the two clerks who had tried to apprehend him.

Thomas returned to his office and reread the pencilled note. *Be home for six, I have news, Helen.*

Wondering what it could be Thomas devoted himself to clearing up all important matters relating to the mill that needed his attention before he left. With Daniel absent because of Susannah's second child, Thomas had been left in charge. No time was set for his brother's return but Thomas believed it might be a while because of the difficult birth. But he knew no more than that.

Helen was quickly into the hall to meet him when she heard the maid open the front door. She glanced at the clock. Her husband was a good time-keeper. She was especially pleased about that this evening. Half an hour – just right.

'A quick cup of tea,' she said to the maid.

'Yes, ma'am. It should be ready shortly.'

'What's all this about?' asked Thomas. 'Why the note?'

'To make sure you wouldn't be late. We are having visitors.'

255

'Oh, I've had a busy day with Daniel not being at the mill. I don't feel like socialising.'

'You will this time.' She smiled at the questioning light in his eyes.

Before he could learn more the maid arrived with the tea and left the room when Helen signified she would pour. She placed the cup in front of Thomas. 'Drink up. I want it cleared away before our visitors arrive at half-past.'

'No biscuit?' he queried.

'I've arranged a light meal for our visitors; the tea is just to put you on.'

'Come on, tell me, otherwise there'll be a half-empty cup to greet them,' he threatened lightly.

'Nathan and Olivia.'

'What? Oh my goodness. When did this happen? I thought nothing had come of the previous contact?'

'Nathan called this morning. He apologised for the delay but said he had much to do. He hopes we will find the wait has been worthwhile.'

'Worthwhile? What does that mean? Didn't he say any more?'

'He asked if you had continued your painting since he last saw us. When I said you had he was pleased. He wouldn't tell me anything else except that he wanted to see us both, together with his wife. As there are more of your paintings to see, I suggested that they should come here this evening and share a light meal with us. Oh, Thomas, this might be just the chance you need – finally.'

'We'll have to wait and see.'

She heard the tremor in his voice. She came to him and slid her arms round his neck. 'I love you, Thomas Bullen. You have changed my life already, just by being you. Now you are going to make me even more proud. Thank you.' She kissed him. When she made to move away he held her tight and gazed directly into her eyes.

'If it hadn't been for you, I would never have received any encouragement to pursue my painting. Whether Mr and Mrs Hopkins bring good news or not, it doesn't matter. I have you.'

'Thank you for saying that.' Helen glanced at the clock. 'You'd better get ready.'

At precisely half-past six the maid heard a knock on the door and admitted the visitors. Helen and Thomas hurried from the drawing-room to welcome them.

'It is delightful to see you again,' said Olivia Hopkins when Helen greeted her. 'It has been too long, but that's the way things turned out.'

'We couldn't neglect a customer with whom we have been dealing with for a considerable time.'

'We understand. Thank you for letting us know you would be out of the country,' said Helen leading the way into the drawing-room.

'That was unexpected and it turned out longer than we thought.'

'And for the best, I hope.'

'Indeed it did,' said Nathan. 'Now we are back we will make sure we have time to deal with Thomas's paintings.' As he was speaking he had crossed the room to look at a landscape that had caught his eye in an alcove to the right of the fireplace. 'Helen,' he called over his shoulder, 'this wasn't here when I last saw you.'

'No, it wasn't.'

'This work is admirable. Such atmosphere, particularly the house. Don't you think so, Olivia?'

'It has,' she replied firmly, 'and it is a friendly one. It comes out in the execution of the work.'

'I am sure that would sell in the London market.'

'It isn't for sale,' replied Thomas. 'It is a present for my sister-in-law. It is the house where she grew up in Lincolnshire.'

Nathan nodded. 'An admirable present. She will love it for the happy memories it will recall.'

'We must let Susannah have it the next time we see her,' Thomas reminded his wife.

'This picture shows your ambition to produce highly saleable work,' Nathan continued. 'I have seen that in the paintings you allowed me to take away. I showed them to some of my connections in London. It would be wrong if I gave you a glowing report, but they did say they recognised a talent that could be nurtured and possibly become out-standing, if the artist were willing to work hard and develop his talent in his own way without being over influenced by their thoughts and suggestions – in other words, they see a natural talent that should be encouraged but allowed to develop in the way the artist wishes. For that you want plenty of time for painting. Is your time still restricted by your commitments at the mill?'

'It is,' replied Thomas, 'but let me say I would welcome the opportunity to paint more.'

'From the evidence of your work so far, that should be arranged as quickly as possible. But before we go any further, let me see what you have been doing since we last spoke.'

'Certainly,' said Thomas, rising to his feet.

He excused himself. Fifteen minutes later he returned to tell them that he had assembled the new paintings in the hall and would bring them in one at a time for Nathan and Olivia to see.

No comment was made as each painting in turn was viewed.

After the last one, the anxiety which Helen and Thomas felt charged the room.

After a few minutes' consideration Nathan spoke. 'This body of work shows me that you have been exploring more than one aspect of your talents. There are some I would suggest you tone down, and others which are more important to your development. Now let us go through each canvas again, so I can discuss their merits and failures. I am doing this not to raise false hopes but to let you see where your talent should best be directed.'

'I do understand that,' said Thomas, and listened to Nathan, carefully taking in all he had to say. When they had finished, Thomas announced sincerely, 'I have learned a great deal from you, sir and am grateful for your frank criticism.'

'Now, where do we go from here?' Nathan mused. 'Well, it will be up to you. It would be ideal if you could pick up your paint brush tomorrow and never do anything else, but that may not be possible. Only you know your financial position. Meanwhile I would like to take to London the four paintings I put aside as we were viewing them.'

'I wondered why you were doing that,' said Helen

Nathan smiled. 'Now you know. May we come again tomorrow and get them ready for transportation?'

'Of course.'

'Let me know then, Thomas, if you have made a firm commitment to a future as an artist. It would be good if I could take that news to London with me.'

'We'll do our best to come to a decision,' said Helen.

When the front door closed behind the Hopkinses, Thomas and Helen stood looking at each other. The silence was charged with expectancy as each waited for the other to speak.

'You should . . . ' started Helen.

In the same moment Thomas said, 'We have to . . . '

Their words broke off into laughter. From the light in their eyes each read what the other had been going to say. Instinctively they flung their arms round each other.

'You are an angel,' gasped Thomas. 'You changed my life by marrying me – and now this.'

'I love you, Thomas Bullen. I know you can succeed as an artist, I just know it.'

'With such faith in me, how can I not?'

32

Penelope relaxed in the contentment she had just brought to the man lying beside her, but a few moments later a small niggling thought made itself felt.

'Daniel,' she said in a quiet, persuasive tone.

He murmured lazily in reply.

'It's three years since you married. You made promises to me then . . . what is to become of them? You've had a son and heir, and you've had a daughter, but what about us?'

He ran his hand across her stomach, sending a shiver of desire through her. 'Aren't you satisfied with the way we are?'

'Of course I am, but you promised me a more permanent relationship. Said I'd be your Lady of the Manor.'

'That will come, love, but I have no control over when Susannah's father dies. When that happens my wife will inherit enormous wealth, which will be mine by right. As I promised, Stockdale Manor will then be ours. That is what I said would happen, and it will. Just be patient. In the meantime I can . . . ' He left that unsaid as he turned towards her, let his hand stray further and then pulled her close.

My dear friend Susannah,

I write with all good wishes to you, and hope you are getting a great deal of pleasure from William and Estelle. They will be grown before you know it. Little Charlie is doing well and is the apple of Henry's eye. I am glad you are enjoying life in Ash Tree Villa and still find time and opportunity to visit the countryside of the Pennines away from the mill towns.

I was sorry to hear from your last letter that Daniel's mother still shows no signs of improvement. It must be trying when she recognises no one and cannot remember aspects of her own life. I think it would be a blessing if she was taken.

I must not end on a dreary note, so will tell you that Roland, in his last letter, wished to be remembered to you. He is very happy with Saskia, and their child is the centre of their lives. Roland has no immediate plans for returning to England. His business development in Holland is making progress that will stand him in good stead when he eventually returns with his family to take over from Father. I am sure they will all love Lincolnshire as we do.

Take care, my dear friend.

Yours with affection,

Rosalind

'It's our monthly meeting this evening unless Daniel cancels it,' said Thomas who was about to leave home for the mill, 'but that seems unlikely.'

'What is the point of them, if he has the final say on everything?' asked Helen, handing him his hat.

'He likes the power these meetings give him. By raising

a discussion he feels he is consulting Ralph and me, though as you say he can over-rule us. I worry a bit. Daniel is not Father. He hasn't the same business acumen; makes some strange decisions which don't always work. I know he loses money sometimes.'

'And you exert a steadying influence?'

'I try to but I'm not often successful. Daniel can be pig-headed and is becoming more antagonistic than ever towards any opposition.'

'Then I'll say it again, you will be better out of it and doing what you want to do. You've no obligation to him.'

'I know, but I think if I walk away I'll be letting my father down. He built that business up to what it is today; it would be a tragedy if Daniel destroyed it.'

Helen came to him and took his hands in hers. 'He won't let that happen. He loves money too much. Daniel won't destroy the mill with bad decisions. Forget that idea. Think of the opportunity you have now we have heard the good news from the Hopkinses.'

Following on from Nathan and Olivia's visit the paintings they had selected were shipped to London. Thomas and Helen had resolved to say nothing about the possibilities ahead for them. If nothing came of this then so be it. Nevertheless, with hope in their minds, they did make some plans. They resolved not to move from Yorkshire; this was where Thomas drew inspiration for his paintings. They made some careful calculations of their financial situation and realised that they could manage on Helen's investments and Thomas's income from his shares in the mill if he received word that there was a strong possibility of selling his work.

Two weeks later they heard from Mr Hopkins that he would like to see Thomas in London.

Arrangements were made but Daniel was not pleased when Thomas told him he wished to take leave of absence.

Sitting comfortably in the railway carriage heading for home, Helen said, 'Thomas, you've not said a word for a quarter of an hour. What's troubling you? You should be delighted with what Mr Hopkins said.'

He gave a little smile. 'Sorry, love. Yes, I am very pleased, but I was wondering what you thought to me leaving the mill now and concentrating on my painting? After all, it will mean more visits to London.'

'Thomas, there is no need to doubt my support. If that is what you want to do, I will be there for you always.'

The following week Thomas and Ralph left the mill together to go to Ash Tree Villa for their meeting. The late-afternoon had turned cool and they buttoned up their overcoats before getting into the trap. Ralph picked up the reins; he always relished this drive from the mill in Keighley to the house in the valley.

'I wonder why Daniel left for home earlier than usual?' said Thomas.

'He didn't say when he poked his head round my door. Just said he was leaving early as he had some figures he wanted to check over before we met.'

'Must be something in the wind; he only keeps the most important documents at home.'

'Could be anything,' observed Ralph. 'He's surprised us in the past. He might again. He's been thoughtful these last few months but he didn't put forward anything new at the last meeting, so maybe we could be in for a shock today.'

On their arrival, the front door was opened by the valet

who greeted them politely. He liked these two unassuming men who were always ready to exchange a pleasantry or two. This evening was no exception as he took their coats.

'Mr Bullen is already in the study,' he informed them.

They knocked on the door and entered to find Daniel gazing down at a sheet of paper. He straightened up and glanced at the wall clock. 'Ah, excellent timing,' he approved. He indicated three chairs drawn close to the crackling log fire. 'Sit down. The whisky's on the table between you.' As he spoke he moved from behind the desk to the third chair alongside its own small table.

'A little less formal this evening,' commented Thomas, wanting to test his elder brother's mood.

'And why not?' said Daniel lightly. 'There is no reason why we shouldn't relax more at these meetings. This evening I think we have every cause to be pleased with ourselves. This last eight weeks I have been compiling figures relating to every aspect of our business.'

Ah, he's trying to soften us up, thought Thomas. He's used the term *our* business whereas in the past it has been *the* business. What's afoot?

'I've come up with some very interesting figures, which of course will be verified by our auditors and bankers at the appropriate time, but I wanted a good idea of how our business stands now. The figures are here for you to see, but I will say that what you will find is that our business is in a very healthy state. I think we should praise ourselves for that.'

'And the workers,' put in Ralph, who had always had a sympathy for the men and women he regarded as the source of their wealth.

'Yes, of course,' his brother agreed, rather too quickly.

'Daniel, you clearly have something in mind and it is not

just to announce that our next dividend will be higher than the last,' put in Thomas.

'Perspicacious as ever,' commented Daniel.

'I need to be when you are in this mood,' replied Thomas. 'So what is it? Do you really need our approval?'

Daniel read what his brother was getting at. Thomas did not like the terms of their father's will that gave Daniel, as eldest son, the final decision on anything connected with the mill.

'I like to keep you informed as to the direction the business is taking,' replied Daniel smoothly, knowing that he was in a position that could not be seriously challenged. He liked exerting the power that kept his brothers dancing to his tune.

'Our payments will be higher, but not as high as they could be because I have decided that we should expand and for that I need capital. That is the reason I have been studying the figures we are generating. They are very good. If we invest a substantial part of our profit we will need only a small loan to expand as I wish to.'

Thomas was wary but wanted to know just what his brother had in mind. He knew that was coming, but Ralph spoke up before Daniel went on.

'It sounds to me that the figures you are talking about will be good, if not very good. Just to verify therefore – you are proposing that we pay ourselves more this year?'

'That is correct,' said Daniel.

Ralph nodded thoughtfully.

'Anything else?' asked Daniel.

'Not at the moment,' replied Ralph.

Daniel was surprised. Ralph was generally the quiet one; the one to be led rather than lead or take a prominent stance on any aspect of work at the mill. But Daniel also recalled that Ralph had acquitted himself well when he and Thomas had worked on the route the fleeces would take from Stockdale Manor to the Keighley mill, and he had been the one to trace Helen as the owner of the derelict property adjacent to the mill.

'What about you, Thomas? Have you any queries?' Daniel asked.

'How can I have? We don't know yet what you are proposing.'

'There is a large plot of unused land about half a mile from the mill. There is also another plot with a medium-sized dilapidated building on it. It would be easy to gain access to both by buying up the strip in between. I have traced the owners of the three parcels of land and they are willing to sell. I propose we buy them, and on the site of the old building erect a shoddy mill.'

'What?' Ralph and Thomas thundered together, their tone and expressions leaving Daniel in no doubt that they would oppose this. But it did not upset him; he knew he had the power to veto their opposition.

'We can make a lot of money out of a shoddy mill. There is only the initial outlay and . . .'

'What about wages?' broke in Ralph.

'Minimum. It's not skilled work.'

'But it's the worst work there is,' pointed out Ralph. 'How would you like to be condemned to sorting and preparing piles of filthy rags that in the grinding stage give off clouds of dirty, choking dust. Have you examined other shoddy mills? They are grey hells, the workers covered in corrosive dust. They wear bandages over their noses and mouths to try to minimise the damage from what they inhale. Is this what you want to damn your fellow human beings to?'

'They don't have to take the work,' countered Daniel.

'They don't,' agreed Thomas testily. 'But remember Father

always believed that looking after the welfare of our workers made for better productivity. Now you are playing on their need to escape poverty in order to line your own pockets. Well, I don't want mine filling at the expense of human suffering.'

'Nor do I,' said Ralph, with more resolve than either of his brothers had seen from him before. 'We'd be better off paying our present workers more to make sure that the mill continues to run smoothly as it stands.'

'Ralph's right,' emphasised Thomas. 'That is by far the better option. Forget a shoddy mill.'

'I worked out the figures, and it is not the better option.'

'In terms of life and how it is lived, it is,' argued Thomas. 'I will not have any part of this.' He stood up as if to emphasise his determination.

'Nor will I,' said Ralph, coming to Thomas's side.

Daniel rose slowly to his feet. A smile of deep satisfaction came in to his eyes. 'But you already are a part of it. You see, I have bought the three parcels of land that are essential to this development. Don't say I had no right to do so . . . you know as well as I do that I had every right. And remember, according to the way Father left the business, I can, if I think it right according to circumstances at the time, pay you a dividend of no more than he stipulated in his will.'

'So you are threatening to hold back the extra dividend you indicated was coming to us? That's blackmail,' snapped Thomas. The extra money would have helped to make his steps into the art world less precarious, but he realised that if he took it, every time he stood in front of his canvas he would see faces swathed in bandages against clouds of choking grey dust. If he did not oppose Daniel's plan he would be haunted by regret for the rest of his life.

He cast a quick glance at Ralph and saw that he too was battling with his conscience. Thomas spoke up. 'I want no part in this scheme. I will not fill my coffers on the back of such slave labour. I withdraw from any part of it, and will draw up a statement of intent accordingly. I will sign a copy and deposit it with my solicitors, and deposit a second copy with a bank. Each will have a note attached saying that they should be made public if ever there is reason for that to happen, so that my name will be exonerated from blame.'

Daniel's face darkened with every word of Thomas's declaration. It darkened even further when Ralph backed his brother in no uncertain terms and then went further. 'I here and now hand in my resignation from the mill. I will write a letter to that effect and hand it to you tomorrow, Daniel.'

Daniel's shock turned to rage. 'You're a fool, Ralph. You have a sound living with the mill. The dividend you receive now will not be sufficient for you to live in the way you are accustomed to. In fact, you will have nowhere to live because I won't have you staying under the same roof as me.' He looked contemptuous. 'This is the way you thank me after all I did to provide you with a home when I got married.'

'I will manage,' Ralph replied defiantly.

'Don't come whining and begging to me when you don't. I'll do nothing for you!'

'Do your worst, brother, but you will not shatter my principles nor Father's,' Ralph hit back firmly.

'Well said, Ralph,' praised Thomas with a satisfaction born of seeing Ralph stand up for himself in this way.

'You know my stance,' said Thomas coldly. 'As a matter of fact, I had come here this evening ready to hand in my own resignation.' He laid an envelope in front of Daniel. 'That is the necessary document. You precipitated this by disclosing your disgusting plans.'

'Damn you!' snarled Daniel. 'You'll leave me high and dry. You're my right-hand man. I need you here.'

'You've never really shown any sign of that.' Daniel started to reply but Thomas stopped him. 'Don't try to persuade me to stay because I won't. There's nothing you can say will stop me pursuing my dreams.'

'Dreams of painting?' Mockery tainted these words and those that followed. 'Pursue the dreams planted in you by your wife? Ruled by a woman? You'll rue the day! But don't come to me when you are on the streets, an impoverished would-be artist, deserted by his wife because he couldn't live up to her unrealistic expectations.'

'There'll be no chance of that,' countered Thomas through tight-drawn lips.

Daniel gave a mocking grunt. 'We'll see.'

Thomas's defiance and self-assurance, and Ralph's certainty, stung Daniel. 'Get out! Get out! Don't either of you ever darken these walls again. Get out!'

'Come on, Ralph,' said Thomas. He turned and strode to the door. Ralph followed and, without losing stride, let it slam behind them. Daniel's curses rang through the room and into the hall. With temper rising he sent everything on his desk clattering to the floor amidst a swirl of paper and pens, leaving ink stains on the carpet.

Startled, Ralph started to turn back but Thomas grabbed his arm. 'Best leave him,' he said. 'Come away.'

They left the house.

Then the reality of what was happening struck Ralph. 'What am I going to do?' he asked. 'I can't go back there.'

'You are coming home with me and we'll sort things out together.'

The crashing noises reached the small drawing-room where Susannah was sitting. They were so startling that shock caused her to drop her book to the floor. She started to get up but sank back on the chair. She should not interfere. Then she heard two voices in the hall and the front door slammed shut, followed by curses coming from the study. She pushed herself from the chair and went into the hall. She could hear Daniel still ranting but there were no voices raised in opposition. She crossed to the door of the study. Here she paused, trembling to think what she might encounter, then cautiously stepped inside, saying, 'Daniel, are you all right?'

Astonished at the scene of destruction, she looked timidly at him for an explanation.

His look was as black as thunder. 'Get out, woman! It has nothing to do with you! Those two bastards have deserted me! Deserted me!' he screamed. He saw her tremble under his tirade. 'Get upstairs, woman, get upstairs!'

Susannah fled, knowing she could do nothing but obey him.

She hadn't reached the top of the stairs before she heard his steps behind her. She felt his grip on her arm and knew from its intensity it would be no good to struggle. He flung open the door of their room, propelled her inside and, as he slammed the door behind him, flung her on to the bed.

'No, Daniel! No!'

'Don't you ever refuse me, woman! Don't you ever do that! Remember, you are mine by right!'

33

Thomas unlocked the front door and flung it open. An oil lamp shed light across the hall. He stepped over the threshold, leaving Ralph to follow and close the door.

'Helen! Helen, we're home!' he shouted, throwing his hat on to a chair, and shedding his coat.

Roused by the unusually boisterous arrival, she hurried to see what it was all about. With a signal she dismissed the maid who had also been startled by the noise.

'We've done it!' Thomas grabbed his wife round the waist and swung her off the ground, letting his laughter boom out. 'We've resigned ... never to go into the mill again!'

Helen was swept up in his mood and joined in the laughter. She became aware of Ralph standing there, amused by the scene and yet appearing to be part of it. Her mind took in Thomas's use of 'we'. 'Ralph, hello,' she said with a note of query in her voice.

'He's resigned too,' said Thomas, lowering her to the ground but keeping one arm round her.

'What?' There was no disguising her surprise.

'Come on, Ralph, get out of that coat. Let's tell Helen everything over a celebratory drink.'

Twenty minutes later, with their glasses half-empty, Helen was in possession of all the facts.

'Well, I was expecting Thomas to return with news of his resignation, after all he had it written out, but I was not expecting anything else. Of course, I knew nothing of Daniel's plans for a shoddy mill nor the views of either of you on that matter.'

'I've always thought conditions for mill workers were far from good,' said Ralph. 'Father saw to it that ours were better off than most. I firmly believe he would never have considered a shoddy mill. I was so relieved when Thomas backed me.'

'And always will,' he said, turning to his wife. 'Ralph can't possibly go back to Ash Tree Villa. Can he come to us until he can get things sorted out?'

'You know there is no need for you to ask that,' replied Helen with a sincerity that settled Ralph's mind.

'I know, but you and I work things out together.'

Ralph thought how refreshing it was to hear those words. He remembered hearing Daniel laying down the law to Susannah about her role in the household, the discipline of the two children, and his expectations of her, even at times to the point of humiliating her. Ralph felt relieved he did not have to return there, but where did his future lie? When he voiced this concern he received a sympathetic hearing from his brother and sister-in-law.

'Something will turn up, I'm sure,' said Helen. 'There is no need to rush to resolve your situation. You are welcome here.'

'You are most kind, but I don't want to impose on you. You two have your own life together.'

'As Helen says, there is no need for you to do anything immediately. I know you want to get your life sorted out, but consider your future carefully. Think about what you would really like to do. You could come to London with us on our next visit. It might give you some ideas. What do you think, Helen?' asked Thomas.

'A new place, different surroundings, might spark off something new. Yes, come with us, Ralph.'

Swept up in their enthusiasm, he said, 'Well, if you don't mind?'

'Of course we don't,' they reassured him together.

Ralph, Thomas and Helen faced their new venture with a modicum of doubt. Though they had experienced the growing conurbation of the West Riding with its factories, mills and narrow streets, the sight of London still overwhelmed them. The streets teemed with people, none of whom seemed to be where they wanted to be, always rushing to find another destination. Street-vendors shouted their wares, beggars held out their hands, urchins darted everywhere as the great city went about its work.

Mr Hopkins had booked them pleasant accommodation in a quiet street which offered a refuge from the continuous bustle of a city that never seemed to sleep. Thomas and Helen gained much from this introduction to the capital's art world. It was an experience that would broaden and deepen Thomas's development as an artist over the years and enable him to look back with satisfaction on the day he and Ralph finally left the wool trade.

Ralph's life did not move forward as quickly as Thomas's; he had come to London with no preconceived idea of what he wanted to do there, and with his working experience limited to the woollen mill there was no immediate outlet for him. One afternoon he was strolling down Oxford Street, his mind not occupied with anything in particular, when a colourful display of woollen shawls and rugs caught his eye. He stopped; perhaps they had come from the Bullen mill. Immediately he remembered the his reason for his confrontation with Daniel – the lot of the workers destined for the shoddy mill. Could he not do more to safeguard their position, and not only theirs but the working conditions of all mill workers? He knew there had been earlier legislation in Parliament aimed at improving these conditions but much more needed to be done. Maybe, with his knowledge of the manufacturing conditions most workers were destined to endure, he could do more to ease their burden.

Lord Carlton was the Parliamentary representative for their district in the West Riding and Ralph knew him to be active in affairs relating to his constituency. Maybe, he thought, my unexpected visit to London, and the sight of these woollen goods, has forged my destiny – to champion the lot of the West Riding mill workers.

On returning to Keighley he would make contact with Lord Carlton and find a sympathetic ear and some guidance towards what he would ensure became a fulfilled life.

It was with this new aim in mind that he told Thomas and Helen that he thought he had found his destiny. They both immediately offered their support for his plan, and looked forward to the time when he would bring them further news.

Spring 1857

My dear friend Rosalind,

I write to you with the news that I am pregnant again but I am sad to say that Daniel shows no interest and my marriage is not as joyful as it was. My husband's attitude to me has changed; he is more irritable and at times deliberately awkward, making mountains out of molehills. I know the mill is a big responsibility and he

275

often works late into the evening, sometimes not returning until the next day, which worries me. Or maybe I am reading more into the situation than there is. After all, apart from the increased pressure of work following Thomas's and Ralph's resignations, he has had the worry of his mother's deterioration and death.

William seems to be the only one who holds his interest. My heart aches for Estelle to whom he shows no love. I try to make up for that loss and have found it drawing us closer, for which I am thankful. She helps to ease my trials. I also find comfort in visits from my sister-in-law, Helen. She is a sweet, considerate person and careful about making her visits as she is aware that Daniel does not approve of them – another stick he wields against me. Thank goodness I have Sally, who married Garth recently; she provides me with a link to Stockdale, which keeps me sane when Daniel's worst side comes out.

I am sorry this is such a gloomy letter. I hope I haven't shocked you but I feel better for pouring out my heart to my closest friend whom I know will understand my need. Please keep this in confidence.

My love to you, Henry and Charlie.

With lasting memories,

Susannah

Daniel had found it hard to fill the gaps left by the departure of his brothers. There were not many employees with the degree of experience and competence he sought. Each night he left the mill in a black mood and carried that home with him. Inevitably he vented his frustration on Susannah, leaving her beaten down by his simmering wrath.

Some respite in his ill humour came when finally the

situation at the mill eased. Two men, who had known each other for ten years and had worked at a Bradford mill for six, were looking for better positions. Daniel studied their credentials in detail and finally employed them as his under-managers.

That evening, when he arrived home, Susannah could tell the situation at the mill must have changed so ventured a query. 'Has the new mill at Saltaire affected your workforce?'

'Of course not, woman!' he replied curtly. 'And I don't want any business talk from you.'

Susannah put her hand protectively to her stomach, as if to protect her unborn child from her husband's wrath. She looked away from him, stricken, remembering the times she had chatted with her father in the peace of the evening about the day's work on the estate.

As her pregnancy progressed even more annoyance and contempt crept into Daniel's words until finally Susannah did not speak unless spoken to. She quickly learned to judge the depth of his mood and the direction that any conversation should take. Thinking of the children, however, she dared one evening to ask, 'Daniel, could you spare some time for us to play with William and Estelle together?'

'Don't be stupid, I have more important things to attend to. I have no interest in the girl, you can do what you like about her, but I will see to William. As he grows up he must take an interest in the mill. It will be his one day.'

One morning in November, Sally came to Susannah's bedroom to see if her mistress needed help dressing, which had become more tiresome for her eight months into her pregnancy. 'Good morning, Maam,' said the maid, but her words froze when she saw Susannah's distressed state.

She rushed to the bedside. Her mistress grasped her hand. 'Send for the doctor,' she gasped. 'There's something wrong!'

Five hours later he looked sadly at her. 'I'm sorry, Mrs Bullen, we have done all we could but your baby was still-born. I have sent for your husband.'

When Daniel arrived home the doctor met him in the hall and immediately led him to the privacy of the small drawing-room.

'Mr Bullen, I'm sorry to tell you, your boy was born dead. Your wife has had a very, very distressing time. There were moments when I thought I was losing her, but she found a fighting spirit from somewhere. Last time I warned you no more children; you said you would tell your wife. It is clear to me you ignored my warning. I did not betray my word to you when Estelle was born, but this time I could not walk away without telling your wife personally that she should have no more children. She wept when I did. Knowing you had hoped for a big family, she feels she is letting you down.' Though he could sense that Daniel was fuming at the reprimand he was being given, the doctor did not hold back. 'You must heed my words, Mr Bullen, or the consequences could be terrible.'

'Are you threatening me?' Daniel demanded, fire in his eyes.

'I am merely stating facts,' replied the doctor coldly.

'And I could imply you did not do all you could for my wife,' hissed Daniel.

The doctor gave a little laugh. 'You forget, Mr Bullen, that I have a witness to what went on at the birth. Not just your wife but the nurse you appointed would testify to the truth.

'Now, sir, this conversation is at an end. I will call here every day to monitor your wife's progress towards good health. You can begin by going to her and offering some comfort, that would be a start, but I warn you that the road will be long and hard and she will need a great deal of understanding from you.' The doctor turned away and walked briskly to the door, calling over his shoulder, 'I will be back tomorrow.'

Daniel glared after him, cursing under his breath. Not wanting to feel the lash of the doctor's tongue again, he waited until he heard the front door close. Then he went slowly up the stairs, reviewing the future in his mind.

As he walked silently over to the bed the nurse left the room. The doctor had insisted that she be on duty at all times until he was satisfied with his patient's recovery, but the grieving couple needed no witness to their loss.

Susannah gave a wan smile and reached out for her husband's hand. She sensed a little reluctance in his touch. 'Oh, Daniel, I'm so sorry.' The tears that had welled in her eyes overflowed and ran silently down her cheeks.

'It can't be helped,' he said quietly. 'You get better.'

She detected no warmth in his voice, no regret. It was as if what had happened was the end of everything; that there was no future left for them.

'Daniel, please don't blame me. I couldn't make the baby as you wanted, and I won't be able to in the future.'

He stared down at her without a shred of compassion, ignoring the tears dampening her pillow. The look in his eyes scared her, but it also made her determined to rise above this life so alien to the one she had known at Stockdale.

He let his hand slip out of hers, then turned and walked away to find solace in the arms of Penelope.

34

'Nurse!' Susannah called weakly.

Mrs Ackroyd, who had been appointed by the doctor six months ago, hurried into the bedroom. Since Susannah's post-puerperal fever she was ever attentive to her patient's needs, only straying from her post if Mrs Bullen's personal maid Sally could be present.

When she reached the bedside, Susannah said, 'Nurse, please get a message to Mrs Thomas Bullen that I would welcome a visit from her. But warn her to be discreet.'

'I understand, Mrs Bullen. I will arrange it with Sally.'

Daniel wrote to Francis:

> Dear Father-in-law,
> I am very sorry to tell you that Susannah is not making the progress I had hoped for. Her melancholic state precludes her having visitors for the foreseeable future. Rest assured, I will let you know when that is possible.
> Your son-in-law,
> Daniel

'Oh, Helen. It's so good to see you again,' said Susannah when her sister-in-law walked in.

'I am pleased too,' she returned, hiding the shock she felt at seeing the pale face against the pillows.

Susannah reached out and took her hand in hers. 'I am so sorry Daniel was not agreeable to your visits in the past. That is why I asked you to be discreet. I am sure he still wouldn't agree to them, but I did so want to see my friend again.'

'Is there any way in which he is more sympathetic?' enquired Helen.

'At times he can still be the man I married, but they are growing infrequent. There are whole days when I don't see him, and he seems to be staying away at night.'

'Maybe life will improve when you are over this weakness, and are up and about more.'

'Maybe,' said Susannah with a doubtful smile.

When Helen returned home she reported to Thomas on Susannah's health and some of what she had learned of Daniel's relationship with his wife. 'The nurse would not be drawn about it but she was definitely critical of his attitude, though very careful what she said. I could tell there was more to it than I could glean. I think Susannah would like me to visit her more often, but I will only do that if you are agreeable.'

'You will have to be extremely careful. Daniel can be a tyrant, and if he had an inkling of any visits made behind his back it could go badly. I don't like the thought of Susannah being isolated from you, though. I think you are good for her, especially at a time when she is getting over the death of a child. So, yes, visit, but be careful.'

Over the next three months, taking every precaution,

Helen visited Susannah twice a week. She was pleased to see an improvement in the patient's health and mental outlook, slow though this was.

'The nurse confirmed it, and told me that yesterday Susannah has started talking about William and Estelle again. I am pleased because that shows she is taking an interest once more, which could stimulate a desire to move out of the seclusion of her room. It won't happen overnight, but the interest in the children is an encouraging sign,' Helen reported.

This news so pleased Thomas that he contemplated visiting his sister-in-law himself but did not pursue the idea, knowing if he were seen at Ash Tree Villa news was sure to reach Daniel, and that could only make things worse for Susannah. He concentrated instead on his painting. Guided by Mr Hopkins he was producing work that was beginning to sell to an informed group of collectors, enabling him to develop the special talent that was becoming evident in him, rather than painting only to commission.

Summer 1860

My dear Rosalind,

I do so enjoy receiving your letters and hearing all the news about your family. Their antics make me smile and spur me on to devote myself more to William and Estelle. It has been a long convalescence but I am pleased to say my strength is finally returning. I am able to get out more and walk in the garden. I enjoy sitting in the sun watching the children play, accompanied by the nurse who has been with us two years now. I dread the day she will leave. When she does, I hope to take the children to see their grandfather at Stockdale again.

Uncle Gideon is well and tries to see me and the children whenever he is at his house in Skipton.

Have you news of Roland?

Please write soon.

You are for ever in my thoughts,

Susannah

Eventually the day came when the nurse was summoned by Daniel one morning before he left for the mill.

'Mrs Ackroyd, I think Mrs Bullen is strong enough for me to dispense with your services. She is walking in the grounds every day now and as you know has started to have a weekly ride in the carriage. You have been with us four years and I am grateful for all you have done.' He placed an envelope on the desk. 'That is your final pay to which I have added a bonus in appreciation of your efforts with a patient who has been trying at times, I know.'

'I thank you, Mr Bullen,' she said, picking up the envelope. 'Mrs Bullen has been a wonderful patient.'

'Though demanding, I have no doubt,' he interposed. A remark she could not help contradicting.

'Not at all. Mrs Bullen was always most considerate and often apologised for any trouble she was causing, though I was careful to reassure her it was not so. She has made excellent progress, especially in the last year. May I suggest something, Mr Bullen?'

He waved a hand in assent.

'When she began to show more interest in the children, especially Estelle, she began to pick up more quickly. I think there is a special bond with her because of the difficult birth. They should be together as much as possible.'

'Thank you,' replied Daniel, without any trace of feeling. 'Goodbye, Nurse.'

In spite of the cold dismissal she said one more thing, 'If Mrs Bullen needs me again, you have my address.'

He nodded.

She walked from the room, knowing it would be best to take note that he was 'dispensing' with her services, and not linger over her departure. She left the next morning.

Her things had been packed and her cases taken downstairs by one of the valets. She collected her coat and hat from her room and went to see Susannah for the final time. 'As I told you when I saw you this morning, Mrs Bullen, this is it. I have come to say goodbye.'

Susannah reached out and they clasped hands.

'Oh, I will so miss you.' Susannah bit her lip to stop the tears

The nurse knew that if she allowed emotion to creep in it would be harder for them both, so she kept it simple. 'I will miss you too. Keep well. If you need me, send a message with Sally.' She squeezed her patient's hand and felt the pressure returned.

Giving the nurse twenty minutes to be clear of the premises, Daniel sat considering the future before he visited Susannah.

'Now, my dear, with the nurse gone you must seize the chance to build on the confidence that has been restored to you. Being less reliant on her should help you to be more yourself. You have nothing to worry you; and there is no reason for you not to make a full recovery.'

'Except that I cannot give you another child,' said Susannah regretfully. Her lips tightened against the tears which threatened.

'Now, my dear, don't ever think of that again, it will only upset you.'

'I think some time at Stockdale would do me good.'

'No!' The word was spoken so viciously that she started in fright. 'No!' Daniel boomed at her again. 'It will only upset you, and anyway your father spoils the children. I explained that to him when he visited after you lost my child.' The blame in the words 'you' and 'my' stung her and stifled any protest. Daniel seized his chance. 'Your father understood and saw it was best that he keep away. I don't want all the good undoing, so you can forget visiting Stockdale for the foreseeable future.'

'But I want to go!' Susannah flared at him.

'No! That is my final word. You will be allowed to go when I say so.'

'My life is . . . '

'Your life is here! I'll hear no more of this. You've ruined my evening, talking like this. I'm going out and I won't be back until morning!'

He strode determinedly towards the door.

'Please, Daniel, don't leave me in this big house alone.'

He stopped and swung round angrily. 'Get a grip on yourself, woman. You won't be alone. The housekeeper's here, the children are here, and some of the servants. Don't show me up by this maudlin behaviour!' He strode out of the room, banging the door behind him.

Tears started to stream silently down her face. She sank to the floor.

Drawn from their rooms by the anger in their father's voice and their mother's loud sobs, two small figures peered from behind the banister on the nursery landing. They drew back, Estelle frightened by the sound of the door to their mother's room crashing open. William flinched, but an eight year old boy was going to hide any sign of weakness from a sister who was a whole year younger.

They saw their father storm down the flight of stairs to his dressing room and a few moments later emerge to hurry down to the hall, losing no time in leaving the house with the front door banging loudly behind him.

'Why is Father angry?' asked Estelle timidly.

'Mother must have upset him again,' said William serious-faced. 'I've heard him scolding her before.'

'I wish he wouldn't be angry. I don't like it.'

'Oh, take no notice. Everything will be all right, it always is.'

Estelle gave a little sniff and bit her lip to keep calm. 'I wish Nurse was still with us. Why did she have to leave?'

'Because Mama was a lot better. We didn't need her any more.'

'So why does Mama still cry?'

'Oh, shut up about it,' snapped William. 'Father knows what he's doing.' He pushed himself to his feet and set off to his room.

'I'm going to help Mama and try to make her better,' called Estelle after his retreating figure. 'You should do the same.'

William grunted, discounting her suggestion. 'Father wouldn't like it. He'd say I was a sissy and shouldn't meddle in things I don't know about.'

'Well, I will go, I'll help her all I can,' the little girl said defiantly. But William was out of earshot of her quietly spoken words.

Six months later life in Ash Tree Villa had settled down. Sensing that Susannah's health was improving further, Daniel had proposed that they should start entertaining again. 'It will help business at the mill. Meeting important customers on a social basis is vital, and greeting rival owners can make for good relationships that help trade. Apart from business, I think we should do more to establish friendships with people in our community. Of course, more importantly,' he added smoothly, 'I believe it would help you to maintain your progress back towards the girl I married.'

There was no mistaking Susannah's joy at this unexpected turn in Daniel's attitude to her. It was as if he had never uttered the words, 'Don't you ever refuse me, woman! Don't you ever do that! Remember, you are mine by right!' which had remained seared on her mind. Could she hope to erase them finally? It would be a huge comfort to her if she were able to, to know that even if she could no longer satisfy his desire for another child he no longer held it against her. Susannah hoped it would be so and would stay that way.

The relationship seemed to her to be strengthened when Daniel proposed that the children should have a governess.

'I think that is a splendid idea,' agreed Susannah. 'It will be pleasant for me too to have someone else to talk to and . . .'

'That isn't the idea,' cut in Daniel sharply, having quickly grasped Susannah's implication. 'Employing a governess is purely for the children's benefit, not to furnish you with a companion.'

'But . . .'

'There are no buts about it. I will carry out the interviews and decide on the most suitable person. I will look for a teacher, male or female, who will live out and come in five days a week, rather than choosing a resident governess. We will use the second drawing-room as the classroom; that will leave the drawing-room and morning room for our own use. The teacher will have his or her meals served in the class-room. Lessons will start at nine and finish at three.' He stopped and eyed Susannah critically. 'You will have no need of any contact with the teacher.'

'But I should like to be involved.'

'No! I said, there is no need. If you don't like my plan, I'll not pursue it. It will be the children who will miss out then, suffering the loss of a good education.'

'Very well,' Susannah sighed, then added hastily, 'I wish you wouldn't shut me out.'

'I'm not doing that,' snapped Daniel. 'I'm saving you worry and trouble. We don't want you having a relapse. Now, I trust you have no objection to that plan?'

'It would be useless for me to do so,' she replied meekly. 'It seems you have everything worked out, though I would have liked you to have consulted me, especially where Estelle is concerned. I think she should have a female's influence.'

Daniel pursed his lips thoughtfully for a moment. 'As I said, I thought I was taking any worry from your shoulders by working this all out. However, I take your point about Estelle. Maybe it would be best if I engaged a husband and wife team.'

'Would you do that, Daniel? It would please me so,' said Susannah with hope in her voice.

'I'll think it over and tell you in the morning.'

Daniel touched his lips with the napkin, leaned back in his chair and smiled across the table at Penelope. 'My dear, that was one of the best meals you have served here.'

'I am so pleased you enjoyed it and that Griffin Manor has lived up to its reputation.'

'Now, I seek your opinion on a family matter. I was proposing to employ a male teacher but Susannah thinks Estelle needs a female influence. You have always shown an interest in the children, what do you think?'

'Susannah is right. Estelle needs someone, as well as her

mother, to help her step into society and find good marriage prospects. I never had that chance. I've done well for myself, but marriage still seems to elude me.' Her eyes settled on Daniel, countering his rueful look with such disdain that he could only reply smoothly, 'Thank you for your considered opinion.'

Spring 1863

Dear Rosalind,

Finally I have good news that has raised my hopes that life with Daniel is improving. He has proposed we should engage a teacher for the children, and much to my surprise has agreed to my suggestion that we need a female teacher for Estelle. In fact, he went further and has now employed a man and wife to teach both children. It is wonderful that he has accepted my idea.

He has also said we should start entertaining again.

This is only a brief note but I wanted you to know that things are looking better.

Be happy for me, dear friend.

Yours as always,

Susannah

One evening, after an enjoyable dinner together, they settled in the drawing-room where, much to Susannah's surprise, Daniel showed no signs of going out.

'My dear,' he began, 'tomorrow I will invite Mr and Mrs Patmore to dine with us in the evening . . . say six-thirty for seven?'

'Patmore? I've never met them. Who are they?' Susannah asked.

'He has a transport business. I've been trying to engage with him this past year but so far I've not managed it. I thought inviting him and his wife here might help towards smoothing the way.'

'I don't think I have met them,' said Susannah.

Daniel seized on the doubtfulness of her tone. 'Of course you have,' he snapped.

'I don't think so.' She drew her words out as if questioning her own memory.

'Yes, you have!' Daniel secretly enjoyed causing such turmoil in her mind.

'I don't . . . '

'Susannah, get a grip on yourself! You must remember them. Don't show me up like this.'

'Have they any children?'

'Yes, a boy and a girl, the same age as our two.'

'If I had seen the children I would have remembered, and even if Mr and Mrs Patmore had only mentioned them, I would surely have recalled it.'

'Susannah, this is getting ridiculous. You have met them. Now that is an end to the matter.'

She felt the sting of his reproach and nodded meekly, but in her mind she was contradicting him.

Daniel knocked on the door of his wife's room and went in. She was seated at her dressing table pinning an unruly wisp of hair into place.

'Hello, Daniel,' she greeted him pleasantly as she smiled at him through the mirror.

'You are looking beautiful tonight,' he said. He placed his hands on her shoulders and bent to kiss her on her forehead. She smiled, reached up and took his hand, saying, 'Thank you. It is a long time since you told me that.'

'You were ill, my dear. It has been too long, but now you look fully recovered and you bloom again.'

'Like a flower?'

'Like a flower,' he confirmed.

He straightened up and fished in his pocket, bringing out a small square velvet box. 'I have a present for you. I would like you to wear it this evening.'

She had watched him in the mirror and now swung round to face him. With excitement dancing in her eyes she took the box from him and opened it to find an oval brooch from which diamonds dazzled in a sparkling display against a thin background of the blackest jet. She gasped at what she was seeing. 'Oh, Daniel, it's so beautiful.' There were tears in her eyes as she added, 'I don't deserve this after all the worry I have caused you.'

'You will repay me by wearing it tonight,' he said gently. 'The Patmores will be here in twenty minutes. I'll see you downstairs in ten.' He walked from the room leaving Susannah gazing at her brooch.

A few minutes later, as she was adjusting her dress in front of her cheval mirror, Estelle ran in. 'Oh, Mama, you look lovely,' she gasped.

Susannah laughed. 'Come and look at this.' She pointed to the brooch she had just pinned to the neck of her dress.

'Oh, it's pretty, Mama. It sparkles like the stars in the sky.'

'Your papa just gave it to me.'

'Does this mean he won't shout at you any more?'

Susannah was a little taken aback at the directness of the question and realised that children take in more than adults imagine. 'I hope so, love,' she replied, seriously.

'So do I, Mama,' the child replied in all seriousness as she ran from the room.

Five minutes later Susannah went downstairs to join her husband and await the Patmores.

'Are William and Estelle settled?' he asked.

'Sally is with them. We'll be able to organise things differently when you have engaged their teachers.'

'Yes. Applications are coming in. I will see that caring for the children on evenings such as this is written into their terms of employment.'

'We mustn't dismiss Sally from such duties altogether, though, especially where Estelle is concerned. She is used to Sally.'

He nodded but made no comment. As Susannah settled herself to await the visitors, his lips tightened – Sally, a daily connection with Stockdale Manor. It irritated him, but he always quelled those thoughts with a reminder of what Stockdale Manor would, one day, mean to Penelope and him.

For now those thoughts were interrupted by the maid announcing the arrival of Mr and Mrs Patmore. Susannah and Daniel went into the hall to greet them. Two maids were already taking coats and hats. Greetings were quickly exchanged and Susannah and Daniel took the new arrivals into the drawing-room. As they settled Mrs Patmore said, 'Mrs Bullen, it is so good to see you again.'

The inference was not lost on either Daniel or Susannah and the glance that passed between them spoke volumes. Susannah felt embarrassed by having denied meeting the Patmores before.

She knew what would happen in the future – Daniel would use this, along with her other perceived shortcomings, to belittle her in front of guests, friends and even the servants. Such jibes and reminders were all the more potent because he used them in the most casual of ways, but always laced with barbs that struck home at her and which only she would recognise as truly hurtful. When they were alone he would berate her with the sharpest of tongues, blaming her for the situation in which she found herself, implying that her mind was weakening and reminding her that he was used to the signs after his mother's decline.

The passing of time did little to change their uneasy relationship, one which Susannah dare not try to break legally. The scandal would hurt her children and devastate her father and uncle. Only her occasional correspondence with Rosalind and Roland brought her some solace.

The times he lashed her with his tongue were always followed by Daniel storming from the house, and, though Susannah suspected he was seeking his pleasures elsewhere, she dare not question him about this. Immediately Daniel left, William would retreat to his room, blaming his mother for the quarrel. Estelle would try to find her own peace while attempting to console her mother. It drew mother and daughter closer but Susannah could not lessen the influence that Daniel exerted over his son by her own advice and example. She was alarmed one evening to overhear him berating his sister in the manner of his father. She put a stop to the tirade but, when she made Daniel aware of the situation, he supported William and made it clear that he would not tolerate any interference from Susannah in his son's upbringing. She was shocked by his unfeeling attitude towards Estelle, which only served to strengthen further the bond between mother and daughter.

35

'Daniel, I am concerned about you,' said Penelope as she eased out of his arms and turned over in bed to look directly into his eyes.

'What concerns you, my sweet?' he replied teasingly.

'Your gambling.'

He laughed aloud. 'Why should that bother you? I do all my gambling here.'

'No, you don't,' she said with conviction, 'and that's what alarms me most. You are heading into the grasp of some very shady characters whose gambling houses set no limits, unlike Griffin Manor where Hugh keeps a strict eye on the betting and considers the welfare of our customers. Word gets around in our line of business, and from what I hear your losses are mounting in more than one house, particularly in Zachariah Cohen's Silver Moon. And he's not a man to cross.'

Daniel frowned angrily. 'You've been spying on me? I don't like that.'

'And I don't like your tone,' Penelope spat back. 'I have not set spies on you! But you know as well as I do that rumours get around in our line of business and often there is truth in them. I hear you are gambling heavily.'

'Then don't believe all you hear,' he snapped.

'I don't, but because these rumours concern you I had them checked out. There is truth in them.' She sensed his anger rising so added quickly, 'Heavy losses are a road to disaster. They can affect other aspects of your life ... '

'See here, Penelope, I ... ' Daniel tried to break in, but she would have none of it.

'No, you hear me out. After all, I have a vested interest in your plan to gain riches from the mill as well as from the estates you expect to come into in Lincolnshire eventually. Yes, all that still tempts me even after all these years, but I won't stand by and watch my dreams frittered away by you at the gambling tables. If you carry on at the rate you are going, then at some stage in the future, you'll run into trouble. The shady characters you are fraternising with will want you to settle your debts; if you can't, they'll get very nasty and resort to violence. And they'll still want their money. You'll have to sell your assets to do that, and then you'll be heading for poverty row. You'd better know now that I won't walk that path with you! If your father were here, what would he think of you selling the beloved mill he worked so hard to acquire and raise to prominence in the area?'

'You forget, I can look after myself,' he countered angrily.

'Daniel,' she snapped back, 'you may think that but there are people who, for payment, would see to it you really did suffer until you cleared your debts. I don't want you damaged and I don't want you to lose the mill and with it our future together. Remember this, Daniel. I've known poverty and, with Hugh's help, fought my way out of it and made something of myself. Then I met you who promised me more. That promise is now compromised. Get those debts paid! And if you want to keep on gambling, then at least confine it to Griffin Manor.'

Daniel met her hard expression with a twitch of his lips. 'All right, my sweet, I will mend my gambling ways. And I will confine myself to your establishment because it holds so many more ways of enjoying myself than other places do.'

'Uncle Gideon!' Susannah jumped out of her chair in the drawing-room when the maid announced his arrival. 'It's been a long while.'

'Too long,' he said in heartfelt apology. 'Not since . . .' He hesitated.

'It's all right, Uncle, you can say it. Not since my child was stillborn.'

He gave a wan smile. 'I only hope you appreciate the difficulties we had then.'

'I did. When I was seriously ill, Daniel was concerned for me and stopped all visiting.'

Gideon nodded. She guessed he had read deeper meaning into Daniel's motives at that time, and was probably aware that he was not far wrong; after all, he conducted business here. No doubt he would have heard rumours about the Bullens' marriage.

But she was delighted that her uncle was here now and she would finally hear how things were with him and her father. It was of Daniel he wished to speak first, however.

'Susannah, I must be truthful with you. I hear things about your husband that concern me.'

'So you've come today because you know that Daniel is away on business?'

Gideon looked embarrassed. 'You are very shrewd, as always.'

'All right, Uncle, say what you have to say and then let us talk of other things. You don't have to rush away, do you?'

He smiled. 'No, I don't. It will be like old times.'

She cast him a doubtful look. 'It can never be like old times; things change; we all do, but let us get the serious side of your visit out of the way.'

He took her hand, sadness plain to see on his familiar face. 'I shouldn't intrude on other people's affairs,' he said, 'but I think so much of my niece that I must speak when I have reason to be concerned for her.'

'So what have you been hearing?' He looked as if he were about to speak then but she stopped him. 'No let me tell you. That I lead a confined life here. That my husband is not at home every night, which leads to the obvious conclusion that he has a paramour or a mistress. Remember, Uncle, the difficult birth of Estelle; a stillborn followed, and with that a doctor's warning about the future. It was a blow to me, but devastating to Daniel. How can I reasonably deny him his pleasure elsewhere?'

'You have talked this over with him?' asked Gideon, surprised by her frankness.

'No, that would have embarrassed him. He believes I don't know. It is best that way.'

'He is being kind to you, though?' Gideon caught her momentary hesitation. 'Susannah, the truth, please!'

'If you are thinking of physical ill treatment, then you have no need to worry.'

'You imply mental cruelty.'

'His behaviour can be embarrassing at times, especially when he deliberately shows me up in front of friends, the children and the servants.' She paused but then, seeing he was expecting more, continued. 'Daniel is very strict, a law unto himself, and expects full obedience from all of us. Oh, I've reached the stage where I don't worry for myself, but it affects the children. Now they are older they know what is going on. William is very much under the influence of his father and seems to believe that Daniel's way of doing things is normal. He browbeats Estelle in the same way as Daniel does me. My husband has little time for his daughter, sadly. You will have to see both the children before you leave.'

'I'd like that. What is happening about their education?'

'Daniel has seen to all that, engaged a pair of teachers who are husband and wife. From what I glean from Estelle, they are very good.'

'Glean from Estelle?' Gideon frowned.

'Oh, I'm forbidden from any contact with them. Daniel says he's imposed that rule to spare me any worry that might trigger my illness again.' She left a little pause then added, 'Ridiculous, really, but I go along with it for the sake of peace and quiet. And, of course, I have Estelle's loving company, which is a comfort.'

Gideon frowned. 'I shall confront him about the matter.'

'Uncle Gideon, you must do no such thing, and you most certainly must not tell my father! It would only make my life more difficult and worry him.'

Gideon held back, racked with indecision. Then he said, 'All right, Susannah, I'll do as you wish on condition that if the situation changes for the worse, in any way whatsoever, you will send a message to me immediately.' She did not agree at once, so he added, 'If you don't promise me that, I will confront Daniel as soon as he is back.'

'All right,' Susannah agreed. 'Now let us have that chat.' As she crossed to the bell-pull she said, 'And we'll have some of your favourite hot chocolate.'

When they were settled, she asked, 'Have you seen Father recently?'

'Yes, three weeks ago I had him over for a few days in Hull. He enjoyed the change but I could tell he was beginning to get restless for Stockdale and his sheep. He told me that Daniel has not really been friendly when he comes to check the fleeces. In fact, he has not come himself these last two years, but handed the task over to one of his managers from the mill.'

'Oh, I am sorry to hear that. I did not know. Father never mentioned it in his letters.'

'I don't think he wanted to worry you after your illness.' Gideon noticed a shadow cross her face, and asked quickly, 'Do you hear much from Rosalind and Roland?'

'Rosalind is good at keeping in touch, not frequently but whenever there is an important event in her life.' Susannah smiled. 'She doesn't seem to alter; at least not judging by her letters. She bubbles with life, seems extremely happy with Henry. Producing a brood for him is her paramount concern, but she says she is drawing the line at seven – one for each day of the week. Her fifth will be two this week. As behoves a person of her social standing she throws herself into char-itable work in the villages within the Smallwood-Browns' estate as well as entertaining frequently at home.'

'And her brother?'

'Roland seems to be thriving in Holland but intends to come back to Harthill one day when the time is right. He now has two children, a girl and a boy. He's pleased there will be an heir to follow him at Harthill. Unfortunately his last letter informed me that his wife was not well, but that was nearly a year ago. Rosalind has not mentioned Saskia in her latest letter so I take it she has shaken off whatever ailed her.'

Susannah found great joy in the pleasant hour they spent together before her uncle rose from his chair to make his goodbyes.

'Take care of yourself, Susannah,' he told her.

'I will. Don't worry about me.'

'But I do. I'm sorry I haven't visited more often.'

'I understand. I know you lead a busy life.'

'That is no excuse.' Gideon took her hands in his. With a serious expression in his eyes which matched the tone of his voice, he said, 'If ever you need me, you know my address in Skipton. You can always get word to me there. I'm glad you still have the faithful Sally and Garth. I'm sure they would see that word got to me.'

Susannah gave a wistful smile. 'My precious links with Stockdale. The one thing I insisted on when Daniel proposed. But I do wish I could visit it again.' Then she added quickly, 'Don't mention that to Daniel, Uncle. It would not do any good at the moment.'

Gideon pondered that request as he walked to the stables to collect his horse and trap, but was comforted by the knowledge that his niece still had Sally and Garth close by. He had not seen the groomsman on his arrival but, as he approached him now, marvelled at how assured the young man seemed. Gideon still remembered him as an apple-cheeked youngster at the Mell Supper all those years ago.

'Mr Charlesworth, how nice to see you, sir.'

'It is good to see you too, Garth. I've had a pleasant talk with Mrs Bullen. I know she thinks highly of you and Sally so I would like you to contact me through my house in Skipton if ever you feel there is any need. I can't say more than that, but I know I can trust you both to remain loyal to Mrs Bullen.'

'Yes, sir. You certainly can. Sally and I have a great deal to thank her for. We will do as you ask, sir.'

'Thank you, Garth. And not a word about this to anyone.'

The younger man nodded. 'My lips are sealed, sir. I'll tell Sally, no one else.'

Gideon felt reassured and easier in his mind as he rode away from Ash Tree Villa.

36

In the passing years Susannah found it easier to tolerate Daniel's attitude rather than challenge it; besides, it avoided what she feared most – violence and its consequences.

Rumours have a habit of rising round men of his type and can trickle into people's lives in insidious ways. Word of Daniel's heavy losses at the gambling tables reached Susannah in a short comment between two of the servants she chanced to overhear, but she dare not question him.

But Penelope had no qualms about challenging him. 'It's six years since I warned you about your gambling; you heeded what I said, fell in with what I suggested but now you've cast that aside and your debts have mounted again!' The accusation in her voice matched the fire in her eyes. 'Carry on and you'll lose everything, even me! I've put up with a lot from you. You say one day you will be rich beyond my dreams but that shows no signs of materialising. In fact if you carry on you'll be impoverished and I'm not prepared for that. Do something about your life, Daniel!'

'Come in!' When Daniel looked up from the accounts he had been studying he found his two managers entering the office.

'We are sorry to bother you, Mr Bullen,' said the older of

the two, 'but we are becoming concerned about the state of the shoddy mill. It is deteriorating fast because a full renovation was not carried out when you bought the building. I drew your attention to it six months ago but nothing has been done.'

Daniel gave the men a withering look. 'Are you criticising me, Benson?'

'No, sir.'

'Are you, Powell?' He eyed his other manager.

'No, sir. We are here to remind you about the state of the building. It really should be seen to before the weakened structure causes an accident and possibly loss of life.'

'Nobody has to work in there unless they want to.' Daniel made his retort pointed and sharp.

'Folk need the money. Living hereabouts isn't easy. But they do expect safe working conditions. Those are bad enough in any shoddy mill, but this one is becoming unsafe.'

'All right, you've made your point. Because you have, I will tell you what I have been contemplating. As a matter of fact, when you came in I was studying the financial state of the business to see if I can afford to put my plan into action. I was wavering but your criticism of the shoddy mill, which has been in operation since you joined this business, has made up my mind for me.'

The two men glanced at each other.

Daniel laughed. 'You've no idea what I'm going to propose?'

'No, sir.'

'I had thought of closing the shoddy mill but it does add to our profits and gives employment to people who haven't the skills to work elsewhere, so I'll keep it but implement the rest of my idea.'

The two men wondered what was coming, and hoped it was going to be something good.

Daniel enjoyed heightening their uncertainty, if only for a few moments. 'In this mill we already prepare wool for spinning, send it elsewhere to be spun, then bring it back here to our weaving looms. I believe we could house more looms and thus increase our output and profits.'

Benson and Powell exchanged surprised glances but backed each other up when they agreed this should make a big difference, both to the profitability of the mill and to employment opportunities for local people.

'For the time being keep, this under your hats. I have more planning to undertake,' said Daniel. 'I must also consider from whom I will buy the new looms, and of course who will repair the shoddy mill. I will keep you informed about this and hope that an increase in your wages of five shillings a week will reward your extra efforts in seeing these changes go smoothly.'

Benson and Powell were taken aback by these unexpected developments. They had come to Mr Bullen's office expecting to meet fierce opposition to their condemnation of the shoddy mill; instead they had encountered a new and beneficial scheme, and one in which they would be involved to their own advantage,

As they left the building, Benson said, 'That's a turnaround.'

'Aye, it is,' agreed Powell. 'He had a fixation with that shoddy mill. Remember when we came here?'

'Aye, that was on the back of his brothers' opposition to it and them leaving. I wonder what they think now, after all this time.'

'I hear snippets that say they're doing all right for themselves, in their different ways.'

'Their leaving turned out well for us.'

'Aye. And that wage increase – he's been a bit tight up to

now. This must be his old man coming through. I'm told he always kept his employees better off than other mill owners did.'

'Well, whatever moved Daniel Bullen to do this, I'm pleased and am certainly not going to say no,' Benson declared.

'Nor I.' Powell grinned and slapped his friend on the back. 'We'll have an extra pint on our way home after work to celebrate.'

'Aye. And no doubt the wife won't be against joining in with the celebrations when I break the news,' Benson added with a grin and a wink.

As the door closed behind Powell and Benson, Daniel leaned back in his chair with a smile of satisfaction. He steepled his hands in front of him and nodded. He had not intended to discuss his plans with the two men, but when they had come to enquire about the shoddy mill it had presented him with an opportunity to set aside their complaint and propose something that would put him in good light with the majority of his employees.

He began to scrutinise the papers that lay across his desk. He still had not completed his assessment of the financial aspect of the proposals he had made and must do so.

An hour later Daniel realised that implementing the scheme he had just precipitately outlined to Powell and Benson was not going to be as easy as he had expected. He cursed, pushing around a sheet of paper on which were the figures that, upon more detailed inspection, showed his scheme could founder. He realised that the building repairs to the shoddy mill were going to be more expensive than he had first calculated and cursed himself again for letting this detail slip. He couldn't lose face and the confidence of his workers by going back on the expansion scheme, for by now news of it would be surging through the mill like wildfire. The name of Daniel Bullen would be on everyone's lips. That would have pleased his father. He must save the situation. He had to!

Daniel pushed himself to his feet, grabbed his coat, and strode determinedly out of the building into the gathering gloom where his horse was tied up. In a matter of minutes he was on the outskirts of Keighley and galloping along a newly familiar route. As he neared the gateway to Griffin Manor he remembered Penelope's warning but shut it from his mind and rode past the gates without turning in.

Another three miles and he was convinced the solution to his problem was within his grasp. He reined his horse to a halt in front of an imposing Palladian-style building overlooking the river. A groomsman was at his side instantly.

'Good evening, Mr Bullen.'

Daniel nodded and took the steps into the house.

'Good evening, sir.' He was greeted by two lackeys, one of whom took his coat and hat; the other halted him with the words, 'I have been instructed to take you to Mr Cohen's office the next time you visited.'

'What on earth for?' snapped Daniel.

'I don't know, sir,' replied the footman. 'I'm only here to carry out orders. Would you follow me, please?'

For a fraction of a second Daniel hesitated but he knew it would be useless to protest further. He followed the man, taking a handkerchief from his pocket as he did so. He mopped his forehead and had the handkerchief out of sight before the footman knocked on a heavy oak door. He paused before he opened it then stepped inside to announce, 'Mr Bullen is here, sir.'

A short impeccably dressed man in his mid-fifties rose

from behind the large mahogany desk situated directly opposite the door. A cabinet of the same wood was set against one wall between two long heavily curtained windows. The first time Daniel had been in this room he had admired the five narrative paintings placed skilfully so that one led the eye naturally to the next. This evening he had no time for such details.

'Good evening, Mr Bullen, it is a pleasure to have you here again,' said Mr Zachariah Cohen, extending his hand.

Daniel took it but almost shuddered at the limp grip he encountered. He saw no warmth in Cohen's smile which resembled the one the spider might have given to the fly.

'You are here to pay off your debt, Mr Bullen?' he enquired.

'Well, I . . . ' Daniel's voice shook a little.

'Oh, Mr Bullen, don't say that is not so? Remember, I did tell you the next time you visited I would expect your debt to be cleared.'

'I know that,' replied Daniel. 'But I was not intending to come this evening so had not got the necessary funds ready. I thought you would overlook the debt when it was a last-minute decision to come to your tables.'

Mr Cohen spread his hands. 'Mr Bullen, you must understand that I cannot run an establishment such as this on promissory notes alone. I need repayment.'

'Let me play tonight . . . '

A cold smile parted Zachariah Cohen's lips. 'I suppose you want me to stake you again? Might I remind you that last time my loan carried ten per cent interest. If I make you another now, it will cost you twenty-five per cent.'

Daniel gasped, 'That's outrageous!'

'Take it or leave it.' Cohen's voice was cold with finality.

Daniel hesitated. Gamble on clearing his debts or walk

away now and find the money elsewhere? Penelope's words of warning rang again in his mind, and he cursed himself for succumbing to the temptation of making a fortune on the vagaries of a ball, dice or card. He really shouldn't dig the pit any deeper by chasing his losses.

'I'll not play tonight,' he resolved.

Mr Cohen gave a tight smile. 'Suit yourself, Mr Bullen. I'll give you four months' grace to repay my money. I am being generous. Four months tonight you had better pay me in full or I cannot be responsible for the consequences.' He was emphasising every word as he approached the door. He opened it for Daniel and said to the lackey, who was still on duty in the hall, 'Bring Mr Bullen's things, he is not staying with us this evening.' He held the door open, 'Good evening, Mr Bullen, no doubt I will be hearing from you soon.'

Daniel strode past without a word, snatched his apparel from the footman and left the building. His seething temper was not eased by the fast ride home, the cool air doing nothing to ease his fear that his whole world was at risk of collapse.

During the next two weeks the household at Ash Tree Villa walked a precarious path as Daniel's temper and moroseness tried everyone around him.

In the middle of the second week, when the housekeeper informed her that several of the staff were talking about leaving, Susannah sought to ease the troubled atmosphere.

'Daniel,' she said as she sat down to breakfast, 'what is ailing you?'

He glared across the table at her. 'What do you mean, woman?'

Susannah plucked up courage to answer frankly, 'You

have been in the foulest of moods with everyone for nearly two weeks. Some of the staff are threatening to leave.'

'Let them!'

'I don't want them to. They have been loyal so far and to find others of the same calibre would be difficult. Will you tell me what the matter is? Let me try to help.'

'You can do nothing, it's work,' he snapped, but the look in his bloodshot eyes disturbed her.

Having regularly experienced Daniel's flaring temper and humiliating rebuffs Susannah almost let the matter drop. Instead she said quietly, as if she hoped he would not hear, 'You should not bring work troubles home with you and vent your disquiet on me, the children and the staff.'

But he caught the words and sprang to his feet, sending his chair crashing backwards to the floor. His eyes bored menacingly into hers as he said, 'I've warned you before – don't tell me what to do! You've no rights in this house. Just do as I say. You can get rid of the teachers for a start, they're an expensive luxury! William can come to the mill with me, and as for your daughter . . . you can do what you like with her.'

The door of the dining-room, which had been slightly ajar, swung sharply open. William and Estelle stood there, visibly shocked by the tirade that had discouraged them from coming into the room.

'William, get your things. You're old enough – time to abandon your books. From now on you will be coming to the mill with me every day!'

As his father strode towards the door William scuttled off to get his coat and hat. Daniel did not alter the direction of his stride. A shocked Estelle, frozen to the spot by what she had just heard, was pushed out of the way. Caught off balance, she stumbled and fell to the floor. Her father ignored her. Susannah was swiftly on her feet and kneeling beside her fourteen-year-old daughter, pulling her comfortingly into her arms, soothing away the tears.

In his fury at Susannah's challenge and Mr Cohen's ultimatum, Daniel urged the horse and trap so fast that even William, in spite of not wanting to appear childish in front of his father, was frightened. He screamed when what could have been a terrible accident was only avoided by the skill of the driver of the other trap, who hauled his horse to a halt. With his passenger preparing to jump out and berate the other for his inconsiderate haste, the driver said, 'It's no good, Mr Charlesworth, he's gone.'

'Fool!' grunted Gideon, glaring after the disappearing trap.

37

Gideon jumped down from the trap and was admitted to the house.

'Mrs Bullen, is she at home?' he asked. 'I'm her uncle.'

Sensing urgency in his tone, the maid answered, 'In the dining-room, sir.' She started across the hall. Opening the dining-room door, she announced, 'Your uncle, Mrs Bullen.'

Susannah rose from her chair and said to Estelle, who was sitting beside her, 'This is a nice surprise! Just the thing to take our minds off ...' She stopped short as Gideon entered the room. 'How lovely to see you.' She held out her hands to him.

He took them and kissed her on the cheek while smiling at Estelle. 'You may not think so when you hear what I have to say.'

Susannah felt a chill envelop her. Her uncle looked so sombre. 'What is it?' she asked

'Are you alone?'

'Yes, except for Estelle. Daniel has taken William to the mill. What brings you here so early? I didn't know you were in Skipton.'

'I wasn't, but I have driven here from Stockdale after we called the doctor to your father last night. I think you should come.'

The colour rapidly drained from Susannah's face and she sank on to a chair beside Estelle who, sensing the seriousness behind Uncle Gideon's words, slid a comforting hand into her mother's.

'How bad?' Susannah asked.

'Francis has not been well for a week or more. I've been with him. He didn't want you worrying, but last night there was a turn for the worse and so I decided I should come.'

'Of course.' She sprang to her feet then and Gideon saw the Susannah he'd once known emerge and take control.

'Uncle, why not rest and eat some breakfast?' She hurried to the bell-pull and, when the maid appeared, told her, 'Sally is to pack my bag and Estelle's. My father is ill, we are going to Stockdale. Will you return with us, Uncle Gideon?'

'Yes. I must be with my brother.'

'Very well. I'll send word to the mill and put the housekeeper in charge here until we return.'

'I'll go and help Sally, Mother.' Estelle hurried away.

'Quite the young lady now,' commented Gideon.

'She is, and such a comfort to me.'

That comment was not lost on her uncle.

'I'll send one of the grooms with a message for Daniel,' Susannah told him.

She left her uncle to his breakfast and went to find the head groom.

'Send someone to the mill and tell my husband and son that my father is ill and they should return immediately. It is extremely important that they do so. Then have a carriage prepared for the family, an unused horse for my uncle's trap, and tell Garth he is to drive it and be at Stockdale for ... I don't know how long.' As soon as Susannah was back in the house she quickly sought out Sally. 'We will leave for

311

Stockdale as soon as possible after Mr Bullen's return from the mill. You are to accompany me.'

Daniel's first irritation on receiving Susannah's message was forgotten once he realised what this might mean – a solution to his problem with Mr Cohen! As he took the reins of his trap he wondered if he really could look that far ahead with confidence. He would know as soon as he reached Stockdale.

'Is Grandfather seriously ill?' queried fifteen-year-old William, who had rushed to the trap at an order from his father.

'It would seem so, otherwise your mother wouldn't have sent for us.'

It was a fast and silent drive back to Ash Tree Villa. When they reached the house they found luggage being packed into their carriage and the trap drawn up in readiness behind it. Susannah was coming down the stairs when they hurried into the hall.

'How bad?' asked Daniel, filling his words with concern to hide the real purpose behind his enquiry.

'Not good,' she replied. 'Uncle Gideon arrived with the news. He thought we should go at once and be prepared to stay.'

Daniel laid a comforting arm around her shoulders. 'I'm sure your father will be all right.'

'I hope so,' said Susannah, a catch in her voice.

'You've got everything organised by the look of it,' he said, casting a glance around the hall.

'I've done what I thought was best. We need your things. And yours, William.'

Daniel and his son had a quick exchange with Gideon, and within half an hour the carriage and trap were driving away from Ash Tree Villa.

*

Stockdale Manor came into sight as they drove up the neat approach to the house; nostalgia flooded Susannah, along with anxiety about her father. It was so good to be here again, back amongst what had once been so familiar. She had been away too long. It must never happen again. This was home; her real home. Now she realised that it always would be; her heart had never left this place.

'Mother, it's so beautiful,' commented Estelle.

Susannah was delighted with her daughter's comment, and pleased that she was now old enough to appreciate it in the manner of a young lady. 'Can't you remember coming here before?'

'Not really, Mother.'

'Maybe you were too young.'

'I can remember Grandfather, but only just.'

The slowing of the carriage prevented any further conversation. Susannah glanced at Daniel and William. They had remained quiet for most of the journey and she knew they were both wishing they were back in the West Riding. At this moment she realised there was a split in her family that might never be breached. But she was newly determined to regain something of what she had lost.

As she entered the familiar place, the house seemed to embrace and welcome her.

The housekeeper hurried into the hall, their anxious expressions fading to one of relief as she said, 'Mrs Bullen.'

'Mrs Grainger, I'm sorry we have not met before, but I am most grateful for what you have done and are doing for my father. My uncle has told me all about you.'

The housekeeper gave a little inclination of her head and said, 'I have tried to keep up the traditions of Mrs Ainsworth.' Susannah quickly introduced Daniel and the children.

Two maids had appeared from a side door as was usual whenever they were aware that visitors had arrived. Mrs Grainger quickly gave them instructions about accommodation for the new arrivals and then turned to Susannah. 'You would like to see your father immediately, I expect. I will take you to him now.' It was obvious that her wording included Daniel, William and Estelle, so they all followed in her footsteps.

'Any change, Mrs Grainger?' Gideon queried as they started for the stairs.

'He's about the same. He settled after I reminded him that you had gone to fetch Mrs Bullen.'

'I'll pop in to see him later,' Gideon announced.

When Mrs Grainger opened the door and stepped out of the way, Susannah apprehensively entered the room.

The curtains at the two large windows were drawn back, allowing the room to be flooded with light as Francis wished. Its tidiness would have struck Susannah had she not been concentrating on the frail figure propped comfortably on a mound of pillows.

'Father!' She was at his bedside in a few strides, taking the thin hand he had raised on hearing her voice.

'Susannah.' He spoke in little above a whisper, but his eyes brightened and shone with joy at the realisation that his daughter, whom he loved so much, was finally with him.

She leaned over and kissed him on the forehead. 'I'm here now, Father. You are going to get well. Daniel is here too, and so are William and Estelle.'

Daniel came forward and pressed Francis's hand. 'We'll soon have you walking those fields again, sir.'

William shook his grandfather's hand and Estelle kissed him on the cheek. 'I am so pleased that you two have come,' he said. 'I've pictured you to myself a good deal over the past few years. You are even better than I'd imagined.'

They both smiled shyly, though William sensed no affinity with this frail spectre of a man. Estelle gazed at him. Their eyes met. In that moment warmth flowed between them as they sensed a special bond between them. For Francis it was like having Susannah back as a child.

Alas, it was to be short-lived. Three days later, he died peacefully.

As shattered as Susannah was, and filled with regret that she had not been strong enough to stand against Daniel's refusal to allow visits to Stockdale, she drew a new strength and determination from the love she had seen blossom between grandfather and granddaughter.

Knowing much more about the locality than Daniel did, Gideon took over all the funeral arrangements and legal technicalities relating to the estate and Francis's assets. Daniel proved willing to carry out any smaller tasks as directed.

The funeral would take place at Thornton Curtis, but with the vicar's other commitments it could not take place for ten days.

'This is a long time for me to be away from the mill,' Daniel said to Susannah. 'My managers are capable, but there are things only I should deal with.'

'You should return,' she replied abruptly, 'but I would like you to be here for the funeral.'

'Of course I will, my dear,' he assured her. 'I must be here to support you.'

'Thank you, Daniel. I appreciate that.'

When William bemoaned the fact that he was to be marooned in the country for nearly a fortnight, Susannah willingly agreed that he might accompany his father, providing he too returned, a point on which Daniel backed her. Estelle made it clear she would stay. Susannah was pleased, and in the days leading up to the funeral she introduced her daughter to the Lincolnshire countryside and its people, chiefly the Websters who were a great support in this trying time.

'Will you be all right on your own, William? I have much to do in the few days we'll be at home. It is not too late to turn back,' Daniel pointed out as they neared the end of the drive from Stockdale Manor.

'I'd rather be with you, Father, and able to spend time at the mill,' he replied.

Daniel was thankful. Over the past few years he had encouraged William to get to know the mill and its workings. His son was the heir to the Bullen enterprise established by his grandfather, expanded by his father, and soon to be safely beyond the grasping fingers of Mr Zachariah Cohen for ever, thanks to his maternal grandfather's riches.

It was late when Daniel and William arrived at Ash Tree Villa but the staff quickly had their rooms ready.

The next morning Daniel took William to the mill, attended to some urgent matters and then went to see Mr Cohen.

'Ah, Mr Bullen, your visit is earlier than I expected. You still have some leeway if you require?' said Zachariah from the comfort of his armchair. He enjoyed having debtors in his clutches and playing them like fish until he decided to haul them in and deal the final blow.

Without being invited, Daniel sat down on the chair opposite his.

'Within three weeks I will be in possession of a great deal of money and other assets,' he said, with an air of confidence that surprised the man sitting opposite.

'That is good news, Mr Bullen,' he said, though Daniel believed there was some disappointment in his tone. 'Can I be assured this true?'

'Certainly, without the shadow of a doubt. It is due to the death of my father-in-law, a prominent landowner and sheep farmer in North Lincolnshire.'

Zachariah Cohen gave a dismissive wave of his hand. 'I am sorry about that. Please give my condolences to your wife.' He smirked, knowing full well that Daniel kept his gambling habit a secret from her. 'Now what are you proposing?'

'That from this moment you relieve me of paying any further interest on my loan.'

Zachariah laughed. 'What? And lose money on what you still owe?'

'Yes.' Daniel met his amusement with hostile narrowed eyes. 'Unless you want me to expose your cheating ways. Don't look shocked. I've known for some time, but you had me hooked and I dare not expose you. Now, without that huge debt hanging over me, I could do so if I chose. Threatening me with physical violence would be no good either because there is a letter in my safe that would expose all the nefarious actions you take at these tables to line your own pockets.'

'In other words, you want a new agreement in force until you clear your debt?'

'Yes.'

'Very well. I will have one drawn up. Visit me again in two days' time.'

Daniel smiled and said no more. He rose from his chair

and left without so much as a farewell. He greatly enjoyed his next call, which was to Griffin Manor.

Even Daniel was surprised by the numbers of people who not only filled the church but stood outside throughout the service, with no one leaving until the coffin holding the much-respected and loved man was lowered to its last resting place.

Two days later the family and employees, all summoned by Gideon, were present when the solicitor read the will. 'A small sum of money has been left to every member of staff serving for more than six months prior to Mr Charlesworth's death, and provision has been made for any retired servants. I don't intend to read through all the names, those in this room know who they are; those who aren't present will be contacted by me or one of my staff. Now I would ask everyone who is not a member of the family to leave.'

Once that was done, the solicitor continued. 'I'll summarise this fairly simple document for you rather than go through all the legal jargon. There are two copies here if anyone wants to read them. Mr Francis Charlesworth leaves the sum of one hundred pounds to his brother Gideon Charlesworth, fifty pounds each to William Bullen and Estelle Bullen. He leaves all the jewellery that belonged to his late wife to his daughter, Susannah Bullen. He also leaves all the horses that might be in his possession at the time of his death to be shared equally between his daughter and brother.' He paused as he started to gather together his papers, and said, 'The will is signed by Francis Charlesworth and witnessed by Mr Henry Smallwood-Brown and Mr Roland Webster, dated 1853.'

The hush that had descended on the room was broken by Susannah. 'May I ask a question?'

'Of course, Mrs Bullen,' the solicitor replied.

'There was no mention of the estate, this house nor any bank account that my father had.'

The very same query had been on Daniel's lips.

'The bank account that your father had has been cleared by the bequests mentioned in the will and the funeral expenses.'

'There is nothing else left?' Susannah queried.

'No, ma'am,' confirmed the solicitor.

'But what about the house and estate? There was no mention of either in the will.'

'They did not belong to your father.'

'What?' Susannah could not disguise her surprise and shock. 'I don't understand . . . '

'I can tell you no more, ma'am.'

'This is ridiculous!' Daniel spoke up, outrage evident in his tone. 'Who do they belong to?'

'I'm sorry, sir, I'm not at liberty to say.'

Ready to seek help to clarify the situation, Susannah turned to her uncle but caught the slight shake of his head and the warning expression on his face. Seeing her husband fuming at what appeared to be a lack of cooperation by the solicitor, she said, 'Daniel, we'll look into this later. The solicitor's hands are tied; he is obviously under orders to say no more. If, indeed, he knows anything else.'

The lawyer, ignoring the exchanges between Mr and Mrs Bullen, gathered up his documents and papers, pushed them neatly into his case, and with a 'Good day', hurried from the room followed by Gideon, who thanked him quickly as he left the house.

With a face black as thunder, his mind tormented by the fact that his arrangement to cancel his gambling debts could not now be honoured, Daniel turned on his wife. 'You know something about this. You'd better put it right or else!'

Estelle, shocked by the ferocity of her father's attitude towards her mother, flinched at what might be the implication behind his words. She looked towards her brother, seeking his support, but all she saw was his blank expression as he followed his father.

'Mother . . . ' she started, her face full of concern.

Susannah gave a little smile and, with one arm round her daughter's shoulder, walked slowly to the door. 'Don't worry, love,' she said gently. 'Whatever happens, just give me your support.'

'I will, Mother, I will.'

'Now I must find my uncle and see what he has to say.'

38

'Uncle Gideon, what was that all about?' Susannah had caught up with him as he re-entered the hall. 'I was shocked by the revelation that Stockdale did not belong to my father. Your little shake of the head indicated you know something about the estate and Father's money?'

He took her arm, saying quietly, 'I do. Let us go outside where we won't be overheard.'

Puzzled, Susannah complied with his request. 'Well?' she said after they had reached the bottom of the steps and turned towards the rose garden.

'Firstly, you must not tell anyone what I am about to reveal.' He paused and looked at her questioningly. She nodded. 'The estate, the house and all your father's assets, including his bank deposits, are now in my name.'

Puzzled by this unexpected and frank admission, she demanded, 'Why?'

'It was an agreement made between your father and myself to prevent them from falling into your husband's hands without benefiting you. You know the rights that can be legally implemented by a husband. You could have been at the mercy of Daniel's actions, even made destitute. As the eldest son, I was the legal heir to Stockdale but got my father to bequeath it to Francis, who in turn passed it back. We were making sure that you would have a source of income you could draw on through me. Some folk might say your father was putting a great deal of trust in me, but, Susannah, you know how close he and I were. And you know my devotion to you. Nevertheless the wording of the document we had drawn up precludes my using the money or assets for any purpose other than meeting your needs.'

Susannah looked thoughtful as she battled to take in the implications of what she had just heard. Gideon judged it best to say no more.

'What made you and Father do this?' she asked cautiously.

'We thought it wise when you married. We knew little of Daniel; he seemed a decent enough young man but came from a completely different background. We feared you might not settle in your new environment, and who knew what the future might bring? So we decided to make provision for the worst that could happen.'

She nodded. 'And do you feel your caution was justified?'

'From things I have heard, which I never disclosed to your father, I am pleased with what we did. You saw Daniel's reaction when he knew there was very little in your name. From a financial aspect, you are safe. As for Daniel—'

Susannah cut him off sharply. 'What do you mean by that?'

'I've heard various rumours about your husband for a long while. I passed them off as just that. But evidence of their veracity has filtered through over a long period of time. More recently Estelle ...'

'You haven't involved her?'

'My dear, you haven't realised that your daughter is now independent-minded. She came to me, seeking advice about what she could do, if anything, to help you resolve your troubles. I was shocked to hear of the abuse and humiliating behaviour you have suffered. I was alarmed that Daniel might have started physically ill treating you, but Estelle assured me that she has not seen any evidence of that. I know I promised not to speak to him about his ill treatment of you but, Susannah, I think the time has come for me to do so.'

'No! No! Please don't do that. It will only make things worse.'

'Susannah, you know how much I care for you, I will do as you say, but I want you to promise me that if the situation gets worse, you will come to me?' Gideon's request was met with silence until he said emphatically, 'Promise me!'

'You are asking me to speak against my husband?'

'Yes, for your own good. There was greed behind his reaction to the will. He knows that this land and house are worth a fortune, and with that added to the mill he would be a very, very rich man. It could drive him to desperate acts. Don't try to protect him. Please, Susannah, promise me what I ask?'

'All right, Uncle,' she said. 'I'll be careful.'

They headed back for the house, but before they left the rose garden an agitated Estelle appeared.

'Oh, there you are. Father's ranting and raging that he can't find you. He wants to leave at once.'

'Impossible. There are things to see to here,' countered Susannah.

'He's in a foul mood,' Estelle informed them. 'I don't think he'll take no for an answer.'

Susannah exchanged looks with her uncle.

'Go to him, Susannah,' Gideon advised. 'If he insists on going, agree. I will look after things here, visit the solicitor and see the estate keeps running. I have a competent staff in

323

Hull and Bradford who will see to the business when I come to Skipton in two weeks' time. I'll call on you then to make sure you are all right.' He turned to Estelle. 'Look after your mother.'

'I will, Uncle Gideon.' She held out her hand to her mother.

There was still doubt in Susannah's eyes that she was doing the right thing.

'Go!' urged Gideon. 'It is the best thing for now.'

She felt regret for the way her life was turning out. Bidding her uncle farewell, she kissed him on the cheek and hurried away with Estelle.

Susannah knew what might await her when she faced Daniel and stiffened her resolve to approach life differently from now on.

'Get ready immediately,' she said to Estelle when they reached the landing outside their rooms. 'No doubt your father will already have instructed William to do so.' With that she stepped inside her bedroom.

'Where the devil have you been, woman?' Daniel's words assailed her as she came into the room. 'I want to get home, away from this damned place!'

She eyed him coldly. 'You never said you would want to leave so soon. You never asked me how long I wanted . . . '

'What *you* wanted?' he broke in. 'What has that to do with our lives? What I say is what you do. Now, pack – and do it quickly.' He hurried from the room, leaving the door ajar.

She heard him kick open another door. 'Are you ready, William?'

'Yes, Father.'

'Good. Get yourself downstairs and await the coach.'

Susannah held her breath; she guessed what was coming next.

Another door crashed.

'Estelle, are you . . . ' His voice rose angrily. 'I told you to get ready!'

Susannah stiffened, recalling how only a few days before they'd left home for Stockdale her daughter had said, 'Mother, you shouldn't let Father browbeat you as he does.' The words had struck home. Now she heard Estelle defy her father with a hostile retort of, 'I am!'

'Don't you answer me in that tone,' he roared.

Estelle did not flinch. 'You don't like it, do you?' she said fiercely. 'Then how do you think Mother feels when you talk to her the way you do?'

Susannah could feel the atmosphere becoming charged. Daniel's response would be a fierce one. She rushed from her room and along the corridor to her daughter's room. Daniel's face was red, his eyes blazing. 'Don't you dare defy me!' He was stepping towards Estelle who stood immobile, facing up to him.

'Daniel! Don't you dare!'

Shaken by this unexpected interference, he swung round, adopting a masterly attitude, expecting his wife to crumble before it. But she stood firm, meeting him eye to eye. Sensing the rising tide of abuse about to break upon them, she said evenly, 'Estelle, finish packing. You have plenty of clothes at home so you needn't take everything. Be in the hall in half an hour.' She started for the door. 'Daniel, leave her to get on with it.'

More than surprised by the cold authority in her voice and by her clear-headedness, he realised there was no point in trying to impose his authority while they were here. And Gideon was still at Stockdale to witness any scene. He walked from the room, saying as he left, 'Half an hour,' his last attempt to exert some authority on the outcome, weakened though he knew it was. But in Keighley he would be master again.

The journey to Ash Tree Villa was tense. Susannah, Estelle and William knew better than to break Daniel's morose silence.

William was less influenced by the atmosphere than the other two were; he was his father's son and judged that whatever mood Daniel expressed, he had good cause to do so. He had learned never to expect an explanation of anything in which his father was involved.

Estelle felt the menace emanating from her father today. The charged atmosphere in the carriage aroused fresh determination in her to look after her mother, and stand firm beside her against any further tirades.

Susannah sat silent, turning over the morning's events, drawing all the threads together – the reading of the will; her beloved Stockdale estate out of Father's hands; Uncle Gideon's explanation lent credence by Daniel's vitriolic reaction to the news. The more she thought about it, the more determined she became to resist any unreasonable demands her husband might make. This morning a bright light had been shed over a dark tunnel in which she had been forced to spend many years. Today's events had showed her that she must protest and see to it that her future was changed, for her own sake and for her daughter's. She had seen a new side to Estelle this morning and was thankful for it – she knew she had a staunch ally there who would shore up her resolve to resist any further browbeating from Daniel.

With the deepest sadness, she had seen her beloved father lowered into the ground. It had seemed the end of the world to her, especially as it had been followed by what had struck her at first as the loss of Stockdale. But was her father not looking after her even now? He had made the arrangement with Uncle Gideon in order to protect her and Stockdale against Daniel's designs. She must draw courage and strength from what they had done for her; she must resist any attempts by Daniel to wrest from her what she had always regarded as her birthright. Susannah felt with satisfaction that the independent spirit of her youth had been reborn in her, thanks to her father's actions. As hard as it might be, she would not let him down.

39

Alerted by the clatter of horses' hoofs and the creak of metal and leather, the household staff appeared outside Ash Tree Villa.

The steaming horses were quickly under the calming influence of the grooms, the carriage door was opened by one of the footmen, who helped Mrs Bullen to the ground and then waited to assist Estelle. Irritated by the delay, Daniel barely curbed his impatience. Once the way was clear he left the carriage quickly with William close behind. Footmen took charge of the heavy luggage while the maids gathered the ladies' lighter bags.

Sensing from Mr Bullen's attitude that all was not well within the family, the servants made their greetings civil and brief.

As Susannah expected, once the maids had left her room Daniel stormed in.

'What the devil was all that about at Stockdale?' he demanded.

'You heard the terms of the will. I know no more than you.'

'I don't believe you,' he sneered with derision. 'You must

have known. A scheme of that nature must have been care-fully planned and it needed more than one person to implement it – your father and uncle and . . . '

'Not me' Susannah cut in. 'I was as surprised as you. You saw my reaction.'

'Put on, to fool me even more.'

Susannah drew herself up and held his gaze with a cold-ness in her eyes that surprised him. 'Don't you dare imply that I am a liar! I did *not* know that Stockdale Manor and all its land belonged to my uncle. I . . . ' Realising what she had revealed, Susannah fell silent, but it was too late.

'Your uncle?' Daniel gasped in astonishment. '*He* owns Stockdale! If you did not know this, then they colluded, without your knowledge, to defraud me of what should have become mine through your inheritance of it.' With that, he snatched Susannah's treasured picture of Stockdale, which Thomas had painted for her, and drove his foot through it.

'So *that's* why you married me! You wanted Stockdale for yourself – no, maybe not, you wanted it for yourself and your mistress, somewhere to conduct your liaison away from the eyes of the world.'

Daniel could not hide his surprise.

Susannah gave a little laugh. 'You thought I didn't know? How naïve can you be? Don't you know people talk? As time passed I realised you were sharing her bed more often than you were in mine, but I tolerated it, said nothing, because it eased your displeasure and spared me the conse-quences. Maybe if I hadn't had such a bad time with Estelle's birth and its consequences, things between us would have been different. Maybe my father and uncle would have had no need to draw up the will we heard today.'

'Damn you! Listen to the truth of it now: I loved Penelope before I ever met you!'

Susannah clenched her fists and tightened her lips in an attempt to control her rising disgust, but words burst from her. 'You selfish, greedy bastard! You were prepared to ruin others' lives to satisfy your own lust. From the start you never intended us to make a satisfactory life together. You even attempted to make it seem as though my mind was affected, so that you could put me away if it came to it. From your first visit to Stockdale you had designs on my home; you charmed and deceived me purely to get your hands on it!' She started to laugh. It grew louder and louder, filled with derision and triumph. 'But you never bargained on my father and uncle seeing right through your selfish plans.'

Daniel's face reddened with mounting anger. Every peal of laughter seemed to madden him further until he could hold back no longer. He strode across the room and struck Susannah hard across the face. Shocked, her laughter stopped as she reeled backwards from the blow. She fell against a table. Raising her hand to her cheek, she stared in disbelief as Daniel stormed out of the room. He slammed the door behind him, sending its reverberations echoing along the landing.

A few moments later a knock on the door brought her back to her senses. Her cheek was stinging. Whoever it was mustn't see. She rushed to her dressing table, grabbed at the powder bowl but in her haste knocked it to the floor, where it left a white trail across the carpet.

The door opened hesitantly. 'Can I come in?' called Estelle.

Susannah swung round, knocking the chair against the dressing table.

'Mother, what's the matter?' Estelle cried. She rushed forward, concern etched on her face. 'What happened? I heard the door slam and saw Father rushing down the stairs – what has he done now?' Her eyes were fixed on the reddening weal on Susannah's face. She reached out to her mother who, overcome, collapsed in her arms with tears streaming down her face.

Estelle held her tight and let her cry. When her mother had stemmed the tears, Estelle asked, 'Did he do that?'

Her mother nodded.

'Then we are leaving!' The girl started to turn away.

'No!'

'But we can't stay here . . . he's a danger to you.'

'It's the first time. It may never happen again.'

'We can't risk it. I've heard enough of his verbal abuse, seen how violently he belittles you, to realise that this could escalate. We can't let that happen.'

'He's still your father,' Susannah pointed out.

'I know, but I have no feelings for him whatsoever and never will after this. When has he shown any love for me? We must get away.'

'But where can we go?'

'To Uncle Thomas and Aunt Helen.'

'I know I could turn to them, but first I will wait and see what course events take here.'

'If that is what you want, but I will be with you at all times. He will *not* strike you again.' Estelle picked up the torn canvas. 'Mother, you will want this. It can be repaired.'

Susannah took the painting and held it to her breast.

When Daniel reached Griffin Manor he dismissed any lackeys who approached him with a wave of his hand, and strode up the stairs without a backward glance. After a sharp rap on Penelope's door he did not wait but walked straight in.

Annoyed by his sudden entry, she glared at him. 'Don't

you ever wait to be invited in? Haven't I told you before not to burst in on me?'

The sharpness of her reproof made him throw up his arms in surrender. 'I'm sorry, but I've had . . .'

' . . . a bad time, judging by the look on your face and the thunder in your eyes.' As she spoke Penelope made her judgement. 'Since you were at Stockdale Manor for your father-in-law's funeral and you are back so soon, I surmise all did not go well.'

'Too bloody true.'

She cast him a thunderous glare. 'You'll curb your tongue in my room, Daniel Bullen, or never step inside again.'

'Oh, how spiky you are too!' As he was speaking he spanned her waist with his hands. 'I like you in this mood.'

She twisted out of his hold but stayed close, facing him in the defiant posture that he knew spelled trouble. 'Why didn't you heed my warning about your gambling?'

'Don't let's get into that!' he countered, trying to head away from the subject.

'And don't you fabricate excuses! You have none. I told you what would happen if you were not careful. Now word has reached me that it has. You are in deep, deep trouble. Zachariah Cohen will want that money by the date he has set; don't think you can escape. I hope you have come away from Stockdale a rich man.' Her voice faded when she saw the look of desolation come into his eyes. 'I can see you haven't. Now, out with it!'

Daniel looked shell-shocked by this sharp criticism but he would not be brow-beaten by a woman. 'You keep out of this. Don't believe all you hear about me and Cohen. He is . . .'

'What I heard was from a reliable source – very reliable. You are in danger if you can't make the payment. Well, can you? And what happened at Stockdale?'

Daniel knew he could not escape Penelope's inquisition. He tried to get it over with quickly, but she, determined to clarify the situation, told him in no uncertain terms to slow down and make no attempt to gloss over things. Finally, when she estimated that she was in full possession of the facts, she accepted he had been outmanoeuvred by two very astute men.

'Well, what are you going to do about it?' she asked when Daniel had finished. 'You are in a deep hole. Don't do anything that will make it deeper.'

He shrugged his shoulders.

'Sell some of the mill. Maybe all of it,' she suggested.

'Never!' he spat. 'That's my life.'

'You won't have one if Zachariah Cohen isn't paid. More than likely you'll end up dead in the River Aire or on some lonely moor. Find a solution, Daniel. I don't want to be left with my memories. I love you, always have. You made promises to me about our life together. Well, time is moving on. I have been content so far with our arrangement, but that is wearing thin. I would like your promises to me fulfilled; if not fully, then partially. Or there's always the begging-bowl.'

'I'll not use that!' he glared. 'I'll not lower myself to beg from the Charlesworths.'

'I suppose you soured the situation there by storming and raving at your wife, as if it was all her fault? If you did and you bear her a grudge, you'd better stay here tonight. We don't want any more trouble from her family. But they may still be the answer to your problem. If you are trying to find another way out of the mess you have created by your gambling, do it quickly. Now, I've work to do here. Sort yourself out, Daniel!' With that order to him, Penelope left the room.

He cursed as the door closed. Anger filled him. He picked

up a cushion and hurled it across the room. His expletives rang out even louder when it sent one of Penelope's favourite figurines crashing to the floor where it shattered into myriad pieces. He grabbed his hat and coat and strode from the room, cursing everyone else for his own shortcomings.

Daniel left Griffin Manor not knowing where he was going, but after nearly an hour, with darkness gathering, he found himself walking beside a high brick wall. He started – the mill! His beloved mill! What had drawn him here? Was it telling him something? Did the answer to his troubles lie here?

He let himself into the yard and walked quickly to the office block. He opened the door to his office, threw his hat on to a chair and, without shedding his coat, sank into the swivel chair behind his desk. He reached to the bottom drawer, picked out a bottle of single malt whisky and a glass. He held the bottle up to eye-level and grunted with satisfaction – nearly full. He poured himself a good measure and leaned back in his chair before taking a drink. He savoured the liquid and gave a nod. His eyes narrowed as his mind sped over recent events in his life. 'Damn all of you,' he muttered. 'You'll not better Daniel Bullen.'

40

'Mother, did Father not come home last night?' Estelle put the question tentatively.

'No.' There was little emotion in Susannah's reply.

'And William?' Estelle queried with a glance at the unoccupied place at the breakfast table.

'He's already left for the mill.'

'Did he make any comment about that?' she asked, indicating the mark on her mother's cheek where the skin had broken under Daniel's blow.

'No,' replied Susannah, with a sad shake of her head.

Estelle's lips tightened. 'Insensitive cur,' she muttered. 'He gets more like Father every day, and now he ignores me just like Father does.'

Susannah was about to spring to their defence but held back, allowing Estelle to go on. 'I was awake most of the night, worrying about you and trying to find a solution. You and I should leave.'

Those words jolted Susannah. 'Leave? Where would we go? Your father would find out, force us to come back, and that would only make matters worse. We can't, Estelle, it isn't possible.'

'We'd go somewhere he wouldn't find us.'

'You make it sound so easy, but it isn't. We would be outcasts and you would be giving up all your future prospects. What would we do for money?'

'We both received a small legacy from Grandfather's will, and I'm sure Uncle Gideon would readily make funds available. Please don't dismiss the idea out of hand. Life here can never be normal again.'

Susannah's mind was in turmoil. She knew Estelle was right, even though her daughter knew nothing of Francis's concealed legacy, but to walk away from a husband, to be condemned by Society, even her friends and relations, would be hard.

Estelle saw she had created havoc in her mother's mind but knew she had to press her or the momentum she was generating would be lost. 'We'd find somewhere away from this area. We could go to Stockdale,' she said, with hope in her voice.

'The first place your father would look,' cut in Susannah.

'I don't mean to stay. Uncle Gideon will still be there if we leave today, and I think he should hear what we plan. He might even advise us on where to go next.' Estelle fell silent then when she saw serious consideration in her mother's expression.

'It will be too difficult to leave William,' pointed out Susannah.

'But, Mother, he's turning out just like Father and you won't be able to alter him,. Besides, you can't go on living in fear. Think of yourself, please.'

Susannah's thoughts drifted. Stockdale, even for a short visit, was tempting, and she just might find a solution there. Uncle Gideon would have to know; after all, she had made a promise to him after the funeral. And there were other friends she could rely on. Rosalind was sure to support the action proposed by Estelle.

A decision made, she stood up sharply. 'All right, I'll do it! But you must stay here. You have all your life before you, and if you leave with me you will be destroying your marriage prospects. Think carefully about that.'

'If I stay, I'd be condemned to live a life like yours, entirely at my father's mercy. Would you want that for me?'

Susannah's lips tightened, turmoil in her mind; whatever happened, her daughter would suffer. She slowly shook her head. 'I would not,' she said quietly.

'Then we'll go. You know it's the right thing, Mother. We must resist any attempt to get you to return, even if Father tries to use force. Life will be different for us but we will make it work.' Estelle grasped her mother's hands. 'We must act quickly. We have no idea when Father and William might return.'

Susannah looked concerned. 'I will not leave Garth and Sally behind to suffer the wrath of my husband. It will be to our benefit to have them with us in any case. Tell Garth to have the carriage ready in half an hour, then pack only the minimum of things. We must travel light.'

As soon as Estelle had left the dining room, Susannah rang the bell for attention. A few minutes later she was instructing the maid who answered the call to tell Sally she was wanted.

Half an hour later, the limited luggage was packed securely in the carriage and Garth and Sally were waiting. As soon as Garth saw his three passengers comfortably seated, he climbed on to his seat and took up the reins.

Not a word was spoken as they drove away from Ash Tree Villa; each had their own feelings but no one wanted to voice them and no one looked back.

*

337

When they reached familiar countryside Susannah's hopes rose. This was her true home. Why had she ever left? Why had she let herself fall for the charms of a young man whose background had been so different from hers? She pushed her regrets away; chances had been lost but now a new future beckoned to her if only she could break the last chains of convention.

'Isn't it wonderful to be home, Ma'am?' Sally blurted out, overcome by seeing Stockdale Manor again. She quickly tried to disown her forwardness. 'Sorry, Ma'am.'

Susannah smiled. 'Don't apologise, Sally. I feel the same.'

Estelle saw the front door opening. 'There's Uncle Gideon!' she called out.

Garth controlled the horse well as it took the curve of the carriage drive. He was quickly on the ground to settle the horse in readiness for his passengers to step down.

Gideon hurried towards them. 'This is a surprise.' Then he noticed their pale, drawn faces. 'You look troubled, what is wrong? He turned a questioning look on Susannah but it was Estelle who quickly answered him. 'We have come to stay, Uncle Gideon.'

He knew there was more behind that simple statement but realised that this was not the time to discuss it.

'You'll remember your way round Stockdale,' said Gideon to Garth and Sally.

'Yes, sir. We'll see to everything.'

As he walked into the house with Susannah and Estelle, Gideon said, 'Why do I have the feeling that you have something of importance to tell me?'

'Because we have,' said Estelle quickly.

'I suspect what brings you back so soon has something to do with Daniel's reaction to the will?'

'It has, Uncle Gideon.' Susannah paused.

Estelle, sensing her mother was embarrassed to reveal what had happened, leaped in and in a matter of minutes Gideon knew all that had happened on their return to Ash Tree Villa.

'Unfortunately there is more to tell, Uncle,' Estelle added.

He looked with concern at Susannah, who held up her hand to stop her daughter from revealing anything else.

'I will tell Uncle Gideon the rest.' She turned her gaze on him. 'As you know, for a long time I suffered verbal abuse and humiliation, in front of strangers, friends, and even the staff. But yesterday my husband struck me.'

Gideon reacted with venom. 'This is abominable behaviour! He should be horse-whipped. That mark on your face?'

Susannah nodded.

'Was there any further trouble this morning?'

'No. Daniel stormed out yesterday, left the house and has not been back. That gave us our chance to leave without his knowing.'

'Good. It also gives us a little space to decide what to do, though I believe this is the first place he will look.'

'So what do you suggest we do?' asked Susannah.

Gideon looked thoughtful. 'I don't think anything will happen until tomorrow. But as a precaution, I suggest we go to the Websters' in the morning. I think they will give you a bed for one night at least. I know Rosalind has stayed on to spend a few days with her mother; Henry has gone to London on business.'

'What will I tell them, Uncle? Do you think they will accept me, now that I'll be shunned by Society?' Susannah dabbed at the tears forming in her eyes.

'The truth, Mother!' Estelle came straight to the point. 'They are your friends. I'm sure they will understand your situation and be only too ready to help.'

339

Gideon, recognising Susannah's reluctance to involve others in her troubles, was loud in his support of Estelle. 'It is the best first step for you, Susannah, and I'm sure your friends will provide a safe haven for the present. It will give us time to decide what to do, but one thing is certain. You are not going back to live with that man.'

At breakfast, Gideon was concerned to see his niece still looking weary. 'Did you sleep at all, my dear?'

'Fitfully.'

'We should leave for the Websters' immediately. We will take Sally and Garth. I'm sure Mrs Webster will approve when she hears the story. It will also mean that your carriage will be nearby if it is needed quickly, and any evidence that you have been here will be gone. I have already told Mrs Grainger to brief the staff that they should say nothing about your stay. If they reveal anything it will mean instant dismissal.

'I did a lot of thinking during the night and I believe it might be a good idea for you to move nearer to Hull. One of my rental properties, about five miles along the Humber, is vacant. We'll give it serious thought when we see how things go with the Websters.'

'I think you are a genius, Uncle Gideon,' said Estelle, sure that the future was looking brighter. Susannah too seemed agreeable to the plan.

Gideon laughed. 'I'm hardly a genius, but I am pleased that my brother and I took the precautions that we did. You are a very rich woman, Susannah. Your money and the estate are safe. If you want anything you have only to ask me. Daniel cannot get his hands on any of it.'

Susannah sighed as she said, 'I may have wealth, but will I still have friends?'

41

'Raincoats,' ordered Gideon when he met Susannah and Estelle in the hall where Sally and Garth were waiting with the luggage.

Ten minutes later, with everyone seated comfortably in the coach, Gideon took the reins and sent the vehicle away from Stockdale Manor.

'I hope this rain isn't a bad omen,' said Susannah, sounding doubtful that their mission would be successful.

'I'm sure it won't be, Mama,' said Estelle, trying to keep up her mother's spirit.

The rain lashed them even harder, adding more gloom to the prospect of the visit. At last Gideon drew the coach to a halt in front of Harthill Priory and jumped to the ground to usher everyone quickly to the shelter of the portico.

The ring of the bell was soon answered by a maid, who instantly recognised Gideon from a previous visit, but did not know the others. She invited them to step inside. 'Mrs Webster would not want you kept waiting in this horrible weather. I'll tell her you are here.' She cast a querying glance at a pale-faced Susannah.

'Tell her Mrs Bullen is here too,' said Susannah.

'Yes, Ma'am. I'll see to your wet things shortly.' She hurried across the hall to the drawing-room.

A few moments later the door burst open and Rosalind flew out. 'Susannah, this is a surprise! I didn't know you were coming back to Stockdale.' She had Susannah in her arms before she had finished speaking. When she broke the hug and stepped back, still holding her by the hands at arm's length, her smile faltered. 'Susannah, you look so pale. Are you not well? Is that why you've come to Stockdale?'

She gave a wan smile. 'Later, Rosalind,' she said quietly, before turning to Mrs Webster who had come from the drawing-room and was greeting Gideon.

'You've chosen a bad day to visit,' she said, then greeted Susannah. 'Lovely to see you, my dear. Your uncle didn't tell us you were coming.'

'He didn't know until I arrived yesterday.'

Marjorie Webster, sharp-minded as usual, picked up on that, but thought it wise to make no comment on the information.

'Need dictated it,' Gideon put in quickly. His sombre expression and words alerted her again to the possibility that something was wrong. 'I'm sorry to arrive unexpectedly, Marjorie.' She waved away his apology. 'But there is an urgent matter we would like to discuss with you.'

'That sounds serious; we'd all better go into the drawing-room.' She led the way in company with Gideon.

'I'd like Peter to be with us,' he said.

She nodded and immediately went to the bell-pull. When the maid appeared Marjorie said, 'You'll find Mr Webster in the study. Tell him I would like to see him in the drawing-room. And then tell Cook we would like chocolate for five.'

'Sorry if we've interrupted something, Peter,' said Gideon after Mr Webster had greeted them.

'Nothing I can't abandon for friends.'

When they were all settled and had been served with a cup of chocolate, Gideon spoke up. 'We have a problem on our hands and we hope you will see your way clear to helping Susannah.'

'We'll do what we can,' Peter spoke up without hesitation.

'Don't say that, Uncle Peter,' said Susannah, 'until you have heard what I have to tell you.'

All eyes turned on her. Embarrassed, she cleared her throat and, with an encouraging look from her uncle, started her story in the way that she and Gideon had decided was best.

'I have left Daniel!'

A moment of silence filled the room.

'What?' Rosalind gasped.

Peter frowned.

Marjorie had sensed there was something troubling them both, but had not expected it to be as dramatic as this.

Susannah did not wait for comment or question but went on with her story, letting the facts speak for themselves.

'Oh, Susannah, I'm so sorry,' said Rosalind. 'This is tragic, but you have done the right thing. Your life could be in danger if you stayed.'

'You did right coming here. Don't you think so, Marjorie?' said Peter.

She tightened her lips. No one spoke; they sensed she was weighing up the situation. 'You should be with your husband, Susannah. You must consider what people will think,' she said evenly.

Susannah saw where this could lead and replied emphatically, 'I am not going back to him. I've told you, he has another woman and only married me to get his hands on Father's wealth.' She raised her eyes skywards as she said, 'Oh, if I had only known!'

'It is no good being wise after the event. I know of other Society women who are in the same situation, but they accept it,' said Marjorie.

'Perhaps,' replied Susannah, 'but I am not going back to Daniel, I'm just *not* going to!' Anguish creased her face. 'I came looking for help and support. Please give me those? You were so much a mother to me when I was growing up, I need your approval now.'

Marjorie turned to Rosalind. 'If we approve of what Susannah has done, where will Henry stand? Be aware this could affect a far wider part of our lives than may at first be apparent.'

Rosalind, who had remained quiet, replied, 'He will understand. I'll see that he does. But I don't think he will need to hear any more than the facts in order to support Susannah. He is a gentleman and would never tolerate any ill treatment of a woman.'

'Quite right,' said Peter, nodding in support of his daughter.

Silence fell on the room as they awaited Marjorie's decision.

When she was ready, she cleared her throat. 'I do understand how you all feel. I don't blame you, and I support your decision.'

'Oh, thank you, Aunt Marjorie,' said Susannah through trembling lips as she pushed herself to her feet. She kissed Marjorie on the cheek and quietly added, 'I knew I could rely on you.'

Rosalind rose to her feet and hugged Susannah. 'Now you have support from us all.'

Marjorie agreed and said, 'All right, we must make plans. Stockdale Manor is the first place Daniel will come looking for you.'

'That is what we thought,' said Gideon, 'which is why I wanted Peter to be here.'

He beamed with pleasure at being included.

'All right, tell me what you have in mind, Gideon?' said Marjorie.

'As you say, Susannah can't stay at Stockdale. This may be a lot to ask of you, but if she and Estelle could stay with you for a few days, until I can get the next part of my plan organised, I would be grateful. But it will mean Sally and Garth would need to be housed here too.'

'That would be no problem,' said Marjorie. 'I will make arrangements for you to stay here now.'

'And I will see to your carriage and horse,' said Peter. 'They will have to be hidden. The horse can be put with ours and can easily be passed off as a new buy; but I don't think anyone will question that. I'll see the carriage housed at Old Griff's.'

'Thank you. One more favour, please?'

'Name it!'

'Loan me a horse? I must return to Stockdale. If Daniel comes looking for Susannah I'll be there to deal with him.'

'Of course. Come, let us get that all sorted out.'

When Penelope woke that same morning she knew Daniel had not slept at Griffin Manor. It caused her no worry because over the years she had grown used to accepting that he had a home of his own to go to whenever he wished. This morning the situation suited her more than usual.

Knowing that Daniel's dilemma must be solved quickly, she had spent much of the night trying to find a solution. She knew she could not raise the necessary money nor would it be any use throwing herself on the mercy of Zachariah Cohen; she was not prepared to meet the special demands he would make on her. One after another she had abandoned possible solutions on seeing the flaws in them, but, as the morning light began to filter through the curtains, she thought of one that might just solve the problem. It was worth a try.

The morning rain would not deter her. After making herself ready to leave from Griffin Manor, she drew her grey mackintosh cape over her dark blue skirt and climbed into the trap. She sent it in the direction of Keighley, to halt discreetly within sight of the Bullen Mill. Daniel must not see her.

'Boy!' she called to two urchins who were running past.

They slid to a halt and looked around to see a lady waving them over. They approached her cautiously.

'Want to earn a couple of pennies, each?' she asked.

They gulped. Two each! That sounded like a fortune. 'Yes, Ma'am.'

'I want you to go to Bullen Mill and find out if Mr Bullen Senior is at work today. You must do it without anyone knowing and you must never say a word about what I'm asking you to do. If you do, there will be big trouble.'

'Yes, Ma'am.'

'Off you go then.'

Penelope waited uneasily for ten minutes and was beginning to think the boys had run out on her when they appeared, panting after their run from the mill.

'He's working, Ma'am.'

'How do I know you're not making that up to get your pennies?'

'Cross our hearts and hope to die,' said the stockier of the two.

'Ask Charlie Spencer on the gate,' said the taller one. 'We wus larkin' round nearby. He told us to "b" off, and when we didn't, threatened to bring Mr Bullen out. We teased him by asking which one? He fell for our trick and said, "Senior". We pretended to be frightened and ran off.'

Penelope, amused by their wiles, took some pennies from her purse. She paid them the promised amount and then added two more each. 'Remember, not a word to anyone.'

'Yes, Ma'am. If you want anything else doin', we's the best.'

'I'll remember.' She grinned and flicked the reins to set the trap in motion. She drove quickly to Ash Tree Villa, planning how she would approach Susannah Bullen.

Though she would never admit it to anyone, Penelope was a little nervous as she walked up the steps to the front door, but she took a grip on her feelings as she tugged the bell-pull.

The door opened easily.

'Good day, Ma'am,' said the maid.

'Good day,' replied Penelope pleasantly. 'I would like to see Mrs Bullen.'

'Are you expected, Ma'am?'

'No, but it is of the utmost importance.'

Struck by the urgency of her tone, the maid replied, 'I'm afraid Mrs Bullen is away, Ma'am.'

'When will she be back?'

'I don't know. I don't think she left any word about that.'

'Oh, dear. It is very important that I see her as soon as possible. Is there anyone who would know?'

'Would you step inside? I'll see if the housekeeper has any information.'

'Thank you,' said Penelope.

A few minutes later the housekeeper, smartly dressed in a well-fitting, plain black dress and holding herself with an air of authority, walked into the hall.

'I'm sorry, Ma'am, I have no information about Mrs Bullen's plans,' she said before Penelope could put a question. 'She left this morning without telling me her intentions.'

Penelope tightened her lips in exasperation. 'It really is urgent that I contact her as soon as possible – a matter of life or death.'

'Mrs Bullen spoke to no one before she left but one of the maids accompanied her, and, as I understand from the head groom, a stable worker drove the trap. I'm sorry, I can't be of any further help. Goodbye, Ma'am.' The housekeeper closed the door.

With her mind in turmoil Penelope left for Griffin Manor. She needed to make some contact with his wife before Daniel discovered what she was up to. She began to turn over what she had learned, but the more she did so, the more hopeless her position seemed to be. She chided herself for allowing her thoughts to wander. When she reached her room she poured herself a whisky and flopped into a chair. Susannah Bullen could be anywhere, but Penelope judged she was not a person who would walk into obscurity. After all, she had children. She must have friends she could turn to; but Penelope knew friendships had not been encouraged by Daniel.

Relations then. She had eliminated Daniel's brothers because she was sure they would have no knowledge of Susannah's whereabouts. Who else was there? She snapped her fingers as she remembered that Susannah had an uncle. Wouldn't it be most likely she would go to him? And he no doubt at Stockdale Manor, seeing to the aftermath of his brother's funeral.

All the facts she had pointed to Susannah Bullen having most likely gone to Stockdale Manor. It was the only possible answer! She must get there before it was too late. Zachariah's repayment date was looming too large.

Penelope called her housekeeper. 'I'm going away for maybe a week. Please see that I have travelling clothes packed for me. I will be travelling on horseback accompanied by one of the groomsmen.' She considered this. 'It had better be Sam, he's the most reliable one. Send that message to the head groom and add that I want everything ready in half-an-hour.'

As her saddlebags were put on her horse, Penelope gave some last instructions to the housekeeper and handed her an envelope. 'Please see this is given to my brother.'

'I'll see to everything, Ma'am, and await your return.'

Sam swung on to his horse. He steadied it whilst Penelope was helped on to hers.

'The clouds are beginning to break, ma'am,' he said. 'I think this rain will soon stop. We could be in for a pleasant ride. May I ask where we are going?'

'Stockdale Manor in North Lincolnshire. I don't know exactly where it is; we'll have to make enquiries when we get to the area. We'll need to find accommodation for the night and hopefully reach Stockdale tomorrow. I have to be there as soon as possible.'

42

The next morning sun was breaking through grey cloud when they pulled their horses to a halt and surveyed the countryside. 'Over there!' cried Penelope with excitement in her voice, as she pointed ahead. In a fold in the rise ahead, they saw a house set low on the hillside as if for protection from anything a north wind could blow at it. Penelope did not hold back; she put her horse to a gallop down the rise, reaching the track which a carved sign declared to be the way to Stockdale Manor. They slowed to a walking pace along a drive which curved gently through finely cut grass that gave way to immaculate lawns running up to the front of the house.

Penelope did not admire the scene. She felt only anger. She inwardly cursed everything this place had done to the life she had dreamed of sharing with Daniel. The day he had come here to vet fleeces and had coveted this estate had changed their lives for ever. When he had made his ideas seem so easy to accomplish, her love for him had blinded her to the torments that lay ahead. She had not realised how much Susannah Charlesworth would stand in the way of realising her dream to become mistress of this magnificent house; nor how the wiles of two men could outsmart Daniel. If only . . .

Penelope curbed her thoughts as she halted her horse at the foot of the steps leading to the door of the Manor.

Sam was out of his saddle and came to assist her to the ground. 'I don't know how long I will be,' she said, 'but hold yourself in readiness for anything.'

'Yes, Ma'am.'

Penelope stood for a moment staring up at the building. She shivered at a sudden feeling that the house was mocking her. She stiffened her spine and tightened her resolve. 'If Daniel's wife is here, I will not walk away without reaching a solution to his future,' she muttered in defiance.

She pulled the doorbell. The house seemed to draw into itself. The summons was ignored for several minutes before a manservant opened the door.

'Good day. I am looking for Mrs Bullen. I believe she may be here,' said Penelope as she handed him her calling card.

'I'm afraid she isn't, Madam.'

Penelope looked crestfallen. All her effort had come to nothing. 'It is imperative that I find her as soon as possible. I thought she had left her home in the West Riding to come here. My enquiries there led us to believe so. I think this used to be her home before her marriage?'

The servant was cautious. This lady looked respectable enough, well dressed, carrying an air of good standing in their own locale. But he had been warned about speaking to casual callers since Mrs Bullen's arrival. 'It did, Madam,' he said, 'but that was many years ago.'

'Is there anybody here who might be able to help me? I really must find her. It is a matter of life or death. I must find Mrs Bullen as soon as possible. I am concerned about the consequences if I don't.'

The servant believed she was genuine in her enquiries and

he did not want the responsibility if something dreadful happened.

'Would you care to wait here a moment, Madam? I'll see if there is anyone here who can help you.' The servant went off, leaving the door slightly ajar.

When the door swung open again, he said, 'Would you please come this way?'

Penelope followed him, glancing around her, taking in the elegance of the hall. He led her straight into the drawing room.

The man who turned away from the window had an elegant bearing, wore his suit well, and exuded an air of confidence. He glanced at the card she had sent in with the servant. 'Good day to you, Miss Huston,' he said coolly. She felt his eyes assessing her.

'I'm grateful to you for seeing me,' said Penelope. 'Firstly, may I express my condolences on the recent loss of your brother?'

'Thank you,' Gideon replied. 'We were close. I miss him and always will, but that is life. Now, I understand from my servant that you were enquiring about my niece?'

'Yes. It is a most urgent matter, one that could end in disaster.'

Gideon was surprised by her air of conviction. 'Really, Miss Huston, it surely cannot be as bad as that.'

'I know it must seem far-fetched but it isn't. If I cannot find Mrs Bullen her husband's life truly is in danger. Please, please, if you know where she is, tell me.'

Gideon looked thoughtful, trying to decide how trustworthy this person was. She was not the type he would have associated with Griffin Manor, which was the address on the card, but rumour had a habit of exaggerating what went on in gambling dens.

'Miss Huston, how do I know that your concern to see my niece is genuine and not some trick to locate her for her husband?'

'Mr Charlesworth, you will have to trust me on this. I love Daniel. Would I have come all this way if his life was not in danger? Please, you must hear what I have to tell you. Then you can make up your own mind. If you don't believe me, I will leave without another word, but that could have dire consequences for Daniel Bullen.'

Gideon was shocked by her revelation and said harshly, 'Why should I help Daniel and you? After all, you have ruined my niece's life?' Their eyes locked for a few seconds. Gideon saw pain in hers and remembered the secret love he had felt for his brother's wife. Before Penelope could answer he said, 'Miss Huston, I know where my niece is, but even after hearing what you have to say, I cannot promise to tell you.'

Penelope shrugged. 'Very well. I accept that. But hear me out.'

'I think you had better sit down and tell me your story.'

When she had finished, Gideon said, 'I think it might be best if I brought Mrs Bullen here.'

Fifteen minutes later he was leaving Stockdale Manor on horseback. These developments had come as a complete surprise. He had thought Daniel might come; instead it had been Miss Huston, who was convinced that the outcome hinged on Susannah. Well, he would soon know if his niece would co-operate, or would her sufferings at Daniel's hands bring instant refusal?

When he was nearing the house Gideon saw Mrs Webster come out of a side door with two black Labradors at her heels. The dogs raced off together.

'Good day, Marjorie. I wish I had as much energy as those two,' said Gideon nodding in the direction of the dogs. He swung down from the saddle.

She laughed and kissed her friend on the cheek. 'Have you come to see your niece? She's in the west garden with Rosalind and her children. The two of them have never stopped talking since you brought her here. She told me she slept well last night. Estelle didn't have such a good night. I think she was still worried for her mother.'

'That's natural,' said Gideon, 'but I'm pleased Susannah slept well. I need to talk seriously with her.'

Marjorie, sensing from his tone and expression that he wanted some private moments with his niece, said, 'I'll come with you to the west garden. Rosalind can walk the dogs with me. If Estelle and the children are with them they can come too, and then you can have Susannah to yourself.'

'You are very perceptive, Marjorie. Thank you.'

She called the dogs and within a few minutes they were walking by her side towards the west garden. After greetings had been exchanged by all, Marjorie said, 'While Gideon has a chat with Susannah, Rosalind and Estelle bring the children and help me keep an eye on them and the dogs.'

Once they had left, Gideon sat down on the seat beside Susannah.

'This seems to be serious,' she said, trying to read his expression.

'It is,' he replied, and took hold of her hand. 'There is a visitor at Stockdale who wants to see you.'

Alarm instantly dismissed any other emotion. 'Not Daniel?' she cried. 'Not him? I won't see him! I won't!'

Gideon gripped her hand tighter, preventing her from rising to escape the danger she felt closing in on her.

'Steady,' he said soothingly. 'It is not Daniel. But I think you should come.'

'Who is it?'

'I think it best if you come and see for yourself.'

Susannah said quietly, 'Let us go.' It was a silent ride back to Stockdale. She had questions but knew from what had already passed between them that her uncle could not or would not give her answers.

Once at Stockdale he led her to the drawing-room. The moment was upon her. The future would now be settled.

43

Susannah stepped into the room and stopped short. A woman turned away from the window. 'Mrs Bullen, I am Miss Penelope Huston and I'm here to help your husband.'

Susannah felt a chill run through her and her face drained of all colour. This was unbelievable. That woman, here? This could only be Daniel's mistress. Feeling utterly betrayed, she turned back to the door.

'Mrs Bullen, please don't go!' The words carried a note of pleading that was not lost on her.

She swung round, glaring at the woman who stood nervously before her. 'Why shouldn't I go? Why should I stay here with the woman who stole my husband from me.'

Penelope stiffened at the accusation. 'I did not steal him,' she said icily. 'I had him before you.'

Susannah ignored that remark. 'What are you doing here?' she asked curtly, sizing up the woman before her.

In a few moments of tense silence they faced up to each other, both drawing on all their reserves to pose the best opposition they could.

Penelope was surprised. She had expected to encounter a meek little thing it would be easy to persuade; someone who, on hearing Daniel's predicament, would instantly give way under the pressure. But now she was not so sure. Mrs Bullen stood in a defiant attitude, holding herself erect, imposing her authority on the situation. The coldness in her eyes was edged with contempt.

Susannah sensed that Miss Huston was uncertain about her; if she summoned up the courage to take the initiative, she could strengthen her stance against whatever Miss Huston had come for.

'You have come a long way to seek me. I am at a loss to understand why. If you have something to tell me, please get on with it.'

Penelope shook off her uncertainty. She must meet Mrs Bullen on equal terms. 'I come not for my sake but for your husband's. I have to tell ... '

Susannah cut in with a mocking laugh, 'Has he sent you? Isn't he man enough to come himself?' Penelope flinched at the sharp and scathing words. From the way they had been delivered she judged that something had happened between man and wife about which she knew nothing.

'Mrs Bullen, Daniel has not sent me,' replied Penelope with cold precise diction. 'He does not know I have come for you.'

'For? Why do you use that word?' Susannah demanded. 'I am *not* returning, no matter how you plead with me.'

'I use it because it is essential that you should.'

'And why should I do that?' Susannah scoffed.

'Because Daniel's life is in danger! You are the only one who can save him.'

Susannah gave a little laugh but it died on her lips when Penelope's serious expression told her there was truth in what she had just said. 'What are you telling me?' asked Susannah.

'Mrs Bullen, may we sit down? It is a long and complicated story.'

Susannah complied with the request and indicated a comfortable armchair while she positioned another so that they faced each other. 'Well?' she prompted.

'As you no doubt know, I own Griffin Manor,' Penelope started, only to be cut off.

'Gambling and girls – a glorified brothel. If I deign to soil my mouth with such a word.'

Penelope smarted under this assessment. 'Mrs Bullen, let me put you straight,' she said stiffly. 'Griffin Manor is no brothel; that is simply a rumour. I will explain more if you want me to, but it is the gambling and your husband I am more concerned about.'

Susannah gave a shrug of her shoulders. 'This is all very well, Miss Huston, but it is not telling me why you are here.'

'I met Daniel when he first visited Griffin Manor. A fine, handsome young man. Who wouldn't have fallen in love? You did.' Susannah was about to make a remark but Penelope stopped her with, 'He loved me before he ever met you.'

'I never knew it was a serious relationship until he told me, only recently. I knew of you, but I thought your role was to be his mistress, and that you accepted it as such.'

Penelope laughed. 'Oh, yes, the accepted ways of Society! It has a great deal to answer for, or maybe I should say it gives us much to be thankful for. Many a woman would be in dire straits if the role of mistress did not exist.'

'And?' Susannah prompted.

'I do honestly believe that in those early days Daniel had real feelings for you and enjoyed your family life, but I began to detect that things were not always smooth-running between you. It was no concern of mine, of course.'

Susannah sensed that this woman did not know how badly their marriage had disintegrated. She had to be told, with nothing held back, in order to understand why Susannah refused to return to Keighley. 'Our marriage had been sinking for a while but it really failed after the stillbirth of our third child, conceived when Daniel raped me.'

The shock of this hit Penelope hard. 'What?' For one moment she doubted Susannah's statement, but the disgust in the other woman's tone convinced her.

'Afterwards I could not fully fulfil his needs. He started humiliating me in all sorts of ways. I'll not go into them, but let me tell you there were several times when I came close to committing suicide. I was only saved by our daughter Estelle. Her father never liked her, and if I had not been there I dread to think what would have happened to her.'

'Mrs Bullen, I am genuinely shocked. This is a side of Daniel I never saw or knew existed.'

Susannah was convinced of the truth of that statement when she saw the pity in Penelope's eyes. 'It is surprising how little we know of the people close to us,' she said. 'I suspect you probably did not know of his desire to own Stockdale and all its assets.'

Penelope held up her hand as she confessed, 'I must be truthful and say that I did, though I had no part in his scheming. I loved him and accepted his explanation of what he was doing and why.'

'Did you hear that he was thwarted by the acumen of my uncle and father?'

Penelope nodded.

'That led to an angry confrontation when we returned home after the reading of the will, resulting in this.' Susannah pushed her hair back to reveal the mark still lingering from his savage blow.

'Oh, no!' Penelope gasped, her own face wreathed in horror. 'I can't believe Daniel could . . .'

'There is the evidence,' cut in Susannah. 'This was the first and only time he hit me. It topped all the humiliation I had suffered, and I swore he would never hit me again. I walked out, encouraged by Estelle. Now, Miss Huston, if you are here to try to get me to return to him, you can forget it.' Susannah was adamant. 'You can go back and tell him that, and emphasise he had better not come after me himself. Tell him I'm looking into the possibility of a divorce. If you still want him, you can have him.'

'Mrs Bullen, the reason I am here has nothing to do with your returning to the West Riding permanently. And after what you have told me, I will quite understand if you refuse to cooperate with my request.'

'So what is it you want of me?' said Susannah haughtily.

'Daniel, against all my warnings, sought to gamble else-where than Griffin Manor. He won some, lost some, but the losses mounted up. He did not know it but he was playing on fixed tables or else with very able card-sharps. He chased his losses and got deeper and deeper into the mire, even to the extent of using mill money to try to over-come his losses. He was called to account by Mr Zachariah Cohen who owns a gambling empire in the West Riding. He is not a man to cross when he wants his money. Failure to comply could be disastrous for Daniel – dead in the River Aire or supposedly lost on the bleak lonely moors.'

'Oh, no! He is in this situation?'

'Yes. I've tried to persuade him to sell part of the mill but he flatly refuses. I can't bail him out because I haven't suf-ficient funds.'

'So you've come all this way to see if I, as his wife, will

help?' asked Susannah, and added ironically, 'You really must love him!'

'After what you have just told me I wouldn't blame you if you refused.' Penelope left the slightest of pauses then said, 'But would you be happy in the knowledge that you abandoned him to his fate?'

Susannah went cold. The arrow had struck home. Could she live with that knowledge for the rest of her life? She sought refuge in, 'But I don't personally have access to any funds that could help.' Although the statement was true, it sounded a weak excuse.

No one spoke. A tense silence filled the room until Penelope broke it. 'Then I will have to accept the consequences of failure, but I had to try. I thank you for listening to me.' She rose from her chair and made towards the door then turned back to Susannah. 'Tell me, Mrs Bullen, if you controlled your own wealth, would you have helped him?'

Susannah did not speak. Penelope's hand was on the door when the reply came. 'Yes, I would,' she said quietly.

'Thank you,' replied Penelope, in all sincerity. 'I thought no less of you, and bear you no grudge because you cannot help.'

The two women locked eyes and each of them knew they still held a spark of love for the same man. One knew she could fan that spark to flames again, if the chance was given her. The other knew that, for the sake of peace in her heart, she would allow the spark to die.

'Maybe I can. Please come and sit down again,' said Susannah, her voice scarcely above a whisper.

Looking dubious, uncertain what this request could mean, Penelope sat down but remained perched on the edge of the seat.

'I will be back in a few minutes,' said Susannah, and left the room without giving an explanation. She went quickly to the morning room. When she opened the door her uncle stopped his impatient pacing.

'Daniel is in serious trouble,' she announced.

Gideon snorted with disgust. 'I know, Miss Huston told me, but I say let him stew in his own juice. After all, how do we know she is telling us the truth?'

'Uncle, please hear me out!' Susannah scolded in such a manner that Gideon was surprised, but in the same time admiring. He saw a change in her and was pleased she was taking charge of the situation.

'I'm sorry,' he apologised.

She nodded in acknowledgement. 'I am convinced it's genuine, and I believe you will be too when I give you all the facts. My husband has large gambling debts and his life is threatened. I think there is a way to help him, but it will need your approval. I want you to release some of my money to help Daniel.'

'Susannah, you can't be serious after what your life with him has been?' he protested.

'Uncle, there have been some good times worth remembering, as well as bad. For their sake, I must help Daniel. I cannot see my husband fall at the mercy of the blackguard who holds a sword over him. Besides, I can see this as a way of being free from him.'

Gideon hesitated thoughtfully before he spoke. He saw determination in his niece's expression and realised that, by complying with her request, he could help purge her mind and heart and lead her to face her life unencumbered.

'All right, Susannah,' he said simply. 'I agree to help you.'

'Thank you,' she replied with relief. The first step had been taken. 'I have had some preliminary thoughts about how I can do this. I will bring Miss Huston, and you will both hear my proposals.'

Penelope rose quickly but nervously when Susannah re-appeared and said, 'Come with me.' Her hope of help was counteracted by Gideon's solemn thoughtful countenance.

When they were seated, Susannah said, 'Miss Huston, I will help but it must be on my terms and with my uncle's approval of them. This is what I propose. Uncle Gideon, you release sufficient of my money to pay Daniel's creditors, but for that, Penelope, I want guarantees in writing. It will be a loan only so that I can reclaim it at any time, but I want it to be couched as an investment in the Bullen Mill, with interest paid to me. In order for this to be implemented, I want a divorce from Daniel. I have no further interest in him. Miss Huston, you will have to agree to be a witness in my case to prove his adultery, cruelty and violence towards me.'

Penelope looked crestfallen at the thought of betraying the man she loved but could see no way out. She nodded in agreement to Susannah, who looked at her uncle 'I know what you are going to say, Uncle – scandal. I could become an outcast, but I will gain peace of mind and I will be able to return to Stockdale Manor, and that will be worth whatever opprobrium is thrown at me. I want a divorce as soon as possible, I have the money. William is his father's boy but I would like occasional contact with him. Estelle will live with me and I must have the right to refuse Daniel any contact with her, unless it has my prior approval and she desires it. There will be other details of the divorce to look into, but Daniel must understand that if he breaks any of the terms I will immediately withdraw my capital. I want no contact with him, so it is up to you, Miss Huston, to persuade him to accept this. You will pass the outcome of that to my uncle. Then, Uncle Gideon, will you please arrange everything so that a reputable lawyer can handle the divorce as quickly as possible?'

Silence fell over the room as Penelope and Gideon let Susannah's terms sink in.

Penelope spoke first. 'I think these conditions are satisfactory, indeed generous. I am sure I can persuade Daniel to accept them. In fact, I can't see that he can do otherwise. The alternative for him is unthinkable.'

'Very well,' said Susannah. 'I leave it to you to inform him of my decision. Documents for his signature will be forthcoming.'

Admiration for his niece had grown in him as Gideon took in all that was being agreed. He realised that she would never have dared to take control of her future in such a way a few years ago, but circumstances had changed her. She had seized unexpected developments in order to turn life in her favour and return to the land she loved. Gideon knew there was no way he could refuse her request. Lives would be destroyed if he did otherwise, and he could not be a party to that.

'I will see to things.' he promised.

'Thank you,' said Susannah with a sense of relief that life was about to change for the better.

'Mrs Bullen, I am grateful. I will write to you about Daniel's decision,' the other woman said.

When she had escorted Penelope to the door, Susannah returned to her uncle. 'Thank you for understanding.'

He took her hands in his. 'I will get the will revoked in your name. As the sole beneficiary, everything will then be yours. I hope you will now be able to enjoy life.'

'Thank you. Now my future is assured. I must return to the Websters'. Rosalind was deeply concerned about Daniel's treatment of me. I must reassure her it is over.

Uncle Gideon, I owe you a great deal.' He waved away her thanks. 'Yes, I do. I will take up residence here immediately but I am not throwing you out – this must always be your home.'

44

Susannah swung her cape around her shoulders, letting its full length fall to her ankles. She adjusted it for comfort, looked in the wall mirror, patted her hair and angled a small-brimmed hat neatly on her head. As she picked up a pair of leather gloves from a table in the hall she looked fondly at Estelle who was coming out of the drawing room.

'It's all over, love. We are home. I'm going to Harthill to see Rosalind. Uncle Gideon is here, you'll be all right. I'll take you to Harthill tomorrow. I'd like to see Rosalind alone.'

'Of course, Mother. I'll occupy myself getting to know my lovely new home.'

Susannah opened the front door and stepped outside. She paused at the top of the steps and surveyed the countryside before her. A sense of peace enveloped her. This was where she belonged. A single tear ran down her cheek. Annoyed, she tightened her lips. Don't look back; this was a vision of the future. It was all around her – the Lincolnshire country-side, and central to it Stockdale Manor and the people who had kept it alive in her absence. Now she felt it close around her as if she had never been away. She moved lightly down the steps, climbed into the trap she had ordered, picked up the reins and drove off, determined that the future would be hers.

She saw the door of Harthill open and Rosalind come out. Susannah waved and her friend waved back.

As they linked arms, Rosalind asked, 'What happened?'

'Walk with me and I'll tell you.'

When her last word faded away it was like setting a seal on her past. Rosalind took Susannah in her arms and hugged her, folding her in the warmth of her love.

'I am never going back,' Susannah whispered.

Rosalind recognised this was a decision not to be questioned; instead she said, 'Oh, it is going to be so good to be near you again. Thank goodness Henry did not want to move away further than Market Rasen. He loves Lincolnshire and knew I wanted to spend most of our time in the north of the county.'

Keighley, April 8th 1869

Mrs Bullen,

I write to tell you that Daniel was more than surprised by your willingness to pay his gambling debts and accepts your conditions. He sees no reason to contest these nor to oppose your divorce.

He was thankful I agreed to stay with him, but I too laid down terms – no more gambling except under my eyes at Griffin Manor.

Penelope Huston

Over the passing weeks Gideon proved to be a pillar of strength and wisdom and Susannah had support from her Lincolnshire friends as well as an understanding letter from Helen, which also told her of Thomas's recent success.

'Susannah, you are looking pale again, just when your

health was improving. Something is troubling you, what is it?' said Mrs Webster one day shortly after it had become publicly known that Susannah was seeking a divorce.

'Several people, some of whom I thought were friends, have shunned me. It hurts.'

'You'll have to get used to it. At times like these you find out who your real friends are.'

'I know. I'm so thankful that Rosalind's in-laws hold a liberal view. They risked being ostracised in Society by receiving me but their understanding has made things easier for me.'

Gideon was pleased that his niece and her daughter had settled into life at Stockdale more easily than he had expected. Rosalind was a frequent casual visitor beyond the formal occasions that saw Susannah gradually making inroads into local society as more people accepted her charm and perspicacity. She was happiest riding around the estate, sharing her time with Estelle.

One day they were both sitting outside at the front of the house when Estelle looked up from the book she was reading.

'Who's this coming to disturb our peace?' she said, looking across the green sward that stretched its luscious grass to the banks of a meandering stream.

Susannah raised her eyes from her book and shaded them against the sun. She could not make out who it was but she kept watching, wondering who was taking such determined strides.

'He means to get here,' commented Estelle.

'He certainly isn't wasting any time.'

'I wonder what he wants.'

'Oh, my goodness,' gasped Susannah and pushed herself to her feet. 'It's Roland!'

'Rosalind's brother?'

'Yes.' Susannah dropped her book on the seat. 'I must go and meet him. I haven't seen him for ages.'

Estelle made to follow then stopped. He was her mother's friend from the past; she didn't even know him, had only heard Rosalind mention him during these last few weeks, generally to say, 'We don't know when he is coming home. He keeps saying: sometime.' Now he was here. Estelle stood watching them. She saw their pace quicken as they neared each other, saw their arms held out in gestures of welcome. She judged their kiss to be light, almost shy.

'It's good to see you, Roland. You look so well. I was sorry to hear about your loss.'

'That's in the past. I've had time to get over it, if you ever get over the loss of someone you love.'

'You'll never get over the loss, but the pain will ease,' said Susannah. 'It will. I know. My little one, to whom I failed to give life, is still with me but the pain of that loss has eased. It will for you too.' She tucked her arm through his. 'Estelle has been a great comfort to me. Your children will be to you. Are they with you?'

'Yes. You will meet Johan and Angelina soon. I left them getting to know their grandparents.'

'It is so good to see you, Roland. Walk with me and tell me about yourself, and then come back with me to meet my daughter.'

'That would be delightful. But it can't be all one-sided. You'll have to tell me something of your life. If we can't get through it all today, we'll have the essentials and hear the rest another time.'

Estelle saw them arm-in-arm walk away from the house. She settled down to her book again.

Half an hour later Susannah stopped. She glanced at the fob watch pinned to the right breast pocket of her jacket. 'I think we had better set off for the house. The same pace as we have been using and we should be there just right for tea. So you've heard the essentials of my story. Now for yours.'

They were still short of the house when Roland stopped and told her, 'You know about me. Well, most of it. All that matters at this stage.'

She started to move on but he held her back and turned her to face him. 'Susannah, I think you will agree that we have both made mistakes in our lives, choosing different worlds as we did. My mistake was in not bringing my wife to England sooner; if I had maybe she would not have contracted the illness from which she died. You, well, your mistake was allowing yourself to be swept off your feet by a charmer. Yes, we both made mistakes. Maybe we should never have moved away from this.' He swept an arm round embracing the land around them. 'Maybe it is now telling us something. Maybe it wants us to stay.'

'I have already decided I am staying. What about you, Roland?'

He hesitated then said, 'I came on this visit to Harthill prepared to make a decision one way or another. I have interests in Holland but can easily dispose of them. Father would like me here to take over from him, he's ailing. But I was still unsure.'

'Was? But you've only just got here. You can't have decided already?'

'Oh, yes, I can. Well, not definitely because my decision to stay depends on one person, and I don't know if it is fair to put the responsibility on her shoulders.'

'The only way is to ask your mother.'

He shook his head. 'I already know my mother's view.'

'Then you have your answer.'

'I haven't. One person has the answer and it isn't Mama. Susannah, our mistakes were really made a long time ago. We never accepted that there was love between us ... maybe we were too young to notice it, maybe we thought too much like brother and sister. Who knows? But with hindsight it was a mistake that we ever parted. I think we should try and rectify that now, as far as is possible. May we try?'

As Susannah considered his question, she saw again the young man who danced with her at the Mell Supper. He read her answer in her smile.

ACKNOWLEDGEMENTS

There are many people involved in the production of a book to get it to the bookshelves; too many to find out who they all are and to mention by name but to all of them, known and unknown, I say a big thank you.

I owe much to my daughter Judith who vetted the manuscript as it was written and offered advice to make the story better. A thank you also to Geraldine, Judith's twin, who read the book when the story was completed and offered final suggestions. Though not directly involved in the production, I know I had the support of my eldest daughter Anne and my son Duncan.

I make a very, very special thank you to Donna Condon who, from joining Piatkus, dealt with all my books through all their stages, and was a pillar of reassurance when Piatkus became an imprint of the Little, Brown Book Group. Sadly, for me, Donna left Little, Brown to take a post with another publisher just before I completed this book. I wish her well wherever life takes her.

I must thank the staff at Piatkus and Little, Brown for the part they have played in getting this book to fruition; with special thanks to Anna Boatman and Caroline Kirkpatrick who both eased me through the changes. I am ever grateful.

I also thank Judy Piatkus who saw the potential in my first Jessica Blair novel.

From that same time comes a freelance editor, Lynn Curtis, who has copy-edited every Jessica Blair book with skill and understanding. I am ever in her debt.

I must thank Paula Walsh, Greg Kotovs and Liz McIvor of the Bradford museums and galleries for kindly providing information on the woollen industry.